Prc

A synopsis from the first four installments of the series,
Chaos in the Blink of an Eye

After countless millions of people silently and mysteriously vanished from the face of the earth—including all small children—in the blink of an eye, the world was plunged into unbridled chaos.

In the days following the Rapture of Christ's Church, the ultimate enemy of God raised up his primary human agent to carry out his diabolical mission, Salvador Romanero.

The *Miracle Maker,* as Romanero was known throughout the world— after various predictions he'd made had all come true—was about to perform his greatest miracle: bringing peace to a tiny country that had lived in constant fear since its inception, the nation of Israel. But instead of a peace treaty being signed, Jerusalem fell under a sneak attack on that day. In just six hours, more blood was shed in the streets of the Holy Land than at any other time in Israel's turbulent history.

Much of the city was in shambles. Smoke smoldered from buildings everywhere. The most notable was the Dome of the Rock. The Muslim shrine that was constructed in Jerusalem back in the 7th century now lay in ruins. Muslims all over the world mourned bitterly.

Mourning very quickly turned into outrage when Salvador Romanero announced to the world that the Dome of the Rock would never be rebuilt. Hundreds of thousands of Muslims flooded the Holy Land seeking revenge.

But it wasn't just Muslims Salvador Romanero was out to silence. Anyone opposing the one world government he was putting in motion— to include a one world religion—would eventually be silenced for good.

As the *Miracle Maker* set out to create a brave new world, children of the Most High God were preparing for the absolute worst. They knew God's unprecedented judgments were coming. After all, it was written.

They also knew Salvador Romanero was the long-foretold Antichrist of the Bible, and there was nothing they could do to stop the Son of Perdition in his quest for global worship.

Initially, Clayton Holmes and Travis Hartings, founders of the *End Times Salvation Movement,* used a website to connect them to other new believers also left behind on that fateful day. Both men prayed for weeks on end that God would give them a surefire sign, so they would know who was trustworthy or not.

For three consecutive nights they had the very same dream. Both heard a voice saying, 'Those who contact you regarding this dream are trustworthy.' Knowing the Most High God was using supernatural dreams to bring His children together in these end times, while many showed interest in joining their rapidly growing organization, only those who'd had certain dreams were deemed trustworthy and invited to live on the properties they would soon have in their possession.

But with the second attempt to sign a peace treaty with Israel now upon them, the chaotic world humanity had inherited after the Rapture would soon come completely unglued.

Instead of peace and prosperity for all, Planet Earth would experience the most turbulent seven years humanity would ever know...

Main Characters:

<u>Clayton Holmes and Travis Hartings</u> – Co-founders of www.LASRglobal.org. Now that Salvador Romanero had been identified as the long-foretold Antichrist of the Bible, the two leaders were putting plans in motion that would hopefully counter some of Romanero's advances. Both knew if they sat back and did nothing, they would be annihilated by the enemy without even putting up a fight.

<u>Pastor Jim Simonton</u> – 48 - Lead Pastor at Southeast Michigan Evangelical Church. Left behind with everyone else, the devastated pastor, after realizing he was a false convert—and that his preaching had led many from his church to be left behind as well—quickly repented of his sins and was determined to never again preach a false or watered-down Gospel. In short: there would be no more false converts at his hands.

<u>Tom Dunleavey</u> – 62 – Catholic priest who tried consulting Brian Mulrooney the day after the disappearances. After both men had similar dreams for three straight nights, they met for a friendly debate. It ultimately led to Tom's leaving the Catholic church.

<u>Dick and Sarah Mulrooney</u> – Married for more than 30 years, the solid relationship they always had was showing small cracks in the dam, after their son Brian converted to Christianity and distanced himself from the Catholic church.

<u>Chelsea Mulrooney</u> – Divorced, and living with her parents, Brian Mulrooney's kid sister was doing all she could to shield herself from the vast chaos in the world. She spent most of her time in her bedroom chatting online with friends looking for comfort in a world where so little comfort was found.

<u>Braxton Rice</u> – Chief of security and vetting for Clayton Holmes and Travis Hartings and their upstart organization the *End Times Salvation Movement.*

<u>Doctor Lee Kim</u> – Lead IT man for the website www.LASRglobal.org, and all other *End Times Salvation Movement* IT operations.

<u>Tamika Moseley</u> – 27 – NYC taxi driver. Lost her two sons, Jamal and Dante, and mother, Ruth Ferguson, on the day of the Rapture. Tamika was driving two businessmen from LaGuardia Airport to the Waldorf-Astoria Hotel when all hell broke loose, and one of her passengers vanished in the back seat of her taxicab.

God ultimately used her to connect Brian Mulrooney and Charles Calloway in the days following the disappearances.

Brian Mulrooney – 33 – Moved from New York City to Ann Arbor, Michigan, after graduating from Notre Dame University and being recruited by the Marriott Corporation. Mulrooney was at Michigan Stadium with his childhood friend, Justin Schroeder, to watch the Ohio State-Michigan football game, when Schroeder suddenly disappeared along with thousands of others.

Justin Schroeder – 33 – Moved from New York City to Boulder, Colorado to attend the University of Colorado. Met his wife Heather at a Bible study in his sophomore year and became a Christ follower soon after that. Both were taken in the Rapture, along with their unborn child. Before going to the football game, Justin left a Bible at Brian Mulrooney's apartment—wrapped as a gift—with a handwritten letter stuffed inside, explaining the many positive changes in his life. His hope was that God would use both items to open his friend's eyes and ears to the Gospel of Jesus Christ.

Renate McCallister – 29 – Like everyone else on the planet, Renate was completely rocked by the disappearances. But she was too blinded spiritually to know what had happened on that fateful day. In her mind, if she couldn't see, hear or feel it, it didn't exist. Renate was the main reason Brian Mulrooney had remained in Michigan the last five years, when he could have transferred elsewhere.

Charles Calloway – 42 – Successful Florida businessman who was in New York City to teach success principles to his fellow colleagues at the time of the disappearances. Calloway was inside Tamika Moseley's cab when his colleague, Richard Figueroa, suddenly vanished in the backseat next to him. The son of a preacher, it didn't take long for Calloway to piece things together and realize it was the Rapture of the Church, and that he had been left behind.

Jacquelyn Swindell – 29 – Lost her husband at Michigan Stadium when he was killed by an object that fell from the sky, after a plane collided with a Goodyear blimp hovering above the stadium. Swindell also lost the child in her womb at that time. After meeting Brian Mulrooney inside the stadium, she offered to drive him home after his car was destroyed in the mayhem. As she did her best to cope in this strange new world, without her husband and unborn child, she was grateful for Brian's friendship, and agreed to join him in his quest for answers...

<u>Craig Rubin</u> – 33 – While his two buddies, Brian Mulrooney and Justin Schroeder, left New York to attend college elsewhere, Craig Rubin remained in the *Big Apple* to work the family business, which consisted of three Jewish delicatessens all bearing the name, Mitzi's. Rubin was en route to Ann Arbor, Michigan to join his two friends when the Rapture occurred. Craig never left New York City.

<u>President Jefferson Danforth and First Lady Melissa Danforth</u> – The First Family were at Camp David with family and friends when the disappearances happened. Many vanished at the Presidential retreat, including the President's and First Lady's daughter, their son-in-law, and all five of their grandchildren (including the unborn child). President Danforth's mother also perished that day. She suffered a fatal heart attack after seeing her grandchildren vanish into thin air.

<u>Salvador Romanero</u> – 30 – As the world mourned the loss of more than a billion people—either by death or disappearance—Satan raised up the young lawyer from Spain as his main agent in human form. No one knew it yet, but the young phenom was about to take the world completely by storm and become the unchallenged leader of the world...

1

PASSOVER WEEK - THREE DAYS AFTER THE SURPRISE ATTACK ON ISRAEL

SALVADOR ROMANERO STOOD BEFORE the Western Wall (also known as the Wailing Wall), wearing a brilliant white custom-tailored suit. It was identical to the one he wore on what turned out to be a scratched peace treaty signing with the nation of Israel.

When bombs started falling from the Israeli sky the other day, Romanero was taken to an underground bunker at the Waldorf-Astoria Hotel. He stripped out of all his clothing and ordered everything burned, including the shoes he wore.

Even the white stallion he rode on that day was put down, never to be mounted again. When news came a short while later that his parents were killed by a bomb that struck the King David Hotel—a bomb meant for *his* destruction—Romanero's rage was such that he felt like burning down the entire city, using his clothing as added kindling.

It took three nights of solitude with the Master Deceiver before he was finally able to calm himself down. Standing on the *Miracle Maker's* right was the Pope, stripped of the futuristic garb he wore last time. Normally when meeting with world leaders and foreign dignitaries, the Pope wore white while everyone else wore dark colors.

That long-time tradition, rule rather, changed once Salvador Romanero became the undisputed leader of the world. Now Romanero wore white. The Pope wore purple and scarlet. He looked more like a glorified cardinal than the Bishop of Rome.

On Romanero's left was Israel's Prime Minister wearing a black suit. The Kippah on his head and neck tie were both pure blue, identical to the color of the Star of David on his country's flag.

Flanking the three men on either side were UN Secretary-General, Li Ping and NATO Secretary-General, Jurgen Staat. Standing behind the five men, on bleachers positioned directly in front of the Western Wall, were the same world leaders as last time. While thousands perished during the botched sneak attack on the Holy Land, everyone from this group was grateful for having survived the mayhem.

Eager as they were to witness the peace treaty signing, they were still too shell-shocked from the ear-splitting explosions the other day to look joyous now. Not only that, they were mourning the deaths of family members, friends and peers who lost their lives in Jerusalem.

In that light, it felt more like another vigil than anything else.

If they needed yet another reminder of what happened the other day, they didn't have to look too far. Directly above them off to the right, out of view of the cameras, the Dome of the Rock lay in ruins after being struck by a bomb meant for the Western Wall.

Even three days later the Muslim holy site, which had stood since 691 A.D., smoldered. To make things worse, the al-Aqsa Mosque and the Islamic Museum—which both stood in the Temple courtyard atop the Western Wall—were stormed the following day by an angry mob of citizens and set ablaze.

Many religious artifacts and symbols were removed from the two holy sites and destroyed in the courtyard for all to see. Muslims were already outraged after Romanero declared that the Dome of the Rock would never be rebuilt. Hundreds of thousands of protesters poured into the Holy Land vowing revenge.

Now this? Their anger couldn't be contained...

None of this would have seemed thinkable three days before. Bombs were being dismantled, guns were being holstered and even destroyed, as the promise of peace lay thick in the air.

After many months of doom and gloom, it was as if Jerusalem had come back from the dead. Tourist sites, restaurants and pubs were full of paying customers, many of whom were famous for something. Record profits were being made.

Marching bands performed in the streets of Jerusalem for the jovial peace-seeking crowds. Teenage Jews and Palestinians played together and even exchanged gifts with one another. Hundreds of white doves were set to take flight from the Wailing Wall the moment the peace treaty was signed.

There was great cause for optimism. Then bombs started falling on them and the numerous celebration festivities leading up to the main event came to a screeching halt.

Tourist sites not destroyed by the bombing were once again cordoned off to visitors and would remain that way for the foreseeable future. Most shops, restaurants and pubs were once again closed for business. Owners of those establishments wondered in silence if they would survive this latest setback.

They feared not.

Hospitals and clinics were bombarded with patients suffering various life-threatening injuries. Triage units were set up in hospital parking lots and in the streets of the Holy Land to accommodate the masses. Limousines used to transport the world's elite to the Wailing Wall the other day were turned into makeshift ambulances, transporting patients to hospitals in the region, as medic helicopters carried critical condition patients to hospitals in Jordan, Lebanon, Syria and Egypt.

Burn units were full beyond capacity. Only patients whose bodies were severely burned in the flames were admitted, leaving those with minor burns to tend to their wounds themselves.

With a world on edge and Jerusalem once again at the epicenter of it all, many who felt so "blessed" to be in the Holy Land had since left for home. As a result, the crowd size had dwindled by at least half.

Those who were unable to travel to Israel were never more grateful to be far away from the Holy Land. Even many miles away, they could almost feel their homes shaking from army tanks making their way up and down the streets of Jerusalem, as armed soldiers and Israeli police blanketed the city armed to the teeth.

Witnessing the mayhem all around them, press members on Romanero's A-List weren't so sure they still wanted the "dubious honor" of being awarded the choicest locations from which to broadcast. They couldn't help but wonder if they were still in harm's way, if imminent danger still lurked in the distance...

Would there be another surprise attack? Who really knew?

Each time they glanced at what was left of the Dome of the Rock, the al-Aqsa Mosque and the Islamic Museum, they wondered in silence if peace in Israel was even attainable. If Salvador Romanero was a *Miracle Maker*, why didn't he prevent it from happening in the first place? Once again, no one knew.

As a whole, world leaders still looked to Romanero as an awesome and mighty source of knowledge, wisdom, and inspiration, but you'd never know it by looking in their eyes.

What caused most faces to quake in anguish—world leader and peace-seeker alike—went beyond the surprise attack and the subsequent destruction of the three Islamic holy sites.

Those things were just the tip of the iceberg.

Two days of chaos followed...

On the night of the attack, Romanero had top military leaders flown to the Holy Land representing many countries. The objective of this global coalition was to bring justice to all countries involved in the sneak attack.

The next day, in between meetings with military strategists, Romanero ordered the arrests of the two men on his security detail who'd wrestled him off the white stallion he was on when warplanes started racing this way and that above the Holy Land. The fact that they had touched him with the eyes of the world upon him—when they were warned repeatedly not to—infuriated Romanero almost as much as those behind the attack.

It was time for payback. To ensure that the right message was sent, Salvador Romanero had their executions carried out on live television, by way of hanging, from an unknown location in Jerusalem.

As his tailor fit him in a new suit, the Man of Peace watched the lifeless bodies of the two men who desecrated him dangling on a large monitor before him, nooses tightly secured around their necks, one head slanted to the left, the other to the right.

Once their dead bodies were removed from the gallows, Romanero's next order was carried out. All air traffic controllers on duty that day were executed in the same manner. It was their incompetence that led to the sneak attack, which ultimately led to his parents being killed.

At least that's what he wanted the world to think. In reality, what happened the other day needed to happen.

The twenty-one men and women were hanged three at a time. The only ATCs spared were Israelis. After all, Romanero was about to deliver peace to their long-besieged country.

Once the last three were hanged and their lifeless bodies were lowered and removed from the nooses, the next three to be hanged were the Middle Eastern pilot who ejected himself from the cockpit—after his plane was shot down by an Israeli fighter pilot just outside Jerusalem—and the Gentile journalist and the cameraman who interviewed him in jail during his interrogation.

When Romanero heard the pilot confess on live TV that Israel's God had changed the path of their rockets in mid-air, even redirecting one of them to the Dome of the Rock, he was incensed. His words should have never left that prison!

11

With nooses fastened around their necks, and their heads covered, the pilot was the easiest to identify from the full body cast he wore after suffering multiple broken bones in the crash.

His face was nearly unrecognizable from the barrage of punches he received at the hands of Israeli authorities upon his capture. Thankfully it was covered.

The command was given and all three fell to their deaths.

Initially, Romanero wanted to have everyone hanged at the Western Wall. He quickly scratched the idea knowing it wouldn't look good with a peace treaty about to be signed from there. The other reason the *Miracle Maker* decided against it were the two mysterious men with wiry gray hair and long gray beards camped out at the Jewish holy site, wearing sackcloth robes and sandals.

No one knew who they were or from where they came. All anyone knew was they suddenly appeared out of nowhere—as if transported by time machine, straight out of the Old Testament and brought to this place—once bombs stopped falling on the world's elite in Israel.

They hadn't left since…

They never spoke; not even between themselves. They gazed out at all who passed by with eyes blazing with power, as if peering into everyone's souls. But not a single word was spoken.

Thanks to the Master Deceiver, Romanero knew they were the Two Witnesses of the Bible. He also knew they had great powers at their disposal and couldn't be touched, let alone killed, until the appointed time came along. Satan explained to his chief human agent why the Dome of the Rock was destroyed and why the al-Aqsa Mosque and Islamic Museum needed to be set ablaze.

As part of the peace agreement with Israel, the Jews would be free to sacrifice to their God from that location. In order for that to happen, the three Muslim holy sites had to be removed—or at least vacated—so the Third Temple could be constructed.

Romanero was told it was written in the Word of God and, therefore, it had to come to pass. He was also informed that the God of Israel was once again with His chosen people.

In short: the Jews would be supernaturally protected from this time on. But the leader of the world was assured by the devil that their demise would come at the appointed time.

This was valuable information. It explained the supernatural stronghold hovering above the nation of Israel the *Miracle Maker* felt deep in his bones.

Remarkably, Romanero never asked his Master about the fate or whereabouts of his parents. It's like he didn't care.

But the most chilling scene shown on global television that day—superseding even the surprise attack on Jerusalem—was when Crown Prince Javier was dragged out of his Madrid, Spain palace in handcuffs, without the slightest resistance by Spain's government, authorities or military.

As dissident number one, Romanero wanted his execution to be carried out first. But after thinking things through he decided to make his execution the last, so it would remain fresh in the minds of the billions watching.

A few steps behind the crown prince were the two men who accompanied him to Brussels, Belgium a few days after the disappearances, to spy on Romanero and report back to the king.

Dissidents two and three were led up wooden steps in handcuffs. Their heads were covered then tightly fastened in thick nooses. When Romanero gave the order from the Holy Land, the wooden floors gave way and the two men fell to their deaths.

More than 50,000 spectators crammed Vicente Calderón Stadium, in the heart of Madrid, to witness the two men being hanged from the gallows at mid-field. Billions more watched on TV and online. It was even shown on the big screen inside the arena.

Once they were confirmed dead the tension became even more palpable when the TV camera was lowered, exposing Prince Javier. His head and hands were secured in wooden stockades. Unlike his two now-dead subordinates, his head wasn't covered.

As the camera slowly pulled back, it became evident that the crown prince wouldn't be hanged like the others. On either side of Crown Prince Javier hung the lifeless bodies of his two fallen countrymen.

When the floor above him gave way, the crown prince felt the earth rumbling all around him. His body quaked in terror when their necks were snapped, and they were instantly killed. He was so frightened that he urinated in his pants.

13

Upon Romanero's command, the heavy vertical blade ten feet above Prince Javier—fastened between two upright posts—was dropped and the guillotine did what it was built to do.

In a matter of seconds, Crown Prince Javier was beheaded as billions watched, thus severing Spain's royal bloodline at the neck. As his head lay on the ground in a pool of his own blood, the stadium grew eerily silent. Emotions were mixed.

Romanero thought back to the night he spent at the king's castle the day after the disappearances. He was forced to listen as Prince Javier barked instructions on what he could and couldn't discuss with world leaders at the Summit in Brussels, Belgium.

"Who's barking instructions now, you weasel!" Romanero whispered to himself.

In a statement posted for his billions of followers on social media, Romanero said he ordered the execution of the crown prince to prove his loyalty wasn't to Spain only, but to the entire world. "At this crucial point in history," he said, "loyalty to all must be placed above loyalty to country!"

Mindful of the bad blood between the two men, most understood Romanero's anger toward Prince Javier. After all, he did try humiliating him in front of so many world leaders last November. But many sensed his "loyalty to all" was secondary to his taking revenge on the late prince for his past actions. Doing it in a stadium full of onlookers proved that much.

Many silently thought it was bad form on his part.

A few hours later, Romanero offered his condolences to Spain on the death of their beloved king, who "allegedly" died of a heart attack while watching his son's head being chopped off in front of the eyes of the world.

While all that was happening, the hundreds of thousands of Muslim protesters who'd stormed Jerusalem demanding justice after the Dome of the Rock was destroyed, were rounded up and detained.

Despite what the Muslim pilot said on international TV that it was their side's fault for firing the missile in the first place, they still blamed the God of Israel. Even in prison Muslims vowed revenge!

Thousands of Christian protesters in the Holy Land were also detained at separate facilities. The only protesters still in the streets of Jerusalem were Jews. The time wasn't yet right to round them up. But that day was coming...

But the carnage didn't end in Israel. Romanero knew practicing Christians and Muslims would never recognize a one world religion that wasn't their own. Which meant they were merely taking up space on the planet, and ultimately needed to be wiped out.

Using facial recognition technology, Christians and Muslims who'd lined the streets in protest around the world, were interviewed on TV, or posted derogatory comments about Romanero online, were identified.

Many were tracked down by their IP addresses. Those who surrendered peacefully were detained at secret internment camps built before the disappearances. Those who didn't surrender peacefully were shot and killed on the spot.

When word got out that millions of their brothers and sisters in the faith were languishing in prisons around the world—or were no longer alive—and with churches, mosques, Christian and Islamic universities and religious training centers being targeted and burned to the ground all over the world, there wasn't a Christian or Muslim protester to be seen anywhere!

It was during this time that surveillance video surfaced, capturing an angry mob of citizens—secretly ordered by Salvador Romanero himself— storming the al-Aqsa Mosque and the Islamic Museum and setting them both ablaze. Both now lay in charred ruins.

With so many Muslims detained, destroying their holy sites wasn't all that difficult to do.

Peace in the Holy Land? What peace? How could anyone be jubilant under such conditions? It was pure chaos again!

And then there were the two long-haired crazed lunatics a short distance away, judging everyone with their eyes. They weren't helping things! Most wished the two creeps would just go away and leave them in peace.

How much worse would it get once the *Man of Peace* declared war on all countries involved in the sneak attack? The man who kept preaching "tolerance for all" apparently wasn't so tolerant after all. It was becoming quite obvious that only those who sided with him would be shown mercy. The rest would be exterminated.

With the peace treaty about to be signed, the blood-thirsty Salvador Romanero "dissident" killing machine was becoming drunk on the blood of all who opposed him.

2

AFTER THE PLAYING OF *Ha Tikva*, Israel's national anthem, Salvador Romanero approached the lectern. The murderous vengeance everyone saw on his face when he addressed the world the day after the bombs stopped falling, was replaced with the usual peace and tranquility he was known for in public.

Dressed in a brilliant white suit, the 30-year-old leader of the world once again looked like the most beautiful person in the universe. Every strand of his soft brown hair was in place. His dark brown eyes were fully aglow. His radiant olive skin made him look like an angel of light. It was hard to find a blemish on the man.

With his right hand, he flashed his now-famous customary peace sign, quickly forming a circle with his right hand, signifying world peace for all, as the three Islamic holy sites smoldered above him. It was bizarre, to say the least; the irony of all ironies.

"Greetings global citizens! I hope this finds each of you well. I want to begin by thanking you, Mister Prime Minister, for welcoming us all so warmly to your country. Shalom!"

"Shalom!" came the reply of the Israeli Prime Minister.

Romanero's smile glistened in the bright sunshine for all to see. "After many years of conflict and failed peace treaty negotiations, the day has finally arrived!"

Even as the words came out of his mouth, the *Miracle Maker* felt nauseous to the point of vomiting. Whenever he was in Israel, which was often of late, he was overcome by this overwhelming sickening feeling. Now about to sign a peace treaty with a race of people he hated with extreme prejudice, his insides were twisted to the point that he could barely stand still.

Knowing their God was the cause of it, Romanero frequently asked the Prince of Darkness to take this "thorn in his side" away.

His request was always denied. Satan assured his top disciple each time that his grace was more than sufficient. But in reality, he didn't have the power to remove it. Only the Most High God had that power.

The Israeli Prime Minister was also battling a nervous stomach. And for good reason. He didn't need the growing number of Jews protesting in the streets of his tiny nation to remind him that he was choosing an outsider, a Gentile, to secure Israel's borders over the supernatural protection of Yahweh God, a power that was put on display the other day for all to see.

Then again, perhaps Salvador Romanero was the one responsible for it? After all, he rightly predicted that no precipitation would fall during the global vigil a few months back.

He was the one who rightly predicted children would once again populate the planet, when no one else dared speculate.

And he was the one who boldly predicted that he would deliver peace to Israel during Passover week.

And here they were...

Whether Yahweh God or Salvador Romanero was responsible for supernaturally protecting the Jews the past few days, the Prime Minister was still unsure. By siding with Romanero, all he could do as Israel's leader was hope for the best outcome.

The tension in Israel was unmistakable...

Romanero went on, "Before we put ink on paper, Mister Prime Minister, I first want to take a moment to update everyone on a few things..." Israel's Prime Minister nodded and Romanero continued, "As you already know by now, we've located all militant rebel forces responsible for the failed attempt to attack us.

"Satellite imagery captured military planes taking off from Beijing, China, Moscow, Russia, Kabul, Afghanistan, Damascus, Syria, Amman, Jordan, Baghdad, Iraq, Beirut, Lebanon, Istanbul, Turkey, Addis Ababa, Ethiopia, Tripoli, Libya and Khartoum, Sudan. Before coming to Israel, they made a brief stop in Tehran, Iran, to refuel and be briefed by Iranian forces before attacking us.

"As far as we can tell, six-hundred enemy warplanes left Iran that day with one collective goal: to silence this beautiful moment in history. Their mission was quickly thwarted. All aircraft used that day have since been destroyed. Soon those nations will have no military aircraft among them.

"With supernatural forces protecting Israel, stronger than anything human, did they really think they could succeed? They should have known their mission was doomed long before it ever started. While it's true that

17

more than one-hundred UN and NATO planes were shot down, not a single Israeli airplane was destroyed, let alone hit by return fire.

"Even more amazing, of the thousands of casualties reported in Jerusalem at the hands of those evildoers, not a single Israeli citizen was found among them—military or civilian!" Romanero shot a quick look at the Israeli Prime Minister, "When I promised to protect Israel, I meant it!"

There was loud cheering. The 300 world leaders gathered behind the *Miracle Maker* stood more erectly. Smiles could be seen for the first time in three days.

Romanero craned his neck back and knew his comment had done what it was intended to do. *You haven't seen anything yet*, Romanero thought, keeping it to himself.

The Prime Minister chuckled nervously seeing the two mysterious men gazing at them in the distance, still judging them with their eyes. A chill shot through him.

Romanero continued, "Not only were the countries already mentioned bent on preventing peace from being offered to the nation of Israel, the stress their actions caused to so many expectant mothers, including many teenagers, led to more than two-hundred thousand innocent lives snuffed out by way of miscarriage.

"I hear your cries, ladies. I also hear the sobs of the innocent unborn victims crying out to me for vengeance. Those who did this will be the next to weep." Romanero's pro-life rhetoric had nothing to do with his championing that particular cause. It was more sinister than that: *You killed my children; my future worshipers!*

Pausing to look out at the anguished expressions on the faces of many peace-loving citizens in his midst, the *Miracle Maker* said, "Yesterday, after meeting with top military officials from around the world, I ordered an all-out attack on the cities already mentioned. I've since had a change of heart, change of approach, rather."

This caused the heads of some of his top military advisers to tilt. Their faces cringed.

"I'm not saying military force won't be used. In fact, as I speak, bombs are now falling on those cities. But only air bases, military locations, nuclear power stations and strategic government buildings are being targeted at this time, to prevent any further attacks from them.

"Once that objective has been met, I will ask my military to stand down. Instead of destroying those cities with military might, the world will watch them collapse under the weight of their deplorable sins against humanity!"

Romanero gazed out at the many gathered before him, "I will not say at this time what will cause their cities to fall, or when, only that it will happen sooner rather than later!"

Most wondered if Romanero was referring to nuclear or biological strikes. With limitless military weaponry at his disposal, he could easily wipe any country off the face of the earth if he chose to.

But why was he sharing military tactics with the enemy? What sense did it make to tell the enemy where he would strike and when?

His top military leaders could only scratch their heads and wait and wonder with the rest of the world...

Romanero continued, "Why the sudden change of tactic? Let's just say that I'm mindful of the many living in those insurgent countries who are loyal global citizens, who long for a better world in which to live. While your countries must suffer, I wish to allow ample time for all compliant citizens who feel threatened within your own borders and wish to flee the coming destruction, to relocate before your cities fall in ruins.

"As we prepare for the arrival of children in a few weeks, women who are pregnant in those countries will be given the first opportunity to relocate. Once your loyalty has been proven to the global community, you will be granted immediate asylum in the country of your choice, no questions asked, and placed in the very best medical care.

"To help make for a smooth transition, everyone relocating will receive free housing and food vouchers for up to one year, as part of a relocation benefits package. In fact, I wish to extend this offer to any citizen on the planet wishing to flee insurgent countries.

"For the next twenty-one days, those of you living in such countries— including the United States of America—will be granted immediate amnesty. But only after your loyalty to the global community has first been proven.

"Part of proving your loyalty will be your pledging allegiance to a one-world government in every way, including a one-world religion. This international decree will transcend the laws and sovereignty of all countries.

"If any country denies passage for any reason, other than incarceration, global officials will step in and see that you are ultimately granted passage to the country of your choice!"

Salvador Romanero gripped the lectern. "My dear citizens, there's no way to sugarcoat it: the only way we can have a one-world religion is by ridding the Earth of all who harbor deeply flawed, mean-spirited religious convictions which differ from ours!

"With children soon to be among us again, we mustn't let their virgin minds and souls be exposed to and corrupted by those who cling to such outdated beliefs. Which is why I ordered the mass detainment of millions of dissident Muslims and Christians.

"Unpleasant as it sounds, in order to rid the world of the scores of religious dissidents, the world population must and will be decreased by one-fourth in the coming months, only to be reduced by another one-third soon after that. Once they are removed from the planet, long term peace will finally be within our reach!"

Israel's Prime Minister glanced over at the Pope with this, "I thought we were here to sign a peace treaty?" look on his face. With all this talk of war and reducing the world populace, it was as if world peace meant nothing to Romanero. At the very least, it wasn't the number one topic of discussion.

The Pope nodded calmly.

Noticing, Romanero said, "Let me close by saying, as we celebrate peace in Israel, I strongly encourage those of you who lost your unborn babies to procreate again. I will see that nothing like this ever happens again. May you all be blessed in my name! Now let's get back to why we have all gathered here..."

After the document for peace was read publicly for all to hear, Romanero smiled at Israel's leader as only he could, "Mister Prime Minister, it is with a humble heart that the world pledges peace in your streets. Not only will your great nation be free from enemy attack for the next seven years, I hereby declare that the three Muslim holy sites will never be rebuilt on this location.

"This means you can begin at once sacrificing to your God according to your laws and traditions. Once all debris has been removed, construction of your Temple can begin immediately."

Israel's Prime Minister nodded gratefully. He took comfort knowing that millions of fanatical Muslims were in prison and couldn't touch him. If they were among the gathering now, they would do all they could to tear him to pieces with their bare hands.

Salvador Romanero ended by saying, "Mister Prime Minister, may every word of the peace agreement you now hold in your hands come to pass precisely as written. Shalom!"

"Shalom!" came the enthusiastic reply.

The peace treaty was signed with the expected pomp and circumstance. As the white doves were released into the air, Israel's Prime Minister beamed as though he'd just been given a priceless treasure. He raised the document high above his head among the enthusiastic cheering.

The smile on his face momentarily vanished when he looked in the direction of the Two Men watching and listening in the distance. The Prime Minister gulped hard. Even in complete silence, he felt the full weight of their stares. It made his insides quake all the more.

But it was nothing compared to what he would face when he stood before the Ancient of Days on Judgment Day, and was forced to give an account as to why he defiled Israel by coming into agreement with the Son of Perdition.

The limelight Israel's Prime Minister now shared with the Antichrist of the Bible—fleeting as it was—would ultimately turn inward and feast on his insides on that Great and terrible Day, as every sin he ever committed was brought to light, especially this one...

Meanwhile, before the ink even dried on the paper, many Jews, their spiritual eyes fully opened, screamed to high Heaven, "Our God would never sanction this! It was Yahweh who protected us the other day when He performed a glorious Passover miracle for His chosen people, not Salvador Romanero! The peace this Gentile promises is a false peace! Only Yahweh can protect us from the constant fear of annihilation!"

Hundreds of millions of Muslims around the world, including the many crammed in prison cells like sardines burned with anger. Who was this infidel to proclaim to their most hated enemy that their three blessed holy sites would never be rebuilt? How dare he!

They cried out to Allah vowing revenge.

The time bomb everyone heard ticking all this time had just exploded, and no one would be able to escape the aftermath.

This was only the beginning...

3

ETSM CABIN – OAK RIDGE, TENNESSEE – 5:30 A.M.

CLAYTON HOLMES STRETCHED HIS hands above his head, "It's official, y'all. With the stroke of a pen, just like that we're Tribulation Saints!" Looking around the room, he said, "Can't help but wonder who among us, if anyone, will still be alive when Christ returns?"

The room grew still as everyone considered the question. Surely there would be casualties among them; many, in fact. Now that the final hourglass of time was turned upside down, it was sobering knowing that every prophecy written about these days would no longer be held back from the planet they still occupied.

With numerous questions swirling in their minds about the surprise attack on Israel, Clayton Holmes and Travis Hartings—co-founders of the *End Times Salvation Movement*—canceled their trip to Atlanta the day after the supposed peace treaty signing.

Both thought it was best to remain at the cabin and pray and study the Word of God, hoping the Most High would shed some light on why everything unfolded the way it had.

The twelve *ETSM* members they were supposed to meet in Georgia, to inspect the seven properties they hoped to have in their possession in the coming weeks—in northwest Georgia, eastern Alabama, southwestern South Carolina and southeast Tennessee—were invited to the cabin in Tennessee instead.

Also invited to this emergency meeting were *ETSM* chief IT man, Dr. Lee Kim from South Korea, former college professor, Xiang Tse Chiang from China, former Muslim Amos Nyarwarta from Algeria, and billionaire Nigel Jones from Australia. Chiang managed to leave China just before bombs started falling on Beijing.

Two other men were also invited to the cabin. Donald Johnson was flown in from Salt Lake City, Utah, and Manuel Jiminez was flown in from Los Angeles, California.

Johnson, who had been a devout Mormon since childhood, was in charge of training missionaries in the Philippines the past 13 years. It took the Rapture for the 47-year-old man to look beyond the book of Mormon as his source of Truth. After reading the Word of God from cover to cover, his eyes were opened.

Johnson sincerely repented of his sins and trusted in Jesus and only Jesus, then worked hard to evangelize those he'd preached a false gospel to in the Philippines, who were also left behind.

He returned to the U.S. after the new year to share the gospel with family members and friends in Utah, with little success. He planned on going back to the Philippines in the coming weeks to help lead the way with other *ETSM* members over there.

Manuel Jiminez was born in Mexico but had lived in Los Angeles since he was a teenager. After coming to faith in Christ, he felt called back to Mexico to win souls for Christ Jesus in his homeland. He planned on relocating there in the coming weeks, but first wanted to spend as much time with those at the top of the organization as they would give him.

ETSM top security man, Braxton Rice drove to Hartsfield International Airport in Atlanta, in a fifteen-passenger van, to fetch the six travelers. Before heading back to the cabin in Tennessee, Rice picked up Charles Calloway at his late parents' house in Atlanta, where he now resided.

The moment they arrived, Braxton Rice placed the cabin on complete lock down. He and his three top security men took turns guarding the outside of the cabin, in shifts, making sure no one was eavesdropping on them. Since the United States stood opposed to a one world government, it was now considered a combatant country.

The tension kept mounting...

Having 25 people staying at the three-bedroom cabin Clayton Holmes and Travis Hartings purchased after the Rapture—including Braxton Rice's three top security associates and Clayton Holmes' 72-year-old aunt, Miss Evelyn—made for tight living quarters. But no one complained. Everyone was grateful just being there.

"Shall I extend the crimson line on the website to Revelation six, verse two?" Dr. Lee Kim asked Travis Hartings, regarding the www.lsarglobal.org website he managed for the *ETSM*, which stood for *Last Shot At Redemption*.

Hartings nodded yes. In his cultured Southern drawl, he said, "And I believe you'll be extending it again soon. Oh, and while you're at it, change the lighter shade of red covering Revelation chapters four and five to scarlet red.

"I feel fairly certain they've since come to pass. Also, with the Two Witnesses now among us, the first four verses of Revelation eleven should also be covered in crimson red."

"You got it, Travis," the MIT graduate from Korea said evenly.

Travis Hartings shook his head in bewilderment. "It's frightening how Romanero's using the Word of God to his advantage..."

"In what way?" Donald Johnson asked.

"Remember what he said about decreasing the population by one-fourth in the coming months, then reducing it again by another one-third soon after that?"

"Yeah?" Then it dawned on Johnson. "He took it from Revelation chapter six, right?"

"The first one-fourth, yes," Clayton Holmes interjected. "The other one-third is found in chapter nine. The only power the devil has in predicting the future comes from the Word of God. Satan knows God's Word cannot fail. He also knows this doesn't bode well for him.

"With his time running short, he's out to destroy as many lives and relationships as he possibly can. As Satan's main man, Romanero must know what's going on. Though I seriously doubt he knows of his eventual doom. His many followers sure don't..."

Nigel Jones weighed in, "His pro-life stance sickens me. What a joke! Isaiah chapter five, verse twenty is coming to life before our very eyes: 'Woe to those who call evil good and good evil, who put darkness for light and light for darkness, who put bitter for sweet and sweet for bitter!'"

Travis Hartings sighed. "Only reason he's interested in protecting life in the womb is because they'll be his future worshipers for the next seven years. Isn't it obvious?"

"To us it is, but not to his many supporters." Xiang Tse Chiang said. "Like Clayton said, they're too blinded spiritually to know all Romanero is doing is sharing the Holy Bible with them. His followers have no idea what the future holds. Only what he tells them. No doubt Antichrist will keep using the Word of God to deceive all who are spiritually blinded and doomed to destruction."

Holmes scratched his head. "Personally, I expected a severe backlash from feminists everywhere for Romanero's stern abortion comments. It's like they've flip-flopped on a woman's right to choose and suddenly embrace life in the womb. They now count it an honor and great privilege to help repopulate the planet."

24

"Never thought I'd see the day," Manuel Jiminez said.

Charles Calloway said, "I heard that! And what about all those pacifists out there suddenly backing a man who just detained millions of Christians and Muslims against their will, and promises to kill millions in the coming months with his pro-war agenda? They're so blind..."

"Speaking of war, what do you think will cause all those cities to fall? Nuclear war?" Manuel Jiminez asked.

Holmes sighed, "Not sure, actually. All we can do is speculate at this point. But whatever it is, it *will* happen. Guess we'll just have to wait and see..."

"Time for breakfast, gentlemen," Miss Evelyn yelled from the kitchen, pulling two pans of bacon and sausage from the oven.

Cooking for 25 people three times a day was a challenge for the 72-year-old woman, but Miss Evelyn didn't mind. It was part of her service to her Maker. Which is why she insisted on doing all the cooking herself.

"Great. I'm starving," Travis Hartings said.

Braxton Rice turned on his walkie-talkie to inform his men outside that it was time to eat, but in shifts. Once everyone was seated Clayton Holmes blessed the food.

Charles Calloway stabbed at the meat on his plate with a fork then placed it in his mouth. It tasted even better than it looked. "Thanks as always, Miss Evelyn, for the scrumptious feast!"

"My duty, my pleasure," came the weary reply. It wasn't the cooking that fatigued the elderly woman so much, but the cleaning up after each meal. After two days, it was taking a toll on her.

There was a pause as everyone ate their meals in silence.

After a while, Travis Hartings said, "Doctor Kim, when do you think we'll be able to use the many drones we have in our possession?"

"The programming's almost completed on the first five-thousand, so I don't see why we can't use them once we take possession of the seven properties," the MIT graduate opined, matter-of-factly. "Once we work all the kinks out, so to speak, we can distribute the drones to all other safe houses."

Manuel Jiminez weighed in, "Including Mexico?"

"Yes, Manuel. The Philippines, too," Dr. Kim said, directing his comment to Donald Johnson. "Drones will prove quite invaluable when delivering intel from one *ETSM* location to another. With so many governments in turmoil, including the United States, if our systems are ever compromised and we can't communicate electronically, drones will be our best way to maintain contact until our systems are restored."

Dr. Kim grew more serious. "Even so, drones can never be considered a 'Be All End All' solution. Once the Mark of the Beast is implemented, we can kiss drones goodbye."

Braxton Rice interjected, "Why do you say that?"

"Among the vast construction taking place in the world, monitors and scanners are being placed on virtually every street corner in all major cities and suburbs. These monitors will have the ability to scan all pedestrians within their range, including those riding in vehicles."

Dr. Kim sighed. "Once the Mark of the Beast is implemented and the scanners are fully functional, any person not recognized will be labeled a rebel and will be incarcerated or killed by universal authorities. These scanners will also detect low flying aircraft, including drones. All aircraft not properly recognized by these scanners will be shot down without warning."

"When will this occur?"

Clayton Holmes said, "At around the halfway point of the Tribulation, give or take." After what had just happened, he didn't want to give an exact timeline just yet.

"So, basically what you're saying is we have three-and-a-half-years?"

"Yes, Braxton."

Dr. Kim took a sip of his coffee, "Even before then, we must find a way to cause any and all intel being transported from one *ETSM* location to the next to self-destruct if one of our drones ever crashes to the ground or is intercepted by the enemy. This is why the programming's not quite completed yet."

Charles Calloway rubbed his chin, "Not to change the topic but can anyone shed light on the significance of the Third Temple?"

All eyes shifted to Clayton Holmes.

"To be honest," Holmes said, "until today, this was a subject I always struggled with. Partly because the Bible never revealed exactly when the Third Temple would be rebuilt. Only that it would be in existence when the prince who is to come reveals himself by entering inside the temple and stopping all sacrifices at the midway point of the Tribulation period.

"Daniel wrote about this in chapter nine of his book, in verse twenty-seven. The Apostle Paul also mentioned it in Second Thessalonians two, verses three and four, declaring that the 'man of lawlessness' will profane the temple by entering it and declaring himself to be God. With the clock now ticking, it doesn't leave the Jews much time. They have three and a half years to finish it."

Holmes paused to take a bite of his food. "Anyway, when I studied the building of the Third Temple, or Ezekiel's Temple, before the Rapture, I always saw three major obstacles which would delay its construction."

"What were they?"

"First and foremost was the location. In order for the Third Temple to be built, the Dome of the Rock, al-Aqsa Mosque and the Islamic Museum first had to be removed.

"The second obstacle was the attitude of the Jewish people and their leaders. For many decades, ultra-Orthodox Jews had a strong passion to build the Temple, but never had the support of the masses. Before the Rapture, the average Israeli was extremely secular." Eyeballing Amos Nyarwarta, Holmes went on, "Their biggest fear was that any attempt to build it would result in a holy war with the Muslims."

Nyarwarta nodded agreement. Even before coming to America, the lifelong Muslim from Algeria sensed in his spirit the religion of his childhood was on its last legs and might not survive.

What took place the past three days further confirmed it. Something deep inside told him the book he was writing for the *ETSM*, comparing Christian eschatology to what Muslims believed would happen in the last days, might not need to be finished after all. For now, Nyarwarta would wait and see.

Holmes continued, "The third obstacle was knowing the identity of Antichrist. After all, he's the one who will defile it. Now that we know for certain 'the prince who is to come' and the 'man of lawlessness' Daniel and Paul were referring to is none other than Salvador Romanero, and since God showed up three days ago and caused a mighty miracle for His chosen people, it's as if a surge of national pride was created.

"With the three Muslim holy sites removed, and with so many Muslims now in prison, Jews everywhere are flocking back to Israel in droves and are suddenly in favor of building a new Temple."

"But don't they need the Temple to be built first?"

Holmes nodded yes. "I believe until a more permanent structure is built, the Jews will erect a temporary tent temple similar to the Tabernacle of Moses. This could be done in no time. Wouldn't be surprised if they resume sacrifices from there in a day or two."

"Makes perfect sense," said Nigel Jones, rubbing his aching forehead. He still had jet-lag after the long flight from Australia.

Travis Hartings weighed in, "How awesome that we all got to witness the removal of the Muslim holy sites with our own two eyes. Even more incredible, at least to me, was hearing the pilot who fired the missile confess that Israel's God flicked it away from the Western Wall into the Dome of the Rock. All I can say is wow!"

Amos Nyarwarta's eyes filled with tears. Fully convinced that the Most High God of Israel really was the One True God, and the Jews—a people he was brainwashed to hate all his life—really were His chosen people, the former Muslim realized just how much his former faith was fueled mostly by hatred and revenge.

Had Yahweh not rescued him from the false religion of Islam, perhaps he, too, would be in prison now, totally bent on revenge against the Jews and Salvador Romanero. Or he'd already be dead and forever doomed.

Feeling overcome by the Holy Spirit, Nyarwarta shouted, "Hallelujah! Let us bless the Lord and give praise to the Most High God of Israel!"

In his deep gravelly voice, Nyarwarta started singing...

"It is well with my soul...
It is well, it is well with my soul..."

Miss Evelyn started singing the first verse of the song...

"When peace like a river, attendeth my way,
When sorrows like sea billows roll
Whatever my lot, thou hast taught me to say
It is well, it is well, with my soul..."

Everyone repeated the chorus lines after her...

"It is well (it is well)
With my soul (with my soul)
It is well, it is well with my soul..."

When they got to the last verse, everyone stood and sang with Miss Evelyn...

"And Lord, haste the day,
when our faith shall be sight,
The clouds be rolled back as a scroll;
The trump shall resound, and the Lord shall descend!
Even so, it is well with my soul..."

It is well (it is well)
With my soul (with my soul)
It is well, it is well with my soul
It is well (it is well)
With my soul (with my soul)
It is well, it is well with my soul..."

When they were finished there wasn't a dry eye inside the *ETSM* cabin. Despite that the seven most horrendous years humanity would ever face were now upon them, the 25 souls in Oak Ridge, Tennessee felt completely protected knowing Yahweh God had commanded angels to guard them in all their ways.

By dwelling in the shelter of the Ancient of Days, they were able to temporarily ignore the turmoil all around them and abide in the shadow of the One who made them.

To the outside world, this would be viewed as sheer madness. But to those who were true children of the Most High God, it made perfect sense...

4

AFTER A LENGTHY PRAISE session to the King of majesty, Charles Calloway dried his moist eyes and excused himself to use the restroom. He turned on his cell phone and saw numerous missed calls from his childhood friend, Santana Jiles.

Charles called him back.

"Hey, bro, are you in Atlanta?" Jiles seemed troubled.

"Not until tomorrow, why? Everything okay?"

"The church is gone."

"My father's church?"

"Yes. Burnt to the ground by arsonists!"

"When?" Calloway's heart throbbed within him. His father had built Mount Zion Baptist Church from the ground up, with his own two hands.

"Early this morning. Been trying to call you all day."

"Sorry. I turned my phone off so I could concentrate on the peace treaty signing..." Calloway didn't tell his friend he was at a cabin in Tennessee. "How do you know it was arson?"

"Deacon Stone drove by the church at five a.m., and saw an unfamiliar car parked in the lot. He went inside to find four masked gunmen ransacking the place. He was no match for them.

"They tied his hands behind his back and covered his mouth with duct tape. I'm at the hospital now. Deacon Stone's in intensive care. He's heavily sedated so it's hard to understand what he's saying."

Calloway grimaced. Ernest Stone was one of the first members at Mount Zion and one of Charles' late father's best friends. Many who were left behind were totally shocked upon learning that the deacon was left behind with them. "Intensive care?"

"Yeah, I'm coming to that. From what I could gather, he watched in stark terror as the thugs emptied desk drawers, filing cabinets and closets, looking for anything of value. They had absolutely no regard for church property. They even made him watch as one of them defecated before the altar, while the other three urinated on Bibles and hymnal books. One of 'em said, 'This is payback from Satan!'"

Calloway grunted, "Seriously?"

"Yeah. He even wiped himself with pages torn out of a Bible. Can't imagine being forced to witness such evil. After ransacking your father's office, they found his safe. Deacon Stone was forced at gunpoint to reveal the combination. At first, he claimed he didn't know it.

"After being struck in the head with one of the assailant's guns, he finally gave it to them. Before opening it, the thugs fired shots through the roof like a bunch of drunken cowboys. Deacon Stone said he felt like he was transported back to the Wild West. He said they had no fear of the police showing up.

"Anyway, when the leader opened the safe and found nothing of value inside, only piles of worthless paperwork, your father's favorite Bible, and a few CDs and DVDs from his past sermons, he was so enraged that he took it out on brother Stone's face."

Jiles sighed. "They beat him pretty bad, bro. He has cuts and bruises all over his face. And a few of his teeth are missing..."

Calloway clenched his fists and did his best to swallow his anger, "He's eighty-two! I wish it would've been me instead of him."

"They're lucky I wasn't there. Wouldn't have gone down without a fight. After rolling the safe into the main sanctuary, they emptied the contents on the floor in front of the altar, then grabbed all Bibles and hymnal books in the pews and threw them on the pile.

"One of them poured gasoline on top and lit a match, shouting 'Hail Satan!' As the flames quickly spread, they fired off more gunshots, poking several more holes in the ceiling, walls and pews. One of them laughed insanely while shooting out all the stained-glass windows.

"The one who defecated in front of the altar pressed his gun up against Deacon Stone's right temple saying, 'Where's your so-called Jesus now? Let Him save you! Long live Satan!' The gun must've been hot because it left a burn mark near his right temple. And he has bruises all over his face. Dark as his skin is, they're still quite visible."

Jiles shook his head. "Before leaving through the back of the sanctuary, the masked gunman slapped Deacon Stone across the face so hard it knocked him off the chair he was loosely tied to.

"Turned out to be a blessing because he was able to free himself. Otherwise, he would have been burned alive inside the church. He spent a few minutes crawling on his hands and knees looking for his glasses one of 'em tossed to the back of the sanctuary. You know how blind he is without 'em."

Charles didn't reply. He was too busy trying to stabilize his breathing.

"Thankfully he found 'em before choking to death on the smoke and was able to escape. He called 911 but it was too late. By the time the fire department arrived, the damage was already done. Paramedics affixed an oxygen mask on Deacon Stone's face and rushed him to the ER."

Hearing all this pained Calloway deeply. "Will he be okay?"

"They put him on a respirator to help clear his lungs from so much smoke inhalation, but the doctors said he'll probably survive. Can't say the same for the church. It's beyond repair. Deacon Stone said he never felt such evil in his life!"

"Text me the hospital address. I'll rearrange my schedule and leave immediately."

"Thanks, Charles. We need you here. As you can imagine, everyone's devastated."

"Tell 'em to remain calm and don't do anything foolish. This is spiritual warfare at the highest level. In the end we win. But until that day comes, we'll face many battles we can't win.

"Tell Deacon Stone I'm coming to see him. If you're still at the hospital when I get there, we can have lunch."

"I'll be here, brother."

"Good. Keep a very close eye on all doctors and nurses until we know whose side they're on. If they know Deacon Stone's a Christian, they may..." Calloway paused.

Jiles knew what he was thinking. "I hear you, bro. Will do."

"See you in a few hours."

Calloway rejoined everyone at the breakfast table.

"Why the long face?" Travis Hartings asked.

"Just got word that my father's church was burned to the ground."

"Sorry to hear that..."

Clayton Holmes said, "Fasten your seat belts, y'all, this is just the beginning. It's about to get a whole lot worse!"

"They went there to rob it but found nothing of value. One of them defecated on the floor before the altar saying, 'Payback from Satan!', while the others urinated on Bibles and hymnal books. Before leaving they set the church ablaze."

"Are you kidding?" Donald Johnson asked.

Calloway rubbed his forehead. "I wish I was. They did quite a number on the oldest living member at the church. He's in the hospital now in intensive care."

"Will he be okay?" Manuel Jiminez asked, concern clearly visible on his face.

"I think so. I know churches are being set ablaze daily. Just never thought it would be my father's church. Deacon Stone's eighty-two. He was one of my father's best friends."

"Oh my..." Miss Evelyn gulped hard, then rose from her seat and gave Calloway a comforting hug. Just hearing that a man ten-years her senior was beaten senseless by four demon-possessed men was unimaginable. It was downright evil!

Braxton Rice weighed in, "Time to start vetting everyone else from your father's church."

"Thanks, Braxton."

"But you know the rules, Charles. Only those who contact us regarding dreams they had are trustworthy. No one else! So not a word until we know for sure they're *ETSM* worthy."

"Understood. I gotta go, y'all. I wanna visit Deacon Stone before visiting hours are over. I still plan on joining you in Atlanta tomorrow to inspect the seven properties. Can you text the meeting location to me?"

Travis Hartings nodded yes.

"Before you go, Charles, let us pray for you," Miss Evelyn said.

"Yes, please!" Calloway was teary eyed. "And please pray for everyone at my father's church as well."

Everyone laid hands on Charles. After a lengthy prayer, Braxton Rice led Calloway outside and gave him the keys to an *ETSM* vehicle. "Godspeed, Charles..."

"See you tomorrow, Braxton."

At that, Calloway drove off. A million thoughts assaulted his mind. He sent a voice text message to Stephen Candelaria from Sarasota Full Gospel Church, warning him to keep a steady eye on the church in Sarasota. Chances were good someone might try to set it ablaze. Then he called Brian Mulrooney.

"Hey, Charles. I was just about to call you to get your take on the peace treaty signing." When Charles didn't reply, Mulrooney said, "Are you okay?"

"Not really. My father's church was burned to the ground early this morning, by four Satan worshipers."

"Oh, man! Sorry to hear that, bro."

"I'm on my way back to Atlanta to see the damage for myself and visit one of my father's best friends in the hospital. When he caught them in the act they beat him to a pulp. He's in intensive care. The worst part is he's eighty-two-years-old, and the oldest remaining member of the church."

Mulrooney winced. "Will he survive?"

"I hope so." There was sniffling. Then, "I need some alone time with God to calm my nerves. Would it be alright if we discussed the peace treaty signing once I get back to Atlanta and see what's what?"

"Sure, but before you go, have you heard from Tamika yet?"

Calloway sighed, "Not a word, bro."

"Think she's still alive?"

"How can we know if she never answers her phone?"

"Just tried calling her again. Was told this time the number could no longer be reached. I'm really concerned for her."

"Me too, Brian. Did you ever contact with your friend who owns those delis? Perhaps he knows something."

"I tried, but still haven't heard from Craig Rubin. It's like he wants nothing to do with me now."

"We both know why. Call him again. This is an emergency. Perhaps you should go to New York and look for Tamika yourself."

"Already thought about that. I need to know either way."

"If her conversion was genuine, at least we can know she's with Jesus now."

"Amen to that. Still, I need to know..."

"Me too. Let me go so I can focus on the road. I'll call you once I'm in Atlanta."

"You got it, Charles."

At that, the call ended.

5

THE FOLLOWING DAY

THEIR VOICES BOOMED THROUGHOUT the Wailing Wall vicinity. Deep, scratchy voices resonated thick in the Jerusalem air from these two rather strange-looking men.

Even without the use of bullhorns or microphones, everyone within a quarter-mile of the Jewish religious site heard them loud and clear. Their voices practically shook the air!

For three straight days they sat in total silence. That all changed the moment the peace treaty was signed. Now they were on their feet, as if roused from a deep slumber. They went from being two mysterious strangers judging everyone with their eyes to two loudmouths condemning everyone with their voices.

With so much chaos in the world, it was only fitting for two unsightly fanatics to rise from the ashes wearing sackcloth clothing, sandals, long wiry gray hair and beards, shouting their full-throated messages of condemnation among the mass destruction.

Authorities were unsuccessful in gathering any kind of intelligence on them. What was there to gather? As far as anyone could tell, they carried no IDs, had no medical or dental records, and they weren't registered in a single database anywhere on the planet.

The only thing authorities knew for sure was that they never left the Wailing Wall vicinity and they rarely slept, if at all. Apparently, they'd lost their minds after sustaining massive shell-shock from the fierce bombing the other day.

Of course, the one place in which they could be traced back was where most never cared to look—God's Holy Word.

From memory, one of them recited Zephaniah 1:2-3: "'I will sweep away everything from the face of the earth,' declares the Lord. "'I will sweep away both man and beast; I will sweep away the birds in the sky and the fish in the sea—and the idols that cause the wicked to stumble.'"

Then the other quoted Isaiah 45:17: "'But Israel is saved by the Lord with everlasting salvation; you shall not be put to shame or confounded to all eternity.'"

Then one quoted Jeremiah 9:23: "'Thus says the Lord: "Let not the wise man boast in his wisdom, let not the mighty man boast in his might, let not the rich man boast in his riches...'"

Then the other recited Jeremiah 9:24: "'But let him who boasts boast in this, that he understands and knows me, that I am the Lord who practices steadfast love, justice, and righteousness in the earth. For in these things I delight, declares the Lord.'"

And on and on they went, back and forth, quoting Scripture upon Scripture, their voices rising high above the landscape. It was evident they weren't there to debate the Word of God, only to preach it. And nothing could drown out their message of impending judgment; it reached the fleshly ears of all who hated God.

In a world full of people preaching sugar, these men clearly were salt! Their message was straight and to the point: "Repent or burn!"

One indisputable fact that couldn't be denied was the total command they both had regarding the Talmud. Even so, the many still-blinded rabbis who'd joined in the fierce protesting against them, were equally appalled at how they kept connecting it to the New Testament, with everything ultimately pointing to one Man, one Savior, Yeshua HaMaschiach.

Each time they did this, the rabbis shouted, "Blasphemy!" at the top of their lungs. "Yeshua?! Yahweh's only begotten Son?" they cried. "Messiah to us Jews? Anathema!"

Ignoring their outrage, one Witness quoted Psalm 31:18 from memory, "'Let the lying lips be mute, which speak insolently against the righteous in pride and contempt.'"

Then the other Witness quoted Psalm 81:11-12, "'But my people did not listen to my voice; Israel would not submit to me. So I gave them over to their stubborn hearts, to follow their own counsels.'"

Then from memory, one of them quoted Psalm 22:1, "'My God, my God, why have you forsaken me? Why are you so far from saving me, from the words of my groaning?'"

All eyes volleyed back to the other Witness when he quoted Psalm 22:14, "'I am poured out like water, and all my bones are out of joint; my heart is like wax; it is melted within my breast...'"

Then the other quoted Psalm 22:15, "'My strength is dried up like a potsherd, and my tongue sticks to my jaws; you lay me in the dust of death.'"

Then the other recited Psalm 22:16, "'For dogs encompass me; a company of evildoers encircles me; they have pierced my hands and feet.'"

Followed by Psalm 22:17, "'I can count all my bones—they stare and gloat over me...'"

Then Psalm 22:18, "'They divide my garments among them, and for my clothing they cast lots...'"

"To whom do you refer?" demanded a red-faced rabbi, already anticipating the reply.

"'The very One you crucified, the Author of life you had delivered over to Pilate. You chose a murderer to be released over Messiah. But Yahweh raised Yeshua HaMaschiach, the Holy and Righteous One from the dead. To this we are His witnesses.'"

Many tore at their robes yelling, "You blasphemers!"

Another rabbi yelled, "In the old days, you would have been stoned to death for saying such things!"

Someone else yelled, "Why can't we stone them now?"

Then another rabbi yelled, "Incarceration is too kind a verdict for them!"

Another man said, "How can you proclaim yourselves to be Jews? Are you aware that we Jews consider Yeshua anathema?"

One of the Witnesses quoted Matthew 23:27-28, "'Woe to you, teachers of the law and Pharisees, you hypocrites! You are like whitewashed tombs, which look beautiful on the outside but on the inside are full of the bones of the dead and everything unclean. In the same way, on the outside you appear to people as righteous but on the inside you are full of hypocrisy and wickedness.'"

This incensed the rabbis even more. Their anger was stoked to even greater heights when the Two Witnesses took turns quoting Isaiah 53, without ever breaking eye contact. They often changed the pronoun from "he" to "Messiah" or "Yeshua" to further demonstrate their point.

From memory, one of them quoted verse three, "'Messiah was despised and rejected by men, a man of sorrows and acquainted with grief; and as one from whom men hide their faces he was despised, and we esteemed him not.'"

Then without missing a beat, the other Witness quoted verse four, "'Surely Messiah has borne our griefs and carried our sorrows; yet we esteemed him stricken, smitten by God, and afflicted.'"

All eyes once again volleyed back to the other Witness when he quoted verse five, "'But Yeshua was pierced for our transgressions; he was crushed for our iniquities; upon him was the chastisement that brought us peace, and with his wounds we are healed.'"

Then the other quoted verse six, "'All we like sheep have gone astray; we have turned—every one—to his own way; and the Lord has laid on Messiah the iniquity of us all.'"

Back and forth they went, pronouncing judgment after judgment on the house of Israel, for their great sin and unbelief. "'Yeshua was oppressed, and he was afflicted, yet he opened not his mouth; like a lamb that is led to the slaughter, and like a sheep that before its shearers is silent, so he opened not his mouth,'" one of them said, quoting verse seven.

Then the other quoted verse eight, "'By oppression and judgment Yeshua was taken away; and as for his generation, who considered that he was cut off out of the land of the living, stricken for the transgression of my people?'"

And back and forth they went reciting Isaiah 53, "'And they made Messiah's grave with the wicked and with a rich man in his death, although he had done no violence, and there was no deceit in his mouth.'"

"'Yet it was the will of the Lord to crush Yeshua; he has put him to grief; when his soul makes an offering for guilt, he shall see his offspring; he shall prolong his days; the will of the Lord shall prosper in his hand.'"

"'Out of the anguish of his soul he shall see and be satisfied; by his knowledge shall the righteous one, my servant, make many to be accounted righteous, and he shall bear their iniquities.'"

"'Therefore I will divide him a portion with the many, and he shall divide the spoil with the strong, because Messiah poured out his soul to death and was numbered with the transgressors; yet he bore the sin of many, and makes intercession for the transgressors.'"

One of the rabbis, knowing they were referring to Yeshua yelled, "Stop this blasphemy!"

Many tore at their robes again.

Before the peace treaty was signed, citizens of Jerusalem kept pleading with their mayor and other local authorities to arrest the two deranged psychopaths.

The mayor was already in crisis management mode removing debris from the streets of Jerusalem, burying the many dead, and preparing for the peace treaty signing. He hadn't the time nor the resources to deal with them.

"My hands are already tied," was his constant reply.

But the real reason the mayor declined to take any significant action came from what took place a few times leading up to the second peace treaty signing. There were several eyewitness reports—including video footage—of citizens tossing rocks at the two men out of frustration, after they refused to answer questions from anyone.

Miraculously, not a single stone connected. Each fell harmlessly to the ground.

Seeing this, the mayor believed they were being supernaturally protected by the very same powerful, unseen shield that had protected Israel when enemy fire killed thousands of Gentiles in Jerusalem, sparing all Jews.

What else could it possibly be?

Aside from perhaps Salvador Romanero, who else on the planet could have stones thrown at them without ever connecting? They were like two strange animals no one knew how to approach, let alone capture.

Now that the peace treaty had been signed, the only thing Israeli officials could do was monitor them very closely and keep them quarantined to the Wailing Wall area. Normally when dealing with two elderly individuals, especially, this wouldn't pose a problem. But these men, despite their age, weren't normal by any stretch of the imagination.

They needed to be closely watched at all times...

As the days passed, the number of insults being hurled at the two loud mouths kept increasing. They were laughed at, mocked and cursed from people of all nations and tongues, including many of the world's most well-known athletes and celebrities.

The mayor's suspicions that the two men were being supernaturally powered and protected from above were heightened considerably when, with cameras running, a flamboyant celebrity approached the two disturbed men.

With his husband standing by his side, the homosexual actor from Hollywood said, "Come on, guys, give it a rest! Hasn't enough already happened? The peace treaty's just been signed. Why don't we all try to be peaceful with each other."

God's Two Witnesses ignored him like he wasn't even there, bruising his ego and upsetting his many fans in the process.

With the eyes of the world watching, the most bizarre thing happened. Fans of this celebrity approached the Two Witnesses, rocks in hand. The instant the four men and two women raised their hands in aggression against the Two Witnesses, without warning, fire shot out of their mouths, quickly devouring all six souls, casting another layer of mysterious fear upon Jerusalem.

After a few startled screams and "oohs and aahs", silence fell upon the Western Wall vicinity. Who were these two men? Everyone wondered with fear and trembling...

But those whose eyes and ears were open to the Word of God knew they were the Two Witnesses of the Book of Revelation and Zechariah chapters 4 and 5. This included the millions who saw them in their dreams the past few weeks—now-former Catholics, Muslims, Hindus and Buddhists.

Salvador Romanero was apprised of the situation and asked what should be done about the two men. Knowing they were the Two Witnesses of the Bible and that he didn't have the power to silence them, the *Miracle Maker* refused to take any course of action. Not yet, anyway!

That would come in time when the Master Deceiver gave him the green light to silence them for good...

IN OAK RIDGE, TENNESSEE, ETSM members were just leaving the cabin to inspect the seven properties they hoped to have in their possession in the coming weeks, when they saw the Two Witnesses breathing fire from their mouths, consuming the six individuals who tried harming them.

After the initial shock had passed, Travis Hartings said, "Doctor Kim, I think it's safe to assume you can extend the crimson red line on the website to Revelation eleven, verse five now."

"Is that the verse describing what we just saw?"

Before Hartings could reply, Clayton Holmes recited it aloud from memory, "'And if anyone would harm them, fire pours from their mouth and consumes their foes. If anyone would harm them, this is how he is doomed to be killed...'"

Dr. Kim said, "Done!" *Crazy times indeed...*

6

ONE WEEK LATER

"HEY, BROTHER TOM, HOW are you?" Brian Mulrooney said, seeing Tom Dunleavey's name appear on his cell phone screen.

"Not so good, I'm afraid," the former Catholic priest said.

Mulrooney sat up in his seat and placed his Bible on the couch next to him. "What's wrong?"

"I'm in serious trouble, Brian, and need your help."

"What kind of trouble?"

"Not on the phone."

Brian scratched his head, "Would you like to meet someplace?"

"Can I stop by your apartment? Many in the community know me. Don't want to be spotted by the wrong people."

What in the world? "Sounds serious. Where are you now?"

"Again, not on the phone. All I'll say for now is I think the Catholic Church wants me dead. After what happened today, I can never go back."

Brian wanted to press on but there was this unmistakable fear in Tom's voice. "I have a second bedroom no one uses. You're welcome to it if you want."

Relief flooded the former Catholic priest's soul. He sighed deeply, "I appreciate it so much..."

"It's the least I can do for a fellow Christ follower. Still know where I live?"

"How could I forget after the way you handed my head to me last time I was there?" Dunleavey said, trying to humor himself. It didn't work.

"It wasn't me, brother, it was all God. At least we're on the same team now."

"Amen to that." Tom Dunleavey grew serious again. "I drove by your place earlier but didn't want to drop by unannounced."

"Wish you would have."

"I was still thinking things through and asking God what to do next."

"Everything will be fine, brother. Come on over. The door will be open."

"Thanks, Brian. See you soon."

The call ended. It didn't take long for Tom Dunleavey to arrive. When he reached Brian's floor, just like last time, he was huffing and puffing considerably, breathing the labored breath of the out-of-shape. He gave a courtesy knock on the door then opened it.

Brian placed his Bible on the table and rose from the couch to welcome his guest.

"I brought donuts."

"Ah, you've discovered one of my weaknesses."

Tom Dunleavey smiled awkwardly and rubbed his belly. "Mine, too, I confess..."

Brian greeted his brother in Christ with a comforting hug. Last time they met, they exchanged handshakes only. Brian felt Tom's inner trembling. "Want me to brew a pot of coffee?"

"Sounds good, actually."

"Take a load off, brother. Make yourself comfortable. It'll be ready in a jiffy."

This was Brian's first time seeing Tom stripped of his priestly garments. He wore gray slacks and a brown sweater. Now that they were on the same side, with nothing left to debate spiritually, the tension they both felt last time was nowhere to be found.

A few moments later, they were seated in the living room.

Brian muted his television, but left it turned on. He always wanted to be ready if and when new news broke anywhere in the world. "So, why do you think the church wants you dead?"

Tom Dunleavey took a gulp from his coffee cup. His eyes projected unending fear and confusion. "A friend of mine who happens to be a higher up in the church sent me a chilling email this morning, advising that I've been placed on the Pope's dissenters list. Not only me but many others in my parish who have also denounced church doctrine and now cling to the Scriptures. Roughly a third of us..."

Brian said, "After the powerful sermon you preached when me and Jacquelyn were there, I'm surprised everyone hasn't been converted. You made it difficult to believe we were in a Catholic Church."

Tom Dunleavey eyeballed Brian, "That's precisely why I'm in trouble. Ever since my conversion, I knew my days at the church were numbered. Just never thought I'd defect this soon. I can't help but feel frightened for those who are on our side. Especially the nuns and priests..."

"Why's that?"

"We're subjected more to the laws of the Church than to the laws of the land. If caught, we'll never stand trial in a court of law. I fear all defectors who are caught will be killed without mercy."

"Where are they now?"

"Don't know. Phone's been off all day. Only turned it on to call you. Then I powered it off again. Before leaving the rectory, I did, however, forward the email I received, informing the three priests and two nuns on our side that I was leaving immediately and suggested they do the same. I warned everyone else to be extremely vigilant, that they may not even be safe at home. Just hope they took my advice...This is totally insane!"

"You can say that again..."

The 62-year-old man took a Dunkin Donuts napkin and cleaned his thick bifocal glasses. "The Church means business, Brian. I'm told hundreds of thousands of Catholic dissenters, worldwide, have recently vanished, never to be heard from again, including a handful of cardinals, if you can believe that. If my source is correct, the church is mainly targeting those over the age of thirty who have been deemed as 'set in their ways.'"

Brian sighed. "That would include me..."

Tom Dunleavey nodded. "The Pope's quite paranoid these days. Just like Romanero has people monitoring social media platforms looking for dissidents speaking out against him—namely evangelical Christians and Muslims—the Pope's doing the same with Catholics who speak out against the Church.

"If my source is correct, as part of Romanero's aggressive plan to drastically shrink the global population, the Pontiff plans to do his part in the coming months, by killing ten million dissidents and defectors who have fallen out of line with Church authority. I'm told many within the church are terrified."

There was a sigh. "With nearly a billion Catholics still on Earth, even if he kills a hundred million, it wouldn't make much of a dent. And that's just for starters. By the time it's all said and done, I wouldn't be surprised if a half-billion Catholics were slaughtered by that monster. Many of them will be our brothers and sisters in Christ."

Tom Dunleavey shook his head in disgust. "I gave my life to the Catholic Church. And how do they repay me? By wanting to kill me?! And for what, preaching the Truth?"

43

"I understand how you feel, brother. At least we can rejoice knowing God saved us both out of that false system."

"Don't get me wrong, Brian. I'm eternally grateful. But things are moving so quickly. I fear for the lives of my flock."

"What made you a target? I mean, you don't seem the type to post disparaging remarks about anyone online, especially the Pope or Salvador Romanero. You're not that foolish."

Tom Dunleavey covered his face with his hands. "Three men visited my church last Sunday."

"Who were they?"

"Spies."

"How can you be so sure?" Mulrooney silently wondered if spies would ever infiltrate the Chadds Ford property, once they were settled on the land? He shivered at the thought.

"Even before the peace treaty signing, the Pope sent out spies to Catholic churches looking for dissidents and defectors. The three men who visited my parish seemed nice enough. Everything went smoothly until..."

"Until what?"

Tom Dunleavey sighed. "Until I told the congregation that in its long and storied history, not a single person had ever been saved by the Catholic church. Only God could save souls, not any particular church and certainly not man. Much of what the Church has set in motion since its inception has only led to eternal destruction for so many."

"Wow!" Brian Mulrooney shook his head. He couldn't be more impressed by Tom's boldness. "I'm proud of you, brother."

"It feels good preaching the Truth for a change. The difference it's making for so many in my parish is nothing short of miraculous. Anyway, after going through the customary piling on of errors handed down by the church—reciting Hail Mary's, praying the rosary, confessing one's sins to a priest, performing various works, the worship of saints and the veneration of angels, to the myth of purgatory, and on and on—I urged my people to seek God above all other things and to read their Bibles on their own, without church supervision.

"That's when the three visitors started getting fidgety. But I was just warming up. The text I chose for that day was the great praise session in Heaven found in Revelation, chapters four and five. After reading it, I asked the congregation if anyone else was being exalted other than Jesus?

"Many heads shook all throughout the sanctuary. I asked if they found it as interesting as I that there was no mention in the text of a single Pope being exalted or worshiped alongside Jesus?

"This caused the three men to grow even more fidgety. I said if they were true vicars of Christ, wouldn't they be exalted in Heaven as well? Wouldn't the Disciple John have seen them in his vision and included them in the text? I believe he would have. But he didn't. And for good reason.

"In fact, there's no mention of any Popes in the Book of Revelation. At least not in a good way. If, by chance, some are in Heaven, it's only because they trusted in Jesus like all other redeemed souls had. Nothing more. Being Pope had nothing to do with their being part of the Body of Christ. If anything, it put distance between themselves and God.

"I then brought to their attention that even Mary wasn't being exalted in the text. I told them she was in Heaven not for bringing Jesus into the world, but for trusting in Him as Lord and Savior.

"I referenced Luke chapter one for this. Seeing so many confused looks in the sanctuary stabbed at my insides, because it further confirmed the so-called gospel I'd been preaching all my life was a false one.

"With a heavy heart I confessed the reason so many Catholics have become children of destruction was because of people like me. Instead of preaching Christ alone at mass, I taught Christ plus works plus many other things equated to one's salvation. That's when I broke down and couldn't stop weeping for the longest time."

Mulrooney covered his mouth with his hands, "What a powerful testimony!"

"I must say I was just as bold with them as you were with me last time." Tom Dunleavey chuckled nervously. Beads of sweat were visible on his nearly bald forehead. "And that's when the three men glared at me angrily and left the church without speaking to anyone.

"The next day they came back revealing their true identities. After a lengthy reprimand, I was placed on administrative leave. It wasn't so much the words they spoke that frightened me, but what I saw in their eyes. I thought they were going to arrest me or even worse..."

Tom Dunleavey had this faraway look on his face. "Scared me so much I stayed in my personal quarters day and night reading the Word of God, until I got the email today. And here I am..."

"Were you able to pack your personal belongings?"

The former Catholic priest yawned and nodded yes. "Wasn't much to pack, actually."

"Give me your car keys. I'll get your things."

Tom Dunleavey didn't protest. He was too drained to. Clearly, he was feeling the effects of the day. He handed Brian his keys, "You'll find everything in the trunk."

"Be back in a jiffy. You've had a rough week. Take it easy. You're safe here."

When Mulrooney returned he led his guest into the spare bedroom. "Sorry in advance for the full closets. My girlfriend, Renate, took this room hostage the day I moved in." Brian sighed, "Soon-to-be former girlfriend, that is..."

Tom Dunleavey looked at Brian strangely. "Renate?"

Mulrooney laughed. "She's the reason I stayed in Michigan all this time. Then came the Rapture. God changed my heart and everything in my former life came crumbling down. Then God led me to Jacquelyn. Guess you can say it was the beginning of my Luke twelve experience."

Tom Dunleavey suppressed another yawn, "Luke twelve experience?"

"You know where Jesus said we'll be divided, father against son and son against father, mother against daughter and daughter against mother, et cetera, et cetera."

Tom Dunleavey pretended not to hear it. Not now, anyway. "The room's just perfect. Thanks for taking me in. You're a real godsend..."

Brian sighed. "Sorry to say, brother, but I'm afraid all I can offer you is temporary shelter. I'll be leaving Michigan soon."

Tom Dunleavey raised an eyebrow. "Where you going?"

"Pennsylvania. But that's all I can tell you. Sorry."

"Interesting..."

"Why's that?"

"I had another dream last night..."

Mulrooney's ears perked up. "What kind of dream?"

"That you moved to a remote location far from Ann Arbor. Not sure where it was, but I'm certain it wasn't in Michigan. I think you and Jacquelyn were married, because I vividly remember seeing you both wearing wedding rings. The two of you were placed in charge of a communal living place, or something like that. I remember seeing many cottages."

Brian's eyes grew wide. "Really?" *Is he ETSM worthy?*

"Yes. Coincidentally, much like the first dream I had, which led to our so-called spiritual showdown, this dream went on for three straight nights. The last one came last night. Then I woke today to the frightening email..."

"Fascinating." Brian wanted to press on, but his guest couldn't stop yawning. It had been a long and stressful day. *Time to call Charles!* "Why don't you rest, brother. We can continue this in the morning."

"Can we pray first?" The desperation in his voice was overpowering. Brian nodded, "I was just about to suggest the same thing."

At that, the two men dropped to their knees on the carpeted floor of the spare bedroom. They held hands and prayed to the God they both thought they knew as Catholics but never really did.

Tom Dunleavey prayed for each member of his now-former church, by name, hoping they, too, had found safe passage. Even if they would never again worship under the same roof, he still felt responsible for them.

When he was finished, Brian prayed that God would provide the necessary grace and strength for the members of Charles Calloway's father's church in Atlanta, especially Elder Stone.

Finally, he prayed for Tamika Moseley. The way he cried out to God on her behalf—with such raw emotion—brought Tom Dunleavey to tears. He didn't know this woman Brian was praying for but, whoever she was, she was obviously special to him.

And Tom Dunleavey was right. Tamika was special to Brian! Not only were they good friends and family in Christ Jesus, she was the one God had used to connect him to Charles Calloway. That alone made her very important to him.

When Brian was finished, both men wiped tears from their eyes.

"Don't know what I'd do without you, Brian."

"Likewise, brother."

Tom suppressed another yawn. "Now that I know I'm safe for the night, it's like all the energy left my body."

"I'll leave you alone so you can rest. See you in the morning." Brian went to his bedroom and called Charles Calloway.

"Hey, Brian," Charles said softly.

"Did I wake you?"

"No. Still at the hospital with Deacon Stone. Been reading the Scriptures to him all night. He finally dozed off. Think I'll spend the night here with him."

"How is he?"

"Still in a lot of pain, but the Doc says his lungs are slowly clearing. When I arrived, the room was full of visitors from church. At Deacon Stone's insistence, they were praying for the four thugs who burned the church to the ground. My heart warmed over hearing them praying like that."

"We just prayed for Deacon Stone. Tamika too."

"We, as in you and Jacquelyn?"

"No. Remember my friend, the former Catholic priest?"

"Tom Dunleavey?"

"Yes. He's on the run from the Catholic Church."

"What? Seriously?"

"Yes. He thinks the Church wants him dead. He told me many Catholics have recently vanished, never to be heard from again."

"Haven't heard anything about it in the news, or anything from Clayton or Travis..."

"According to him, you won't. Looks like he'll be staying with me until I move to Pennsylvania. Anyway, he had another dream..."

"What kind of dream, Brian?"

"Our kind. He saw me and Jacquelyn far away from Ann Arbor, Michigan in charge of a 'commune', to use his word. I believe God's leading him to the *ETSM*."

"Your timing's impeccable. I'm in the process of emailing Braxton Rice with the rest of the names from my father's church, so they can be vetted. Would you like me to include brother Tom?"

"Yes, please."

"It could take weeks before I hear back from Travis on this matter. But since brother Tom had our kind of dream, it puts him on the fast track. Many of the names I'm sending haven't had dreams yet. Guess you can say they'll be preemptively vetted, just in case."

"Let's hope they have the dream soon."

"Amen to that." Charles sighed. "When I think about what those cowards did to an elderly man, I can't control my anger. Why couldn't it have been me instead of Deacon Stone?" Calloway sniffled. "The items they destroyed in my father's safe were the closest links I had to his preaching. They're irreplaceable."

"I can only imagine how you feel, Charles. But never forget they can take your father's things but they can never remove him from your memory."

48

"I know, Brian, but right now I feel nothing but hatred toward them."

"It sounds to me that Deacon Stone was the ultimate victim. Yet, he asked everyone to pray for his tormentors. I suggest you do the same. Never forget, if they don't repent and trust in Jesus soon, they'll end up eternally doomed. What can be worse than that?"

"Thanks, Brian. I needed to hear that."

"Why don't we pray now and ask God to remove the anger from your heart?"

"Go ahead. I'll listen. Don't wanna wake Deacon Stone."

Both men closed their eyes and Brian began. This was something they did every night since meeting at the Waldorf-Astoria Hotel. They never missed a night since.

Once Brian was finished, Charles Calloway whispered a simple "Amen" and the call ended.

Mulrooney sat on the edge of his bed and took a few deep breaths, hoping the room would stop spinning soon. It was hard to believe that only a week had passed since the signing of the peace treaty, yet so much had happened in that short span of time.

First it was the many hangings shown on live television, followed by the beheading of the crown prince of Spain—at a packed coliseum of all places—at the hands of his chief nemesis, Salvador Romanero.

Then to see millions of American citizens on TV waiting in long lines to take advantage of Romanero's relocation offer. Most interviewed couldn't wait to denounce their citizenship as Americans and move to other countries. Millions had already been processed. Millions more were still waiting to be interviewed.

All this as bombs kept pounding enemy cities. It was too much to absorb.

Add into the mix the arson of Charles' father's church, not to mention Tom Dunleavey's being on the run from the Catholic church for preaching the Truth, and it was easy to understand why the room was spinning!

Brian knew this time was coming. He just hoped things would slow down a little, so he could catch his breath.

How much worse could it get? Mulrooney knew the answer.

This was only the beginning of what was still to come.

Brian shivered at the thought...

7

TWO WEEKS LATER

IN THE TWENTY-ONE DAYS since Salvador Romanero declared all borders temporarily open, nearly 600,000,000 citizens willingly denounced citizenship in the countries of their birth in order to relocate, making this, by far, the largest global population shift in the history of the world.

Due to the overwhelming response, though the deadline was now upon them, millions still waited in long lines to be processed. Those who were smart began the tedious process of filling out forms and answering questions online. They got to wait in lines that moved more briskly before taking the oath of allegiance.

That part needed to be done in person. No exceptions!

Pregnant women didn't have to wait in line at all. While their paperwork was being processed they reclined indoors in total comfort until it was time to take the oath.

The countless benefits to being pregnant inspired teenagers everywhere to want to experience what Romanero called, "the boundless joys of motherhood".

Suddenly getting pregnant was more chic than going to college or climbing the extremely-shaky corporate ladders of the world. And the benefits were infinitely better. Add to the fact that, like everyone else, they would receive free housing and food vouchers for up to one year—as part of Romanero's relocation benefits package—and the decision to get pregnant was a no-brainer.

Without giving it a second thought, scores of young women quit jobs and dropped out of high school and college, leaving many concerned parents in their wake, especially those who'd recently come to faith in Christ.

These parents were fearful for their daughters and prayed that God would rescue them before it was too late. In many cases, they begged their offspring not to leave the countries of their birth.

Most were unsuccessful.

These parents loathed Salvador Romanero for separating what was left of their families but dared not badmouth the *Miracle Maker* publicly for fear that if their daughters—who were still kids themselves—confessed their parents' hatred of Salvador Romanero during the interview process, it could mean death for them.

In the United States of America alone, a staggering 70,000,000 citizens were among those seeking relocation to Canada, Mexico or halfway around the world.

Not surprisingly, the largest demographic seeking relocation were Muslims, equating to 200,000,000. What was alarming to some was that many hardcore Middle Eastern Muslims—those vowing revenge on Salvador Romanero for the recent mishaps in Israel—chose to relocate to countries in the Western Hemisphere.

But with everything moving so briskly, and with the deadline now upon them, there was no time to protest or challenge it.

All in all, regardless of country, those relocating came from all walks of life and from most religious groups. Some did it to be with someone they'd met online halfway around the world. Others were living in countries illegally and wanted to move elsewhere without fear of incarceration.

Some had lengthy criminal records. Some were drug addicts. Even low-level criminals were being released from prison for the sole purpose of relocating to other countries to begin life anew.

In the end, one's past mattered not. Morals and character weren't nearly as important as accepting the terms set forth by the global community, namely Salvador Romanero.

For those who were cash-strapped—the vast majority—having free food and housing for one year made this their big chance to finally experience life in other countries.

What went unspoken but had actually made Romanero's relocation benefits package feasible was that, because of the disappearances, many homes on the planet no longer had people living in them.

As for the food, most would come from the various food banks around the world. But providing so much food to hundreds of millions of people, all at once, would prove foolish in the months to come...

Most Americans who relocated said they did it because of President Danforth's defiant opposition to Salvador Romanero.

They detested him for it.

Fearing bad things would soon happen to the United States, they didn't want to still be around when it happened.

When it came time to take the oath, instead of placing hands on the Holy Bible or the Quran, oath-takers raised one hand and placed the other on the documents they would sign after pledging their complete loyalty and total submission to Salvador Romanero and his one world government and religion.

Once allegiance was sworn, the person taking the oath was asked, "Do you understand the terms set forth in the document upon which your left hand rests?"

"I do," was the standard reply.

"Do you agree to all terms?"

"Yes."

"Do you understand that once relocation has been granted, the penalty for disloyalty after agreeing to the terms will mean death for you? No exceptions!"

"Yes, I do."

"Congratulations! You are free to relocate. Once you arrive there, someone will be waiting to take you to your temporary housing. Enjoy your new life!"

The entire oath-taking process was recorded and stored onto the computer system in Brussels, Belgium known as the Beast. So advanced was this system it had the capability of storing every detail on every person on the planet—including their complete DNA make up and the numbers of hairs on their heads—with the slightest of ease.

Of the 200,000,000 Muslims taking this oath, half were nominal in their faith and were labeled as "secular" by hardcore Muslims. All they wanted was a better life for their families far away from the chaos invading their countries. If it meant forgoing what the Quran taught to achieve this goal, so be it.

The other half were staunch jihadists in every sense of the word. With their nations under siege, if they had any hope of obtaining global domination, relocation was deemed necessary for now. It was vital, in fact.

The required oath they'd made to Romanero's one-world religion was as worthless as the paper on which their signatures were recorded. Islam was the only true religion. Everything else was pagan at best, advanced by enemy infidels.

The fact that they'd lied in order to gain passage elsewhere meant nothing to them. They were taught it was okay to lie to the infidels if it served a greater purpose for the cause.

With three of their venerated holy sites in Israel destroyed, and with Romanero vowing they would never be rebuilt, all that mattered to them now was revenge!

Another major setback they faced was that some of their underground arsenals, stockpiled with massive amounts of chemical, biological and nuclear weaponry, were confiscated by Romanero's forces or destroyed during the fierce bombing campaign.

But as divine providence would have it, most of it went undetected and was still hidden deep beneath the Earth's surface in remote areas far from their larger cities. They would remain buried until these Islamic jihadists were resettled and had ample time to reorganize.

When the time was right, they'd be unearthed for the sole purpose of striking back at the infidels. Every last resource they had would be squandered away on achieving three main objectives: destroying the nation of Israel, followed by the United States of America, and killing Salvador Romanero.

Once those three objectives were achieved, everything else would fall into place.

While wiping Israel off the face of the Earth would always be their top priority, the fact that the tiny country was being supernaturally protected by their God, meant their focus had to be on the two other objectives for the time being.

If they could somehow find a way to bring America to its knees in the coming months and assassinate Salvador Romanero, they could then unearth their remaining resources and kill all Jews everywhere.

Thousands of bombs with Psalm 83:4 hand-painted on them declaring, "Come," they say, "let us destroy them as a nation, that the name of Israel be remembered no more" were still in their possession waiting to be unleashed on Israel.

Despite how dark and gloomy things looked now, when the time was right, Israel would cease to exist...

JUST AS THE WORDS Salvador Romanero spoke about "countries falling under the weight of their own sins", were starting to fade into the backdrop of society, he appeared on international television with what could only be described as the appearance of someone concealing a mighty secret that no one else knew.

After spending a full night in his meditation room with the Master Deceiver, the *Miracle Maker* looked confidently determined. The aura he gave off was that the entire universe was subject to his control. It was impossible not to notice it.

His address was short and to the point, "After being assured that all enemy air bases, military locations, nuclear power stations and strategic government buildings were dismantled and utterly destroyed, I've called for an immediate ceasefire on the twelve countries responsible for their coordinated attempt to thwart the peace treaty signing in Israel.

"Where ornate palaces, government buildings, military facilities, churches, mosques, and all other threats once stood in those countries, little remains now but smoldering wreckage.

"All of their nuclear forces and military bases have either been confiscated by us or destroyed, and many of their armed forces, including most who were deployed to Israel in the days leading up to the original peace treaty signing, have been silenced for good."

As Romanero spoke, viewers saw on a split screen the destruction in Moscow, Russia. The Kremlin, Red Square, and most of Moscow's government and research buildings lay in ruins.

Viewers then saw footage of the destruction in Tehran, Iran, followed by Istanbul, Turkey, then Damascus, Syria, and on and on...

"At this time, I wish to commend my military on a near-flawless campaign. Your efforts were quite extraordinary. Now I'm asking you to step down as I finish it without your assistance!"

With an assuring grin on his face, Romanero said, "Within twenty-four hours after the last global citizen has been relocated, you will witness with your own two eyes the words I spoke coming to pass precisely as stated, without the use of a single weapon.

"But nothing will happen until everyone seeking relocation has been processed. If you are still waiting in line, let me assure you that you *will* be processed. To help move things along more efficiently, I've ordered for a doubling of case workers at each location. Not only that, many more aircraft have been repositioned to help transport those who have already been processed. Remain patient a little longer.

"Not surprisingly, the response in the United States has been overwhelming. More than seventy million have forfeited their rights as American citizens in order to be part of something far greater.

"I find it quite interesting that if this offer had been made prior to the disappearances, the U.S. population would have easily doubled, if not tripled. Now, save for a small fraction, most seem to want nothing to do with that once mighty nation."

Romanero paused to let his comment hang thick in the air, knowing President Danforth was undoubtedly watching from the White House. "In closing, those of you not living in the twelve insurgent countries who have chosen not to relocate at this time, let me assure you that there will be other opportunities down the road.

"But for now, aside from those already waiting in line, I hereby declare all borders closed so caseworkers can focus all their time on processing the many who are still waiting in line.

"Once that objective has been reached and everyone has reached their new destinations, sit back and watch in awe as I finish what my brave and mighty military started. Until then, may you all be blessed in my name."

At that, the camera faded to black in Madrid, Spain, and newscasters started dissecting Romanero's address. Even with his "no weapons" comment, a nervous energy circled the planet, as citizens of the world braced for impact. Not knowing what to expect, grocery store shelves were laid bare all over the world.

Lost among the flurry of activity was that not a single Christian was among the massive global exodus. Whereas Muslims were taught it was okay to lie to further their agenda, Christians were taught otherwise.

They knew this wasn't the implementation of the Mark of the Beast; but it was the initial shake up, so to speak, the pulling up of roots and planting them into an unknown, shallow soil.

Christ followers knew there was still time for those relocating to repent and come to faith in Jesus. Perhaps moving away from their familiar surroundings would cause them to contemplate life on a much-deeper level.

Hopefully God would give them new hearts and put His Spirit inside them, as written in Ezekiel 36:26-27. That would be the ongoing prayer of the Christian community from this point forward.

But once the future chip was implemented there could be no turning back for all who willingly took it into their bodies. Their fate would be sealed, and their souls would ultimately be sent to the eternal lake of fire.

What Christians didn't presently know was while the super computer in Brussels recorded every pledge of allegiance to Salvador Romanero, it also flagged every citizen on the planet who chose not to relocate.

This was the main reason the offer was made in the first place...

8

ONE MONTH AFTER THE PEACE TREATY SIGNING

THIRTEEN HOURS AFTER THE last person was relocated, it happened: the ground started shaking in Tehran, Iran. At first, it was enough to rattle a few buildings and fill those living there with mild concern.

When the shaking didn't stop but kept getting stronger—and infinitely more violent—mild concern quickly mushroomed into full blown fear and panic. Normally earthquakes lasted only a few seconds, but not this one.

Suddenly, like a throttle turned on full blast, the ground started shaking ever so violently. It was unlike anything past earthquake survivors had ever experienced before.

People were thrown around like rag dolls. Some slammed into walls. Others went flying through plate glass windows. Some fell many stories to their deaths below.

In the end, with the ground shaking violently beneath their feet, there was no safe place to hide. Normally it wasn't the earthquake itself that claimed so many lives; it was what happened after the quake—the destruction of man-made roads and structures, landslides, avalanches, tsunamis, and so forth. But not this time.

It didn't take long for the news unfolding in Tehran, Iran to break. The world watched in horror as an earthquake registering a magnitude 9.9 quickly reduced buildings to rubble, as if made out of paper mâché. Even buildings deemed "earthquake proof" collapsed without posing the slightest challenge.

Streets and roadways were turned into angry waves traveling on a violent ocean, flicking vehicles of all shapes and sizes hundreds of feet in the air before falling back to Earth a good distance away. Many gas and water lines recently repaired after the disappearances had ruptured again. Power lines were down as far as the eye could see, causing countless fires and explosions.

Smoke billowed up everywhere.

In just minutes, the city of Tehran was completely leveled. There was no need to fear aftershocks. The city lay in ruins. Power was out everywhere.

Watching in stunned horror, many covered their hearts and mouths with their hands, gasping for breath. The words, "collapsing under the weight of deplorable sins" was at the forefront of every sound mind on the planet.

It was frightening and incredibly awe-inspiring at the same time how Salvador Romanero the Great had predicted something so massively destructive like this in advance.

There simply were no words to describe it.

Just as everyone was slowly coming to grips with what their eyes had been exposed to, there was breaking news in Iran's second most populated city, Mashhad, situated in the Razavi Khorasan province. In a matter of minutes, a 9.5 quake rocked the city, destroying everything in its path, leaving scores of dead bodies in the aftermath.

A few minutes later, there was breaking news in Iran's third most populated city, Isfahan. A 9.4 quake this time creating more death and destruction. Then there was breaking news in Iran's fourth most populated city, Karaj, followed by Iran's next most populated city, Tabriz.

Citizens of the world watched in total disbelief.

Suddenly, there was breaking news in Shanghai, China. A 9.8 earthquake shook the city for nearly three minutes, completely leveling the many skyscrapers which had stood so proudly for many years in the city also known as the "Paris of the East".

Then news broke in Beijing of a 9.7 quake. Total destruction and mass chaos ensued. Earthquakes were then reported in the cities of Guangzhou, Shenzhen, Tianjin, Taipei (located on the north coast of Taiwan) and Hong Kong.

Needless to say, these once-sprawling cities no longer looked recognizable.

A few minutes later, as news stations struggled mightily to keep up with the breaking news in Iran and China, there was breaking news in Moscow, Russia, followed by Saint Petersburg, Novosibirsk and Yekaterinburg.

Simultaneously a Domino effect of earthquakes caused the entire world to tremble in horror. All major cities were destroyed in Afghanistan, Syria, Jordan, Iraq, Lebanon, Turkey, Ethiopia, Libya and Sudan.

In just a few seconds their major cities, some of which were hotbeds of Islamic radicalism, lay in ruins.

It took roughly an hour, but every large city within the twelve enemy countries were reduced to rubble. Light tremors were felt in neighboring countries, but the epicenters were clearly based in and around the cities in which Romanero had pronounced judgment.

For the first time in recorded history, multiple earthquakes struck Planet Earth simultaneously, each registering a mind-numbing magnitude 9.0 or above. Death and carnage were visible as far as the eye could see where the earthquakes had struck, were targeted, rather. Buildings lay smoldering in ruins in many cities.

Unlike all past catastrophes, there would be no international relief this time. As far as the *Miracle Maker* was concerned, those cities no longer mattered. They were mere footnotes in the history of civilization, and a necessary part of the massive population reduction.

As impressive as Romanero's military had been in destroying key strategic locations beforehand, it couldn't compare to this. There wasn't an army or terrorist organization on the planet that could hope to achieve what the *Miracle Maker* had just accomplished in sixty minutes.

It made his top military advisers fear and respect him even more.

The chief concern coming from the scientific communities of the world was that the enormous seismic waves created by the multiple quakes might weaken the tops of magma chambers—large underground pools of liquid rock found beneath the surface of the Earth—or disturb the gases inside the chambers, potentially causing volcanic eruptions in many places.

Geologists, seismologists and scientists at the Institute of Volcanology and Seismology at Hokkaido University in Japan monitored all volcanic activity very closely.

Given what had just happened, even the slightest hiccup registered anywhere on the planet caused fear to snake through them.

They warned that with so much friction generated from tectonic plates grinding and scraping against each other in so many places—all caused by the many earthquakes—the massive waves of energy traveling through the earth at blinding speed needed to escape somewhere.

Would it lead to volcanic eruptions or perhaps tsunamis at some point? It was too soon to know for sure...

The only thing preventing full-blown panic from pushing them into a permanent state of hopelessness was that 75 percent of the world's volcanoes—active and dormant—were situated along the Pacific rim. This region was called the "Ring of Fire" because it circled the Pacific Ocean and was home to 452 volcanoes.

This was also where 80 percent of all earthquakes on the planet occurred. Since the quakes took place far from those regions, they were kept off the "imminent danger" list for now.

The other possible danger they faced was with nuclear power plants. Had any suffered structural damage in the quakes? If so, it could lead to massive meltdown in some places. Scientists at the National Earthquake Information Center (NEIC) would keep monitoring things very closely for the foreseeable future.

But even without volcanic eruptions or meltdowns at nuclear power plants, the stress the earthquakes caused to the planet would have a devastating impact on the environment and the world economy as a whole.

In many places, the costs would be incalculable. No country would be spared.

Even so, in the coming days, the world would marvel all the more—friend of Romanero and foe alike—when scientists, seismologists and geologists would confirm the quakes weren't generated by man, as some were speculating. They came naturally.

In other words, the ground wasn't manipulated by man in any way, as documented in the past in the United States, Japan, and Canada. Most human-induced earthquakes were caused by the injection of fluids into deep wells for waste disposal, or when scouting for oil. Others were caused by deep mining and nuclear testing.

But those quakes were only felt in the immediate area surrounding the test sites, and were so minor they barely registered, if at all.

Scientists, seismologists and geologists couldn't help but be completely baffled by Salvador Romanero, mystified even.

Some of his past so-called miracles could easily be explained away, but not this one. Clearly this man had special powers and insights no one else had. Many threw in the towel, confessing what happened could only be explained as something they were trained not to believe in, a true miracle.

"Could there be any doubt now that Romanero was god?" said a scientist from India.

"Who else could order 9.0 earthquakes to strike various locations of his choosing?" said another from Costa Rica. "Surely not Jesus! Surely not Allah or Confucius or Buddha!"

The overall consensus among scientists was that only Salvador Romanero the Great was capable of performing this sign of all signs. And to further prove his divine nature, he graciously spared so many lives by allowing them ample time to relocate to other countries before the grounds started quaking.

As the world marveled at the *Miracle Maker,* in truth, only Yahweh had the power to send the devastating earthquakes. The very same supernatural power hovering above the nation of Israel, protecting the city and the Two Messengers God had sent back to Planet Earth to fulfill prophecy, was the very same power that had caused those cities to collapse under the weight of their own sins.

The Most High sent the quakes for their failed attempt to strike the land of Yahweh's beloved people during Passover Week.

Only those who were blinded to the Truth—the vast majority—were totally unaware of it...

9

THE FOLLOWING WEEK

PRESIDENT JEFFERSON DANFORTH FIRST met with Clayton Holmes and Travis Hartings at an underground bunker somewhere in the foothill mountains of northern Virginia.

After offering to assist their growing organization, the President arranged for the two leaders of the *End Times Salvation Movement* to meet a second time at the White House. That meeting took place last month. Much was accomplished.

They made tentative plans to meet three months later so they could start implementing those plans. But after watching Salvador Romanero's forces surgically destroy multiple cities, before Romanero completely leveled them with devastating earthquakes, just as he had predicted, the President was suddenly fearful for his life.

After placing America on Threat Con Delta, the highest level, he quickly rearranged his schedule. He couldn't help but wonder if the *Miracle Maker* would send earthquakes to America next?

Rumors were already spreading...

The very thought of American cities collapsing at the command of a madman nearly caused the President's heart to give out on him. As it was, Southern California averaged roughly 10,000 earthquakes per year. The vast-majority went unnoticed. But even the slightest tremor filled most with stark terror now.

Everyone was understandably on edge.

But that was just the beginning of President Danforth's troubles. The massive security meltdown in Israel, which led to the surprise attack last month, still had his stomach in knots.

Under normal circumstances, the vast military coalition in Iran would have never gone undetected by U.S. intelligence agencies. Never! It would have been the first thing listed in the President's daily intelligence briefings. But there was no mention of it.

So glaringly obvious was this military buildup that even third-world countries could have detected it with their sub-par spying capabilities. Who knows, perhaps they did?

When Salvador Romanero shared what happened in Iran with the world the following day—naming all twelve countries involved in the surprise attack without even batting an eye—it made President Danforth look even more powerless and pathetic.

I should have been the one sharing it with the world, not him! But how could he possibly share intelligence with others that he never received in the first place?

Even if he had advance knowledge of the sneak attack, what could he have possibly done to prevent it? Who would want to ally with the United States, after 70,000,000 of its own citizens had left the country for greener pastures, so to speak?

The answer was glaringly obvious: no one. The biggest question on President Danforth's mind now was what had prevented intelligence from reaching his desk? He feared a "deep state" or shadow government was in place, coordinated by career government employees, private citizens, and who knew who else, to influence state and national policy without regard for democratically elected leadership.

President Danforth wondered how many in the government had already detached themselves from their sworn duties to the United States, and were now secretly working for the enemy? He feared this breach of protocol was widespread. This meant it was just a matter of time before some in his administration betrayed him.

He knew Vice President Everett Ashford, Chief of Staff Aaron Gillespie, National Security Adviser Nelson Casanieves and Joint Chief of Staff, William Messersmith were with him. Other than them, who really knew?

With hundreds of thousands on the government payroll, it was frightening to think just how deep the espionage went?

Convinced beyond all doubt he could never compete with Salvador Romanero; after all, his name was written in the Word of God—not by name but by title, Antichrist—it was time to stop trying. The man had supernatural powers others didn't have.

He really was a *Miracle Maker* after all.

Besides, how could he possibly cross swords with the young man globally, when he couldn't even govern his own citizens, what was left of them anyway? With rumors abounding that America was next to be targeted, how many more Americans would soon flee the country?

If President Danforth couldn't find a way to stop this invisible government, massive decisions would soon be made on behalf of the United States without his knowledge or permission, and the turmoil unfolding across the Atlantic and Pacific oceans would visit American shores with little or no warning.

Those closest to Jefferson Danforth knew he wanted to resign his Presidency. But for the time being he needed to remain on office. Too many safeguards needed to be put in place before he could ever think about stepping down.

Unless, of course, he was forced out or carried out in a casket. Was it possible that what happened to the crown prince of Spain on live television—with zero resistance from Spain's government or military—could happen to him as well? What was unthinkable just a few short months ago could no longer be ignored.

Hence, the need for greater urgency and efficiency.

Which is why Clayton Holmes and Travis Hartings were back at the White House two months sooner than scheduled.

But they weren't alone this time. Two other men representing another grassroots organization rapidly gaining steam in the United States were also in the Oval Office meeting with President Danforth—the *American Freedom Keepers*.

Much like the *ETSM*, the *AFK* was adding thousands to their fold each week. Comprised mostly of military personnel—both active and retired—these men and women believed America should remain the Super Power of the world. They were willing to fight and die, if necessary, to keep the United States a sovereign nation.

America's truest twenty-first century patriots were fed up and weren't about to lie down and let some young, egotistical foreigner take their country away from them without giving it their best fight. If other countries—and weak-willed Americans for that matter—were willing to yield to Romanero's New World Order, that was their problem.

Their courage was commendable, as was their determination, but no matter how much they steeled themselves against the enemy, they had to come to grips with the fact that America would never again be the super power it once was. In short, they were still in denial.

The three most obvious differences between both groups was 1) whereas the *AFK* was willing to accept anyone sharing the same love of country and disdain for Salvador Romanero into their group, the *ETSM* was an invitation-only clandestine group in which its members had to have similar dreams in order to join; 2) whereas members of the *AFK* were deluded into thinking they could ultimately defeat the *Miracle Maker* and his global coalition, members of the *ETSM* knew this was an impossibility—after all, it was written; 3) the *AFK* was more militarily minded, and willing to do whatever it took to preserve the United States of America, while the *ETSM* was more concerned with the soul of the nation.

The four men were ordered to take separate commercial flights to Washington D.C. Upon landing, to avoid being followed, all were given precise instructions to adhere to, which resembled your basic wild goose chase, before finally arriving at their designated pickup locations.

From there, they were met individually by secret service agents of the President's choosing and driven to the White House in government-issued vehicles, then smuggled inside without incident.

Even though President Danforth no longer was the most powerful man on the planet, and the country they loved had shrunken by nearly half since the Rapture, it was impossible not to feel the full weight of being ushered into the Oval Office to meet the man.

As America's highest civil servant, the President still had access to every perk and luxury afforded his position. No one had to remind the four men that having him on their side was a major asset. It gave them access to numerous resources.

The President began, "Thanks for coming on such short notice, gentlemen."

"Our pleasure, Sir," the four visitors said in unison. It was evident to each of them that the President was under severe duress. He looked consumed by anxiety.

President Danforth placed his hands behind his head and stretched his arms upward, "Time is short, so I'll be brief. Instead of shaping world events like America's done for many generations, it seems we're suddenly at the mercy of them."

The President leaned forward in his seat, "Especially if we don't stop the shadow government Salvador Romanero has put in place, with the help of many willing Americans—government official and private citizen alike.

"Essentially what this means, gentlemen, is the real power no longer resides with our publicly elected officials, but with many others exercising power behind the scenes, beyond the scrutiny of our democratic institutions. I don't know when this new shadow government was formed. But what I do know is if we sit back and do nothing, it won't take long before America is reduced to ashes."

President Danforth winced at his own words, "reduced to ashes". They made him think of the earthquakes, which, in turn, made him think of the supernatural power his chief nemesis possessed in great quantities. *Are we really the next to be leveled?*

Brushing off a shiver, he went on, "It's with that in mind, gentlemen, that I'm in the process of creating a secret counter government, if you will. If everything goes as planned, and that's a big 'if', this shadow government will once again become the true executive and military power. Only those who have proven their loyalty to us will be part of it.

"As promised in our prior meetings, both of your groups will be awarded underground properties scattered all across the mainland. Due to lack of use, most are in need of complete overhauls. All will be fully mobilized with the most advanced and secure military-strength technologies available to man.

"Each will be stocked with food and water supplies to get many of you through the next seven years. Jesus will return long before the expiration dates pass on the MREs (Meals, Ready-to-eat)."

The two *AFK* leaders nodded politely.

The two *ETSM* leaders, on the other hand, wanted to high-five each other.

"The good news is you won't be the only ones living in sub-terrain structures. In fact, most of the new construction taking place in the world is being done far beneath the earth's surface.

"People are frightened and are moving underground in record numbers. Many living in the central U.S. are reconstructing tornado shelters and underground crawl spaces just in case. This will only increase in the coming days.

"Which is why I've ordered for a quadrupling of underground shelters through this invisible government, effective immediately. Aside from your basic construction machinery, I have secret access to dozens of tunnel boring machines, also known as 'metal earthworms'. They're quite remarkable."

Travis Hartings said, "I once saw a documentary on it. Fascinating."

"Yeah," the President said in reply. "They're guided by laser light and can break apart a hundred feet of earth in a day, six feet at a time. Using hydraulics, eighteen-ton concrete blocks are constructed as makeshift walls to maintain the tunnel's integrity.

"Once the walls are in place, the TBM rotates in round, circular motions, easily removing the earth like it wasn't even there. The dirt is then placed on conveyor belts and moved to the back. Thousands are in use as we speak.

"Naturally, all locations you inhabit will eventually have the proper sewage, air and water filtration and ventilation units in place. Without these things, long term survival underground would be impossible. Not only that, most will be built fifty feet beneath the earth's surface and will be able to withstand a twenty-kiloton nuclear blast. But earthquakes are altogether different, I'm afraid. There isn't much we can do to protect from them."

No one dared asked him to further elaborate. They knew exactly what he meant.

Travis Hartings said, "What about above ground locations?"

"Those, too, will be needed in great quantities," the President said in reply. "But it will raise the stakes by making us more out in the open. I happen to have secret access to dozens of mobile bricklaying robots which are earmarked for your organizations."

"What are those?" asked one of the *AFK* leaders.

"Let's just say they can build homes very quickly and cheaply. They can lay a thousand bricks per hour, twenty-four hours a day, which means above ground homes can be built in a day or two.

"Much like TBM's they are laser guided so each brick is stacked perfectly. Once programmed, the bricks interlock like Legos and are sealed with a special glue, leaving room for windows and doors, which are added last.

"Once above ground locations are built or refurbished, walls and rooftops will need to be lined with copper a few inches thick, which I'll also be providing for you. The hope is that it will prevent the enemy from honing-in with high-tech satellite surveillance devices, including sonar and thermal imaging.

"Each above ground house you plan on occupying should be hermetically sealed with additional thick inner wall walls built approximately a foot or so away from outside walls. This will help prevent heat seeking technologies from detecting human body heat inside. If you really want to get creative, you can wallpaper them to project images of dining rooms, living rooms, kitchens or bedrooms."

What a great idea! Travis Hartings thought. He was partly embarrassed for not thinking it up himself.

"Gentlemen, I plan on making dozens of mobile bricklaying robots and tunnel boring machines available for your exclusive use. That said, I'd suggest you start purchasing as much land as you possibly can.

"Don't concern yourselves too much with the condition of above ground structures. Chances are they'll be leveled anyway. The key is to acquire vast amounts of land fast, so we can build upon it quickly, above ground and below."

"Sounds like a plan, Mister President," Travis Hartings said.

President Danforth said, "There will be another meeting next week at the same location where we first met. I'll need the names of the top five-hundred leaders from both of your organizations.

"Since the properties you'll be living on will be scattered across the country, I'll want all states represented. I'll need their names by the end of the day, so they can be properly vetted."

"Yes, Mister President," all four men said at the same time.

"Everyone on the list will be placed under constant surveillance, including the four of you. Until cleared, no one can know anything about the meeting. If at any time someone is viewed as a potential threat, they will be scratched off the list. Are we clear, gentlemen?"

"Yes, Mister President," all four men said again.

"Very good then. A final list will be emailed to you two days before we meet."

"Understood, Mister President," Clayton Holmes said.

The President looked at his watch. "Thanks for stopping by the White House, gentlemen. I'll advise the four of you to exercise extreme caution from here on out, especially when you're no longer under the protection of the secret service."

"It's an honor seeing you again, Sir," said one of the *AFK* leaders, before he and his partner were escorted out of the Oval Office.

President Danforth motioned for Holmes and Hartings to remain seated. Pulling a Bible from his desk drawer, the President said, "I've been reading it ever since our first meeting. I still have many questions, and was wondering if the two of you could help me make better sense of it..."

Holmes and Hartings glanced at each other. Holmes quickly looked away, seeing tears in his partner's eyes.

"It would be an honor, Sir," Holmes managed to say.

"The First Lady will join us shortly for lunch. I hope someday soon she, too, will be eager to read it. For security reasons, we'll adjourn to a more secure location for lunch. Don't know how many in the White House can be trusted..."

"As you say, Mister President."

10

THE SECURE LOCATION ENDED up being an underground bunker just beneath the White House Situation Room. With lunch finished, the President crisscrossed his knife and fork over his plate and motioned for the two men to proceed. He was eager to begin.

The same couldn't be said about the First Lady. She was completely unmoved by her husband's newfound spiritual enlightenment. In fact, it was starting to irritate her.

"Shall we, gentlemen?"

Travis Hartings said, "Where would you like to begin, Mister President?"

"Since the two of you understand the Word of God better than me, why don't you tell me?"

Travis glanced at his partner and Clayton Holmes leaned up in his chair. "The only way to fully understand the Word of God, Sir, is by having a proper understanding of the Gospel of Jesus Christ.

"The word 'gospel' actually means Good News. But in order for it to be seen as good news, I believe we first must consider the bad news. Namely, our sin condition. Because of sin, God can't even look at us."

Grabbing the Bible on the table before him, Holmes gazed deep into the President's eyes, "Sadly, most people read this Book for all the wrong reasons. Some read it hoping to increase their knowledge. Others read it seeking wisdom. Many more read it to gain a broader sense of Jewish and church history. As a known historian, I'm sure this is of particular interest to you as well."

President Danforth nodded politely.

Holmes went on, "That's all well and good, Sir, but did you know countless multitudes have read this Book over the centuries only to end up in hell?"

President Danforth winced.

"It's true. In and of itself Bible history has never saved anyone's soul. Anyone can read the Word of God from cover to cover a hundred times, a thousand times even, but only those who approach it with repentant hearts and broken spirits can gain a clear understanding the Gospel of Jesus

Christ. It's impossible to come into proper fellowship with the Most High God any other way."

Holmes grew more solemn, "Believe me, I know what I'm talking about. Before the Rapture, I was considered by many to be an expert on Bible prophecy and history. And look where it got me? My still being here proves I was nothing but a false convert.

"Not to come off as disrespectful, Sir, but when it comes to God's salvation, being President of the United States counts for nothing..."

President Danforth gulped, then looked at his lunch guest blankly. Having listened to his preaching online the past few months, he knew not to expect sugarcoating. It was too late in the game for that.

The First Lady flinched and shifted uncomfortably in her seat. She waited for Holmes to tell her being First Lady couldn't save her either. Thankfully he spared her that rebuke.

Holmes noticed her uneasiness but went on. It was that important. "Bottom line: our sin is an affront to God's holiness. And who, being of sin, can atone for sin? The answer is no one.

"Here's why: regardless of where we end up in life, whether one becomes president or merely a pauper, we all start out at the exact same place: spiritually dead. In other words, the moment we come out of our mothers' wombs, we're physically alive, but from a spiritual standpoint we enter this world dead on arrival..."

President Danforth nodded thoughtfully, as if in total agreement.

The First Lady shot Holmes an almost sarcastic sideways look. "Why are we born 'spiritually dead', as you say? I'm having difficulty wrapping my mind around it."

Holmes chuckled to himself. He sort of felt like Jesus explaining to Nicodemus what it meant to be born again. Only the First Lady didn't ask if she must crawl back inside her mother's womb. "Like I already said, Madam First Lady, because we're all born of sin, just like our parents, grandparents and great grandparents were. This dates all the way back to Adam and Eve."

Melissa Danforth looked increasingly confused. This way of thinking went against her belief that humans were inherently good, unlike what this man was suggesting.

Clayton Holmes said, "I agree it's difficult looking at newborn infants and having even the slightest inkling that they could possibly be born of sin. Newborns look so innocent. On some levels they are. After all, what infant commits sin? None, right?"

The Danforths both nodded agreement.

"It won't be long before children populate the planet again. Despite what Romanero says about creating a new utopia for all children, once they grow into toddlers, we'll get to see first-hand the sin-effect they inherited at birth. No one will have to teach them how to sin. They'll do it naturally, just like we do. No one's free from this curse, Madam First Lady, no one."

The way Holmes said it caused Melissa Danforth to break eye contact with him. She, too, was familiar with his deep booming voice. He was the reason she wore earplugs to sleep most nights. Her husband loved listening to his preaching as the couple lay in bed. The First Lady looked at her fingernails, totally stone-faced, slowly shrinking away from the conversation.

Holmes went on, "Personally, I believe the next generation of children will be even worse than past generations. How could they not, being raised by those who were left behind because they weren't deemed worthy to be part of the Church Age? I shudder at the thought."

"Now, if you're wondering what we must be saved from, Madam First Lady, the answer is an eternity in hell separated from God. And not because God is cruel, but that we're so sinful.

"This creates a serious dilemma with the Most High. We've already been born once. That was physically. But only those who are supernaturally born a second time, or born again, can be forgiven by God and rightly be called His children."

President Danforth rubbed his chin. "Never thought of it that way. Makes sense."

The First Lady, on the other hand, was becoming even more irritated. "And just how is one born again, Mister Holmes?"

"By faith in Jesus Christ, Madam First Lady. On the surface, it sounds quite simple, I know. Prior to last November, like so many other false converts, I actually thought I had something to do with obtaining my salvation.

Holmes shook his head. "How foolish I was to think a spiritually dead sinner like myself could take the first step to initiating my salvation. I've since discovered that if we humans had anything to do with obtaining the salvation of God, the Creator of the universe would cease at once from being sovereign."

Holmes leaned up in his chair, "I can assure you there never was a time when the Most High had His fingers crossed in Heaven hoping that humanity would choose Him over the world. Those who think they're doing God a favor by choosing Jesus as Lord and Savior, have zero understanding of the Gospel. Sounds a little silly hearing it from this perspective, doesn't it?"

"Yes, it does," President Danforth said, shifting his weight in his chair. "No wonder the church was so messed up prior to the Rapture."

Holmes shook his head in disgust, "Indeed. The simple truth is as spiritually dead sinners, we're completely incapable of choosing God. Nor do we want to choose Him! God must choose us, not the other way around!

"In short: there's no place in which man can initiate salvation. We do indeed make a choice to receive Christ, but only after our hearts have first been regenerated by the power of the Holy Spirit."

Melissa Danforth was still skeptical. "Okay, so how does someone know if they are among God's chosen or not?"

"In a nutshell, Madam First Lady, they respond to the Call. When confronted with the Gospel, they suddenly see their hopeless condition and how their sin has alienated them from the One who created them, the very One who has the power to destroy them.

"This leads to deep grief in their spirits, which ultimately leads to genuine repentance. They start looking to God for answers to their many life questions instead of man.

"The more God reveals Himself, the less the things of this world matter to them. This leads to a constant hungering and thirsting for His Word above all other things..."

"If you're so smart and proclaim what happened last year was the Rapture, Mister Holmes, why are you still here?"

Haven't you been listening? "It's only the repentant soul that God will accept, the heart that is broken, not the mouth that professes faith then defies it by their actions. I was the one who professed faith then defied it by my self-centered actions..."

The First Lady blinked hard.

Travis Hartings noticed and interjected, "When Clayton tried explaining that he was nothing but a false convert before the Rapture, I refused to believe him. How could I when he was the godliest man I'd ever known?

"Then God opened my eyes and ears spiritually and what never made sense to me suddenly became crystal clear..."

Clayton Holmes sighed, "In truth, Madam First Lady, it's easy for anyone to obtain knowledge of the mysteries of the Gospel. All they have to do is open the Word of God and start reading it. That was me. I constantly read the Bible and was always learning from it, but I never arrived at the Truth. It was all for show."

Travis Hartings could tell by looking at the First Lady the words coming from his partner's mouth were utter foolishness to her. And this could only mean one thing: she was spiritually dead. It was time to try a different approach.

Said Hartings, "Madam First Lady, the reason my partner keeps referring to false converts is that after praying with someone to receive Christ as Lord and Savior, many get emotional thinking they've just been made right with God.

"But because they have no true understanding of the Gospel, they have no idea what it means to truly repent. Because of this, they end up going back to their sinful lifestyles.

"In short, they become false converts. They fail to realize true repentance is a change of mind that leads to a change of heart which leads to a change of actions. This change involves both a turning from sin and a turning to God. That's when we can know for sure we are saved."

Clayton Holmes looked impressed. *Nice going Mister Chief Facilitator!*

Melissa Danforth felt herself shrinking even further away from the conversation. She was still fragile after her failed suicide attempt last Thanksgiving. Now this?

She rose from her seat. "Thank you, gentlemen, for your input. If you'll excuse me, I think I'll take a nap..."

"It was a pleasure meeting you, Madam First Lady. We'll be praying for you."

Melissa Danforth snickered and, without saying another word, left the room.

When the door closed, President Danforth started weeping. The two *ETSM* leaders looked at each other blankly, not knowing what to do. What does one say when seated before a weeping President?

Holmes and Hartings sat silently looking down at their feet.

After a while, President Danforth dabbed at his wet eyes with a handkerchief. "My tears represent great joy and deep sadness. The joyous tears come from knowing I'm a child of the Most High God. I've already surrendered my life to King Jesus. Thank you, gentlemen, for confirming what I had already come to understand."

The two leaders of the *ETSM* couldn't contain their joy.

President Danforth sighed. "The tears of sadness are for my wife. Now that I've been awakened from within, I see just how spiritually blinded she is. If God does the choosing as you said earlier, let's just pray that God has chosen her as well."

"It would be our pleasure, sir," Clayton Holmes said.

The three men joined hands and prayed for more than an hour for their country, his leadership, and for the First Lady of the United States.

During this time a bond was formed between the three men that not even the shrinking American population, or the many calamities striking the planet, could break apart...

11

CLAYTON HOLMES AND TRAVIS Hartings ended up spending the entire day at the White House. This was President Danforth's first time experiencing true Christian fellowship at this place, or at any other place for that matter. He didn't want it to end.

With a world seemingly against him, just being in the presence of the two *ETSM* leaders greatly comforted his troubled spirit. He wished they could remain at 1600 Pennsylvania Avenue until the end of his term.

After dinner, the three men retreated to the underground bunker beneath the White House Situation Room one last time. The President clasped his hands together. It was time to ask the question that had been at the forefront of his mind all day.

Said he, "Okay, gentlemen, now that the peace treaty's been signed for real, who or what was the cause of the three-day delay?"

Clayton Holmes said, "We believe God was shaking the Holy Land one last time, so His chosen people would finally wake up and see that He, not Salvador Romanero, is still in control. It was God who paved the way for the Third Temple construction to begin, not Romanero."

"Hmm. Sounds logical to me."

Travis Hartings interjected, "Yet, Romanero's trying to take credit for what God did, by using the Bible to his advantage."

President Danforth shook his head, "This is deep, gentlemen."

Holmes said, "By being part of Satan's unholy trinity, Romanero's role is to imitate Jesus, which explains the many miracles. Everything he said in his speech about the population being cut by one-quarter, only to be followed up with another one-third, were spoken by Jesus and recorded in the Book of Revelation by the Disciple John."

The President nodded thoughtfully. "I thought it sounded familiar."

Travis Hartings took a swig from his water bottle, "According to Daniel eight, verses twenty-four and twenty-five, we can know for sure that Romanero will be unstoppable, at least for the time being."

President Danforth was intrigued. "What exactly does it say?"

Hartings opened his Bible and flipped to the Book of Daniel. '*His power shall be great—but not by his own power; and he shall cause fearful destruction and shall succeed in what he does, and destroy mighty men and the people who are the saints.*

By his cunning he shall make deceit prosper under his hand, and in his own mind he shall become great. Without warning he shall destroy many. And he shall even rise up against the Prince of princes, and he shall be broken—but by no human hand.'

Clayton Holmes jumped in, "There are several things we can learn about Romanero from these two passages. We already know he's the Antichrist. Verse twenty-four clearly states his power shall be great—but it won't be by his own power. Who else, other than God, has the power to send earthquakes to the places of his choosing?"

President Danforth shrank back in his chair. A chill raced through him. "I met the man twice. Once in Brussels and once here at the White House. Never felt such evil coming from a person in all my life. And believe me, gentlemen, I've met my share of evil people! But I also felt his power. Truth be told, it ripped right through me."

Holmes said, "I can believe that. Even on TV he makes my skin crawl. According to the text, he'll cause fearful destruction and will succeed in what he does, even destroying God's saints. By his cunning he shall make deceit prosper under his hand, and in his own mind he shall become great. Without warning he shall destroy many. And he shall even rise up against the Prince of princes, and he shall be broken—but by no human hand."

"This sounds just like Satan, whose pride got him kicked out of Heaven for wanting to be like the Most High God. So cunning was he that one-third of the angels went with him. That's the kind of supernatural power Romanero now has. But when he rises up against Christ Jesus, he will be broken."

"Tell me about God's Two Witnesses in Jerusalem?" The President was becoming more familiar with what the Bible had to say about them, but he wanted to know what the two *ETSM* leaders had to say.

Holmes said, "Some believe they are Elijah and Enoch, because both men never died physical deaths. Others believe they are Elijah and Moses because both were with Jesus in the Garden of Gethsemane leading up to His crucifixion."

"Who do you think they are?"

"Not sure, Sir. All I know is they're the two olive trees and the two lampstands that stand before the Lord of the earth, as mentioned in the Book of Revelation, chapter eleven. They've been anointed by the Holy

Spirit to bring forth light to a dark, lost world. If anyone attempts to harm them fire will supernaturally come out of their mouths to devour them. Scripture says that anyone who tries harming them must die that way."

The President shook his head in disbelief. "Truthfully, when I saw it happen, I couldn't believe my eyes!"

"You and me both. I always thought it was more metaphorical than anything else. They'll also have the power to seal the sky, so no rain will fall while they're prophesying. According to the Word of God, for the next three and a half years, they'll have power to turn water into blood, and to strike the earth with every kind of plague, as often as they want to, very much resembling Old Testament times."

Hartings marveled. "The fact that they're performing Old Testament miracles further confirms this isn't the time for the Church, but for God to rescue His people, the Jews."

Clayton Holmes eyeballed his partner. "Good point, Travis..."

Before Travis could reply, the President said, "Are you suggesting they're untouchables?"

Hartings shook his head, "For the next three-and-a-half-years, yes. No one will be able to harm them until God's needs have been fully served. Only then will the Most High allow Antichrist to overpower His Two Witnesses and kill them.

"Romanero will put their dead bodies on display in the streets of Jerusalem. People from every nation and tongue will celebrate their demise with great joy, and even send gifts to each other, as those in the Holy Land gloat over their dead bodies. Imagine that...

"After three days have passed, Yahweh God will breathe life back into his Two Witnesses and they will rise to their feet, striking terror into the hearts of all who personally witness it. Then they'll be taken up to Heaven before the eyes of the world, much like Jesus on the day of Pentecost.

"Immediately after that, an intense earthquake will rock Jerusalem, and one-tenth of the city will collapse, killing seven-thousand of the earth's elite."

Seeing the President shaking his head in disbelief, Travis Hartings said, "I know, like we really need more earthquakes, right? Anyway, the Bible states all who survive will be terrified and will give glory to the God of Heaven."

President Danforth scratched his head, "This is fascinating, gentlemen. I can't help but be impressed by your knowledge of the Bible."

Clayton Holmes grabbed his Bible off the table, "Mister President, the intelligence you have at your fingertips, impressive as it is, can't come close to comparing to the intelligence in this Book. Even Jesus prophesied on these days, in Matthew chapter twenty-four, Luke chapters seventeen and twenty-one, and in Mark chapter thirteen."

"Yeah. Been reading the Gospels a lot lately. Jesus spoke of wars and rumors of wars and many other things leading up to these days, right?"

"Exactly. I still find it amazing that after the people of Israel had finally determined that Jesus wasn't the Messiah—in fact, they thought He was demonic—He did only what God could do, predict the future. Everything He taught His disciples about these days was one-hundred percent accurate. Mere man could never do that!"

President Danforth shook his head in wonderment. "Okay, now that the peace treaty's been signed, what comes next?"

"Already happening, Mister President. The Four Horsemen in Revelation six," Clayton Holmes said.

"Care to expound on it for me?"

Hartings went to the www.lsarglobal.org website and clicked on Revelation six. He read the first two verses. "*'I watched as the Lamb opened the first of the seven seals. Then I heard one of the four living creatures say in a voice like thunder, "Come and see!" I looked, and there before me was a white horse! Its rider held a bow, and he was given a crown, and he rode out as a conqueror bent on conquest.'*"

"Romanero, right?"

"Yes, Sir. He's the rider on the white horse."

"What about the other three?"

"Let's begin with the Red Horse..."

Hartings read Revelation 6:3-4: '*When the Lamb opened the second seal, I heard the second living creature say, "Come and see!" Then another horse came out, a fiery red one. Its rider was given power to take peace from the earth and to make men slay each other. To him was given a large sword.*'

Once his partner was finished reading, Holmes weighed in, "The second horse represents war, which explains the fiery red color. This rider was given a large sword with which to take peace from the earth. The sword suggests much blood will be spilled."

"Now let's examine the Black Horse in Revelation 6:5-6. Hartings read the text, '*When the Lamb opened the third seal, I heard the third living creature say, "Come and see!" I looked, and there before me was a black horse! Its rider was holding a pair of scales in his hand. Then I heard what sounded like a voice among the four living creatures, saying, "A quart of wheat for a day's wages, and three quarts of barley for a day's wages, and do not damage the oil and the wine!"'*

Once again, Holmes weighed in, "The rider on the black horse will bring famine upon the whole earth. Men and women will work all day just to earn enough money to buy a loaf of bread for their families.

"Not everyone will be destitute, but the majority will. Surely it will be a time of great depression on Planet Earth. I wonder if last week's earthquakes will trigger extreme food rationing..."

Holmes nodded at his partner and Hartings read Revelation 6:7-8, *'When the Lamb opened the fourth seal, I heard the voice of the fourth living creature say, "Come and see!" I looked and there before me was a pale horse! Its rider was named Death, and Hades was following close behind him. They were given power over a fourth of the earth to kill by sword, famine, and plague, and by the wild beasts of the earth.'*

Holmes leaned back in his seat, "As you can see by reading the text, Mister President, the rider on the fourth horse is the only one given a specific name. And that name is 'Death', because he will bring death to the earth.

"This rider will have the power to kill one fourth of the world's population by unspeakable tragedy. This is the very text from which Romanero derived his facts. Even he knows the Word of God is infallible."

President Danforth sighed. "Scary stuff. Doesn't look good for us."

"Short term, no. But once we get to Revelation nineteen, life will be just perfect for us Christians. But before that glorious time arrives, we will literally go through hell."

"Would you mind giving me a glimpse into this perfect life, as you say?"

"Sure. Chapter nineteen describes another praise session in Heaven, preceding Christ's glorious return to earth with His Bride—the Redeemed souls of the ages. With God's twenty-one Judgments satisfied the multitude in Heaven rejoice saying, 'Hallelujah! Salvation and glory and power belong to our God, for true and just are his judgments.'"

"Again the great multitude, like the roar of many waters and like loud peals of thunder will exclaim, 'Hallelujah! For our Lord God Almighty reigns. Let us rejoice and be glad and give him glory! For the wedding of the Lamb has come, and his bride (the believers) has made herself ready. Fine linen—signifying the righteous acts of the saints—bright and clean, was given to her to wear.'"

"Chapter twenty describes three major events: Christ's thousand-year reign on earth as KING OF KINGS AND LORD OF LORDS—Satan's doom—and the judgment of the dead at the Great White Throne.

"Chapters twenty-one and twenty-two describe the New Jerusalem, where the believers of the ages will spend eternity. But those who die in their sins will be ushered into Hades, to await the Great White Judgment. They'll be forced to give an account for everything they did in human form. After that, they'll receive their final eternal sentence—the Lake of Fire, where there will be constant weeping and gnashing of teeth."

President Danforth sighed. "It's only seven years away but by the time it finally gets here, I'm sure it'll feel more like seventy years. After all, the past seven months has felt like seven years.

"True, but once this time passes, Sir, it'll be just the beginning of the beginning of eternal bliss for all who are children of the Most High God."

The comment earned Travis Hartings a smile from the President. "I think that is the perfect place to end our discussion, gentlemen..."

"We're so grateful, Sir, for everything you're doing for us."

"My sentiments exactly. See you next weekend."

"We look forward to it, Mister President," Travis Hartings said, on behalf of himself and his partner.

At that, two secret servicemen escorted Clayton Holmes and Travis Hartings out of the White House...

12

SIX DAYS LATER

BRIAN MULROONEY WAS AWAKENED at 5 a.m., after being notified on his cell phone that he'd just received a secure email from Travis Hartings. He sat up in bed, rubbed sleep from his eyes, and signed onto the secure site.

Squinting in the darkness he read the email: *Good morning, Brian. Your immediate presence is requested in Washington D.C. A plane ticket has been purchased for you. Your flight leaves at 9 a.m., out of Detroit Metro. Flight details have been sent in a second email, which was programmed to be sent upon your receipt of this one.*

Sure enough, Mulrooney was notified that he'd received a new email.

Sorry for the short notice. You'll receive further instructions once you arrive in D.C. Until then, do not reply to this text message or contact anyone else, not even Jacquelyn. We'll inform her that you're away on official ETSM business, and you'll be out of town for a couple of days. Have a safe flight. See you there. Godspeed.

Mulrooney ran his fingers through his hair. His head still throbbed from the five trips made the day before, from Ann Arbor to Southeast Michigan Evangelical Church, in Sterling Heights, Michigan. Each round trip took roughly two hours.

When Brian explained Tom Dunleavey's dire situation to Jim Simonton, the lead pastor at Southeast Michigan Evangelical Church contacted a few of his trusted brethren asking if they would join him in providing temporary shelter for former members of a Catholic Church in Ann Arbor, who'd recently converted to Christianity.

The response was overwhelmingly positive.

With everything set, Brian drove Tom Dunleavey to Sterling Heights the next day. Mulrooney then took the church van and began the tedious task of transporting folks from Ann Arbor to Sterling Heights, as Tom remained behind with Pastor Simonton. It took five trips, but he managed to successfully smuggle everyone to safety.

With hatred for Christians so widespread, Brian was increasingly paranoid driving a church vehicle. So much so that he called Pastor

Simonton urging him to strip all church advertising off the van as soon as possible, to prevent someone from pulling up next to whoever was driving it and blowing their brains out simply for being a Christian.

Tom Dunleavey rejoiced upon seeing his displaced flock again. They shared many tearful embraces. There were also tears of sorrow for two who were still among the missing: Brother Virgil, a former priest, and sister Mary Catherine, a former nun. Both had yet to be contacted.

Tom had a sinking feeling they both fell off the planet, never to be heard from again. Though saddened by this realization, they rejoiced knowing they would see their brother and sister again on the other side, the Good side.

Pastor Simonton arranged for a potluck dinner so he could introduce his new brothers and sisters in Christ to the families or individuals who'd agreed to take them in.

No one complained that the portions were much smaller than they were before the Rapture. It was agreed by many in the Christian communities to start rationing food and water now, to hopefully prevent from going without in the days to come.

As a result, most believers were noticeably thinner.

By the time Brian and Tom returned to the apartment in Ann Arbor, Brian was so tired his eyes were already closed before his head hit the pillow. He never bothered setting the alarm. Starved for sleep, his plan was to sleep in for a change.

Travis Hartings changed all that. But as one of the first full time members of the organization, Mulrooney had to be ready to go anywhere he was asked to go on a moment's notice, no questions asked.

What made this trip significant was that he would finally meet the *ETSM* leaders, at least Travis Hartings. It would also be his first time flying on an airplane since the Rapture. Brian was nervous and excited at the same time.

What made it significantly different from the first two trips—Chicago for the formation of the *ETSM*, and Chadds Ford, Pennsylvania to scout out the first *ETSM* property—was that Jacquelyn wouldn't accompany him this time.

Mulrooney showered, took two Tylenol, and knocked on the spare bedroom door.

"Brother Tom, are you awake?" There was no answer. Brian knocked again a little harder, finally rousing his house guest from his sleep.

"I'm awake. I'm awake." Tom, too, had a throbbing headache.

"May I come in?"

"Yes."

Mulrooney entered.

Tom Dunleavey sat up in bed. "Everything okay?"

"Yeah. I was wondering if you could give me a ride to the airport?"

"How funny that you should ask me that question..."

"Why?"

"I was just dreaming that you woke me needing a ride to the airport."

"Are you serious?" *Wow!*

"Yes. In my dream you were going to Washington D.C. for some sort of secret meeting. I feel certain it's connected to the last dream I had."

Brian's mind was blown. It was evident on his face. "Hmm, what else did you see in the dream?"

"It was a clandestine gathering of sorts. Underground, I believe. Don't laugh but President Danforth was there..."

"What if I told you I *was* going to Washington..."

"Given this strange new climate, I wouldn't be overly surprised."

"Not sure about the 'the President being there part'," Mulrooney said, using his fingers as quotation marks, "but there will be other important people there who mean more to me than President Danforth. This'll be my first time meeting them in person."

Wish I was going with you... "What time's your flight?"

"Nine a.m. I need to leave in an hour. I've already showered. I'm about to cook some eggs and brew a pot of coffee. Want some?"

"Sounds good. I'll be ready to go by the time breakfast is ready."

They arrived at Detroit Metro at 7:30., giving Mulrooney ample time to be cleared through security.

Tom Dunleavey was still chomping at the bit to know who Brian would be meeting with in Washington. "When will you be back?"

"Sunday night. Ten-fifteen, give or take."

"Short trip."

"Yeah. Needless to say, I won't be back in time for church."

"I still plan on going. Though it will be a little strange sitting with my flock instead of preaching to them. I'm sure we'll learn so much from Pastor Jim about these crazy times."

"Indeed, you will. Even if most of what he teaches is terrifying, at least it's the Truth, right?" Brian looked at his watch. "Gotta go."

84

"See you in two days. Enjoy the flight."

"Make yourself comfortable at the apartment while I'm gone."

"Thanks, Brian."

"The only possible snag is Renate. She has a key to my apartment. I have a hunch she snoops on me when I'm out of town. If she sees my car's not there, she may go inside. Which is why I asked for a ride. Other than her, you should have no other visitors."

"What should I do if she stops by?"

"I doubt she will. We haven't spoken in weeks. But if she does, just be yourself. You're my friend. Nuff said." Brian got out of the car. "Enjoy church on Sunday. And tell Pastor Jim I said hi."

"I'll do that, Brian."

Brian Mulrooney went inside the airport terminal not knowing Pastor Jim Simonton had received the same encrypted email from Travis Hartings, and that he, too, was at Detroit Metro parking his car, before boarding a separate flight to Washington National Airport.

Since President Danforth wanted members to come from across the country, Brian and Jacquelyn were the first two selected from Michigan. But since it was a men's only meeting, Simonton would go in her place.

ETSM membership had swelled to nearly ten thousand full time members. It was difficult selecting only five hundred, but that's all they could invite.

Pastor Jim Simonton wasn't invited to the formation of the *ETSM* a few months back because he didn't have the dream everyone else invited had had. That all changed on the night of the surprise attack on Israel, when Simonton was rocked by a series of dreams that went on for three straight nights.

Because he vividly saw Brian and Jacquelyn in his dream, Jim was eagerly to share it with them. They received it with great joy, then shared it with Charles Calloway, who then shared it with Clayton Holmes and Travis Hartings.

Since Simonton was a pastor of a fairly-large church, and since he'd already gone through the vetting process—even if he didn't know it—now that he had the dream, inviting him was a no-brainer.

UPON LANDING IN D.C. Mulrooney turned on his phone and had three new text messages. One was from Travis Hartings, informing him to check his secure email.

He sat on a chair in the lobby where no one could see his phone screen and signed in: *I wired a thousand dollars to your bank to help pay your hotel and rental car expenses. Expect another email upon receipt of this one with the hotel reservation info for tonight. You'll receive a final email tomorrow morning with more instructions.*

Until then, be extremely careful out there. Chances are you're being watched not only by us. It's time to develop trust. We'll be watching and listening. Sleep early tonight. You'll need it. See you in the morning. TH.

The second text message was from Jacquelyn: *Hi sweetie! Have a safe trip wherever you are! I know you can't reply back. I also know you'll comply with all orders. I miss you so much already. See you soon. I love you, Brian, and I'm praying for you always!*

A smile crossed Brian's face. Jacquelyn's words warmed him like no one else could, including Renate.

The third text message was from Twitter, informing Brian that he had a new follower. There was no profile picture. Under normal circumstances, he would have ignored it like he did all who hid behind online profiles choosing not to identify themselves.

But the name caught his attention: *NYCTaxiDriver111. Tamika?* Mulrooney read the message: *Hi Brian. This is your favorite taxi driver. I'm in serious trouble and need your help!*

Brian's hands started trembling. Tears flooded his eyes, "You're alive! Thank you, Lord!" He typed back: *Is this who I think it is? If so, what's wrong?*

Just as he was about to send it, he remembered what Travis Hartings had said about not contacting anyone. They were watching and listening. Which meant they were also monitoring his online activity. The last thing he wanted was to lose the trust of those at the top of the organization.

With a sharp pain in his heart, Mulrooney deleted the message and powered down his phone. *Hang in there, sis. Help is on the way. Just need a few days...*

13

MEANWHILE, TAMIKA MOSELEY BRUSHED back fresh tears of her own. The one person she thought she could count on more than anyone else never replied to her desperate plea for help. *Where are you, Brian?* Her heart sunk deep in her chest.

Tamika deactivated her newly-created Twitter account but wouldn't permanently delete it until she contacted Brian Mulrooney or Charles Calloway. If she contacted them...

If Charles had a Twitter account, it was under a different name. She did find a Facebook account linked to him, but there was no activity whatsoever since before the Rapture.

Tamika couldn't afford to waste time sending emails to dead-end accounts. As it was, she was taking a big risk just being at this place.

Still on the run for the *Graveyard Incident*, the former New York City taxi driver was still living in her mother's Oldsmobile Cutlass Supreme with her pet cat, Cocoa.

Even if the allegations against her were false, which they were—after all, the only thing she was remotely guilty of was breaking into the cemetery and opening her grandfather's casket—proving her innocence would be difficult.

Tamika had nothing to do with the $45K worth of bronze vases that were "allegedly" stolen that night. If anything, she left the cemetery that frigid morning with less than she went there with. The pick and shovel she'd borrowed from the janitor at her apartment complex were never returned.

Tamika dropped them to the ground while trying to escape being captured by the two security guards. Thanks to the two Doberman Pinschers, she also left the cemetery with less blood in her body. The dogs clamped onto her legs just as she was climbing the fence to escape and pulled her back to the surface with the greatest of ease, tearing into her flesh with their razor-sharp teeth.

Had Tamika not been carrying mace, they would have kept chomping away on her until all her flesh was gone and perhaps she wouldn't be able to walk now.

Thankfully the pain had subsided considerably. But pus still protruded from her still-unhealed wounds. It looked and smelled nasty. The infection wouldn't go away until someone examined her and gave her antibiotics, and perhaps a few stitches.

As much as she wanted to go to a hospital, it was out of the question. As a wanna-be nurse, she felt she could treat herself, but she didn't have the proper medical equipment. She, did, however, clean her leg twice a day with diluted peroxide mixed with water, before wrapping duct tape she found in the trunk of her mother's car around her legs to keep the new gauze in place.

In God's eyes, Tamika knew she was innocent of the grand theft charges filed against her. But convincing a New York City jury of her innocence would be no easy matter. In the courtroom of public opinion, most living in the *Big Apple* had already judged her guilty as charged.

What angered them more than the grand larceny charges was that she desecrated the grave of a decorated military veteran, who just happened to be her own grandfather! Who did such things? Only a raving lunatic did!

If there was one thing Tamika was thankful for regarding the "Earthquakes Miracle", and the 70,000,000 Americans who recently left the country for greener pastures—3,000,000 alone within a 50-mile radius of New York City—it's that it pushed her story far from the front pages.

In normal times, Tamika had no trouble believing the *Graveyard Incident* was worthy of being a front-page story. But in these bizarre times, it should have been buried deep within the pages of the newspaper, if that. Even if the story had died down considerably, that didn't change the fact that Tamika Moseley was still a wanted woman. If anyone recognized her she'd be placed in handcuffs and carted off to jail, no questions asked.

If she could somehow contact Brian Mulrooney or Charles Calloway, they would remind her this was spiritual warfare, that Satan and his hordes of demons were doing all they could to silence those who were children of the Most High God, and on and on. As much as their words had always annoyed her before her conversion, she longed to hear them now.

If this is spiritual warfare, I'm not sure how much more of it I can take!

The very thought of incarceration nearly paralyzed her from stepping foot inside the local library in Patterson, New Jersey in the first place. Everything inside told her not to do it, especially since going inside meant she needed to remove the bandanna that had covered most of her face the past few weeks.

It was yet another forgotten item she found in her closet when police came banging on her door on what seemed like eons ago. What once was a worthless bandanna suddenly became the most important accessory Tamika Moseley owned.

She knew exposing her face for all to see could be dangerous, but she was desperate to contact her two spiritual mentors.

If she still had her cell phone, there would be no need to come to this place. But she didn't have it. She threw it in the trash weeks ago, so authorities wouldn't track her down with it.

Even if she could borrow someone's phone, it would do her no good. When she tossed her broken cell phone in the trash can, Brian's and Charles' numbers went with it. She never bothered committing them to memory. But who did these days?

In that light, the library was the only viable option Tamika had. Once a computer finally became available to her, she took time to familiarize herself with the online world. The first thing she did was to create a temporary Gmail account. She then joined Twitter and silently rejoiced upon locating Brian Mulrooney's profile.

She waited two hours for Brian to reply to her message, looking over her shoulders and praying for God's protection the whole time, but he never did. It was like a knife in her heart.

Tamika left the library feeling even more hopeless. She pulled the bandanna dangling around her neck up to cover her face.

In a twisted sense of irony, if there was another benefit to the many calamities bombarding the planet, citizens were urged to wear surgical masks to hopefully shield their lungs from the deadly toxins still feared present in the atmosphere.

Tamika didn't have a surgical mask and wasn't about to go to a hospital to get one, even if they were giving them away for free.

It would be too risky.

The worn-out bandanna she wore, with an American flag on it, was good enough, because it covered more of her face than a surgical mask could. Perhaps it made her look a little thuggish, but as long as it kept her face covered she could care less what others thought.

But even with a bandanna, Tamika needed to remain on high alert at all times and do her best to avoid making any missteps. One false move is all it would take to make her life even more miserable than it already was. *All this for a crime I didn't even commit!*

Though innocent of the charges leveled against her, Tamika had no one to blame for her current predicament but herself. Even if she'd somehow escaped the clutches of the two Doberman Pinschers, her fate was already sealed when she drove to the cemetery on the day of the break-in, asking for directions to her grandfather's site.

That was mistake number one. Mistake number two was pulling up in a taxicab. No one had to tell her it was a dumb thing to do. *It wasn't dumb—it was insanely stupid!*

Before getting in her mother's car, Tamika took a good look around to make sure no one was watching her.

Satisfied the coast was clear, she climbed inside and scooped her pet feline onto her lap. At least Cocoa was happy to see her.

Desperate as she was to leave the tri-state area, with only forty dollars left to her name, she wouldn't get too far. As it was, she only had a quarter-tank of gasoline left in the car. And with fuel prices averaging $12 a gallon, forty bucks wouldn't even make a dent in the gas tank.

Tamika Moseley felt completely trapped. She was tired, broke, hungry and frightened for her life. And on top of that, she felt dirty all the way down to the soul.

With her two sons, Jamal and Dante, and her mother now in Heaven, and with a warrant out for her arrest, nothing was keeping her from leaving the area. But in order to do that, she desperately needed Brian or Charles to help her.

With that justification, risky or not, Tamika would try her luck again at the Patterson, New Jersey library in the morning.

Help me, Lord!

Sighing, she said, "Still just you and I against the world, Cocoa..."

14

THE NEXT DAY

THE ELEVATOR CAME TO a stop. Once passengers were unloaded, the elevator car shot back up the shaft at a very brisk pace to retrieve more people.

An identical elevator on the opposite side of the base of the mountain worked just as effortlessly depositing its passengers 300 feet beneath the earth's surface.

By design, there were no buttons or gadgets inside the elevator cars, only phones in case the elevators ever broke down and stranded passengers needed assistance. Other than that, they were one-stop machines—top to bottom, bottom to top.

But blindfolded passengers were totally unaware of it. All they knew was they were inside an elevator car descending at a fairly-rapid speed. Nothing more, including that they'd been dropped inside a mountain of all places, a very secure mountain.

With a thousand people being covertly taken to the same place, it took many trips to transport everyone. The first buses pulled into the mountain just after midnight. This was the ninth of ten trips being made. Members from both groups in this shift were ordered to be at their designated pickup locations at four-thirty a.m.

All were within close-proximity to the Washington D.C. Metroplex. Members of the *End Times Salvation Movement* met at various locations in Northeast Virginia, while members of the *American Freedom Keepers* met at various locations in Southeast Maryland.

Like all other *ETSM* members, Brian Mulrooney received the final encrypted email from Travis Hartings at 3 a.m., with instructions on where to go next. He Googled the pickup location in northern Virginia. It was less than five miles from his hotel, giving him plenty of time.

Government-issued armored Suburbans were dispatched to each group. If anyone was late by even one minute, they would be left behind. Those waiting to be picked-up were ordered to remain in their vehicles and were prohibited from speaking to anyone until they reached their final destination.

The only thing they were allowed to bring with them were the clothes on their backs. Nothing more.

At exactly four-thirty, a black Chevy Suburban arrived at each location to pick everyone up. As was fully anticipated, no one was late. Passengers were hurried inside the SUVs and frisked, then scanned for weapons, cell phones, cameras and all other possible recording devices, before being blindfolded by secret service agents.

As quickly as the SUVs appeared, they vanished just as fast. The black Suburbans drove a short distance to a vacant warehouse. Blindfolded passengers got out of the SUVs and were placed on board buses parked inside the warehouse.

From there they were taken to the meeting location.

Ironically, no one seemed scared. A little jittery, which was fully expected, but certainly not fearful. Passengers remained silent as instructed. Not only were they totally unaware of their whereabouts, they were prohibited from asking questions.

All they knew was higher ups in their organizations had set this meeting in place, after powerful individuals in Washington had requested an audience with them—including top-ranking U.S. Military officials—in a hopeful attempt to form a secret alliance of sorts with the two groups, at least on some levels.

They had no idea whose presence they would soon be in...

Less than an hour later, still under a canopy of darkness, the buses arrived at either side of the undisclosed meeting location, and quickly vanished inside the mountain located 50 miles west of Washington D.C.

Passengers were then placed inside the stealthy elevators, depending on which group they represented. One elevator was for the *ETSM*. The other was for the *AFK*.

Upon reaching the bottom of the shaft, blindfolds were removed, and they were led to a massive full-service cafeteria-size kitchen, which could easily accommodate 500 meals per sitting. They were free to help themselves to a continental breakfast and engage in conversation with members of their respective groups.

Combined, the three-story sub-terrain shelter took up 10,000 square foot of space. It was partitioned into many sections, including a military-style sleeping quarters easily capable of sleeping 500 people per shift, and ten shower rooms equipped with ten toilets and shower stalls.

Three-thousand square feet was used for work space, to include a large auditorium-style conference room which was dubbed "the Chamber Room". The walls surrounding the underground structure were ten feet thick, made of solid steel, insulated with the purest copper known to man. To further safeguard from outside eavesdroppers, both were hermetically sealed with additional thick inner walls made from the same materials, making outside interference virtually impossible.

An underground tunnel connected to another one-story sub-terrain location, which was used to house a state of the art command center. It was revamped and fully stocked with all the latest in high tech communication gizmos so advanced that, aside from someone committing espionage on the inside, it would take outsiders many years before they could ever hope to pinpoint this, or any other subsequent locations.

And even that would require the world's most skilled computer hackers to pull it off. In short, it was an extremely secure location.

But for now, this part was off limits to all *ETSM* and *AFK* members.

With the air completely filtered and pressurized, those invited would be hard pressed to believe they were 300 feet below the earth's surface. When push came to shove, and all hell broke loose, thousands from one of these two groups would reside at this location.

The final two busloads were en route and would arrive momentarily. The one carrying *AFK* members was short by six passengers, after they failed background checks and were removed from the list they never even knew they were on.

For added security purposes, a handful of U.S. military personnel safeguarded the premises above ground and below. They were joined by a few trusted agents from the CIA, FBI, NSA and USSS (the United States Secret Service).

Pastor Jim Simonton exited the elevator car and was shocked to see Brian Mulrooney pouring a cup of coffee for himself in the cafeteria. He was so excited he could hardly contain himself. Sneaking up behind him, Jim covered Brian's eyes with his hands.

"Guess who?" Pastor Jim said, disguising his voice.

"Oh no, not another blindfold," said Mulrooney, jokingly. "Charles?"

"Nice try." Jim released his grip.

Brian craned his neck back. His eyes widened. "Pastor Jim! What are *you* doing here?"

"I could ask you the same thing?"

93

"I've been a member since last March. Jacquelyn too."

Jim Simonton raised an eyebrow. "Really now? Well then, surprise!"

"How could it be? I know you had dreams and all, but you weren't even invited to the formation of the *ETSM*."

"Given the current state of the world, I was told they're speeding up the process with everyone."

"This is answered prayer! Jacquelyn will be thrilled with the news. But who will preach at church tomorrow?"

"Brother Tom, only he doesn't know it yet."

"You're right about that, pastor. He fully expects to see you tomorrow. Told me at the airport he looks forward to hearing everything you have to say."

"As the saying goes, 'When you least expect it, you're elected.' Besides, he's been through a lot. I think it'll be good for him to preach this weekend." Jim poured himself a cup of coffee and grabbed a blueberry muffin. He took a bite and blew into his cup before venturing a sip. "Does Jacquelyn know you're here?"

Mulrooney shook his head. "She knows I'm away on official *ETSM* business. Nothing more." Swallowing the food in his mouth, he said, "Speaking of Jacquelyn, I have something very important to ask you, pastor."

"Good news or bad?"

A smile broke across Brian's face.

Noticing his pink cheeks, Pastor Simonton said, "Am I allowed to venture a guess?"

"Sure, but after the meeting. I wanna remain focused while I'm here."

Pastor Jim nodded agreement. "Let's meet tomorrow then. I know just the place."

"Sounds like a plan. I can't tell you how excited I am to finally meet Clayton and Travis. Wasn't sure the day would ever come..."

"I must be really blessed to meet them right off the bat."

"Indeed, you are, Pastor." Brian scanned the lobby looking for Charles Calloway. He didn't see him but would be shocked if his good friend wasn't invited as well. "Who in the world has this kind of power and connections to pull something like this together so discreetly."

"Someone with serious clout backing them."

94

"You can say that again." Brian filled a plastic cup full of orange juice. "Reminds me of the formation of the *End Times Salvation Movement* last March. Only this is far more secure and sophisticated."

Just as Simonton was about to say something, the elevator door opened, and Charles Calloway disembarked with a dozen or so other *ETSM* members. All were blindfolded.

Brian smiled, "That's Charles Calloway..."

Once the blindfold was removed, Calloway saw Brian and went off in his direction.

"Charles, good to see you again, man!" They embraced. "Good news. I think our prayer's been answered..."

Charles raised an eyebrow, "What prayer?"

"I heard from Tamika. She found me on Twitter of all places."

"Really? That's a relief! How is she?"

"Well, she's in serious trouble."

"What kind of trouble?"

"Don't know, Charles. I wanted to reply to her message, and almost did, in fact, but I was warned not to contact anyone until the meeting's over."

"At least we know she's alive, right?"

"Amen to that. The moment I hear from her again, you'll be the first to know."

Before Pastor Jim could say a word, Charles said, "Pastor Simonton?"

Jim Simonton smiled. "Finally, we meet face to face."

"Your Christmas message messed me up for the longest time!"

"Messed me up too, believe me."

The two men had spoken on the phone a few times and exchanged e-mails and text messages on numerous occasions, but this was their first time meeting in person.

Brian jumped in, "Where are Clayton and Travis?"

"They're here somewhere. Guess we'll find out soon enough. All I know is we'll be meeting with members of another group similar to ours, whatever that means. Couldn't pry any more information out of them. But they sounded optimistic."

"Can't wait to finally meet them," said Brian.

"Soon enough, my brother, soon enough."

Calloway's eyes swept the room. Many nodded and waved at him. It felt good to be recognized again as a leader of a large group. But this was infinitely more gratifying than Cell-U-Loss International. Instead of winning customers for himself, Calloway was winning souls for Christ. The payment received also differed: temporal versus eternal.

Charles saw Donald Johnson and waved to him. Johnson was flanked by at least 20 *ETSM* members.

"Who's that?" said Brian.

"Donald Johnson. He's an ex-Mormon from Salt Lake City. Used to be a missionary in the Philippines. Plans on going back, only this time he'll be preaching the Truth, the whole Truth, and nothing but the Truth. He's an interesting guy. The man to his right is Manuel Jiminez from L.A. I met them both last week."

"They're quite popular," Jim Simonton said, adding the right mixture of cream and sugar to his second cup of coffee. He wanted to ask where they had met but thought better of it. Like everyone else, he was on a need-to-know-basis.

"Yeah," Calloway replied. "We speak once a week. Manuel's a good man. He figures to assume a big role with the *ETSM* down in Mexico."

"Can we go over and meet them?" Brian said.

"Sure. Go on fellas," said Charles, "I'll join you after I grab a cup of java."

"Sounds good."

"I think everyone here in this gathering is *ETSM*. But until you know for sure, not a word to anyone about the organization. Even if some proclaim to be believers, not a word. Understood?"

"Yes, sir!" Brian and Jim both said.

"Good. Go introduce yourselves. I'll join you shortly..."

96

15

AT EXACTLY 5:45 A.M., the stealthy elevators made their final trips down into the bowels of the earth. After dropping off the final passenger loads, the elevators shot back up to the earth's surface where they would remain under heavy guard until the meeting concluded sometime the following day.

After allowing a few minutes for latecomers to eat and drink, the command was given for everyone to take their refreshments and proceed to the main chamber room.

Members of the *End Times Salvation Movement* entered through one door. Members of the *American Freedom Keepers* entered through another door on the opposite side of the auditorium.

Clayton Holmes and Travis Hartings were seated on the auditorium stage with two other men no one from the *ETSM* recognized. The two *ETSM* founders acknowledged the members from their group with nods and waves as they found their seats.

Charles Calloway and Donald Johnson sat in the front row.

"Must be the leaders from the other group," Johnson whispered in Calloway's ear, referring to the two men seated next to Holmes and Hartings.

Charles nodded agreement.

Brian Mulrooney and Pastor Jim Simonton joined them in the front row.

Not counting the six vacant seats from the *AFK* members who failed background checks, the thousand-seat meeting room was at full capacity.

Once everyone was seated, the room grew eerily silent. Everyone shifted uncomfortably in their seats, shooting anxious looks at one another, wondering what would happen next.

Suddenly Vice-President Everett Ashford, National Security Adviser Nelson Casanieves, the Joint Chief of Staff, William Messersmith, and the President's chief-of-staff, Aaron Gillespie, emerged from a side door and took their seats on stage.

Just when Brian Mulrooney thought he couldn't be anymore wowed, out of nowhere, *Hail to the Chief* started playing. *Could it be?* Everyone stood, as President Jefferson Danforth emerged from a separate door.

Tom Dunleavey was right! Mulrooney's mind was completely blown! What Brian had brushed aside as only a dream had become a reality after all.

President Danforth arrived at the mountain the day before, through an off-road hidden garage only few knew about. It descended to the connecting sub-terrain location his 994 guests knew nothing about. It was revamped with everything he would need to govern the country from there, if he wanted or needed to.

Everyone remained standing as the Pledge of Allegiance and National Anthem followed. Once finished, the President motioned for everyone to be seated.

Without the use of a microphone or Teleprompter, the President said, "Greetings, my fellow Americans!" His once salt-and-pepper-colored hair was mostly all salt now.

"Greetings, Mister President!"

"Please be seated. I want to thank you all for coming on such short notice. Life sure has grown unpredictable, hasn't it?" The President managed a humorless chuckle. "These days, it's impossible knowing what will happen on any given day. The slightest tremor in the ground creates instant panic among our citizens. What's left of them, anyway.

"While all of you were en route, a five-point-two quake struck just north of Anchorage, Alaska. Needless to say, many up there are freaking out! People are literally tiptoeing up and down the streets hoping not to upset the Earth. It's quite surreal."

President Danforth scratched his head, "Now, I'm the first to admit that some of Romanero's so-called miracles could easily be explained away, but not this one. We all saw it with our own two eyes. Despite what some may say, there's no scientific way of predicting earthquakes. General predictions are made all the time in earthquake-prone locations, but how often do they get it right? Very seldom. There is no exact science.

"This proves the *Miracle Maker* really does have supernatural powers no one else has, including myself. That's why this meeting was called in the first place. The reason you've all been invited is that the men seated behind me thought you were worthy of an invite."

Heads nodded thoughtfully throughout the room.

"Gentlemen, putting the earthquakes aside for now, as a dissident country, we must always be on the highest alert! Mostly thanks to me, Romanero sees America as the biggest threat to his one world government. It's frightening to think that he's still in the infancy stage. Once fully operational, he'll have little trouble annihilating any country that stands in his way..."

President Danforth glanced at the *AFK* side of the auditorium. "Including the United States. I'm sure it didn't escape your attention that the only country he named in his 'relocation' speech was ours. There's no way to sugarcoat it, gentlemen, America's in deep trouble.

"With one-third of our population gone, by way of the disappearances, and with seventy million more recently vacated, we really have become a shadow of who we once were. Prior to the disappearances, America was the third most populated country in the world. Soon, we'll be lucky to remain in the top ten."

President Danforth looked deeply troubled, "Did you ever think you'd see the day when millions would denounce their citizenship as Americans? I must say Romanero was right on one front: had borders been opened prior to the disappearances, our population would have increased exponentially. Now millions have pledged their undying support to a thirty-year-old foreigner in order to gain the full protection of the New World Order."

"Let 'em leave!" yelled a member of the *AFK*.

A chuckle rippled through the room. Even President Danforth laughed. Pointing to the man he did not know, but had all sorts of intelligence on, the President said, "Sir, your 'do or die' spirit very much embodies the characteristics our forefathers possessed way back when. That's exactly the kind of attitude we'll all need if we are to succeed with the monumental challenge at hand."

The salty old veteran stiffened up, his pride bolstered.

President Danforth went on, "But I'm afraid Salvador Romanero isn't our only problem, gentlemen. While bombs haven't yet reached the Western Hemisphere, intel reports suggest that many of the Muslims who relocated to countries in our hemisphere are hardcore Islamic jihadists in every sense of the word.

"We think they're planning a massive attack on our side of the world. Details are sketchy, but suffice it to say, we believe an attack of some sort is imminent. We just don't know when or from where it will come. But America *will* be the bull's eye."

President Danforth craned his neck to glance at the two *AFK* leaders, "Naturally, I'll do everything in my power to make sure our military is steadfast in its protection of our remaining citizens. Having so many top military officials sharing our common mindset gives us access to secret arsenals not even Congress knows about.

"When America is invaded, strong measures will need to be taken to protect lives. Let me assure you, gentlemen, that we will not go down without a fight! Even if it means using nuclear weapons it will be done. But more on that another time."

The two *AFK* leaders, both military veterans with many years of service, straightened up in their seats. Clearly, this was the best thing they'd heard so far.

"For now, as the now-former world super power, it pains me to say that our biggest task, at least for now, is more of a defensive approach. We need to fortify our positions, not on the front line but beneath the earth's surface," the President said evenly.

"It's with that in mind that I wish to announce my intent to make many underground facilities similar to this one available to both of your respective organizations.

"I'm prepared to provide everything you'll need to sustain yourselves for the longest possible time; things you could never obtain on your own. Your leaders have already been briefed on this matter. The rest of you will know more as time goes on..."

"Naturally, once I leave office or I'm forced out, I'll be stripped of the countless resources I have full access to as America's highest civil servant. With that in mind, we must act quickly and be hunkered down before the storm comes.

"I must warn, gentlemen, that the safety isn't the bunker itself, but in getting you there without being exposed. If you have enough food and water—which I'll personally see that you do, at least initially—and no one knows you're there, you can remain underground indefinitely.

"I hate to cut it short but as you can imagine, my plate's quite full now. So let me close by saying we will have another meeting a week from now. Those invited will spend a full week here and get a real taste of what true communal living is all about.

100

"The week after that we'll do it again. This time women from your groups will be invited. By that time, I hope to start awarding properties. But for now, though only for one night, consider yourselves our Guinea pigs, so to speak.

"Once you've been assigned to your rooms, you'll find a change of clothing and a night bag full of toiletries. I look forward to seeing some of you again next week. God bless you and God bless America."

At that, President Danforth left through the same door from which he entered. What he didn't say was that a dozen or so licensed behavior specialists were listening and observing from behind closed doors, studying the facial gestures and body movements of everyone very closely.

Some even mingled among them.

The only red flag to go up so far was when the President first appeared on stage. *ETSM* members were genuinely surprised to see him. But the same couldn't be said about the two *AFK* leaders.

Many of their members looked as though they fully expected to see the President. If true, how could they be trusted with top-secret information as time marched on?

The licensed behavior specialists would keep monitoring them very carefully...

16

THE NEXT DAY

PASTOR JIM SIMONTON LOOKED up from the newspaper he was reading and spotted Brian Mulrooney. He was gazing into the pane glass window of the greasy spoon diner, watching a short-order cook skillfully stacking freshly grilled hot cakes onto a plate. Scooping a dollop of butter onto the steamy pile, he rang the bell for the waitress to pick up her order. Once eye contact was made, the Michigan pastor motioned his good friend and fellow *ETSM* colleague inside.

Simonton discovered this place the day before, while en route to his designated pickup spot before being shuttled off to the underground meeting location an hour or so away from D.C. Even at 4 a.m., the aroma was so rich he didn't need to waste time thinking of where to meet for breakfast this morning. "Trouble finding it?"

"Piece of cake, brother," Mulrooney said, taking a seat opposite his pastor. Even with GPS, it was oftentimes tricky for newcomers to the D.C. area to navigate the complex 68-square-mile city, but Brian found it rather easily. "Coffee any good here?"

"Adequate, I suppose."

"Yummy," came the reply, jokingly. "Anything good in the news?"

"Sure, if you're a Salvador Romanero fan."

"No thanks," Brian said. "I keep waiting for the ground to start shaking beneath my feet."

Jim Simonton shook his head. "So, what's so important that it can't wait?"

"The final payment's been received in Pennsylvania. All that's needed now are signatures, which means soon I'll be living in the Keystone State."

"Are you up to the challenge?" Simonton already knew Brian would manage a safe house in Pennsylvania, he just didn't know where.

"I think so. But my heart's heavy knowing I'll be cutting ties with my former life." Brian sighed. "Including my family..."

Jim slouched in his seat. "I can imagine. Just glad my parents died before the Rapture. I'd hate to see them have to go through all this. I'm even more grateful I was an only child.

"What really blows my mind is when my folks went to be with Jesus, they didn't have glorified bodies yet. Now that the Rapture's come and gone, they do. Can't wait to see how it all unfolds on the other side."

"So that's how it works, huh?"

"Yes, sir. First Corinthians fifteen confirms it."

Both men were silent as they tried measuring the weight of Jim's statement.

Finally, Brian said, "As you know, Pastor, Jacquelyn will accompany me to Pennsylvania..."

Pastor Simonton gazed deep into Brian's eyes. "Something tells me you're about to make another significant lifestyle change. Am I right?"

A smile broke across Mulrooney's face.

"Does it have anything to do with the joining of two people?"

Brian nodded yes.

"Thought so. When?"

"As soon as possible."

"Does Jacquelyn know?"

"No, but I don't think she'll be too surprised."

"I'm sure she'll be thrilled to accept your hand in marriage."

"I hope so. If we wanna share the same bed, we must become husband and wife, right?"

"Yes."

"There's nothing more I want. I love her, Pastor, and don't wanna face the future without her."

"I understand your feelings. But as exciting as it is to find true love at this point in history, there's a serious downside to consider. Actually, there are many unknowns."

"Yeah. My biggest question is if we miraculously survive the next seven years, will we remain husband and wife during Christ's thousand-year reign on Planet Earth?"

"Hmm...Far as I know, yes. You'll move into the millennial period and raise your children in a era of peace, with Jesus ruling the planet from Jerusalem. Those who were part of the Church Age leading up to the Rapture will come back with Jesus in their glorified bodies. Unlike those still in human form, they won't be able to procreate."

"Does this mean we'll be alive for the entire thousand years?"

"Still not sure of that. I'm studying the Scriptures asking God for the wisdom to know more about the Millennial period. Until I know more, I'd rather not say."

"I understand, Pastor. Is it selfish to want Jacquelyn and I to both be alive when Jesus comes back?"

"Not at all, Brian. That's what I want, too. I can imagine how much more you'll want it if you and Jacquelyn ever bring children into the world."

Brian grinned at the prospect. "I'd love to be married to her for a thousand years."

Pastor Jim smiled, thinking how blessed Brian was to find a good woman to love in such desperate times.

The waiter approached, and they ordered breakfast.

Once he left, Brian said, "Will you marry us, Pastor?"

"I would consider it a great honor, Brian. Do you plan to get married at the church?"

Mulrooney bit his lower lip. "Naturally, that would be my choice. But since it isn't a Catholic church, I seriously doubt my parents will attend, especially my Dad. Not sure about Jacquelyn's parents either. They already think we're out of our minds..."

"Well, considering they're not Christ followers, everything we do will be viewed by them as utter foolishness."

"Don't I know it!"

"Normally our church doesn't marry couples who haven't gone through a marriage counseling class first. But given the times, I think it can be overlooked."

"Thank you, Pastor."

"Don't thank me just yet; not until Jacquelyn accepts your proposal!" Pastor Simonton winked at Brian.

Mulrooney laughed. "Good point." Brian took a sip of coffee and grew more serious. "I plan on asking Charles to be my best man."

"He would make the perfect choice."

"Yeah, I wanted him to hear the news firsthand. He planned on joining us here, but his schedule changed. Said it was *ETSM* business at the highest level."

Pastor Jim said, "As an *ETSM* higher-up, chit-chatting with friends in diners is a luxury Charles no longer has time for."

"I know. You're right, Pastor."

"But don't worry, you and I both know he'll be happy with the news." Mulrooney smiled at the thought, then shivered knowing Jacquelyn still had to agree to marry him. It wasn't a question about love. Brian knew she loved him as much as he loved her.

But with life so unpredictable, not to mention that she lost her first husband not too long ago, perhaps she might reject him on the grounds that the timing just wasn't right. *Thy will be done, Lord...*

Seeing that Brian was a million miles away, Pastor Simonton said, "Next weekend's service will be dedicated to baptisms only. Everyone will be there. Why don't you pop the question then? This way, you can save on wedding invitations."

"Not a bad idea. Think I'll do that."

The waiter came with their meals. Pastor Simonton blessed it.

Brian put a fork full of pancakes in his mouth and swallowed. "What time's your flight back to Detroit?"

"Five-thirty p.m., out of Washington National. You?"

"Six-fifteen, out of Ronald Reagan."

"Did you park your car at Detroit Metro?"

"No. Brother Tom dropped me off."

Pastor Jim said, "I'll gladly drive you to your place if you want."

"Sounds good. Why make Tom drive all that way when you'll already be there, right?"

"Exactly. By the time I get my car, you'll have already landed."

"I appreciate it, Pastor."

Pastor Jim took the last sip of coffee in his cup, "Figured I'd do a little sightseeing in our nation's capitol before heading to the airport. Care to join me?"

"Sure, why not? Always wanted to see D.C. If not now, I may never get to see it. Could be turned into rubble at any time..."

"My thoughts exactly."

Pastor Simonton tossed a few dollar bills and some coins on the table for a tip, and the two *ETSM* members left to take in the sights...

17

WHAT CHARLES CALLOWAY DIDN'T mention in his text message, couldn't say, was that he was no longer in the Washington D.C. vicinity. As everyone was blindfolded and taken back to their personal vehicles in shifts, Calloway was approached by two secret service agents and told to stay put.

After the last bus left the mountain, Calloway, Donald Johnson and Manuel Jiminez—also asked to remain behind—left through another door. The three men were blindfolded then driven out of the underground bunker in a black Suburban and taken a short distance away to a waiting non-white-top military helicopter.

They relaxed when their blindfolds were removed, and they saw Clayton Holmes and Travis Hartings on board the chopper waiting for them. The five men were flown a relatively short distance deep in the heart of the Catoctin Mountains, in Western Maryland. Only Holmes and Hartings knew where they were going.

Upon landing, under heavy guard, they were hurried to another government-issued black Suburban and taken to a remote location, where they waited a half-hour for the call to move on to the next location.

The reason for the delay was that secret service agents Daniel Sullivan and Guillermo Sanchez conducted numerous electronic counter sweeps of the President's retreat looking for bombs, listening devices and all other electronic counter measures.

With a shadow government in place, they wanted to make sure no one would be eavesdropping on them in the form of espionage.

Once Camp David was deemed "bug free", Agent Sullivan called secret service agent Anthony Galiano, who was waiting nearby with the President in an unmarked car, "Bring POTUS here immediately!"

"Yes, sir! Right away!"

President Danforth arrived a few minutes later with absolutely no fanfare. There were no press members, foreign dignitaries or welcoming committees to greet him. Also absent was the playing of "Hail to the Chief" announcing his arrival.

Once President Danforth was situated, his five invited guests were brought to him. "Welcome to Camp David, gentlemen!" he said, greeting them at the front door.

Clayton Holmes and Travis Hartings remained calm. Charles Calloway, Donald Johnson and Manuel Jiminez, on the other hand, couldn't contain their excitement.

Meeting the President of the United States at an underground shelter was one thing. Being invited to his personal retreat was beyond description.

"I can't believe I'm at Camp David!" Calloway mumbled to himself.

Even among the impending doom, President Danforth chuckled to himself. He was reminded of his first visit to the White House at the ripe young age of twelve. He very much looked the way Charles did now. "This is my first time back since last November's tragedy."

"That's right! I remember you were here when it happened..." Calloway said.

"Was sitting over there by the fireplace," the President said somberly, pointing over in that direction, shaking his head at the painful memory, "watching the Ohio State-Michigan football game. Seems like long ago."

Revisiting the place where so many loved ones breathed their last breath in human form filled the President with great dread and sadness. Horrific thoughts fought hard to flood his mind. He fought even harder to push them away.

Prior to the Rapture, Jefferson Danforth considered Camp David as perhaps the greatest benefit to being President. This place would never again be considered a peaceful retreat. It was hallowed ground now.

This was the first time the First Lady didn't accompany him. She told her husband on the day of the Rapture that she would never step foot inside Camp David again.

Aside from White House Head Chef Amy Wong, who was flown to Camp David from Washington, no one else was privy to this "unofficial" covert gathering at Camp David.

Not even Press Secretary Jordan Kendall knew his whereabouts. She knew her boss was meeting covertly with anti-globalists who loved America and detested Salvador Romanero as much as he did. She just didn't know who they were or where the meeting was taking place.

"I'm sorry, Sir," was all Calloway could think to say.

"Where were you at the time, Charles?"

"In a taxicab in New York City, with a business associate of mine who suddenly vanished into thin air."

Thanks to the secret service, President Danforth already knew so much of Calloway's past. Braxton Rice and his team were doing a good job of spying and vetting for the *ETSM*, but they didn't have the kind of access the United States Secret Service had at their disposal.

Because of them—much like he did with Donald Johnson and Manuel Jiminez—the President knew the family members Charles Calloway had lost last November, and pretty much everything he did leading up to the Rapture.

What he didn't know from Calloway's extensive background check was his exact whereabouts at 12:01 that afternoon, when life was forever changed for everyone on Planet Earth. He knew Charles was in New York City for a business convention, but nothing more.

"Must have been quite a traumatic experience for you."

"You can say that again, Sir."

"Who could have ever predicted that day?" asked the President.

Charles looked down at his feet. "My father. He didn't know the exact hour or day, but he knew this moment was fast approaching. Just wish I'd listened to him."

"I'm sure he'd be relieved knowing you're a believer now."

Tears welled up in Calloway's eyes. "I was blessed with such amazing parents."

President Danforth thought about his own parents. From a worldly standpoint, he couldn't have asked for anyone better. But now that his spiritual eyes had been opened, he seriously doubted if they ever knew Jesus intimately.

He was saddened to think of the eternal consequences his deceased parents were now suffering, based solely on the choices and decisions they'd made while still alive in the flesh.

Jefferson Danforth kept these agonizing thoughts to himself. Placing his right hand on Calloway's shoulder, he squeezed gently, "I'm sure they'll be thrilled beyond measure to see you again."

"Thanks, Mister President, I needed to hear that." Calloway smiled. Then it dawned on him: "Are you a Christ follower?"

"As a matter of fact, I am. Guess you could say this is my coming out party. Now that I know the Truth and have been set free by it, I covet the prayers of God's true saints."

Before Calloway could reply, President Danforth glanced over at Clayton Holmes and Travis Hartings. The two men approached him. Of his own free will, President Jefferson Danforth knelt before everyone. Looking up into Holmes' sparkling eyes, the President reached for his humongous hands, which all but swallowed up his own hands.

Clayton Holmes said, "Gather around the President, y'all, and lay hands on him."

Once everyone had inched in as close as they could get and laid their hands upon him, Holmes began, "Lord Father God, our hearts are filled with joy knowing our President is among those of Your choosing. We lift up our brother knowing dark clouds loom on the horizon.

"Soon he'll be forced to make decisions no other American President has ever had to seriously contemplate, let alone execute. Please strengthen him daily, Lord, and be his Rock and Comforter. Grant him the wisdom only You can provide. In fact, grant each of us the wisdom to do what is just and right in Your sight.

"On a personal note, I feel so humbled to participate in perhaps the most significant event to ever transpire at Camp David. It would be difficult imagining anything topping this. I can't help but wonder if genuine Christian fellowship has ever taken place here prior to now.

"Thanks again for the provisions provided to us by President Danforth, and for the privilege of allowing me to represent Your Kingdom here on Earth. May You always be enthroned on the praises of Your People! I ask these things in Jesus' matchless, mighty name, Amen."

"Amen!" was the reply in unison.

Holmes paused to wipe his eyes. "Anything you'd like to add, Mister President?"

The President glanced skyward, "Thank You, Lord, for sending these fine men to help me better understand Your Word, and for letting me see just how lost and sinful I really was. Jesus, I know my sins are what caused You to die so brutally on that cross..."

The President took a deep breath then started weeping, "How can I possibly fathom that You would curse Your only begotten Son for my sake, Father, by treating Him on the cross as if He lived my sinful life? You punished *Him* for the countless sins I've committed. How could I possibly repay You for that? Words fail me..."

The President sniffled, "All I can do is thank You again for looking beyond my sin and declaring me righteous and worthy to spend eternity with You..."

Clayton Holmes was deeply touched by the President's repentant words. The hair on the back of his neck stood at full attention, rendering the giant of a man momentarily speechless. He paused to collect himself.

With tears in his eyes, he tightened his grip on the President's hands, and cleared his throat, "Wow! Thank you, Father! What love indeed! How could we not bow down in worship of You? Your steadfast love and grace are too wonderful to tell. We love You, and exalt you, Lord Jesus!"

For White House Chef Amy Wong, to see her boss, a man she deeply admired and respected, on his knees praying as common citizens towered high above him, was the most beautiful experience of her life. She felt highly favored to be able to witness this intimately beautiful moment.

The Holy Spirit flooded each heart and soul. Had it happened just a few months ago, Wong might have rejected it as sheer religiosity coming from the man who just happened to be her boss.

But that was then...

Chef Wong was first exposed to the Gospel by her late friend and former White House Chief Baker, Edna Brown. Edna was always talking about the love of Jesus, but Wong always ignored her.

Upon hearing that Brown was among the disappearances at Camp David, Wong mourned bitterly for her friend. But after hearing it was Christian in nature, she felt drawn to the Book Edna Brown was always quoting, the same Book she always ignored.

Now that Wong was a believer, she was eager to see Edna Brown again someday. She couldn't wait to tell her friend that after being saved, she started having weekly Bible readings at the White House.

On Clayton Holmes' and Travis Hartings' first visit to the White House, Wong pulled the two *ETSM* leaders aside before they left that night and asked if they would be willing to share the Gospel with the three men who joined her each week to read the Word of God: secret service agents Daniel Sullivan, Guillermo Sanchez and Anthony Galiano.

Holmes explained God's plan of salvation to them in the clearest possible way. All three men, feeling utterly filthy and helpless, saw Jesus for who He really was; the only One who could rescue their souls from eternal damnation. They repented of their many sins that night and trusted in Jesus as Lord and Savior.

Glancing around the room, Chef Wong finally understood why her boss had instructed her to leave her entire staff back at 1600 Pennsylvania Avenue. They weren't Christ followers. Her only regret was that the First Lady wasn't with them. Wong would never stop praying for her. For now, she rejoiced knowing that her boss, the President of the United States, was a new Christ follower. To have the distinct privilege of laying hands on her boss and praying with him in such an intimate way was too amazing to put into words.

Moved by the power of the Holy Spirit, the White House head chef dropped to her knees, raised her hands skyward, and started singing with a voice that was glad...

"I exalt thee,
I exalt thee,
I exalt thee, Oh Lord..."

At first, President Danforth shot her a sideways look. Seeing the shy-by-nature Asian woman on her knees, with her hands lifted high above her head, praising her Maker was so out of character for her. The unbridled joy in her voice and on her face brought fresh tears to his eyes.

The second time through, Clayton Holmes dropped to his knees, raised his hands toward the ceiling, and joined her...

"I exalt thee,
I exalt thee,
I exalt thee, Oh Lord..."

Everyone was on their knees the third time through. Travis Hartings changed the pronoun from 'I' to 'we' and lent his voice to the singing.

Then Donald Johnson joined in.

Charles Calloway slowly swayed side to side on his knees, with his head down, eyes closed and a smile on his face. He was drinking it all in.

Finally, he shouted, "Hallelujah!" and joined in the singing.

After a while, everyone stood and formed a circle and joined hands...

"We exalt thee,
We exalt thee,
We exalt thee, Oh Lord..."

The next time through, Agent Sullivan joined in. President Danforth remained silent and listened as the beautiful melody washed over him.

When they were finished, President Danforth couldn't remember feeling any better. "So, this is what true Christian fellowship feels like? Could you imagine what would happen if the press got wind of this?"

Travis Hartings marveled at the expression on the President's face. It looked as if God had momentarily lifted the oppressive weight of an American Presidency off his shoulders.

"In all my years in public service," President Danforth said, "I've never felt a sense of genuine camaraderie like I do right now. It can only be God at work in us."

White House Head Chef Amy Wong wiped tears from her eyes and excused herself, so she could get busy in the kitchen. She still had a job to do. The President requested Mexican food before leaving the White House and Wong delivered.

When the last plate was brought from the kitchen everyone sat down to eat, including Chef Wong. This was a day of firsts for her.

For starters, it was her first time cooking a meal for an American President—President Danforth being her third—without the full assistance of her staff.

It was also her first time being asked to dine with those for whom she'd just cooked. It was almost too much to absorb at once.

Travis Hartings blessed the food, and everyone dug in. It was as delicious as it looked.

President Danforth took a bite of his enchilada. Swallowing, he said, "By choosing to align myself with your two groups, even if secretly, I'm placing myself directly in harm's way.

"If word ever got out that I'm supplying everything from food to shelter to military-strength weaponry to known Salvador Romanero dissidents, it could mean grave danger for me."

"We know, Sir, and we appreciate everything you're doing for us."

"It goes both ways, gentlemen. With so many Americans wanting my head on a plate, I feel comforted in your presence. Besides, if anyone deserves my support, it's you.

"But we mustn't be naive. With a shadow government in place, word will eventually get out." The President sighed, "Until that day comes, no one aside from those in your organization can know I'm a Christian."

112

"We understand, Mister President."

"Wish I could say the same for most members of the *American Freedom Keepers*. Don't get me wrong: they're extremely valuable to us in that they're willing to fight Romanero to the death. But, as you all know, they're wrong in thinking they can somehow remove him from power, or that America will become the super power it once was.

"With dark powerful forces controlling Romanero, the next seven years are his for the taking. There's nothing I can do to stop him. The fact that most *AFK* members are ignorant to this exposes their lack of spiritual depth regarding the Word of God."

Travis Hartings cleared his throat, "This is why we cannot form a total joint venture with them. Our differences are spiritual in nature."

President Danforth straightened up in his seat, "I'm sure some in that group are believers. But until we're one-hundred percent certain where they stand in Christ Jesus, ally or not, they need to be kept at arm's length. Under no condition can we reveal any of your locations to them."

Clayton Holmes weighed in, "Agreed. In the end, patriot or not, when it comes to one's spiritual affiliation, everyone eventually needs to choose a side. *AFK* members who reject Jesus will ultimately accept the Mark of the Beast. Otherwise they won't be able to buy, sell or eat. Once that happens, they'll succumb to Satan's deceptive spirit and will ultimately become our staunch enemies."

President Danforth gulped hard. *Will Melissa one day become my staunch enemy?* It was enough to choke on. "Can we pray for the First Lady?"

"Yes, Mister President..."

Once they had finished praying, the meeting at Camp David came to a close...

18

TAMIKA MOSELEY LOWERED THE bandanna covering her face. She gulped hard, prayed for God's protection and went inside the library in Patterson, New Jersey for the second straight day.

Once a computer became available, Tamika reactivated her Twitter account. She had three new followers, whatever that meant.

Whoever they were, she wasn't interested in getting to know them. All that mattered was contacting Brian Mulrooney. Seeing no messages from him shredded her heart a little more. Out of desperation, she sent him another message: *Hi Brian. This is your favorite taxi driver. Did you get my last message? I'm in serious trouble and really need your help!*

If Brian didn't reply this time, Tamika would perform another online search for Charles Calloway. Her last search had proved fruitless.

Brian Mulrooney's phone was turned off as he went through airport security at Ronald Reagan National Airport. Upon turning it on, he was informed he had a new Twitter message from *NYCTaxiDriver111*.

He raced to his gate and signed into his Twitter account. His heart raced with anticipation. *Is this who I think it is? If so, what's wrong?*

Tamika's hands started flailing over the keyboard when she received a reply from Brian. She replied: *Yes, it's me. Can't explain online. Please come to New York as soon as possible. I'll pick you up at the airport. I'm begging you!*

Brian replied: *What happened to your phone? I've tried calling you a million times!*

Tamika replied: *I'll explain later. For now, please come!*

Sensing her great despair, and with a strong inner-prompting, Mulrooney turned on his laptop and booked a flight to New York as they chatted online. *Just booked a flight. Be there in 2 days...*

Relief flooded over her: *Thanks so much, Brian!*

No problem. Here's my flight information. Gotta jet. Don't wanna miss my plane back to Michigan! Stay safe there. See you soon...

Tamika jotted down Brian's flight information on a piece of paper. She couldn't help but wonder if he would still come to New York had he known she was a fugitive on the run. Part of her was surprised he didn't know by now. It seemed everyone else knew.

Before signing off the computer, Tamika Moseley deleted her Twitter account. Then it was off to share the good news with Cocoa...

BRIAN MULROONEY FOUND HIS seat on the plane and sent a text message to Charles Calloway: *Just chatted with Tamika. She wouldn't tell me what kind of trouble she's in. She wants to tell me in person. I'm going to New York in 2 days to meet her. Talk about answered prayer!*
Calloway replied: *Amen! Thanks for the update. Keep me informed...*
Mulrooney replied: *You know I will.*

Brian then sent a text message to Tom Dunleavey informing that Pastor Simonton would drive him home from the airport, and that he would explain everything later.

After that Brian called Jacquelyn. Just hearing her voice again soothed his nerves like no one else could. They didn't discuss anything important, including the news regarding Tamika Moseley—that would come later. Brian was just happy to speak to her again. They remained on the phone until he was ordered to power down his phone in preparation for takeoff.

When Brian landed in Detroit, Pastor Jim was waiting outside the baggage claim area for him. Mulrooney climbed into his truck.

"Hey stranger, long time no see! How was the flight?"

Brian laughed then grew serious. "I chatted with Tamika before boarding the plane."

"Is she okay?"

"Well, she's in trouble, but wouldn't tell me online. Said she was too afraid. She begged me to come to New York immediately."

"So, what will you do?"

"Already booked a flight. I leave in two days. While I'm there, I plan to meet my mother. Time to tell her I'm leaving Michigan." Brian took a deep breath. "And getting married..."

"What about your father?"

There was this pained expression on Brian's face. "Still haven't spoken to him since I shared my dream about the Catholic church with him. I think he hates me."

"The great separation has begun, Brian. All we can do is pray that God will change your father's heart."

"That's my daily prayer for him."

"From now on, I'll join you in praying for him."

115

Brian was deeply touched by his pastor's gesture. "Thanks, brother. I can't wait to tell Jacquelyn you're an *ETSM* member. She'll be thrilled with the news."

"After meeting Clayton and Travis, I have no doubt God has ordained them for this time."

"I thank God every day for them. If I had to endure all this craziness alone, I don't know what I'd do, especially knowing what's still coming. Don't know what I'd do without Jacquelyn, either. With dark clouds gathering in the distance, she's my warm blanket on a cold day. Speaking of Jacquelyn, would it be okay if we were the last to be baptized?"

Sensing Brian's reasoning, Pastor Simonton said, "As you wish."

"Other than you, Charles and brother Tom, I plan on telling no one else. They'll know soon enough."

"Your secret's safe with me, Brian. Good news travels quickly these days."

"You're right about that!" A few moments later, they reached Brian's apartment. "Don't think I'll see you until next Sunday at church. Until then, take care of yourself."

"You too, brother. Have a safe flight to New York. See you next weekend."

"Oh, there's something I've been longing to say to you for the longest time, Pastor."

"Oh, yeah, what's that?"

"Keep fighting the Good Fight. Pray for me as I pray for you. God is with us."

The comment made Jim Simonton grin from ear to ear. "You too, Brian."

Brian climbed the three flights of stairs and opened the door to his apartment. Tom Dunleavey was sitting on the living room couch reading the Word of God.

The TV was on, but the sound was muted. Whenever the Two Witnesses appeared on TV, the former Catholic priest stopped everything he was doing to watch and listen ever so carefully.

Seeing the same two men who'd disrupted his dream world for three straight nights, consuming all who became too aggressive with them by breathing fire from their mouths, was the most bizarre thing his eyes had ever seen. It was impossible to put into words.

"Welcome back home, Brian. How was the flight?"

116

"She's alive!"

"Who?"

"Tamika, the woman we prayed for the other night. Talk about a huge load off my chest! The not-knowing was making me crazy."

"Why'd she wait so long to contact you?"

"She's in serious trouble."

"What kind of trouble?"

"Don't know. She wouldn't tell me online. I'm going to New York in two days to see her. While I'm there, I plan to meet my mother. It's time to tell her I'm leaving Michigan and getting married..."

Tom Dunleavey raised an eyebrow. "Married?"

"Yes. Just like in your dream. Decided on the plane that when I return from New York, I'll spend what little money left I have on an engagement ring. Only you, Charles, and Pastor Jim know for now. I'd like to keep it that way."

"I won't tell a soul. You have my word. Speaking of Pastor Jim, did he tell you why he wasn't at church today?"

Brian shook his head. "He was in Washington D.C. with me..."

"Seriously?" Tom Dunleavey's curiosity shot into the stratosphere.

Seeing the shock on his face, Brian said, "Believe me, I was just as surprised as you. Didn't know until I saw him at the meeting. I was equally surprised when he told me you'd be preaching in his absence."

"That would be correct..."

"How'd it go?"

"Well, it went..." Tom Dunleavey laughed at his own statement. "Actually, it went very well. I admit I felt out of sorts at first. And nervous, mostly because I didn't want to drag any old habits from my years as a Catholic priest into the sanctuary."

"What did you preach on?"

"Since I had no time to prepare a message, I preached the same message I gave at my old church in Ann Arbor, Revelation chapters four and five. Thankfully, it was well received by everyone..."

"I'm sure it was, brother..."

Tom Dunleavey eyeballed Brian carefully, "I must say I'm even more curious about this Christian group you're involved with..."

"Hopefully soon, you'll know more." Brian rubbed his throbbing forehead. It had been a long day. *Hope I don't regret saying this.* "By the way, you were right..."

"In what way?"

"President Danforth *was* there!"

"Not surprised to hear you say that. After all, I had the same dream both nights you were gone."

Brian's eyes grew big as silver dollar pancakes. "Seriously? I wasn't supposed to tell you that. Had it not been for your dream I wouldn't have said a word."

"Hope someday soon you can tell me more."

"That's the plan, brother. Let's just say because of the dreams you've had, the ball's already rolling. But the decision's not mine to make. It's out of my hands."

Tom saw the sincerity in Brian's eyes. "I understand. Guess you'll be needing a ride to the airport again?"

"Actually, I think I'll ask Jacquelyn this time. It'll be the last time I see her before the Sunday baptism service. That's where I plan to ask for her hand in marriage. But thanks, anyway."

"For the record, I think you make the perfect couple."

Brian Mulrooney didn't reply, but from what Tom saw on his face, his comment had hit the mark. It was priceless.

Little did they know the turmoil in their lives was about to be taken to a whole new level.

This was only the beginning...

19

TWO DAYS LATER

TAMIKA MOSELEY CIRCLED LAGUARDIA Airport for the third time, doing her best to avoid being seen by anyone, especially the police! Perhaps the soon-to-be 28-year-old woman was being overly paranoid, but even with her face covered with a bandanna it seemed everyone was staring at her. That's what being on the run from authorities did to a person.

Tamika spent every-last dollar she had on gas and tolls just to get to LaGuardia. But what other choice did she have? She was lonely and terrified and in desperate need of a friend; which is why she risked coming here in the first place—to fetch Brian Mulrooney.

Brian's flight was due in at 3:16. It was now 3:47 p.m. and still no sign of him. Tamika knew his plane had already landed, after foolishly going inside the terminal to check the ARRIVALS board. She covered her dark-skinned face with her bandanna, left her pet cat, Cocoa, in the car and hurried inside. Her heart pumped wildly every step of the way.

Sure, it was potentially dangerous, but with no cell phone, how else would she know if his plane had landed or not? Tamika was learning first hand just how difficult it was navigating life in the twenty-first century without a mobile device, especially as a wanted woman!

"Where are you, Brian?" Tamika grunted under her breath and circled again. A million thoughts assaulted her brain. Had New York City authorities already tracked her down to her mother's vehicle? Was there a BOLO (Be On the Look Out) for the car she was driving?

Would airport police officers who were out ticketing and towing illegally parked and unattended vehicles recognize her at some point?

Even worse, had someone known she'd communicated with Brian on Twitter, brief as it was? If so, was Brian detained by airport police upon landing? If not, would someone follow his every move hoping he would lead authorities straight to her?

Nothing could be ruled out. Every fiber in Tamika's body was on full alert. Part of her wanted to flee back to New Jersey where she felt slightly safer. But she couldn't; she really needed Brian's help.

"Please protect me, Father!"

Finally, at 3:58 p.m., after circling LaGuardia Airport for the seventh time, Tamika spotted Brian Mulrooney out of the corner of her eye and pulled to the curb.

Brian wore a New York Mets baseball cap just like he said he would. For added measure, the surgical mask he wore on the plane now dangled from his neck, so Tamika could easily recognize him. He looked a little pale. Other than that, nothing had changed.

"She's here now," said Brian to Charles Calloway, noticing her. "I'll call later with an update. If you could contact Pastor Jim and brother Tom and tell them I arrived safely, I'd appreciate it."

"Will do, Brian."

"Thanks, Charles." Mulrooney ended the call, covered his face with the surgical mask, and lowered himself into the late model Oldsmobile. "Hey, stranger, we meet again. Are you ever a sight for sore eyes! Talk about answered prayer!"

"Good to see you, too, Brian..."

"Sorry for the delay. We waited on the plane for nearly a half hour before a jet way finally opened up."

"Just glad you're here!" Tamika breathed a sigh of relief. She suddenly felt safe, at least as safe as one could feel given her dire situation.

Mulrooney reached over and hugged Tamika, doing his best to ignore that his friend looked ghastly thin. She was perhaps 20 pounds lighter than when they'd first met last November. She was bordering on skeletal. Bones protruded through her facial features.

"Who's this little guy?" Brian asked, noticing a cat in the back seat.

"Her name's Cocoa."

"Nice to meet you, Cocoa," Brian scooped the cat into his arms, looking more at Tamika than her pet feline. He couldn't overlook the fear in her eyes. Nor could he avoid the overpowering foul odor in the car. It took all his strength to keep from gagging. It smelled more like a homeless shelter than a vehicle.

Mulrooney tried not to sniff it in, for fear he might have an asthma attack. "Looks like you're moving up in the world. Least this car has no dents or holes in the floor."

Tamika tried to laugh but couldn't. She half-smiled through her bandanna.

120

Brian fastened his seat belt. "So, what's so important that I had to travel all this way to see you?"

"Ever since I received Christ as Lord and Savior, my life's been turned completely upside down. And not in a good way..."

"I can relate."

"Not sure you will after you hear what I have to say."

The way she said it made Mulrooney squirm in his seat. "What's going on, Tamika? You had us worried."

"Search my name online and see for yourself."

Brian did as he was instructed and took his time reading all about the graveyard incident. The more he read the more breathless he became. His shock knew no bounds.

Tamika's head remained down the entire time.

Finished reading it, Mulrooney's eyes narrowed. "Did you do this?"

Tamika shook her head no. "Only thing I did was open my grandfather's casket."

"Why would you do such a thing, Tamika?"

"To see if the Rapture theory was true or not..."

Brian gasped. His eyes grew wide. "Are you saying you went there looking for your grandfather's remains?"

Tamika nodded yes. "That's when I came to faith in Jesus."

Brian knew Tamika recently became a believer, but never in a million lifetimes would he have ever guessed her method of finding the Truth. Had it happened before the Rapture, he would have thought she was a demented psychopath like everyone else.

"Man, oh man! Wait until Charles hears this!" *First Tom Dunleavey? Now Tamika?*

"It's quite a story, I know. Can't help but wonder if God's punishing me for it now? But what a moment it will be for Momma when she sees me in Heaven!"

"Amen to that." Brian looked forward to meeting Ruth in Heaven too. His list of saints kept growing! "Hungry?"

"I could eat," Tamika said.

"Let's eat then. My treat!"

"Where to?"

"As much as I'd like to see Craig again, I'm afraid *Mitzi's* is out of the question."

"I heard that."

121

"Hmm, why's that, Tamika?"

"I'm no longer welcome there. Craig sent me a text message the moment he saw my face on TV. He urged me to turn myself in and let justice prevail. I told him the charges against me were false. I admitted to opening my grandfather's casket, but everything else was untrue."

Though Brian hadn't heard from Craig Rubin in many months, he was mildly surprised his old friend hadn't contacted him by now, regarding this serious matter. "Are you saying the forty-five thousand dollars worth of stolen vases was made up?"

"All I can say is if it happened, I had nothing to do with it." Tamika let out a deep exhale, "Craig never even offered to help me."

"Can't say I'm surprised. All we can do is pray for him."

"Been doing that nightly. Anyway, when I got home that night, I parked my car a few blocks from my apartment building and limped home, after being bit by two cemetery dogs.

"Turned out to be a good move. Had I parked outside the apartment building, there's no way I would have escaped that night. Cops had the place surrounded."

"Amazing!" Brian took this as evidence that her conversion was genuine.

"Yeah. Been sleeping in my car ever since, mostly in vacant parking lots in New Jersey. Which explains the unpleasant odor you may be smelling. I also have a serious leg infection. Looks nasty and full of pus. I'll show you later..."

Brian thought about Jacquelyn's leg and how she had needed 72 stitches. And she wasn't bitten by dogs! "We need to find a way to have your leg looked at."

"No chance I'm going to a doctor now, or back to my apartment. Too many doors been knocked-in over the years by police officers out to make an arrest. Don't want the next felon hauled out of the complex in handcuffs to be me. Besides, I didn't pay the rent the last two months. So, on top of everything else, I'm sure they trying to evict me by now."

"Why didn't you contact me or Charles sooner? We could have helped you."

"I tried. The moment I heard my name on the radio I called you both. Got your voice mails. Got so frustrated I smashed my phone on the sidewalk. Been without one ever since."

122

Mulrooney sighed, "I remember seeing a missed call from you. We were busy with an important matter and our phones were temporarily confiscated. We tried calling you many times since.

"Would've Googled your name, but I knew I'd never find you on social media. I can't tell you how frustrating it was not hearing from you all this time. I thought you were dead."

"Well, I'm not dead, but this is no way to live."

"I think your life is a microcosm of things to come for all believers."

"Hmm." Tamika's shoulders slumped. She lowered her head.

It was time to change the subject. Brian said, "Do you like Chinese food?"

"Yes."

"Tell you what, let's order Chinese and take it back to my hotel room. You'll be safe there."

"Okay." Tamika knew she could trust Brian.

"Move it or get a ticket!" barked a burly police officer out of nowhere, startling Tamika. Seeing it was a cop, she turned her head the other way and shrank in her seat.

The man glared at her wondering why she looked so familiar to him. Unable to connect the dots, he shrugged it off and kept walking. Had he remained there a moment longer he would have seen Tamika Moseley hyperventilating.

Brian saw the fear in her eyes. "Think it might be best if I drive."

"I was hoping you'd say that," Tamika said, in between breaths.

Mulrooney removed his baseball cap. "Put this on."

Tamika did as she was instructed.

Brian got out and Tamika slid over to the passenger side. After their seat belts were fastened, they drove off.

Mulrooney pulled his cell phone out of his coat pocket and called the hotel. A woman at the front desk answered. "I have a reservation for the next two nights. The reason I called is that I think I failed to mention that I brought my pet cat with me." *Sorry, Lord, for my dishonesty...*

"I'll be happy to check for you, sir. Name?"

"Brian Mulrooney."

"Let me check your reservation." The woman perused the computer screen in front of her. "There's no mention of a cat, sir."

"That's what I thought. Sorry, it was a last-minute decision to bring her along with me. If I have to pay extra, I will."

"That shouldn't be a problem, sir. We'll just put a larger hold on your credit card, just in case."

"That'll be fine. See you shortly."

The call ended.

Even through her worn out bandanna, Brian knew Tamika was smiling. *Finally!*

20

BRIAN MULROONEY AND TAMIKA Moseley arrived at the hotel an hour later. Knowing her frail body lacked nutrients, Mulrooney ordered enough Chinese food for eight people.

"Why don't you park the car while I get us checked in?"

"Okay."

Brian handed Tamika his cell phone. "Give me a few minutes, then call the front desk asking for me. I'll give you my room number. Check my call history. It's the last call I made."

"Okay."

"See you soon. Do your best to avoid making eye contact with anyone."

"Been doing that for many weeks."

"Well then, this should be easy," Mulrooney said, with a half-smile.

Tamika didn't smile back. She was still trembling from the brief encounter with the airport policeman.

"Don't worry, sis, God is with us."

I sure hope so...

Brian shouldered his garment bag and scooped Cocoa up in his arms. "I'll leave the Chinese food with you. This way, if someone becomes suspicious, just tell 'em you're delivering it to me."

Tamika nodded her head. "Least someone's thinking."

"See you soon." Mulrooney closed the car door and went inside to check in.

Tamika scooted over to the driver's side and took in her surroundings to make sure no one was watching. Satisfied that the coast was clear, she parked the car on a side street two blocks away and remained inside the vehicle until it was time to call the hotel.

After asking for Brian Mulrooney, the woman at the front desk put her through to his room. "NYC taxi driver?"

"Yup..."

"I'm in room five-eighteen. Once you enter the hotel, the elevators will be off to the left. Do your best to avoid the front desk."

"On my way." Tamika grabbed the Chinese food, made sure all the car doors were locked, and left at once for the hotel. The only time she raised her head was to avoid bumping into someone, or when she passed a street light pole, to make sure there weren't any WANTED posters with her name and face posted on them. She was relieved to see none.

Tamika reached the hotel lobby and saw the bank of elevators exactly where Brian had said they would be. She rushed off in that direction as quickly as she could without ever glancing at the front desk. Facemask on, she was determined not to be spotted by someone. She was too close now.

Brian was in the hallway on the fifth floor holding Cocoa waiting for her. "Thank you, Lord, for the protection," he said, seeing her.

They hurried inside the room. For the first time in many weeks, Tamika Moseley finally felt safe. Relief washed over her.

"Please make yourself comfortable," Mulrooney said, placing Cocoa onto the plush, carpeted floor.

Tamika lowered her bandanna. "Mind if I use your shower before we eat? Hungry as I am, I feel so dirty."

"Sure. Take all the time you need. We can always reheat the food in the microwave. Do you have clean clothes in the car?"

Tamika suddenly looked embarrassed. "No..."

"I see. Tell you what, take my robe. It's clean. In the meantime, I'll go to the front desk and get some coins, so we can wash your clothes after we eat, okay?"

Tamika smiled faintly and went to the bathroom.

After a refreshing shower, Brian reheated the food. Blessing it, they dug in. It tasted as good as it smelled.

Brian twirled Lo Mein noodles on his paper plate with a white plastic fork, "It's kinda strange to be staying in a hotel in New York City. If my folks only knew I was here..."

"Do you plan on seeing them while you're here?"

"Hopefully my mother. If so, I already fear the outcome..."

"Why's that?"

Brian gazed out the window and sighed.

Seeing sadness creeping onto his face, Tamika changed the subject. "How's Jacquelyn?"

"As good as can be expected. She's a wonderful woman!"

"Yeah. You tell me that every time we talk!"

"What can I say, Tamika, I love her. Truth is, I plan on proposing to her when I get back to Michigan."

A smile broke across Tamika's face. "Wow! Really?"

Brian nodded. "Just hope she says yes."

"I'm sure she will. You're a great guy. I hope to meet Jacquelyn someday."

Brian took a gulp of his soft drink. "She looks forward to meeting you as well."

Tamika swallowed the food in her mouth. "Does she know I'm with you now?"

Brian nodded yes. "I called when you were in the shower. When I told her how you came to faith in Jesus, she rejoiced. And guess what?"

"What?"

"When I told her you've been sleeping in your car all this time, she insisted that you stay at the hotel with me."

Tamika's face lit up. She got teary-eyed. "Really? She said that?"

"Yup. I was going to extend the offer myself. Jacquelyn just happened to beat me to it."

"I don't know what to say..."

"There's nothing to say. Just accept the offer. If anyone needs a good night's sleep, it's you. I'm booked here the next two nights. Bad news is I can't afford another room. But I only need one bed."

"Actually, I feel safer knowin' you're here."

Brian smiled. "Well then, take a load off. You're safe here."

With so much venomous hatred being spewed at her by so many in her city, Brian's words washed over her like a soothing spring rain. Even with serious charges filed against her, Brian and Jacquelyn still trusted her. It gave Tamika hope to want to continue on her journey. *Thank you, Jesus!*

When they finished eating, Brian noticed Tamika's energy level had decreased. Now that she felt safe, much like Tom Dunleavey the other day, the constant adrenaline pumping through her body from being on the run had slowly dissipated. The poor woman looked completely exhausted. Her eyes grew heavy.

"Why don't we start your laundry before we both fall asleep?"

Tamika got up out of her chair. "Sounds like a plan."

"Think I should go to the car for you. Just tell me what to get."

"I dunno. The trunk's loaded with dirty laundry."

"I'll grab everything I can. Whatever's left over, we can always wash tomorrow."

Tamika sat on the couch in stunned silence as Brian emptied his suitcase, so he could put her dirty clothes inside. "I'd like to do my own laundry if you don't mind. Even if I have to put dirty clothes back on for now."

"By all means. Though I suggest you wear the baseball cap and bandanna whenever you leave the room."

"Believe me, I have no plans of going anywhere without them."

Tamika handed Brian her car keys and told him where her car was parked. Brian left at once.

At midnight, Tamika came back to the room with the last of the clean clothes.

Brian suddenly looked ashen. "Remember I told you earlier that I hope to meet with my mother in the morning?"

"Yeah?"

"The reason I fear the outcome is she doesn't know I'm moving to Pennsylvania, or that I'm about to propose to a woman she's never even met."

Tamika shot Brian a sideways look, "Pennsylvania?"

"Yes, to manage a safe house for exiled believers. That's all I can tell you for the time being. Sorry. Hopefully soon you'll know more. Lord willing."

"I understand..." *Safe house?* Tamika liked the sound of it.

"For now, just pray all goes well with me and my mother. That is, if she agrees to even meet me."

"You got it."

"Anything else I can do for you before I go to sleep?"

"I'd really like to brush my teeth."

"Let me guess, your tooth brush is in the car, right?"

Tamika nodded yes. "In my son's backpack in the back seat with all my toiletries. Also, would you mind bringing a can of cat food for Cocoa and one of her toys?"

"Okay, but once I get back, it's bed time for me. I'm bushed."

"I heard that."

When Brian returned, Tamika and Cocoa were both sound asleep in Tamika's bed. "Guess you're not brushing your teeth after all," he whispered softly so she wouldn't hear him.

128

Before calling it a night, Brian showered and sent a text message to his mother informing that he was in New York and wanted to meet her in the morning at their favorite diner up the street from her house. Mulrooney flicked off the light switch and climbed into bed. Within minutes he, too, was sound asleep...

21

THE NEXT MORNING

AT NINE A.M. BRIAN Mulrooney peeked through the window of a half-full restaurant. Seeing his mother seated at a booth set for two, he thanked God under his breath and went inside.

By the time Sarah replied to his text message, he was already sleeping. It said: *Will do my best. Wish you had given me a little more notice. Love you too.* Brian read it the moment he woke up. It was like music to his soul.

"Thanks for coming, Ma. So nice to see you again." Brian kissed his mother's right cheek. He silently gasped seeing her face up close. It was as if she'd aged ten years from when he saw her last Thanksgiving. Brian knew she occasionally dyed her hair prior to last November. It was almost completely gray now.

In the days leading up to the Rapture, Sarah Mulrooney was a happy-go-lucky woman. Her deep blue friendly eyes were always lively; her hair was always combed to perfection. Nary a strand was ever out of place.

It's like she no longer cared. For the first time ever, she looked like an old woman.

Sarah noticed her son staring at her. "You'll have to pardon my appearance. Coming here was no easy task."

"I appreciate it more than you know." Brian did all he could to ignore the tension he saw on his mother's face. It reflected someone who was barely hanging on. It pained him knowing much of it was there because of him; his father too, stemming from how badly things had deteriorated between the two of them.

The waiter approached with another coffee cup and a fresh pot of coffee. He poured a steaming cup for Brian and refilled Sarah's half-empty cup.

Sarah ventured a sip, all the while thinking how dreadful it was that a mother had to do all this sneaking around just to see her son. It was pure insanity. The only way she was able to pull it off was by lying to her husband and telling him she had a hair salon appointment.

Perhaps she would stop by the salon later, just to cover her tracks. She hated being dishonest with Dick, but felt she had no choice in the matter. He followed her everywhere she went these days.

Sarah sighed, "Who would have ever imagined life turning out like this?"

"Only gonna get worse, Ma." *How much worse after this meeting?* Brian shivered at the thought, especially if she knew her own flesh and blood was harboring one of New York City's most hated fugitives in his hotel room.

"Yeah. You keep telling me that."

"Come on, Ma, what's it gonna take for you to come to faith in Christ? Do you really think the ground has shaken for the last time, or that bombs will stop falling from the sky? Romanero's a madman! He's the son of Perdition! His power comes from Satan himself. Sorry to say this but it won't be long before bombs start falling on Manhattan. Perhaps earthquakes too. Everything man-made will soon be destroyed."

Brian paused after his mother flinched. Her posture begged him to stop preaching to her, but her eyes motioned for him to continue. "From what I'm learning in Scripture, God's about to get everyone's attention again. I'm sure you're aware by now that Salvador Romanero is predicting that twenty-five percent of humanity will soon be wiped off the map, followed by another one-third after that."

Sarah nodded yes.

"What he didn't say was that he got that information from the Bible, in the Book of Revelation. God's causing all of this to happen, not Romanero! And that's just round one!"

Brian scanned the restaurant with a paranoid twitch, before continuing. "What assurance do you have that you'll be fine either way?"

"Hmm."

"Now more than ever, you need God's eternal protection. I can tell you to place your trust in Christ as Lord and Savior till I'm blue in the face, Ma, but the decision is entirely yours to make." Brian paused to sip his coffee. "Who knows, once your eyes and ears are opened spiritually and you receive Christ as Lord and Savior, perhaps Chelsea will follow."

"Don't hold your breath. We hardly speak anymore." Sarah seemed agitated. "I'm afraid she's become a prisoner to social media. She locks herself in her bedroom chatting with friends all night. Only time she comes out is to eat, shower or use the restroom."

"Be patient with her, Ma. Insomnia's on the rise worldwide. Most people are too terrified to leave the house these days. They prefer to remain in their comfort zones, where it's so much safer than venturing outside. For Chelsea, that place just happens to be her bedroom."

"I understand that, Brian."

"We're all trying to define our new normal. Chelsea's lost and needs Jesus.

"I know, but it's just so hard..."

"As my sister and only sibling, it pains me too." Brian took another sip of coffee. "Almost as much as my relationship with Dad has caused you so much pain."

The waiter approached, and they ordered breakfast. When he left them, Brian said, "Until Dad realizes the Catholic Church can't save his soul, he'll never have peace with God. The very place he goes to for peace and solace just happens to be one of the biggest obstacles in his path.

"I'm sure he knows Catholics are reading their Bibles and are coming to faith in Jesus in record numbers! That's my prayer for Dad, too." Brian took a sip of coffee. "What if I told you a former Catholic priest from the church in Ann Arbor is staying at my apartment?"

"Not sure how to respond to that..."

"He's on the run from the church. Wanna know what made him a defector?" When Sarah didn't reply, Brian said, "Preaching the Truth. Can you believe that? He gave his whole life to the Catholic church and now they wanna kill him. He's turned into a mighty man of God and has become a dear friend to me.

"We met because of similar dreams we both had. It led to a spiritual debate. Now he's on my side. God's side, rather. I'm sure if Dad met him, he would hate him as much as he hates me."

Sarah stared at her coffee cup and shifted uncomfortably in her seat in total silence. Brian would rejoice if he knew she was reading the Bible meant for Justin Schroeder's now-deceased parents every day and having spiritual dreams of her own.

Yet, she was too scared to take the next step and go all in. It wasn't the life-altering message the Word of God offered that kept her from jumping in head first; it was the fear of losing her husband. The last thing Sarah wanted was to put even more strain on her 35-year marriage.

The waiter approached again. "Your order will be right up." He refilled their coffee cups and quickly left them.

They sat in silence a moment until, against his better judgment, Brian said, "You'll never guess who I met last week."

"Who?"

Brian let his eyes wander the half-full restaurant, to make sure no one was eavesdropping on them. He couldn't be too careful now. He leaned forward in his seat and spoke in a near whisper, "President Danforth."

Sarah's face said it all: unbridled shock. "Are you kidding me?"

"No." Brian half-smiled. It quickly faded knowing he was betraying the trust *ETSM* leaders had placed in him, by sharing this little tidbit with his mother.

"What was the nature of your business with the President of the United States? You're a hotel manager, not a senator or governor."

Brian looked down at his coffee cup and sighed. "I'm afraid I can't share that with you, Mom." When Sarah didn't reply, Brian said, "There's something else I need to tell you."

"What is it?"

Brian grimaced. "I'm moving to Pennsylvania."

Sarah blinked hard. "You're moving where?"

"Pennsylvania," came the reply.

"I thought you loved Michigan?" Sarah was clearly puzzled.

"I do, Ma, but it's time to move on."

"Why Pennsylvania?"

"It's where the Lord wants me to go."

"What about Renate?"

"We're history."

Sarah raised an eyebrow.

"Come on, Mom, you know we've been drifting apart for many months now. She's not a Christian. And there's no way I can love someone who loves Salvador Romanero. He's the Antichrist of the Bible!"

Sarah looked down at the table, hoping no one had heard her son's outrageous remark. Even if true—which even Sarah thought it was—it was a potentially dangerous thing to say.

Brian took a moment to formulate his next thoughts. "Besides, I've met someone else."

Sarah steadied her gaze on Brian, "What? Who?"

"Remember Jacquelyn, the one whose husband was killed at the football game?"

"Yes."

"We're in love. In fact, when I get back to Michigan, I'm going to ask her to marry me."

Sarah's eyes widened. "Is this some kind of joke?"

"I'm afraid not..." Brian was unable to maintain eye contact with his mother.

"I still remember what you told me last November when the topic of marriage came up. You said, 'What's the point. Why be married for only seven years?' I can still hear your words ringing in my ears."

"What can I say, Ma? I love Jacquelyn and can't live without her."

Sarah was mindful of how badly things had deteriorated between Brian and Renate. She also knew it was purely spiritual. But in love again so soon?

For the first time ever, Sarah Mulrooney felt like an outsider in her son's life. "We'll practically be neighbors." This was said with little enthusiasm. In normal times, Sarah would be thrilled that her son was moving to one of New York's neighboring states. Pennsylvania was so much closer than Michigan. But try as she might, she couldn't mask the betrayal on her face. She took a sip of coffee. "Where in Pennsylvania?"

"That's just it." Brian took a deep breath. This wasn't going to be easy. "I can't say. Only that I'll be managing a safe house for Christians. You see how hated we are."

"But I'm your mother..." Sarah's voice quivered, and her moist eyes drifted away. She watched a cook dishing up an order of bacon, eggs and hash browns, then scooting it up on the counter. A waitress quickly grabbed the hot plate and delivered it to a man sitting at the counter.

Brian cleared his throat. "Sorry, Ma, but only those who are part of the Movement can know my exact whereabouts."

"Why not just move to Mars then!"

"I'm not purposely trying to upset you, Mom. You know how hard this is for me. But I'm under strict orders."

"Orders from whom?"

"Those at the top of the organization."

Sarah felt panicked, "Will I, we, ever see you again?"

"Hard to say. The later it gets in the game, the more persecuted Christ followers will become. The millions killed so far is only a drop in the bucket. With so much technology out there, soon it'll be impossible for me to be seen anywhere in public.

"Once the chip becomes mandatory, and scanners are set up worldwide, no one will be able to buy or sell anything without first accepting the Mark of the Beast."

Sarah didn't reply to her son's outlandish comment. How could she when she knew he was right?

"Once I reject Salvador Romanero's Mark, which I most certainly will, I'll be considered a fugitive from justice by local and universal law enforcement agencies. If I live that long..."

Brian looked at his mother carefully. "Believe me, I'm not looking forward to being a hunted fugitive, especially if captured by those who hate me. Nor do I look forward to being separated from loved ones. But I gotta do what I gotta do."

"When will this chip become mandatory?"

"Can't say for sure, but if I had to guess I'd say three years or so."

Seeing fresh tears pouring out of his mother's eyes, Brian frowned and looked away. "I don't like this any more than you do, but if you know where I am, the enemy'll use any method to force you to reveal my whereabouts, including torture. I'm talking unspeakable torture, Ma."

"And just how do you expect me to tell your father all this?"

"I'm hoping you won't tell him for now."

"What's to tell. You haven't told me anything," Sarah said, her voice elevating.

Brian scanned the restaurant once more to make sure no one was watching. "To tell you the truth, I've already said too much."

"Too much? Ha! I don't even know where you're staying in my city." Sarah looked out the window. Air got caught in her chest. She had difficulty breathing, wondering what would come out of her son's mouth next?

Sensing her dilemma, Brian moved to her side of the booth and wrapped his right arm around his mother. "I've had this pit in my stomach for many days trying to think of the best way to tell you all this. But as much as it hurts, nothing'll change my mind. If you think the gap between me and Dad is huge now, if he doesn't repent, it will only get worse.

"The animosity's coming from him, not me. He has this religious, self-righteous spirit inside that isn't from above. It's not a spirit of love and, therefore, not the Spirit of God. If his heart isn't changed soon, he and I will drift even further apart. The consequences are eternal. I fear for him."

135

Sarah couldn't argue the point. She couldn't argue any of Brian's points, in fact. He made too much sense. And he was right: the hatred wasn't coming from Christians, it was being directed at them! One did not have to be a rocket-scientist to see it.

The waiter approached: "How was everything?"

"Fine, thanks," Brian said.

"More coffee?"

"No thanks," he said again.

Sarah looked up with sad eyes and put a hand up in polite refusal.

"Be right back with your check."

The waiter cleared the breakfast plates from the table. Sarah's meal was only half-eaten. How could she eat when this might be the last time ever seeing her son in person?

"When are you leaving?"

"Tomorrow morning."

"Are you driving?"

Brian shook his head, "Flying. Out of LaGuardia."

"Would you like me to see you off?"

"Of course, I would, Ma. But under the circumstances, it's probably not a good idea. Dad may find out."

Sarah looked greatly disappointed. And dejected. "As you wish, son..."

Brian searched his mother's eyes. Distant eyes stared back. He just did the one thing he thought he'd never do in a million years—break his mother's heart. But his heart was also broken.

The waiter dropped the check and they stood to leave.

Brian paid the bill, then braced for an agonizing departure.

Sarah tried not to make a scene but failed miserably. Many heard her sobs and stared at them.

They walked outside and shared another tearful embrace before Sarah turned and walked away. It was a wonder she didn't bump into someone or something with her vision blurred from so many tears. Her pace was clumsy and slow.

Her head was down, like a little girl who'd just lost her best friend. Her whole world kept falling apart a little more each day. She needed Jesus more than ever.

It took every ounce of strength Brian possessed not to chase after his mother and wrap his arms around her once more.

136

Overcome with grief, Brian Mulrooney fell to his knees on the Manhattan sidewalk, "I hate you, Satan!" He knew it was foolish and potentially dangerous being so vulnerable in this uncertain climate, but that didn't stop him from raising his hands skyward and crying, "Father in Heaven, give me the strength to endure all this. My mother, too. I'm begging You."

"This ain't no church, you psycho!" said a passerby.

"Get outta here, you bum!" said a police officer out walking the beat.

And to think this was happening to millions of families all over the world...

22

BRIAN MULROONEY PICKED HIMSELF up off the pavement ever so gingerly and brushed dirt off his jeans.

He could almost hear the people still inside the restaurant sneering at him for bringing his mother to tears the way he had.

Mulrooney was too afraid to look back, for fear that they might poke their judgmental fingers at the pane glass window as if jabbing him in the chest.

He took a couple deep breaths and rushed off to check on something he'd found online before breakfast. After what had just transpired with his mother, he prayed his next encounter would have a more positive outcome.

When he arrived, it was easy to spot the boarding house he was looking for. A sign was posted on the window. It read:

> VACANCY
> WEEKLY RENTALS
> NO CREDIT CHECK
> NO CRIMINALS!

Mulrooney went inside to find a heavyset woman on the other side of the bullet proof glass, at the check-in desk, arguing with someone on the phone.

She held a land line phone in one hand, and a lit cigarette in the other. Without the slightest discretion she barked into the phone, "I want the rent money today or the next one banging on your door will be the police!"

The way she presented herself, it was as if she was absent the day the world was forever changed last November. Her gravelly voice from chain-smoking for so many years was so loud that it practically shook the glass.

After one last tirade with the poor soul on the other end, she slammed down the phone, took a long drag from the cigarette and blew it straight at Brian. "Yes?"

Thankfully the bullet proof glass dividing them prevented the thick cloud of smoke from reaching him. It was the last thing his asthmatic lungs needed. "How much are your weekly rentals?"

"How many people?"

"Just me."

"Two-fifty per week, plus tax," the woman said, glancing at the security monitors on the wall to her left.

Brian couldn't feign his surprise. Shock was more like it. Prior to the disappearances, even fleabag places like this would have cost at least twice that much.

"I don't need it until tomorrow," he said. "But I'd still like to see it first if you don't mind."

"Valid ID?"

Mulrooney pulled his wallet from his back pocket and slid his Michigan driver's license through the well beneath the bullet proof glass.

The heavyset woman lit another cigarette and briefly glanced at his license, before sliding him a room key. "Down the hall on your left." She was clearly unconcerned that this was a smoke-free lobby.

Brian pulled his surgical mask over his face and left to inspect the room. It was equipped with a queen-size bed, an old worn-out couch, a wooden coffee table from a generation long gone, a phone that would never be used, a TV, an old coffee maker that Mulrooney hoped still worked, an even older microwave, and a small refrigerator.

Convinced Tamika would be comfortable at this place for the next two weeks or so, Brian closed the door and went back to the lobby. He slid the key through the well beneath the glass. "Looks fine. I'll be back tomorrow."

"If you like it so much, why don't you pay for it now?"

Brian looked at her skeptically. "Tomorrow!"

"Okay, geez!" She returned his driver's license.

Mulrooney left the boarding house and walked the perimeter of the building looking for all possible exit strategies, in case someone learned of Tamika's whereabouts and she needed to make a quick escape.

It became apparent that her only option would be the back-door exit, which emptied onto a small side street. She'd have to do all her coming and going from there. Hopefully she wouldn't leave at all. She couldn't be seen by anyone.

The biggest red flag Brian saw was the woman at the front desk. Clearly, she ran a very tight ship at her establishment. She watched the monitors in her office like a hawk. If she came knocking on Tamika's door for any reason, it could pose a serious problem.

Before going back to his hotel, Mulrooney went to a store across the street and roamed the aisles to make sure they had the necessary items Tamika would need for two weeks, including cat food. Satisfied that they did, he would come back in the morning to purchase everything after paying for the room.

After that, Brian went to a local bookstore and purchased a few crossword puzzles and a Bible for Tamika. He was mildly shocked to see Bibles still for sale. From there he went to an electronics store and purchased a new cell phone.

Brian arrived back at the hotel two hours later. Tamika was still sleeping. He placed the Bible and crossword puzzles in his suitcase, then sat quietly on the couch careful not to make too much noise. He opened his Bible to the Book of Ezekiel and started reading.

Tamika woke up soon after. She saw Brian and nearly jumped out of her skin. "Ooh, you scared me!"

Brian closed the Bible and placed it on the table. "Good afternoon."

"Afternoon? Are you kidding?"

"It's one-thirty, but who's counting?"

"Wow!" Tamika sat up and rubbed sleep from her eyes. "I really needed that."

"Why don't you go back to sleep?"

"I'm good, thanks. Best sleep I had in weeks."

"Hungry?"

"I could eat."

"How does pastrami and Swiss on rye sound?"

Tamika yawned, "Sounds good, actually."

"There are two sandwiches in the fridge. I'll eat mine later. Still full from breakfast."

"How was your meeting?"

Brian frowned. "One of the most difficult of my life. I'm still reeling from it."

"Why's that?"

"Because I broke my mother's heart..."

"Oh, my! Sorry to hear that. You really did have a bad morning." Tamika got out of bed and sat on the chair next to Brian's. She ran her fingers through her hair, "What a strange dream I had..."

"Oh yeah? What kind of dream?"

140

"Perhaps it's because of what you said about Christians living in hiding, but that's exactly what I saw in my dream. You were there. Jacquelyn too. And a few others I didn't know. It was completely-surrounded by trees and nature. Nothing like the city. It was beautiful. I felt safe there."

Brian's eyes widened.

"Anything else?"

"No. That's pretty much it."

"Interesting dream you had." Mulrooney changed the subject so he wouldn't say something he wasn't supposed to. "By the way, I have something for you."

"What is it?"

Brian handed her a new cell phone. "It's linked to my account, so you should be fine using it. Even so, only use it in an emergency."

Tamika blinked a few times, "Why are you being so nice to me?"

"Because you're my sister in Christ."

It was enough to bring Tamika to tears. With so many in the city pitted against her, Brian's act of genuine kindness gave her the shot in the arm she desperately needed.

She couldn't remember feeling any more comforted in friendship than she did with Brian. Though this was only their second face to face meeting, he had an uncanny way of softening the tough exterior she'd developed over the years as a New York City cab driver.

Wiping her eyes, she said, "Thank you, Brian."

"You're welcome."

After Tamika finished eating her pastrami and Swiss cheese sandwich, they spent the rest of the day reading the Word of God together.

She went to sleep that night even more determined to leave New York City than ever before. With her face constantly splashed all over the local media for a crime she never committed, if there was any chance she could somehow escape to Pennsylvania with Brian, she'd jump all over it. She would travel to Siberia if the opportunity ever arose, anything to escape this nightmare!

Tamika couldn't help but wonder if the dream she'd had was somehow connected to the place in Pennsylvania. All she knew for now was that Brian would manage a safe house for exiled believers. The very thought of joining him and Jacquelyn breathed new life into her.

That is, until her thoughts shifted to the grim reality that she would be homeless again come daybreak. As Brian left the *Big Apple* to begin life anew with Jacquelyn Swindell, Tamika would once again do all she could to avoid capture by authorities, without a cent to her name. She didn't even have the money to go back to New Jersey, thus dashing her hopes again.

Tamika sighed in the darkness, then softly whispered, "Please rescue me, Lord, from my crazy situation."

Lying in the bed next to hers, Brian heard her desperate cry for help. If there was any good news, now that she'd had the dream, the vetting process would begin immediately. And like all others who'd had dreams, Tamika would be fast-tracked.

Brian felt reasonably certain they were compatible enough to co-exist on the same property. The more Tamika spoke, the more convinced he was that her conversion was genuine. Clearly, she wasn't the same person he'd met last November. Not even close. It had to be the Holy Spirit at work in her.

Knowing how God was using supernatural dreams to call many to salvation, Brian felt with everything in him that Tamika was part of this wondrous end times tapestry.

The fact that she was saved proved that much. And it started with a bizarre dream about her grandfather...

Did her second dream merely confirm that she would be someday invited to join the *ETSM*? It sure felt that way...

Even so, until Mulrooney heard from those at the top of the organization, Tamika was still an outsider and, therefore, couldn't know anything about the Movement he was involved with.

As it was, he'd already told her too much.

"Open this door for her, Father, as only You can..."

At that, Brian Mulrooney drifted off to sleep...

23

THE FOLLOWING DAY

"HELLO," BRIAN MULROONEY SAID, groggily.

"Good morning, my brother."

"Hey, Charles! Sorry I didn't call you back yesterday. Was busy all day. Time slipped away."

"Figured that much. Busy here too with you know who doing you know what!" Calloway was referring to the seven properties the *ETSM* was in the process of purchasing near Atlanta, Georgia. They hoped to have them in their possession soon. "How'd it go with your Momma?"

"Not so good. It was one of the most difficult moments of my life."

"Figured that much. Are you okay?"

"I will be. Thanks for the concern."

"What about Tamika?"

"Where shall I begin?"

"Is it good or bad?"

"Both, actually. Very good and very bad."

"Are you suggesting that..."

"No!" Brian knew what Charles was getting at. "I'm beyond convinced she's a true Christ follower. Once you hear her story, you'll be convinced too." He glanced over at Tamika. The ringing cell phone woke her.

"Well then, Hallelujah!"

"But you'll never guess in a million years how she came to faith in Christ."

Calloway sat up in his chair, "Indulge me."

Brian glanced at Tamika and cupped the phone. "Want me to tell him?"

Tamika nodded affirmatively.

Brian told Charles everything. While listening, Calloway Googled the *Graveyard Incident* in New York City and read all about it. "So that's why we haven't heard from her all this time."

"She's been running scared, bro. Ditched her cell phone weeks ago, so the police couldn't track her down with it."

"Is she the one responsible for all this?"

"According to her, the only thing she's guilty of is digging up her grandfather's grave to see if his remains were still there or not. Nothing more."

"Do you believe her?"

"I do."

"If she's innocent, why doesn't she turn herself in and face the music?"

"She's terrified of being incarcerated. I don't think you realize how hated she is here in the *Big Apple*. They wanna throw the book at her!"

"I can appreciate that." Charles paused a moment to let it all sink in. "For someone to do something so outrageous, her conversion must be genuine, right?"

"Yup."

"Where's she been staying?"

"In her car in New Jersey with her pet cat."

"How's her health?"

"She's a little on the thin side. And she has a leg infection that needs to be looked at ASAP. Other than that, she seems fine."

"That's good. Do you think she's *ETSM* worthy?"

"All I can say is she had a dream."

"Our kind?"

"Yup. Tell you more about it later."

"Should I call Braxton Rice?"

"Yes. Call him."

"Check. Where will Tamika stay tonight?"

"Got it covered, bro."

"Care to share it with me?"

"Later."

"Check."

"Not to cut it short, but I need to shower and head to the airport."

"What time's your flight?"

"Noon. But I need to make a stop along the way," Brian said, in a near whisper.

"Call me later when you're free to talk."

"You got it, man."

"Have a safe flight, Brian. Godspeed."

"Thanks, Charles. Wanna say hi to Tamika?"

"Yeah, put her on."

Brian handed Tamika his phone. "Hey, Charles."

"How's my dear sister in Christ?"

"How would you be if you were me?"

"Now, there's a question! One thing I know is I'd be reading the Word day and night and praying for God's constant protection."

"My Bible's still at my apartment. Even if I had it, it would've been impossible to read it in the car when always on the lookout for the police." Tamika scratched her head. "They think I'm a monster, Charles."

"Hang in there, sis. This, too, will pass."

"I can't be locked up now. I just can't be! Innocent or not, stealing forty-five thousand dollars worth of stuff will get me at least five years. I can't do that, especially for something I didn't even do..."

"We'll figure something out. For now, just try to remain calm. And do your best to stay out of trouble."

Tamika took a sip of water. "I'm tryin'."

"So, you dug up your Grandpa's grave. Looks like we have another 'Doubting T' on our hands..."

"What do you mean, Charles?"

"Instead of doubting Thomas, you're doubting Tamika. I mean, look how far you went to try proving us wrong..."

"Ha ha ha, very funny." Tamika paused to take a breath, "Brian's such an amazing friend. Don't know what I'd do without him."

"Yeah, he's a true brother. You can trust what he tells you."

"I believe that."

"We got your back, Tamika. Just hang in there. It'll all work out."

"Thanks, Charles."

"No problem. Family always takes care of their own, right?" Calloway sighed. "You had us so concerned."

"Sorry, Charles."

"I forgive you. Just don't let it happen again. Hear me?"

"Loud and clear! It won't happen again. Promise."

"Okay, sis, it's over and done with. Least now we know why we haven't heard from you. You've really been through it. Brian said you had a strange dream last night. Care to share with me?"

"I was living somewhere far from here in a cottage in the woods. There were many cottages there. Brian and Jacquelyn were there too with many others I didn't know. It felt like we was one big family. It was comforting."

Thank you, Lord! "Quite a dream you had."

"Didn't tell Brian yet, but I had the same dream again last night."

Time to call Braxton Rice... "I gotta run now, Tamika. Nice hearing from you again. Praise God you're safe. God bless and keep you."

"God bless and keep you, too, Charles."

The call ended, and Charles Calloway sent a text message to Braxton Rice, updating him on the developing situation...

24

BRIAN MULROONEY AND TAMIKA Moseley were en route to LaGuardia Airport. Brian navigated the vehicle down the street, doing his best to conceal the excitement in his voice. "Where will you sleep tonight?"

Tamika sighed, "Not sure yet. But definitely not here in the city. Probably go back to Jersey."

Brian shook his head. "Hmm."

"It's okay, Brian. I'll manage. Thanks to you, I had two days of much needed rest. It was badly needed. I feel rejuvenated."

Instead of taking the Queensboro Bridge to LaGuardia, Mulrooney went off in the opposite direction.

"You're going the wrong way," the former taxi driver said.

"I need to make a quick stop first."

"Where to?"

"You'll see soon enough."

When they arrived at the location, Brian parked the vehicle. "This may take a few minutes. Do your best not to be seen by anyone."

Tamika lowered the baseball cap on her head and watched Brian until he went inside a building across the street.

"Good morning."

"Morning," the heavyset woman said to Brian, blowing smoke from her cigarette in his direction. The smoke hit the bullet proof glass and scattered in all directions.

"As promised, I'm back." *Talk about a chain smoker!*

"I see," the woman said matter-of-factly.

"Still have vacancies?"

"Uh-huh!" It was almost as if she didn't need his business.

The cruise director on Titanic probably had a better attitude than this woman, even after hitting the iceberg! Mulrooney chuckled at the thought then cleared his throat. "I'd like a room in the back of the building please."

The woman stiffened then shifted her weight in her stool chair. "Oh, yeah, why's that?"

"Just a preference I have..."

147

The heavyset woman pointed her plump stubby pointer finger through the cloud of smoke she'd created on her side of the bullet proof glass. Scowl on her face she said, "Listen, Mister, I don't want no funny stuff at my establishment! Do you hear me?"

"Okay, you got me. Truth is, I brought my pet cat to New York with me. Cocoa likes quiet places. I figured the back of the building would be the quietest." *Sorry, Lord...*

The woman's eyes narrowed. "And just where is this cat of yours?"

"Out in the car."

"Anything else I need to know before handing you a room key?"

Mulrooney gulped hard, "No ma'am."

She glared at Brian suspiciously, "Hmm. Better not be!"

Brian flashed a small wad of cash in her face. The greed factor kicked in and she refocused. "Before I pay you, I'd like to inspect the room to see if it's as clean as the one I saw yesterday." He didn't want it to be so unpleasant that Tamika would say, "No thanks. I'd rather sleep in my car."

"ID?" Brian slid his Michigan driver's license through the well beneath the bullet proof glass.

The plump woman studied it this time as if something had changed since the last time she saw it. "I'd like to see the cat." Before Brian could ask why, she said, "I always like knowing who's staying at my establishment, including pets."

"You'll see Cocoa when I come back with my things."

"Just don't forget!" she said, sliding him a key to a room on the fourth floor.

Brian glared at her angrily. He wanted to say, "Are you like this with all your guests?" But after hearing her yelling on the phone the other day, he knew the answer was yes. He took a deep breath, "Be right back."

Mulrooney took the stairs two at a time up to the fourth floor. After a quick inspection, he was satisfied and closed the door behind him. He paid for the room for two weeks, then crossed the street and stocked up on things Tamika would need for that amount of time.

Seeing two large black suitcases for sale, Brian purchased them both and asked the clerk to hold them for him for a few minutes.

Finally, he grabbed a bouquet of flowers, then spent a few minutes back in the room doing his best to make it as cozy as possible for his sister in Christ. She was clearly at a point where she needed something good to happen to her.

Tamika silently rejoiced when she saw Brian walking toward her mother's Oldsmobile Cutlass Supreme carrying two black suitcases. "Are those for me?"

"Yes, but that's not all. See that building over there?"

"Yeah?"

"It's a boarding house. Consider it your home for the next two weeks."

Tamika's face lit up. "Are you serious?"

"I found it yesterday after meeting with my mother. Sorry for waiting so long but I wanted to surprise you."

Tamika looked down as if to cry but was able to compose herself. "You never cease to amaze me, Brian! I don't know what to say. Thank you, thank you, thank you!"

"It's not me, Tamika, but the Spirit of God at work inside me."

"I want the kind of faith you have."

"You already have it, sis. Just needs to be further developed."

"Hope so, cause time's running out."

"You're right about that. Let's fill these suitcases with your belongings so I can take them up to your room. It's in my name so you should be fine, so long as you don't cause a disturbance. Even so, I wouldn't recommend leaving unless absolutely necessary. Also, phone contact between us should be extremely limited. You never know, right?"

Tamika lowered her head again, totally overwhelmed by her friend's generosity.

"Come on, Tamika, did you really think I'd leave you here all alone to fend for yourself?" Tamika flashed the biggest and brightest smile Brian Mulrooney had ever seen on her usually sullen face. "It isn't the Ritz-Carlton, but at least it's clean."

"It's perfect, Brian. Just perfect. You just lifted a heavy weight off my shoulders."

Not wanting to violate his privilege by squandering away *ETSM* funds that weren't his to begin with, Brian paid for the room, and everything else, with his own money.

His Bible told him not to let his left hand know what his right hand was doing. All that mattered was that God knew, and that He loved a cheerful giver—especially an anonymous one. This was a good time for Brian to put that Godly principle into practice.

"Thank you, Brian, from the bottom of my heart."

Seeing the sincerity in her eyes, Mulrooney said, "You're welcome, my dear sister." It felt good doing this for her. It was evident in his blue eyes; they were fully sparkling.

"It's nice knowin' I have a place to stay for the next two weeks. I'm all Jersey'd out. You're taking a huge risk for me."

"I'm not too concerned about myself, but I am concerned about my family. I don't want anyone linking you to them, especially the police. So please be extremely careful."

"I will, promise."

"After thinking it through and praying about it, I don't think you should take me to the airport. Too risky. I also don't think you should leave your car parked out on the streets. If you do, you'd have to keep feeding the meters, which means you'd constantly have to leave the room. Not good."

"What are you getting at, Brian?"

"In friendship, trust goes both ways, right?"

"Yeah?"

"I need you to trust me with your mother's car."

"In what way?"

"I'm thinking I should drive myself to the airport and park the car there. If the cops ever link you to your mother's car, it's best they find it far from this place. If they find it at the airport, perhaps they'll think you already left town."

"Hmm, not a bad thought."

"Don't worry, I plan on coming back in two weeks to hopefully get you out of here. Once I land, they'll be no need to rent a car. I'll come get you in your mother's car."

"What if something happens and I need the car?"

"Do you have a second set of keys?"

Tamika nodded yes.

"Once I park it in the airport garage, I'll text you with the exact parking space in case you need it. Let's just hope it doesn't come to that."

"I heard that!" Tamika grimaced. "When you come back to get me, where will you take me?"

"Not sure yet. All I know is God will lead the way. For now, just know Charles and I got your back." Seeing Tamika getting emotional again, Brian backpedaled, "There's a fridge in your room and a microwave, so you can reheat the leftover Chinese food from last night."

"Okay."

"Be careful with the woman who owns the place. She could pose a problem."

"Why?"

Brian answered, "She's not the friendliest woman on the planet. She runs a very tight ship so be sure to avoid her at all costs."

"I have no plans on introducing myself to her."

"Good, because if she sees you, no doubt you'll be hammered with questions. Least she knows about Cocoa, so you should be fine there. Just hope your pet doesn't get cabin fever being inside the room day and night."

"She's a house cat. Long as she's fed, she won't be a problem."

"Very good then." Brian looked at his watch. "Let's focus on getting you safely up to your room. After I bring your things up there, I gotta jet."

"Understood."

It took longer than expected for Brian to take Tamika's things to the room. After seeing Cocoa with her own two eyes, the boarding house owner made him sign a waiver holding him responsible for any damage the cat might cause to the room, including carpet stains. Mulrooney nearly laughed. The carpets were already severely stained.

When Brian returned to the car, Tamika was distraught.

"What's wrong?"

"Three cop cars came and went while you were gone..."

"Remain vigilant, Tamika. We're almost there. Cocoa's safe in the room. After I take the last of your things upstairs, it'll be your turn to move. Then no one will bother you. Okay?"

Tamika nodded yes.

"Okay, good. I'll text you just before I leave the room. That'll be your signal to head for the back door immediately. It's the only door back there, so you won't have any trouble finding it.

"Once you're there, I'll be holding it open for you, key in hand. Then you'll take the stairs up to the fourth floor as quickly as you can and pray she isn't watching you on camera. Your room's the first one on the left, number four-twenty-nine."

"Okay," Tamika said, almost stuttering.

Brian saw the fear in her eyes. "Everything's gonna be fine. But I need you to stay focused. Can you do that for me?"

Tamika nodded yes.

"Good." Brian looked at his watch. "We need to do this now."

"I'm ready."

Mulrooney dropped a few more coins in the parking meter, just in case, grabbed the rest of Tamika's things and went back inside. The boarding house owner was on the phone yelling at someone, so Brian kept walking.

After checking once more to make sure he hadn't forgotten to do something, Brian closed the door and texted Tamika: *It's time...*

As Mulrooney descended the stairs two at a time, Tamika lowered the baseball cap over her head, pulled her bandanna up to cover her face and ran to the back door exit as quickly as she could.

Brian was waiting for her, key in hand. "Whatever you do, don't look up while in the stairwell. There are cameras there."

"Okay."

Brian hugged Tamika and handed her the room key. "See you in two weeks."

"Have a safe flight."

"Love ya, sis! God be with you!"

"Love you, too, Brian."

Brian slid behind the wheel of Tamika's mother's car and left for the airport. He was about to embark on the biggest journey of his life. He would purchase an engagement ring in the morning and ask Jacquelyn's hand in marriage at church this upcoming Sunday.

If all goes well, it'll be Jacquelyn Mulrooney soon. Then they could move to Pennsylvania as husband and wife. A smile broke across Brian's face. It was nice thinking happy thoughts again for a change.

TAMIKA MOSELEY DASHED UP the stairs to the fourth floor and entered the room without incident. Locking the door behind her, she leaned up against it and closed her eyes. She lowered her bandanna. Her chest heaved up and down. She took a few deep breaths to compose herself.

Once her breathing had stabilized, Tamika thanked God for delivering her safely to her room. For the next two weeks anyway.

When she opened her eyes and saw flowers on the table, the tears came. Not only had Brian provided her with a place to stay for the next two weeks, he stocked the room with enough food—including cat food for Cocoa—to last throughout her stay, not to mention plenty of toiletries, including a new toothbrush, and even ointment for her leg.

But that wasn't the end of his generosity. Brian also left three-hundred dollars in cash, a few Crossword puzzle magazines, and most importantly, a new Bible for her.

Tamika sat on the couch and shook her head. This was Christian love at its finest. Who would have ever thought that a chance encounter with Brian Mulrooney in a dented taxicab last November would have led to all this?

Tamika wasn't even supposed to work on that fateful day. If she needed further evidence that God still worked through His faithful servants in the most mysterious of ways, she had it.

"Thank You, Lord, for blessing me with such wonderful friends," Tamika said softly through her sniffles. "Please bless Brian and Charles for their kindness to me! I love them both dearly."

Tamika fed Cocoa, ate leftover Chinese food, then took a two-hour nap. She woke and made a pot of hot water for tea, then spent the rest of the evening reading the Word of God in peace and quiet, with four walls and a roof over her head.

Her goal until Brian came back was simple: absorb as much of God's Word as two weeks would allow and pray without ceasing that Brian and Charles would find a way to smuggle her out of the *Big Apple*.

There was nothing keeping her in the Empire State, not even Isaac. With their most common links now gone—Dante and Jamal—they had little else in common, including religion.

Tamika would try to find a way to share the Word of God with him, but if the opportunity arose, she would leave New York City in a New York minute!

That would be her constant prayer from this day forward...

153

25

THE FOLLOWING WEEKEND

"BECAUSE OF YOUR OPEN stance for Christ Jesus and your overall obedience to His Holy command, it is my great privilege to baptize you, brother Tom, in the name of the Father, Son and Holy Spirit," Pastor Jim Simonton declared to Tom Dunleavey, submerging him beneath the water. The former Catholic priest came up out of the baptismal pool to a rousing ovation. He raised his hands above his head and shouted, "Hallelujah!" at the top of his lungs.

Even dripping wet, Tom Dunleavey clung to his pastor weeping tears of joy. He couldn't stop thanking God for allowing him to be part of something so magnificently beautiful, especially knowing nearly 50 new believers from his former church in Ann Arbor would also be baptized this day.

Prior to his "true" conversion a few months back, Tom Dunleavey would have scoffed at the notion of dedicating an entire Sunday to baptisms only, with no other services performed.

Who did such absurd things? Not only that, the thought of being baptized as an adult—none other than by a non-Catholic clergyman— would have never entered into his mind. Never!

What sounded sacrilege a few months back now made perfect sense to him. Joy flooded his soul knowing the Most High had delivered him from the religiosity he fiercely clung to as a Catholic priest.

In the three weeks Tom had attended Southeast Michigan Evangelical Church, his knowledge of the Word of God had increased drastically. With his spiritual eyes and ears now fully open, the words exploded off the pages straight into his heart and mind. It's like he was reading an entirely different Book.

Before baptizing Tom Dunleavey, Jim Simonton was the first to be dunked under the water. Unlike Tom, Jim was baptized as a young adult long before the Rapture.

Now that the new lead pastor at SMEC was saved for real, it was only right to take the plunge again for real...

With Brian Mulrooney's assistance, Tom Dunleavey had the distinct honor of baptizing his pastor in front of the entire congregation. He knew it was wrong, but he took comfort knowing he wasn't the only one who needed to be baptized a second time.

Pastor Simonton came out of the water ever so jubilantly to a thunderous ovation from a full congregation. He was embraced heartily by his two brothers.

Everyone baptized after him received similar receptions.

Seven hours later, after performing nearly 700 baptisms, sometimes as many as three at a time—including the 50 new converts from Tom Dunleavey's flock in Ann Arbor—they neared the end of the line.

The former Catholic priest counted it a great privilege to baptize those he'd led astray for so many years. It was self-healing. Still in hiding from the Catholic Church, they were extremely grateful to their brothers and sisters for opening their hearts and homes to them in these extremely turbulent times.

By choice, the last two to be baptized were Brian Mulrooney and Jacquelyn Swindell. When Jacquelyn stepped into the baptismal pool, Brian remained outside.

"Pastor, before we continue, would it be okay if I say something?"

"By all means!" Pastor Jim handed Mulrooney the microphone.

Taking a knee beside the baptismal pool, Brian faced Jacquelyn and exhaled deeply. Sensing what was about to happen, an energy of excitement filled the church.

Jacquelyn's shy demeanor surfaced. Her face turned a deep shade of pink.

Taking her hand into his, Brian looked deep into her eyes, "Jacquelyn, I think you know how much I love you. At least I hope you do."

Jacquelyn's head tilted in astonishment; her heart raced. She gulped in air to keep from fainting.

Pulling a small black box from his shorts pocket, his voice cracked, "I don't want to spend another day on this crazy planet without having you by my side." Brian paused a moment to avoid getting all choked up. "If you feel the same way, please honor me by marrying me..."

Gazing deep into Brian's tear-filled eyes, with two of her own, she sniffled softly then whispered, "Of course, I'll marry you!"

They embraced. Everyone cheered and applauded wildly.

"I'd like to do it as quickly as possible, if you don't mind."

155

"How quickly?"

"Next week, if possible."

"Hmm..." Jacquelyn looked skyward and rubbed her chin as if suddenly deep in thought. "Yep, free all next week!" Laughter erupted throughout the congregation. "I'd marry you tomorrow, Brian. Even today, in fact. Geez, what took you so long?"

Everyone laughed again.

Brian placed the ring on Jacquelyn's finger and the congregation rose to give them a standing ovation.

"Pastor Jim, would you be so kind to marry us?" Though he already asked his friend a week ago, he wanted to make it official.

"It would be my pleasure, guys."

"Will next Saturday work for you?"

Mimicking Jacquelyn's earlier gesture, Pastor Jim looked skyward and rubbed his chin with his fingers, "Yep. I'm free!"

Once again, the sanctuary was filled with laughter.

"Perfect!" Facing the congregation, Brian said, "I'm sure I speak on Jacquelyn's behalf when I say we'd be honored if you all attended our wedding next week. With time being so short, consider this announcement the only invitation you will receive."

"We'll be there," yelled a fellow church member.

"Us too!" yelled another couple.

And on and on it went.

When it finally quieted down, Brian placed the now-empty black box on the floor next to the blow-up baptismal pool and stepped inside with Jacquelyn. Reaching for his fianceé's hand, the newly engaged man said, "Okay, Pastor, we're ready."

Pastor Simonton motioned for Tom Dunleavey to help submerge them both under the water. "Upon your confession of faith in Jesus Christ as Lord and Savior, it's *our* pleasure," Pastor Jim said, glancing over at Tom Dunleavey, "to baptize you both, in the name of the Father, Son and Holy Spirit."

The moment they came up out of the water, they embraced.

Thunderous applause ensued. But the sheer jubilation the newly engaged couple now felt wouldn't last...

26

THE FOLLOWING DAY

"I'M GETTING MARRIED," JACQUELYN Swindell blurted out to her parents. Her voice trembled through each syllable.

Fearing a less than gracious response from her parents, Jacquelyn drove to Irish Hills, Michigan, without her fiancé of just one day. As much as she had wished to draw upon Brian's strength, seeing the shocked, angered expressions on her parents' faces, confirmed that she'd made the right decision by going alone.

Jacquelyn braced for impact.

After taking a few deep audible breaths, and blinking hard a few times, George Legler finally said, "Come again?" Those were the very last words he ever expected to hear come out of his daughter's mouth. It was outrageous, bizarre really.

"Brian asked me to marry him at church yesterday, and I said yes. I love him, Pop."

"What a weasel!" George snapped. His body started twitching uncontrollably. "At least Tom had the decency to ask me in advance for your hand in marriage."

"I know, Pop, but these are different times!"

"Blah, blah, blah," came the reply. "I believe you've lost your marbles, young lady."

Sheila Legler sat next to her daughter and stroked her hair. "You're still not thinking clearly, sweetheart. You're still distraught over the loss of Tom. It's never good to cling to the first man who takes an interest in you, especially when in mourning."

"Come on, Mom, you know me better than that..."

"Listen to your mother, Jacquelyn!" George snapped again.

"Remain obedient," the newly engaged woman whispered to herself, trying to suppress the uneasiness she felt building inside.

Sheila went on, "After everything you've endured the past few months, I'm sure you really do think you love Brian. But he just happened to be there when you desperately needed someone. What if it turns out to be nothing more than a rebound?"

"It's not like that, Mom. I love him in a way that I never loved Tom."

"Don't say that, dear."

"It's true."

Sheila shook her head. "But you barely know Brian!"

"I know how it looks to the both of you, but for the first time in my life I know what true love feels like." Jacquelyn knew her words were falling on deaf ears.

"We understand you want another child, Jacquelyn. Even we want that for you. But you don't have to get married for that. If you think Brian's the right one to give you a baby, who are we to object? We just want to be grandparents again."

"Not sure I want to bring a child into this crazy world..."

"Don't say that. With Salvador Romanero leading the way, the future's bright, right George?"

George nodded agreement, but ever so reluctantly.

"I agree." Jacquelyn frowned. "But only for those who belong to Christ Jesus. Everyone else will be eternally damned..."

"It's like Dennis all over again," George barked, folding his arms across his chest. "Do you plan to become a walking talking Bible like your brother was?"

Jacquelyn straightened up in her seat, "Hopefully."

"This is unbelievable!" Prior to the Rapture, save for when his son came on too strongly with all his "Jesus talk", George Legler—who was of German descent—was a rather calm, level-headed man.

Sheila, on the other hand, had inherited a feisty Italian temper from her parents. She was usually the first to get angry. It's as if they'd switched personalities.

Jacquelyn exhaled deeply. This wasn't going to be easy. Looking down at the floor, she said, "There's more. I'm moving to Pennsylvania."

"What?!" George Legler struggled to lean up in his chair, so he could eyeball his daughter more carefully. He was on the verge of exploding. "Are you on drugs?!"

"No, Pop, I'm not..." Jacquelyn bit her tongue. Having never tried drugs a single day in her life, her father's question really stung. She wanted to react but kept quiet.

"Where in Pennsylvania?" Sheila said, trying to preemptively defuse what was brewing beneath the surface.

Jacquelyn looked down at the floor again. "Can't say..."

"What do you mean you can't say, sweetie?" Sheila glanced at her husband and saw the utter betrayal on his face. He was crushed. So was she.

George Legler couldn't believe what his ears were hearing. "Excuse me, young lady?"

"Sorry, Pop. All I can say is Christians will need safe places to live in once Salvador Romanero declares all-out war on us. He's not the man you think he is. He's the Antichrist of the Bible Dennis always warned about. Even if you don't believe it, there's no doubt in my mind."

"And you're not being brainwashed?! I think you need professional help. You really have lost your mind."

To lose a son, daughter-in-law and three grandchildren on the same day was already difficult enough to cope with. Now this? Their own daughter couldn't say where she was moving? Who in their right mind did such nonsensical things? It was pure insanity.

It made the Leglers hate Brian Mulrooney even more!

"I can see why you might think that way, Pop. I'll admit on the surface it does seem rather strange. But I assure you my fiancé isn't brainwashing me. I know exactly what I'm doing. In fact, I've never thought more clearly in all my life! Crazy as it sounds, I'm convinced Pennsylvania's where God wants me to go. As Brian's wife!"

Noticing the tear build-up in his wife's eyes, George Legler could take no more. He erupted: "You've fallen prey to a madman, Jacquelyn. You just don't know it yet."

"Calm down, Pop!"

George Legler clenched his fists. "Calm down?! You come here telling us you're getting married next week and moving to Pennsylvania to begin life anew, and you want me to calm down?"

"Oh, that Brian's good, alright! A real piece of work! How could you possibly love someone like him? Can't you see how cunning and deceptive he is? What a snake! How dare he prey upon you like this when you're still in mourning over Tom!"

"I respectfully disagree with you, Pop." Jacquelyn shivered. She remembered that glare all too well. She half expected her father to kick her out of the house, like she'd witnessed on a few occasions with Dennis. But he never did. Perhaps it was because she was moving out of Michigan and he feared he might never see her again.

The room grew silent as George took a few deep breaths to calm himself down. He knew the situation required a delicate balance. He didn't want to say something that would potentially cause him to lose his daughter forever.

Painful as it was to admit, it dawned on George that he and Sheila were failures when it came to their offspring. Simply put: George and Sheila Legler were good life partners, but when it came to making babies they were simply incompatible. Perhaps it was a breakdown in their DNA. What else could it be?

Perhaps Jacquelyn's right. Perhaps it's best if we don't have more grandchildren...

Sheila Legler chimed in, "Your situation with Brian has all the makings of two desperate people bonding after surviving a deeply traumatic moment together. It's natural to develop strong feelings under such trying conditions.

"The problem is, you reconnected to society by vesting all your still raw, undisciplined emotions into the same religion that recently destroyed Dennis, Michele, and our three grandchildren."

"They weren't destroyed, Mom. They're in Heaven now. Dennis was right all along." Jacquelyn sighed. "Just wish I'd listened to them all those years. If you choose to remain defiant to the Word of God by not believing it, that's your choice. But it doesn't make it any less true. The message of the Cross may be utter foolishness to the two of you, but to me it's the power of the living God unto salvation."

Defiant? She really is being brainwashed! Sheila shook her head in protest, then glanced at her husband. His head was buried in his hands. "It pains me to see you so caught up in the very same deception as your brother was."

"I'm not being deceived, Mom, you are. You too, Pop."

George took a deep breath to prevent a new burst of anger from escaping his mouth. "Do you even watch the news, Jacquelyn? Millions of Christians are in prison and millions more are dead for believing what you believe."

"I'm aware of that, Pop."

"Is that what you want for yourself?"

"No, but if I'm killed for my faith in Jesus, so be it. Just hope someday you'll both come around and receive Jesus as Lord and Savior before it's too late."

160

"Come around?!" Try as he might, George Legler couldn't hold back his temper. The level of disgust in his voice was palpable.

"Yes, Pop," Jacquelyn said softly. The distant faraway look in her mother's eyes confirmed that they knew her mind was made up. There was nothing they could do or say to change it. No matter how much pressure they applied, their daughter would never divulge her future location in Pennsylvania to them.

As Jacquelyn stood to leave, George and Sheila Legler could only shake their heads. They never bothered walking their daughter out to her car, like they always did, or watch her drive off.

They were too busy trying to piece together this next onslaught of sheer madness which had become their lives.

It was a bitter pill to swallow.

Jacquelyn had to pull her vehicle to the side of the road three times while driving back to her house. Her vision was blurred from so many tears.

"Please rescue my parents, Father, before it's too late..."

27

MEANWHILE, BRIAN MULROONEY SHIVERED when his apartment front door opened. This wasn't something he looked forward to, but it had to be done. And it had to be done now, while Tom Dunleavey wasn't here.

Renate McCallister looked beautiful as ever, dressed to the nines, in a white button-down silk blouse, short black skirt and high heels. After not seeing her boyfriend in more than a month, she was full of cautious anticipation.

It didn't take long for the smile on her face to vanish. Something was wrong. Boxes littered the living room floor. Some even had her name written on them. And what she saw on Brian's face was anything but comforting.

An alarm went off inside her head. Renate gulped in some air. "What's with all the boxes?"

"You may want to sit down..."

Renate reluctantly did as she was told. "Are you moving?"

Brian took a seat opposite her, "Yes."

Renate flinched. "Are you breaking up with me?"

Mulrooney closed his eyes and nodded yes, "I'm sorry, Renate."

Renate started trembling. "It's because of Jacquelyn, isn't it?"

"No." Brian lowered his head. "Not entirely, anyway..."

"What's that supposed to mean?"

"Come on, Renate, you know we've been drifting apart since the Rapture."

"Rapture? Ha! I think what you really mean is ever since Jacquelyn..."

"I'm sure it looks that way to you, but it simply isn't so." *I can't love someone who loves Salvador Romanero!*

Renate snickered but remained silent.

"Truth is," Brian said, "had the Rapture not happened, I'm sure we'd still be together. But now that my eyes have been opened, even had I not met Jacquelyn at the football game, it would still be over between us. Our situation is spiritual in nature. And eternal. At least to me."

"Whatever..." Renate rolled her eyes. There was a sarcastic expression on her face, but inside she felt like she was dying.

162

"Look, Renate, this isn't easy for me. We've had five good years together. I was good to you just as you were to me. Again, it's more spiritual than anything else."

"What if I become a Christian?" Renate said out of desperation.

"You can't choose Jesus merely to get something you want. True Christianity doesn't work that way. Besides, we don't choose Jesus. He chooses us..."

"What are you getting at?" *Boy, he's out there...*

"If you truly were searching for God, I think you'd understand. In fact, I know you would."

"Are you saying I'm not searching?"

"Let me put it this way. In the five years we were together, the one sure thing in your life, not counting me, was protecting the environment. The energy and passion you put into that cause is the very same passion I now have for Jesus. Only more.

"Sorry to say, Renate, but whereas my cause leads to eternal assurance, yours ultimately leads to a horrific dead end."

Renate shot Brian a sideways look but remained silent.

Brian looked at her carefully and went on, "Not trying to rain on your parade, but despite what your boy Romanero preaches, this world—including the environment—can't be saved. What's coming our way is far worse than any scientist or environmental alarmist could ever predict. For those who belong to God, soon there will be a new Heaven and Earth. But only to those who trust in Jesus as Lord and Savior."

"You know my love for you was deeper than my concern for the environment, Brian. Hasn't *your* God confirmed that to you by now?"

"I can never go back to the worldly love we shared."

"Excuse me, Brian?!" *Worldly love?*

"I'm sorry, Renate, but I no longer love you the way I once did. Even if you became a Christ follower, it would still be over between us." Brian shook his head, "That part of my heart's now occupied by Jacquelyn..."

After waiting for a reply and not getting one, he went on, "You're a beautiful woman. You'll have little trouble finding someone else. My real prayer is that you'll come into proper relationship with the One who made you..."

"How do you know I haven't already found someone?"

"What are you saying?"

"Nothing. None of your business," Renate said angrily.

"Who is he?"

"Someone Rachel set me up with."

"Wow, you cheated on me?"

Renate ignored his question. "Speaking of Rachel, she's three months pregnant. Who knows, perhaps I am too..."

"Seriously?"

"Does it really matter at this point?"

"I suppose not." Brian closed his eyes and gulped. It was time. "I'm getting married..."

The room turned icy cold. Tears formed in Renate's eyes. "I knew it the first time I saw the two of you together!"

"What you saw that night was nothing more than two frightened people searching for answers. It wasn't until we both became Christians that our relationship deepened. I'm sorry, Renate. I never meant to hurt you."

"How can you be so heartless after all this time?"

"I'm not being heartless."

"Really? I come here hoping to make up with you and this is what I get in return? Not only are you ending our relationship, you're getting married to someone else, yet you're not being heartless?!"

Brian sighed then lowered his head. "I see your point." There was a long silence. "But nothing will change my mind."

"Where are you moving to?"

"Can't say..."

"Close by?"

"No."

"Back to New York?"

"No."

"Out of Michigan?"

"Can't say, swee...Renate," Mulrooney said, nearly calling her "sweetie", like he'd habitually done the past five years.

There was another prolonged silence as Renate pieced it all together in her mind. Brian was taken back to when he met with Jacquelyn to tell her that her husband was forever doomed. It had that same feel to it.

That is until, as a last-ditch effort, Renate raised her skirt just high enough for Brian to see what she was wearing underneath. If logic couldn't rescue him from the doldrums to which he had sunk and win him back, perhaps seduction could.

Brian turned his head away. "This isn't happening, Renate."

"You haven't touched me since before the disappearances, Brian Mulrooney! This time last year you could hardly keep your hands off me. Now you're suddenly rejecting *me* because you've become religious? You and I both know you're no priest!"

Thank God for that! "Like I said, I'm not the same man I once was..."

"That's for sure!" Renate grunted. "So, when are you getting married?"

"Soon..."

"When?"

"Soon, okay?"

Full blown panic set in. Renate inched in closer once more to seduce Brian.

Brian grabbed her shoulders and kept her at arm's length before their lips could touch. "I said no!"

Renate let out a God-awful scream, "Mark never rejected me! Not even once!"

"Mark?"

"Never mind." The old Brian would have been insanely jealous knowing she'd cheated on him. But not now. His silence only served to incense her even more.

Renate picked up Brian's half full glass of water and threw it at him with all her strength. It just missed his head. It hit the wall behind him sending glass and water in all directions. She stood and removed the apartment key from her key ring.

Brian could no longer maintain eye contact with her, "When would you like me to drop your things at your parents' house?"

"Are you serious? That's all you can say?" Renate slammed the key on the coffee table then slapped Brian across the face with all her strength, leaving a mark. "I hate you, Brian Mulrooney and never want to see you again!"

Renate McCallister stormed out of the apartment, knowing it was for the last time. Her heart broke a little more with each step she took. The pain was so intense. *Perhaps it's time to call Mark and give him a chance!*

Though she'd met him a few times, she never seriously entertained him because her hope all along was that Brian would eventually come back to his senses.

165

Renate now had every reason to believe it would never happen. *Yeah, it's time to give him a chance!*

She pulled her cell phone out of her purse and called Mark.

BRIAN CALLED TOM DUNLEAVEY informing that Renate had just left and he was free to come back to the apartment. Then Mulrooney drove to Livonia, Michigan to meet with his manager Susan Marlucci to officially tender his resignation, effective immediately.

Marlucci listened thoughtfully, then said, "Not giving us ample notice won't look good on your resume, Brian."

"I know and I'm sorry. You know me. Normally I wouldn't do this. But something came up and I need to leave Michigan as soon as possible." Seeing a framed picture of Salvador Romanero hanging on the wall behind his boss made him want to vomit. "It's sort of an emergency."

"Are you sick or in legal trouble?"

"No. Nothing like that."

"Is Renate going with you?"

Mulrooney sighed. "No. We're through..."

"I thought you loved each other?"

"Lately we've been going in different directions..."

"When did you break up?"

"Today, actually."

Susan Marlucci wasn't overly surprised. It seemed most people who were in relationships prior to the disappearances were no longer together.

In that light, this was simply par for the course. There was no need to discuss the matter any further. But leaving the job he loved so much was altogether different.

"Try as I might, I can't seem to wrap my mind around this. You're not even on the layoff list. You were deemed too valuable to the organization to be let go, even despite our shrinking profits. You've overcome so much to get to your position, Brian. Now this? Are you sure you're okay?"

Mulrooney nodded yes. "On many levels, I've never been better."

"What do you mean by that?"

"Nothing."

Marlucci shook her head. "Call it woman's intuition, but why do I feel I should be concerned for you?"

"I'm fine, really..." *Infinitely better than you!* he thought, glancing up at Romanero's picture again.

"I want to believe you, Brian, I really do, but cutting ties so suddenly and walking away from the position you've worked so hard for is so unlike you. Aside from the increased sick days you've taken of late, you've been an exemplary employee. I'd hate to see you throw it all away so suddenly..."

Brian sighed and looked down at his feet.

Once eye contact was established again, Susan Marlucci gazed deep into his eyes, a little more skeptically this time, "Did one of our competitors steal you away?"

Mulrooney shook his head. "It's nothing like that. Promise."

Time will tell. It always does. "I ask because you're not even asking for a transfer."

Brian took a deep breath, "Let's just say I'm in need of a serious life change, one that has nothing to do with the hotel business."

"What kind of life change?"

"Perhaps another time. I need to get going. Lots of packing to do." Brian rose from his seat and extended his right hand, "Thanks again, Susan, for hiring me way back when. I really enjoyed my time here. Sorry again for the lack of notice. Hope you can forgive me."

"Good luck, Brian." Susan Marlucci shook his hand knowing something wasn't right. She could feel it in her bones. She was deeply concerned for her now-former employee.

Marlucci added *Call Renate McCallister* to her "To Do" list.

Brian Mulrooney left the Marriott Hotel in Livonia, Michigan, officially retired from the hotel business and from mainstream life as a whole.

Little did he know he would be forced to drop out of mainstream life sooner than even he expected...

28

ONE WEEK LATER

"WAIT!" TAMIKA MOSELEY WHISPERED into the cell phone Brian Mulrooney had purchased for her. She was putting ointment on her leg when he called.

Just like last time Brian called to check up on her, Tamika turned up the volume on the TV then dashed to the bathroom and turned on the ceiling exhaust fan.

Knowing how flimsy the walls were—after all, she heard every sound in the hallways and in the adjoining rooms—she turned on the shower to further drown out her voice.

"Okay, we can talk now."

"How ya holding up, sis?"

"I'm fine. But every time I hear someone out in the hallway, I pray they don't start banging on the door."

"Have you gone outside at all?"

"No. But I ordered a pizza last night."

There was silence.

"Don't worry, Brian, the delivery man only saw my hand when I gave him the money. And I made sure to wear gloves. Told him to put the pizza on the floor cause I had a very bad cold and didn't want him to catch it."

"Think it worked?"

"Let me put it this way: After doing all I could to sound like a man, he said, 'Thank you, sir' before leaving."

The way she said it made Brian laugh. "That's good. Anyway, I call bearing good news."

Tamika braced herself, "Oh yeah? What news?"

"Jacquelyn said yes."

"That's fantastic!" Tamika practically shouted, before quickly toning it down a few notches. "Congratulations to you both. When's the big day?"

"Four days from now, here in Michigan."

"I'm so happy for you, Brian."

"Jacquelyn and I want you to be one of the bridesmaids."

"But I don't even know her..."

"You're my friend. And that's good enough for her. Besides, Jacquelyn feels like she already knows you."

"I don't know what to say..."

"Honor us by accepting."

"Okay, I accept." Tamika sighed, "But what about my situation here?"

"That's the other reason I'm calling. There's been a slight change of plans. I know you weren't expecting to check out until tomorrow, but our good friend from the Sunshine State's coming to smuggle you out of the city instead of me.

"Sorry for not giving you more advance-notice, sis, but he has another matter in Manhattan to take care of. We figured it was best to kill two birds with one stone. Since he's the one who will be picking you up, I mailed your mother's car keys to him."

The old Tamika Moseley might have protested, but after everything Brian had done for her, she knew she could trust his plan. The prospect of finally leaving New York thrilled her to no end. "When will he be here?"

"Not sure, exactly. All I know is he lands early this evening. He's not sure how long the other thing will take. He told me to tell you to be ready at any time."

"My things are already packed. All I gotta do is shower and I'm good to go." After two weeks, Tamika was getting a little stir crazy.

"Once you get to Michigan, you'll stay with Jacquelyn until we figure where to go from there."

Tamika's soul flooded with joy upon hearing this. It was really happening. Just as she was about to share her gratitude with Brian, there was a gasp. Then, "Oh, no!"

"What is it, Tamika?"

"I think they linked me to my mother's car."

Mulrooney felt this sharp pain in his temples. "Why do you say that?"

"I see my face on TV and the license plate numbers from my mother's car. Hold on." Tamika left the bathroom and sat on the bed. She watched and listened. Her body trembled so much, she could barely hold the phone in her hand. "I'm toast. Won't be long before they find me."

"Remain calm, Tamika. Don't panic. If you start freaking out, you may do something foolish. If they find your mother's car parked at the airport, perhaps they'll think you already skipped town. The room's in my name so there's no way they can track you there. Just do your best to remain calm while I think up a Plan B."

"What do you mean?"

"For starters, there's no way Charles can use your mother's car now."

"So, what will we do?"

Brian rubbed his throbbing forehead. "Not sure yet. I need a little time to think things through. But chances are good they'll find your mother's car soon enough, which means you can kiss it goodbye."

Brian took a deep breath, "Don't expect to hear from me tonight. In fact, the moment the call ends, turn off your phone and keep it off. I'll do all the coordinating with our friend from the Sunshine State."

"I need to get out of here, Brian. I can feel the walls closing in on me."

"I know. Be ready to leave in a moment's notice. Until then, try and remain calm. Turn off the TV and read the Bible. And keep praying."

"Please hurry, Brian. I'm scared to death."

"Relax, my dear sister. We'll get through this. God is with us."

The call ended, and Tamika powered down her phone. But it was too late. The damage was already done. Brian Mulrooney unknowingly just gave New York City authorities the big break they'd been waiting for.

With so much ongoing tragedy in the world, the *Graveyard Incident* story had died down considerably. But once the media got wind of this latest development, pressure was once again applied for authorities to find Moseley and finally put an end to it all.

Knowing most fugitives on the run still used cell phones and social media, that was always the next step in the process. But since Moseley ditched her phone weeks ago, and authorities couldn't find her anywhere on social media, both avenues turned out to be dead ends.

If she was online, she was completely invisible.

The only other shot they had was to enter certain keywords into their voice recognition system and hope something would flush out at some point. Those words were *Tamika – Moseley – Graveyard – Incident*. Whenever they were mentioned in New York and the surrounding areas, either by phone call, email or text message, it was immediately red flagged and sent off for further analysis.

At first, with so many New Yorkers still talking about the *Graveyard Incident*, those two words turned out to be more white noise than anything else. And with hundreds of "Tamikas" living in the region, it was almost like finding a needle in a haystack.

Brian Mulrooney changed everything.

Thanks to him, both his and Tamika's voices were stored away in the universal voice recognition system which boasted a 99.9999998 percent accuracy capability. Their voices would remain in the system forever. After listening to the call, authorities suddenly had a treasure trove of information to go on. They knew a "Brian" and a "Jacquelyn" were involved, who just happened to be getting married in four days in the state of Michigan. They knew there was a man from the Sunshine State named "Charles" who was coming to New York to smuggle their fugitive to safety.

They also knew their final destination was Michigan.

The most damning evidence they had on Moseley was when she told Brian they'd linked her to her mother's car, and it wouldn't be long before they find her. It was all on audiotape.

After putting a "BOLO" (Be On The Lookout) for a late-model Oldsmobile Cutlass Supreme belonging to Ruth Ferguson—Tamika Moseley's mother—authorities scanned all flights originating in Florida scheduled to land either at JFK, LaGuardia or Newark, looking for a man named Charles.

Then, without obtaining a warrant, they dispatched a Pilatus PC-12 airplane to circle the skies above the *Big Apple*, equipped with "dirtbox" technology, which essentially allowed for the scanning of phone calls.

Since the device acted like a cell phone tower, and since cell phones automatically locked on to the nearest possible towers, by flying overhead it could detect anyone using a cell phone within its target range and track their movements.

What the "dirtbox" couldn't do was listen to calls or intercept data. All it could do was track locations. Now that they "potentially" had Moseley's new number, they would wait until she used it again, track her exact location, and place her under arrest.

If they needed more help putting the pieces of the case together, they had it in the person of Craig Rubin.

The moment Rubin saw the commotion on TV, he called authorities saying he was a friend of the man named "Brian" they were interested in, until he found Jesus and went off the deep end.

After providing authorities with Brian's full name, Rubin told them how Brian and Tamika had met. He also told them the fugitive contacted him on the day the warrant was issued for her arrest, and that he told Tamika to turn herself in.

171

What Rubin couldn't provide was Jacquelyn's and Charles' last names. He did, however, give them Brian's girlfriend's first name, but couldn't for the life in him remember Renate's last name.

Authorities thanked Rubin for his assistance. With a unique name like "Renate", she might be the easiest one to find. But by the time detectives found Renate McCallister, it would be too late...

29

"I SEE IT, BRO," Charles Calloway said, locating Tamika Moseley's late mother's Oldsmobile Cutlass. It was parked on the third floor of a parking garage at LaGuardia Airport, exactly where Brian said it would be.

"Whatever you do, don't go anywhere near the vehicle," Brian said in a panic.

Calloway stopped dead in his tracks in the parking garage. "Why not?"

Mulrooney sighed. "So much happened when you were on the plane."

"Like what?"

"They linked you know who to her mother's car. They gave an exact description and license plate number. Just as the story was starting to die down, it's all over the news again."

"Great! Just wonderful!" Calloway's pulse raced in his ears. "Guess this mission won't be as easy as I thought." *Should've drove to New York instead!*

Brian gulped. "It gets worse. Brother Tom and I have been monitoring news agencies in New York while waiting for your call. They have all kinds of information on us."

"What? How?"

"It's all my fault. I accidentally mentioned you know who's name on the phone. Yours too, I'm afraid. But only your first names. Even so, the moment her name was mentioned, it was entered into some voice recognition system they have and was red-flagged and sent off for further analysis."

"What do they know about me?"

"Basically, that you're from the Sunshine State and you're coming to the *Big Apple* to smuggle their fugitive out of the city."

"You can't be serious!" *Thank God I no longer live in Florida...*

"Wish I was joking. It was stupid of me!"

"So, what now?"

"Do you have a Florida driver's license?"

"Not anymore, why?"

"Good. Rent a car as quickly as you can. Our friend fears they'll start banging on her door any minute. Needless to say, she's petrified. Just glad my folks are already en route to Michigan, so my sister could be fitted for her dress. Hope they don't find out about this until after the wedding..."

Charles Calloway wasn't a happy man. His tone of voice dictated that much. "I gotta go. Talk to you later."

"Sorry for all this, Charles. I know you're using a Satphone. Even so, you're in their coverage area now so be extremely careful."

Calloway ended the call and went back inside the airport terminal suddenly feeling like a fugitive himself. *Thank God I exchanged my Florida driver's license!*

The man with the Georgia driver's license searched for the closest rental car agency, a paranoid spirit led the way. He rented the smallest, cheapest car they had, which wasn't so cheap after all. Had he rented it prior to the disappearances, it would have been so much cheaper.

Calloway found the car, placed his suitcase in the trunk and slid behind the steering wheel. Part of him wanted to ditch his first meeting and focus on rescuing Tamika Moseley before the police found her.

But since his main reason for coming to New York dealt with a dream he was convinced came from God, Charles felt with everything in him that he needed to press on and meet Mary Johnston, even if she had no idea he was coming to see her.

After this latest development, who knew if or when he'd ever step foot in this city again? Yes, he had to meet her now.

Calloway just hoped Mary had the same dream, and that she would be expecting him when he arrived.

Charles Calloway programmed the Waldorf-Astoria into his GPS and left immediately. Once there, he waited patiently in line at the registration desk. A million thoughts assaulted his brain from his last visit to this establishment.

Mary Johnston was checking in a guest when she noticed Calloway standing in line. Rattled by the look of recognition on his face, she shot him a curious look.

Charles noticed and gulped. When it was his turn in line, Mary was still busy with a guest, so he let the couple behind him go before him.

Finally, Mary Johnston waved him over. "Welcome to the Waldorf-Astoria Hotel! Checking in, sir?"

"No, I'm not. Do you remember me?"

"I can't recall your name for the life in me, but I remember checking you in on the day of the disappearances. I've had dreams about you lately."

Yes! Calloway's eyes darted left to right to make sure no one was watching or listening. "What kind of dreams?"

"Dream, rather. Hard to explain, but I kept seeing myself far away from my job and this city. Other than that, it was rather vague. Except for you, that is. You took me to a place and people that made me feel safe. Thought it was just a crazy dream until now. Truthfully, I've been sort of expecting to see you again."

"What if I told you your dream was from God?"

"Are you a Christian?"

"I am. You?"

Mary smiled and nodded yes. *Thank you, Lord!*

"Can you take a short break?"

Mary shook her head no. "Just got back from my break fifteen minutes ago."

Charles lowered his head and sighed. "What if I told you I had a similar dream myself, and that's why I'm here?"

"I would be fully intrigued. Why couldn't you have come earlier?" Mary sighed. "My shift's over at nine."

"Unfortunately, I can't wait around. I have an emergency and need to leave town immediately."

Seeing perspiration forming on Calloway's forehead brought Mary Johnston back to the day their paths first crossed. Only it was mixed with blood last time. She still remembered how bad it looked. How could she forget? "Is everything okay?"

"Not really..."

"Are you in danger?"

"Aren't all Christians?"

When Mary didn't answer, Calloway's eyes darted left to right to make sure no one was listening.

He reached for a pen and paper. "Here's my cell phone number. Please text me so I have yours as well. I look forward to having a lengthy discussion with you about all this. Hopefully it will make more sense by then."

"Me too."

"I gotta go now."

"Okay, Mister Calloway."

"Please call me, Charles."

Mary smiled faintly. "I very much look forward to hearing from you again, Mister Calloway. I can't explain it but, ironically, your visit makes me feel hopeful in these crazy times."

"Glory to God, Mary! Expect a call from me in the coming weeks. Until then, keep fighting the Good Fight. Pray for me as I pray for you. God is with us."

The comment earned him a warm smile. The hotel employee said, "I'll do that."

At that, Charles Calloway left the Waldorf-Astoria Hotel with a pretty good feeling that Mary Johnston was *ETSM* worthy. As much as he wanted to send a text message to Braxton Rice to get the ball rolling, he had to maintain a razor-sharp focus until he and Tamika were off this forsaken island. He had no plan of calling Brian until they were in Jersey.

Charles slid behind the wheel of the rental car, programmed the address where Tamika was staying into his GPS, and drove off into the night. His senses were on full alert. After making a quick stop at a local pizzeria, Calloway arrived at the boarding house with a large pepperoni pizza and a two liter of Sprite.

"Can I help you?" said the heavyset woman Brian had warned him about.

"Here to deliver a pizza."

"Name and room number?"

Calloway looked at the receipt. "Mulrooney. Four-twenty-nine."

"Oh, you mean the ghost..."

"What do you mean by that?"

"Haven't seen him since he checked in two weeks ago. Or his cat. I know he's up there. I can hear him in his room. Every time I knock to see if he's okay, he ignores me. Came close to calling the police on him..."

"Are you saying I'm wasting my time coming here?"

"No. He'll open for you, just like the other night when he had a pizza delivered. Thankfully he's leaving in the morning. Something about him rubs me the wrong way."

Calloway wanted to say, "Why are you telling me this? I'm just a pizza deliveryman," but he remained silent.

The boarding house owner gave Charles a good looking over. "Take the stairs up to the fourth floor. His room's the las' one on the right."

"Thanks." Calloway took the steps two at a time until he reached the fourth floor. He banged on the door. There was no answer. "Pizza delivery for Brian Mulrooney!"

When Tamika didn't answer, Calloway grunted. In a loud whisper, he said, "Open the door, Tamika! It's me, Charles!"

Tamika opened the door and quickly waved Charles in. Had he not been holding a pizza in his hands she might have jumped into his arms.

"Whoa! Your hair's gone!"

"Took it all the way down. Trying to look different."

"It'll grow back, Tamika. Right now, your hair's the least of your problems. Your leg too, for that matter. We need to get you out of here right now. I think the woman at the front desk has been keeping tabs on you."

"She's so nosy! She knocked on my door the past three days. Las' night she asked if I was going to extend my stay, but I didn't answer her. No way I was openin' that door for her! I kept praying she would leave without trying to come in. Had that chair pressed up against the door just in case."

Calloway said, "She said she came close to calling the police on you."

Tamika looked up at the ceiling, "Thank you, Lord, for the protection."

"Amen!" Calloway said in a whisper. "Anyway, we have plenty of time to discuss all this on the way to Michigan. Everything packed and ready to go?"

"Yeah..."

"Is that the rear exit door?"

Tamika nodded yes.

"Time to get a move on. This is a one trip deal. I'll grab whatever I can and take it down to the car. Whatever I can't carry stays behind."

"Understood."

"Give me a two-minute head start so I can put your things in the trunk and start the car. Can you carry the cat and the pizza? We can always eat it in the car."

Tamika nodded yes. "I'll put the Sprite in my backpack."

"Good. Soon as I see you, I'll flash my headlights. Brian told me the owner watches the monitors in her office like a hawk. So make sure you cover your face. And be quick about it."

"Okay. Can we pray first? I can't stop shaking."

"Of course!" In a near whisper, Calloway prayed a short prayer asking for God's protection, then left at once for the back stairwell so the woman at the front desk wouldn't see him carrying her things.

A few moments later, Tamika emerged from the back of the building, bandanna covering her face up to her eyes and a New York Mets baseball cap on her head.

Calloway flashed his headlights.

Tamika saw it and held the pizza box with two hands, with Cocoa on top of it. She picked up her pace and hurried to the car as quickly as she could.

Once she was in, Charles put the car in drive and drove off. "Michigan, here we come!"

"I won't feel safe 'til we're outta New York!"

"I heard that!" Fear twisted through Calloway. If they got caught before leaving Manhattan, he'd be taken into custody too, for aiding, abetting and harboring a known fugitive. "Please protect us, Lord!"

Charles turned on his phone to check for any text messages from Brian Mulrooney. There was one: *Take Holland Tunnel to Jersey. No outbound toll. But there will be at least one toll booth in N.J. Other than that, try to avoid all toll roads if you can. Less eyes looking at you. Also, I recommend alternative routes. You have three days to get here so take your time. And watch your speed. Always use cruise control. Last thing you need is a speeding ticket. Let's have no further contact until you arrive, unless absolutely necessary. God bless you both.*

Calloway powered off his phone where it would remain until they reached Michigan. "What's the quickest way to the Holland Tunnel?" he asked Tamika.

Tamika had him take all the back roads. It ended up saving them 15 minutes. It was nice knowing her days of taxi driving had come in handy.

Once they passed through the Holland Tunnel and crossed into New Jersey, they both breathed a sigh of relief.

"Thank God there's no toll in this direction," Calloway said.

"Don't get too excited. There's one coming up soon..."

Calloway gulped hard at Tamika's words. If the authorities knew she was headed to Michigan, chances were good there was an All Point's Bulletin (APB) extending all the way to Ann Arbor where the call had originated. Toll booth collectors would surely be among the first to be notified.

Pulling up to the toll booth, Calloway's heart pounded like a bass drum. "Put your seat back and lower the cap to cover your face."

Tamika did as she was told, turning her head away from the toll collector.

If there was an APB on them, this man seemingly knew nothing about it. If anything, he looked bored to death and couldn't wait for his shift to be over.

Calloway handed the man a twenty-dollar bill, "I'm going to Pennsylvania but I'm running low on funds. Is there a road I can take without tolls?"

"Yup, but it'll take longer."

"That's fine."

The man gave Charles directions and they were off again.

For now, they were safe.

"Mind passing me a slice of pizza?"

Tamika opened the pizza box. It was cold, but the smell was still heavenly.

Charles sunk his teeth in. Just one bite took him back to when he first tasted authentic New York City pizza while stranded in the *Big Apple* after the Rapture. Even cold, it still was the best pizza on the planet.

Tamika took a bite and swallowed. "How'd your meeting go?"

"Short but productive. I went to the Waldorf-Astoria to see a woman who checked me in on the day of the Rapture. Her name's Mary. I'm convinced God wanted me to meet her."

"How can you know for sure?"

"From dreams we both had. God's communicating to His children using dreams, just like He did with you. Just pray we can get Mary safely out of the city someday..."

As if on cue, Tamika momentarily forgot about her own problems and started praying for Mary Johnston, a woman she'd never met, but you'd never know it by the way Tamika prayed for her. The words she spoke were bold and genuinely heartfelt.

If Charles needed a sign that Tamika was a true sister in Christ, something he could see with his own two eyes and hear with his own two ears, she'd just provided it for him...

179

30

THE NEXT DAY

WE'RE HERE.

Brian Mulrooney replied to Charles Calloway's text message. *Find a payphone as quickly as you can and call this number. Have a pen and paper ready. Hurry.*

Calloway did as he was instructed. "Hey, Brian, we..."

"Jot down this address," said the voice on the other end, "and leave immediately!"

At first, Calloway looked at the receiver in his hand skeptically, thinking he'd dialed the wrong number. The voice on the other end clearly wasn't Brian's. Then he recognized it: Braxton Rice. *The man's everywhere!* Calloway wrote down the address.

"When you get there," Rice commanded, "stay in your car until I arrive."

Before Calloway could respond the line went dead. He programmed the address into the GPS on the rental car. *A hotel?*

They left at once.

Braxton Rice was already there when they arrived. He pulled up next to the rental car in a white van with dark tinted side windows. Lowering the passenger front window, he didn't look happy. "Throw your stuff in the back. Quickly!"

To Tamika, Rice said, "Get in the back seat!"

Charles placed the final suitcase in the back of the van and climbed in the front passenger seat.

Rice eyeballed him steadily. "Now go inside the hotel and reserve a room for the next four nights."

Calloway shot Rice a suspicious look. "Why?"

"Just do it. I'll explain later. The money will be reimbursed to you later."

Calloway was clearly confused but did as he was told.

A few moments later, he was back inside the van. "Done."

"Do you have insurance on the rental car?"

Charles nodded yes.

Without saying another word, Rice got out of the vehicle and, using a pocket knife, slashed two of the car tires. *Sorry for this, Lord.*

Charles and Tamika watched in near-disbelief but didn't ask any questions.

Calloway craned his neck back, "Don't worry, Tamika. He's a good man. I'm sure there's a good reason for all this."

Tamika didn't reply. What could she possibly say?

Rice got back in the van and they drove across the street to an adjoining hotel and parked.

After a moment of uneasy silence, Rice eyeballed Charles again, "Now go back to the hotel and tell 'em someone slashed your tires while you were checking in. Then call the rental company and tell 'em what happened. Tell 'em you're late for a meeting and you can't wait around. Tell 'em you'll leave the car keys at the front desk and that you won't be needing the car anymore. After they fix the tires, they can take the car back. Insurance will cover the damage. When the rental car company inquires, they'll see you're staying there. Only you won't be!"

"But why do all this?"

"The fact that your first name's Charles and you rented the car at an airport in New York City might cause authorities to want to make further inquiries. If so, you won't be at the hotel, right?"

Calloway shifted in his seat. "Yeah, but why four days?"

"I'll explain the rest later. Now hurry!"

Without saying another word, Calloway jumped out of the van.

Rice rolled down the passenger front window. "Be creative coming back."

"Check!" Calloway crossed the street and picked up the pace.

Tamika wanted to strike up a conversation with Braxton, but he clearly wasn't in the mood for idle talk. She couldn't help but be impressed by the way he took charge of the situation without even breaking a sweat.

The reason Rice was so cranky was that he, too, was starved for sleep after driving straight through the night, just like Charles and Tamika had done.

Rice had just returned to Tennessee after a two-day trip, when he received a desperate text message from Brian Mulrooney with the news.

Rice replied: *Are you serious? Man, oh man! Not good!!! See you in the morning. Don't reply back!*

Rice showered and, though totally sleep-deprived, left the cabin in Tennessee and drove all night to Michigan. True to his word, he was at Mulrooney's apartment at six a.m. He sent another text message: *I'm out front of your apartment. Hurry!*

Mulrooney got dressed and ran down the stairs as quickly as he could. He climbed inside the white van. "Good morning, brother," Brian had said. Rice didn't reply. He drove off, totally stone-faced much like now. That was only their second-time meeting in person and Brian sensed Braxton already wanted to strangle him.

When the two men arrived at Jacquelyn's house, Rice managed to take a two-hour nap. Other than that, he kept to himself, replying to secure emails and text messages, and frequently staring out the front window, deep in thought, waiting for Charles and Tamika to arrive in Michigan.

Calloway climbed back inside the van, breaking Rice from his reverie. "Rental car company will be here in an hour."

Without saying a word, Rice put the car in drive and they left at once for Jacquelyn Swindell's house, in total silence. Upon arriving, Rice remotely opened the garage door.

The three hurried inside the house starved for sleep. Tamika removed her bandanna and baseball cap, and let her face and scalp breathe.

"Whoa! You cut off your hair!" Brian was astonished.

Tamika rubbed her scalp and nodded yes. There was sadness in her eyes. Her hairstyle had always accentuated her spunky personality. Now it was gone. Everything was gone. Even fully dressed, Tamika Moseley felt completely naked.

"I'd like you to meet Jacquelyn."

"Nice to finally meet you, Jacquelyn."

The two women hugged. Jacquelyn was happy to finally meet Tamika, but you'd never know it by looking in her eyes. She looked nothing like a radiant bride-to-be.

Tamika was consumed by guilt. This was all her fault. She started weeping uncontrollably. "Sorry for causing so much trouble on your wedding week."

Brian chimed in, "It's not your fault, Tamika. I should have been more careful."

"You got that right, Brian. It's your fault..." said Braxton Rice, with a hint of anger in his voice. "Do you realize the potential danger your phone call may have on us?"

"You're right. I need to be more careful..."

Rice shook his head. "And to think you'll be in charge of the first safe house! You should have thought this through, man, especially knowin' the real estate agent knows your name. Both of you, in fact."

Rice had held his tongue all day waiting for Charles and Tamika to arrive, so everyone could hear the same message from the same source at the same time. As chief of security, the onus fell on Rice to protect the Movement to the best of his ability. *If I can't protect this small number of people, how can I possibly provide security for ETSM members worldwide?*

Brian looked down at his feet. "It won't happen again, Braxton."

Rice sighed, then toned it down a few notches. "Sorry for my outburst. I know you're getting married tomorrow. It was an honest mistake. What you did for Tamika was noble. But even noble acts of kindness need serious planning these days."

Looking at Jacquelyn, Rice said, "You may not be linked to Tamika yet but, by marrying Brian, soon you will be. You both need to be more careful in the future."

Jacquelyn took a moment to clear her throat. "Yes, sir. Won't happen again."

"It better not. If a simple unsecured phone call can lead to all this, it won't take much for something very serious to happen. What has me most upset is the timing of it all."

Rice handed wrapped boxes to Brian and Jacquelyn.

Brian gave Braxton a sideways look, "What's this?"

"Wedding gifts, compliments of the *ETSM*. Go on, open them."

Brian and Jacquelyn did as they were told but without the usual excitement newlyweds displayed when opening wedding gifts.

Before they could inquire, Rice said, "They're Satphones given to us from the person we met in D.C. a few weeks ago." With Tamika present, Rice didn't mention President Danforth by name. "They're unregistered, untraceable, and each call made comes up as 'restricted'. The phones are swept each day for bugs to ensure against eavesdropping or counter-espionage. All text and voice messages are deleted with each new sweep. One day later and your call would've been untraceable."

Mulrooney once again lowered his head in shame.

Rice reiterated, "Like I said, it's all about timing..."

183

Jacquelyn gulped hard, realizing the potential danger she may have brought upon the *ETSM* by telling her parents she was relocating to Pennsylvania. Would their real estate agent, Rhonda Kimmel, someday lead authorities to the property? She prayed not.

"Is your apartment empty of your things?" Rice said to Mulrooney.

"Pretty much, but I have a friend staying there."

"I know. Tom Dunleavey, right?"

Brian nodded yes. There was no need to ask how he knew.

"He's coming to the wedding, right?"

Brian nodded yes again. "I've asked him to be one of my groomsmen."

"Might be time for him to move out. And kiss goodbye whatever else is still there, furniture and the like."

"Most of my things are here at Jacquelyn's."

"Good, because you can't go back there. Too risky. If I understand the situation clearly, the only thing we still got going for us is the cops don't know Jacquelyn's last name. Even your buddy in New York with the Jewish delis doesn't know."

Rice shifted his attention to Charles, "Far as I can tell, they don't know your last name either. Least for now. The reason I told you to book the hotel room for four days is that Brian told me he plans to leave Michigan four days from now. If they connect the two of you, which, at some point they will, they'll stake out a hotel you'll never go back to, one that's an hour away from the church."

Charles nodded. "Good thinking."

Brian jumped in, "My parents know Jacquelyn's last name."

"Let's just pray your folks don't hear about all this nonsense until after the wedding." Rice shook his head. "Suddenly your big day's not as problem free as we had thought. I mean, what assurance do we have that law enforcement won't show up tomorrow? If they do, how can I possibly protect you both?"

Jacquelyn sighed. The thought of police disrupting her wedding and taking Brian and Tamika into custody, and perhaps even Charles, frightened her to no end.

Without even asking Jacquelyn, Rice made a command decision. "We all stay here tonight. Call Pastor Jim and bring him up to speed. Then call Tom Dunleavey and tell him to pack his things and come here until we decide where to go from here."

Brian reached for his cell phone.

Rice grabbed his arm. "Use my phone until your new phone's fully charged. It's secure. Your phone's the reason we're in this mess in the first place!"

"Oh yeah. Sorry again..." Mulrooney said sheepishly.

Braxton Rice could only shake his head. *Amateurs!*

Brian called Tom Dunleavey. Given his situation, Brian wasn't surprised his house guest didn't answer the phone. All his calls were screened. "Brother Tom, it's Brian. Call me back as soon as you get this message. Call this number. It's very important."

It didn't take long for Tom to call back. "Hey, Brian, what's wrong?"

"Sorry to change our plans for tonight, but I'm afraid I won't be home."

"What a shame. I was really looking forward to our last night together."

"Me too, but it seems I've spent my last night at the apartment. I recommend you don't sleep there, either. In fact, I must insist that you leave. If police come knocking on the door, they might ask to see your ID. Not good, if you know what I mean!"

Police? Tom Dunleavey felt his pulse race. "What's going on, Brian?"

"Not on the phone. But suffice it to say my situation's starting to mirror yours." Mulrooney sighed. "Could you pack a few things I'll need from the apartment, including my suit for tomorrow? It's already laid out on my bed."

"Of course."

"This may be the only chance I have to get my things from the apartment, so you may need to make a few trips to the car."

"I'll do what I can, Brian." Tom Dunleavey grimaced. He envisioned himself lumbering up and down three flights of steps carrying many things, sweating like a long-distance runner after a ten-mile run. His lower back hurt just thinking about it.

"I would do it myself, but it would be too risky."

"It's okay, Brian, I'll manage."

"I really appreciate it, brother. I'll email you with the things I need and the address here. Everything will be explained when you get here."

Tom had a thought. "Since we're all going to be in Sterling Heights tomorrow, would it be okay if I brought your things there instead? I think this is answered prayer. Perhaps it's time for me to join my flock there. As you know, I already have a place to stay."

Brian eyeballed Braxton Rice who was listening.

"Even better," Rice whispered, realizing Tom Dunleavey might be a good man to have around to do favors in the coming days.

Brian said, "Sounds like a plan, brother Tom. Like you said, we're all gonna be there anyway, right?"

"So, I'll see you tomorrow then?"

"Lord willing. Expect a text message soon. And be extremely vigilant."

"I will."

The call ended. Tom Dunleavey's heart sank deep in his chest. If only he knew his own situation, dire as it was, paled in comparison to what Brian Mulrooney would face in the coming days, perhaps his old heart would simply give out on him...

31

THE FOLLOWING DAY

GLASS-ENCASED CANDLES WERE perched atop six-foot high white wooden candle holders. They lined the aisle-way leading to the altar at Southeast Michigan Evangelical Church. All were adorned with fresh-cut flowers plucked from the gardens of some church members and adorned with white ribbons.

Braxton Rice and his three top associates were put in charge of security. Since no invitations were mailed out, Rice requested a list with the names of all invitees on it. Not only was everyone asked to arrive two hours early, they had to show photo identification to his three associates and reveal the secret code that was texted to them, before entering the church. It took just under two hours, but the 800 invited guests were finally cleared through.

Now that Rice had a list of the names of most church members, the vetting process could begin with them.

The four *ETSM* security men would remain outside the church during the ceremony, guarding the outside perimeter and praying that authorities wouldn't show up at some point.

Now just minutes away from starting, every pew in the sanctuary was full, except for the front rows, which were reserved for family members only.

On the bride's side, George and Sheila Legler sat alone. They strongly urged friends and family members not to attend, which only made them look even more out of place, in an otherwise jammed packed church.

Both were visibly uncomfortable and couldn't wait for the shenanigans to end, so they could go home and do their best to forget the whole thing. What made this already bizarre day even more bizarre for George and Sheila Legler was that they didn't know a single person in their daughter's bridal party.

The front row on the groom's side bore a similar resemblance. Aside from Chelsea, who was asked to be one of the four bridesmaids, Dick and Sarah Mulrooney knew no one else. Much like the Leglers, they sat alone.

For the first time since the disappearances, Sarah dyed her hair for the wedding. She looked infinitely better than when Brian last saw her in New York. She looked almost back to normal, in fact.

The same couldn't be said for Dick Mulrooney. The expression on his face very much resembled George Legler's.

As it was, this was the first time Dick had seen his son since Brian shared his dream about the Catholic church a few months back. It was a fiery phone conversation to say the least.

At least Chelsea seemed happy for her older brother. Even though he'd caused so much trouble on the home front, and nearly destroyed the family in the process, she was honored to be part of the wedding party.

Charles Calloway stood next to the groom, honored to be Brian's best man. Three groomsmen stood next to Calloway: Clayton Holmes, Travis Hartings and Tom Dunleavey. All four wore black tuxedos adorned with lavender bow ties.

Craig Rubin was invited to be one of Brian's three groomsmen. Mindful that Brian was harboring Tamika Moseley, he declined. Refused was more like it. But instead of calling Brian, Craig sent a text message to Sarah Mulrooney stating his unwillingness to attend her son's wedding. Thankfully, he left it at that, without mentioning Tamika Moseley.

When Sarah forwarded the text message to her son, Brian wasn't the least bit surprised. He hadn't heard a word from Craig in many months. Even had he attended, Charles Calloway was still Brian's only choice as best man. Tom Dunleavey stood in Craig Rubin's absence.

Everyone stood when the organist, along with a quartet of violins started playing, "Mendelssohn's Wedding March". All eyes were glued on Jacquelyn Swindell, as she slowly but steadily inched her way to her awaiting groom.

On the surface, it looked like a normal wedding, but there was an uneasy spirit inside the church that most clearly felt.

What didn't go unnoticed by anyone was that Jacquelyn's father wasn't by her side as she made her way to the altar.

George Legler flat-out refused to give his daughter away to Brian Mulrooney. As far as he was concerned, Jacquelyn was lucky he came at all! Marrying Brian was the ultimate sign of disrespect to his late son-in-law. Tom Swindell was a good man, a responsible man.

In George's not-so-humble opinion, Brian Mulrooney wasn't even close to being in the same league as Tom!

Seated next to her husband, Sheila Legler was thinking similar thoughts. She couldn't comprehend how her own daughter could be getting married so quickly.

Only seven months had passed since Tom tragically perished. This wasn't the normal behavior of a grieving woman on the verge of turning 30, but of an 18-year-old teenager.

Hadn't they already endured enough heartache and tragedy? Now this slap in the face from their only daughter?

In the end, the only reason the Leglers finally decided to come was that both feared it might be the last time they would see their troubled daughter again.

Jacquelyn sensed what they were thinking. But after shedding buckets full of tears over her disintegrating relationship with her parents, the bride-to-be finally came to accept it all for what it was: spiritual warfare, plain and simple! But nothing would stop her from becoming Mrs. Jacquelyn Mulrooney.

Even so, to keep from completely losing it, Brian and Jacquelyn both agreed to block everyone and everything out and lock eyes on each other—from start to finish—as they said their "I do's".

Watching his radiant bride approaching, Mulrooney didn't need any such agreement; not even someone pouring acid in his eyes could pry them away from her. Jacquelyn looked breathtakingly beautiful in a gown designed by someone at church. Brian did his best to compose himself but failed miserably. Her cobalt blue eyes alone stopped his breath in his throat. He became teary-eyed.

Pastor Jim Simonton waited patiently, thrilled to be able to witness genuine Christian love, amid the fake worldly love being forced down the throats of the masses. He couldn't help but wonder if this, his very first wedding ceremony performed, would also be his last.

The moment Jacquelyn joined Brian at the altar the music stopped playing.

Pastor Simonton wasted no time: "We are gathered here today to join two beautiful souls together in Holy matrimony. Even among so much chaos and despair in the world, I can't help but rejoice joining man and woman together in true Christian love."

Dick Mulrooney snorted, then shifted uncomfortably in his seat. Even though he never met Jacquelyn, he already disliked the woman. She wasn't supposed to be his daughter-in-law. Renate was!

While Jacquelyn could make him a grandfather someday, this wasn't part of the plan; part of the dream. Dick would never be free to indoctrinate that grandchild into the Catholic Church, like he knew he could with the son Renate gave birth to in his dream for three straight nights.

If anything, this was a cruel and ridiculous nightmare.

Dick eyeballed the woman to Chelsea's left, wondering why she looked so familiar to him. He squinted at the wedding program in his hand and adjusted his reading glasses.

He read her name: *Tamika Moseley*. It dawned on him. *The fugitive? Is my daughter standing alongside a known criminal?* He quickly dismissed the thought. After all, they were in Michigan, not New York.

That couldn't be her, could it? Her hair was much shorter than in the photograph he'd seen numerous times on TV, but fugitives often changed their appearances to avoid capture.

Dick Googled her name and his shock soared to a whole new level. Glaring back at him on his phone screen side by side with Tamika Moseley was his own son's image in a New York City news feed.

Dick Mulrooney gulped hard. He adjusted his glasses and read how New York City prosecutors were considering pressing charges against his son for aiding and abetting a known criminal.

Not only was Moseley's cell phone linked to Brian's account, the boarding house she was staying at was also in his son's name. That is, until a man from Florida named Charles smuggled her out of the city.

Dick referenced the wedding program: Charles Calloway. *Is he the man from Florida?* Dick plugged his earpiece into his phone and listened to a video feed of the owner of the boarding house telling reporters what she said in her police affidavit.

"I was suspicious of him the instant I laid eyes on him," the woman said regarding Brian Mulrooney, "especially after he insisted on having a room in the back of the building. He said the reason was because he brought his pet cat with him, when it wasn't even his cat to begin with; it was Moseley's.

"Now I know why he never left the room. It was Tamika Moseley all along! I saw her leaving my building the night she escaped. The so-called pizza delivery man smuggled her out the back door to safety. Had I known it was her, she wouldn't have gotten away. She'd be sitting in a jail cell. Him too!"

Finished listening, Dick Mulrooney removed his earpiece and glared angrily at Tamika Moseley. His gaze held her captive. Her knees grew weak. She suddenly felt naked without her bandanna. *He knows who I am!* Dick pointed his cell phone at her and started snapping away. Tamika lowered her head and took deep breaths to prevent from fainting.

Dick then took pictures of Charles Calloway. Surely, he was the man from Florida.

At first, Chelsea Mulrooney thought her father was taking pictures of her. She smiled as her father kept snapping away. It quickly became apparent she wasn't the object of her father's frenzied picture taking.

Dick Mulrooney glared at his son, "A fugitive as one of your bridesmaids?" he said under his breath, so no one heard him. "Really? You gotta be kidding me!"

His eyes narrowed and shifted to Charles Calloway. Gritting his teeth, he said, "I know who you are, buster! You won't get away with what you did!" After a brief stare-down, Dick Mulrooney rose from his seat and stormed out of the church, unable to fathom how his own flesh and blood could allow a woman on the run from police to participate in his wedding.

This wasn't a Christian wedding; it was a dangerous cult gathering, and his son was one of the criminal ringleaders. It was the beautiful side of evil in disguise. What other logical explanation could there be other than his son and daughter-in-law were demon possessed?

Many in the church shook their heads in bewilderment.

Brian shot a desperate look at his mother.

Sarah shrugged her shoulders. She had no idea what had provoked her husband to leave so suddenly. Even if she did, there was no way she would leave her son's wedding. It would have to wait until later.

Like everyone else, the Leglers didn't know why Dick Mulrooney left so suddenly. But nobody comes unglued like that unless they had a strong suspicion. Whatever it was, undoubtedly it was all Brian's fault.

Tamika's trembling increased. Her eyes darted left and right looking for the best way to escape before law enforcement showed up. *On the run again!* It's like she'd jumped out of the frying pan and straight into the fire. It felt as if her last breath had just been sucked out of her lungs.

"Help me, Lord!" Tamika whispered skyward.

Clayton Holmes excused himself from the bridal party and escorted Tamika out of the church. He could feel her left arm trembling. "Relax. We'll get you out of here..."

191

Holmes opened the church door and did a quick sweep of the area looking for Brian Mulrooney's father. Seeing him driving off in a rental car, he said, "Stay here," to Tamika, then joined Braxton Rice outside.

Rice looked at Clayton quizzically, "What's wrong, boss?"

"Tell me again about Tamika Moseley's background check..."

Rice was about to ask why. But seeing his boss drinking in his surroundings without making eye contact with him was so unlike Clayton. Something was wrong.

"Came back clean. You know about her legal issues, right?"

Holmes nodded yes.

"Brian and Charles don't believe it's true. Nor do I. She dug up her grandfather's grave to see if the Rapture was true or not. She didn't rob nobody. The only possible red flag would be her husband."

"Husband?"

"Yeah. They separated after he became a Muslim. I checked him out, too."

"And?"

"Seems they haven't communicated in years."

"What's your gut telling you?"

"She's *ETSM* material. After all, she did have the dream."

"Take her to the cabin immediately. Charles too," Holmes said. "Your three associates can ride back with us later."

Rice knew what that meant: the safe-house in Tennessee. "Where are they?"

"Charles is still inside the sanctuary. Tamika's waiting on the other side of the door."

"I'll get the van ready, boss."

Clayton Holmes nodded then went back inside and briefed Tamika on what would happen next. After that, he went back inside the sanctuary to give Charles his instructions.

Calloway left at once and Holmes rejoined the bridal party.

Meanwhile, Rice huddled with his three associates outside. After a brief explanation, he placed one of them in charge, and went inside to get Tamika. "Follow me."

Tamika said nothing but followed Braxton Rice to the same white van she was in the day before; it was one of many owned by the *ETSM*.

"Get in," Rice said, opening the side door.

"Where you taking me?"

"To Jacquelyn's to get your things. Just waiting on Charles."

"And after that?"

"Tennessee."

"Where in Tennessee?"

"At this point, does it matter?"

"I suppose not..." Tamika climbed in the back seat.

Rice looked in his rear-view mirror and saw the fear in her eyes, "Don't worry. I'm taking you someplace safe. So long as the cops don't find us first."

Tamika was too frightened to utter a reply.

Calloway climbed inside the van and Braxton Rice left at once. They rode mostly in silence until Rice pulled into Jacquelyn's driveway an hour later. "Let's be quick about this. We need to get out of Michigan ASAP."

Before getting out of the van, Tamika said, "I can't leave my cat behind. He must come with me."

Under normal conditions, Rice would never agree to such emotional wishes. But what he saw in the rear-view mirror was a woman about to become completely unhinged. "Suit yourself."

Rice got out and punched in the code to unlock the door to Jacquelyn's house. Tamika only had two suitcases and a backpack to collect. Calloway had even less than that.

They were in and out in just minutes.

Tamika climbed in the backseat of the van and took a few deep breaths to steady her erratic breathing. It was like New York City all over again. Only she was unaware of her surroundings and, therefore, wasn't sure which state line she was desperate to cross this time.

"We'll be driving a while. Why don't you both try to take a nap..."

Calloway remained silent. His mind was full of thoughts...

Tamika sighed, "Thanks for saving me, Braxton."

Rice looked in the rear-view mirror. "Wait till we get there before thanking me."

"You got it." Tamika stroked Cocoa's fur. "Looks like we're homeless again, girl..."

32

AND IF ALL THAT wasn't enough, it was about to get a whole lot crazier inside Southeast Michigan Evangelical Church.

Entering through the same back door that Tamika Moseley and Charles Calloway had just left were Renate McCallister's sister, Megan, accompanied by her father.

Renate wasn't with them. Neither was her mother, Rose.

Brian winced. He couldn't believe what his eyes were seeing. *Why are they here? How did they even know about it?*

Dressed all in black, Dylan and Megan McCallister looked more like they were attending a funeral than a wedding. Both appeared grief-stricken, as if in deep mourning.

Side by side, the two walked the entire aisle way before taking a seat in the front row, a few spaces away from Sarah Mulrooney.

Sarah's eyes nearly popped out of her head upon seeing them. She gasped, then nodded politely.

They didn't nod back.

Brian then nodded nervously at his two uninvited guests. Instead of nodding back, they glared at the groom somberly with no emotion whatsoever. They looked tired, numb.

Seeing Jacquelyn's brow furrow, Brian whispered to her, "Renate's father and sister."

Jacquelyn sighed, closed her eyes and lowered her head. *Can it get any worse?*

"Remain focused. Let's finish this," said Pastor Simonton to Brian and Jacquelyn, in a near whisper. But even Jim was having difficulty wrapping his mind around what was going on. The wedding had barely even started, yet it couldn't be any more bizarre!

Brian looked at Clayton Holmes. His spiritual mentor nodded as if everything was okay with Tamika.

The groom snapped out of it. "I'm okay, Pastor! Let's do this."

Tom Dunleavey stood two spaces away from Brian Mulrooney and was able to hear his whispering. His heart sank for his good friend.

Brian briefly glanced at the McCallisters again. How could he possibly ignore them when they were seated in the front row with his mother? As uncomfortable as seeing them made him feel, Mulrooney knew in his heart that he was always faithful to Renate, in the five-and-a-half years they were together. Then he became a Christian and everything changed. He never planned for any of this to happen. It just happened.

Even so, just seeing them caused guilt to mushroom through him.

Brian looked away from them and shot a quick glance at his soon-to-be father-in-law. He was thankful Jacquelyn couldn't see him. If she looked at her father for even a split second, she would completely unravel and start weeping hysterically. But she remained true to her promise, never once breaking eye contact with the one she was about to marry.

Brian had already accepted that unless his in-laws became Christians, there would be no relationship with them of any kind. It pained him to think such unhealthy thoughts, especially while in the process of marrying their only daughter, but it was something he needed to accept.

Usually when couples exchanged wedding vows, they planned far into the future together as husband and wife, starting with being parents and ultimately becoming grandparents. And if they were truly blessed, great-grandparents.

But Brian and Jacquelyn didn't have the luxury of thinking along those lines. The remaining sand at the top of the hourglass was steadily finding its way to the bottom. There was nothing they could do to stop it.

Unless they miraculously survived the next seven years, their time together as husband and wife would be short, and filled with constant challenges, to say the least.

The positive side to exchanging vows under such adverse conditions was that it heightened overall awareness by creating a sense of urgency, which allowed the couple to fully embrace each moment spent together.

By only having so much time with which to work, emotions were naturally deepened and intensified on all levels, thus safeguarding the marriage, and protecting it from experiencing a season of inertia, or possibly even a time of unfaithfulness.

After sharing the Gospel message of Jesus Christ—a message originally prepared for the parents of the bride and groom; everyone else was saved—Pastor Simonton said, "Does anyone here object? If so, speak now or forever hold your peace."

Brian and Jacquelyn braced themselves fearing the worst. Both expected Jacquelyn's father to rise from his seat and condemn the marriage as a sham. Miraculously, he remained seated.

Their eyes quickly shifted to Dylan and Megan McCallister. As if on cue, they rose as one, causing all eyes to focus on them. An awkward silence fell upon the church that hung thick in the air for what seemed an eternity.

Scowl on his face, Dylan McCallister pointed his trembling finger at Brian Mulrooney. Just as he was about to say something, the grieved man started sobbing loudly.

After a few uneasy moments, Dylan McCallister wiped tears from his eyes and uttered something unintelligible before he and his daughter left the church. Their pace was dreadfully slow.

Everyone shifted uncomfortably in their seats waiting for them to finally reach the back of the congregation.

The tension was palpable.

This caused yet another alarm to go off in George and Sheila Legler's minds. First Brian's father, now this bombshell? They both feared for their daughter, who stood beside this maniac with her head down, trembling more than Dylan McCallister's finger a few moments ago.

It made them detest Brian Mulrooney even more.

Seeing that Jacquelyn was a breath away from coming apart at the seams, Sheila Legler stood to comfort her daughter.

George Legler grabbed his wife's arm: "She made her bed, Sheila. Let her sleep in it a while until she finally wakes up and sees her husband is nothing but trouble. Hopefully soon she'll come to her senses and leave him! Then the healing process can finally begin for us."

Sheila sheepishly sat down.

The Leglers didn't know what had caused Brian and Renate to go their separate ways—only what Jacquelyn had told them—but this sudden outburst from the McCallisters told them all they needed to know: Brian must have brainwashed their daughter into thinking she loved him when she really didn't, much like he did with Jacquelyn.

They glared at their son-in-law with growing contempt. *How dare you subject our daughter to such madness!*

Brian gazed out at the congregation looking completely disheveled. Many shot comforting looks at him, but it wasn't enough to remove this new coating of shock from his face.

"Come on, Brian, stay focused," said Pastor Simonton in a near whisper. "Let's make it official."

Brian cleared his throat, "I'm okay, Pastor. Let's finish this!"

Pastor Simonton cleared his throat, trying to alleviate the uneasy tension everyone felt, and said, "Brian and Jacquelyn, turn and face each other. Brian, repeat after me: Jacquelyn, with this ring, I thee wed."

Brian did as he was instructed, shaky voice and all. He was clearly rattled.

Then to Jacquelyn: "Jacquelyn, repeat after me: Brian, with this ring, I thee wed."

Jacquelyn repeated her vows.

"By the authority vested in me by the state of Michigan, and more importantly, in the name of the Father, the Son, and the Holy Spirit, I now pronounce you husband and wife. Brian, you may now kiss your bride."

Not counting the Leglers, everyone else rose to their feet and gave the newlyweds a thunderous ovation.

Once everyone calmed down, Pastor Simonton said, "For those of you who are unfamiliar with our church, the dinner reception will be held down in the basement. Once you leave through the back doors, you'll be directed to a side door which will lead you there. See you all down there..."

Leaving the church, everyone saw two large cardboard boxes on either side of the rear exit doors full of wrapped gifts. A sign was posted on each box: *Please take one. Love, Brian and Jacquelyn Mulrooney.*

Jacquelyn noticed them—it was impossible not to—but didn't know what was inside the boxes. All she knew was they weren't there earlier. A smile crossed her face. Was it Pastor Simonton's idea?

The new bride had no idea that Dylan and Megan McCallister had placed the boxes there, not her pastor or anyone else from the church. It took some doing, but they were finally able to convince the three men Braxton Rice left behind to safeguard the church that the gifts were DVDs for wedding guests to take home with them.

Since they were unable to confirm it—after all, the wedding had already started—the three security men let down their guards and even helped the McCallisters place the boxes by the rear door exits so everyone would grab a gift on the way out.

Totally oblivious to this, Jacquelyn stood alongside her husband and greeted everyone as they filed out of the church and made their way down to the basement.

She wasn't expecting her parents to join them for dinner, but when they left the church without saying a word to anyone, including her, her heart ached.

Jacquelyn knew they were totally against the wedding. She also knew they despised Brian. But they never even bothered to congratulate their own daughter. Nor did they bother taking a wrapped gift home with them.

Soon, very soon, the new bride would rejoice knowing they didn't take one...

CLAYTON HOLMES STEPPED OUTSIDE and called Braxton Rice on the secure Satphone he obtained from President Danforth.

"Hey, boss..."

"Where are you?"

"I-75 south near Lima, Ohio. Hope to be there in about six hours."

"Glad you're out of Michigan. Man, oh man! What a mess this day turned out to be."

"I heard that..."

"You only saw Round One."

"What did we miss?" The way Rice said it made Calloway look his way.

"Tell you later. Travis and I will be leaving soon. Hope to see you late tonight or early in the morning."

"Okay, boss."

"How are Charles and Tamika?"

Rice looked into his rear-view mirror, "Charles is fine. Tamika's sleeping."

"Let's not wake her then. Get on down the road. Call me when you get there."

"You got it." Rice placed another phone call. "Hi, Miss Evelyn. It's Braxton."

"Everything okay?"

"Just dodged a bullet," Rice said in a near whisper. "I'll explain later. For now, can you prepare a room for a young woman who's with me now. Her name's Tamika? Charles is with us as well."

"When will you be here?"

"Not for a few hours. I'm sure we'll be hungry by then. Also, can you call our doctor friend?"

"What for?"

198

"Tamika was bitten by two dogs a while back and has a serious leg infection. It needs to be treated immediately. Perhaps Doctor Singh could examine her."

"Just get her here. I'll take care of the rest. It'll be nice having a woman around for a change," Clayton Holmes' aunt replied.

"I'll call again when I'm twenty minutes out. Pray for us."

"You know I will."

Charles Calloway said, "What would we do without you, Miss Evelyn..."

"Lots of cooking and washing your own dishes..."

Her reply caught both men by surprise. Their laughter was loud enough that it rattled their sleeping passenger in the back seat.

"See you soon, Miss Evelyn."

"Be safe out there."

"We will," Calloway said.

The call ended.

Braxton Rice looked in his rear-view mirror again to find Tamika Moseley staring at him.

Seeing his facial features soften while on the phone with Miss Evelyn—whoever she was—comforted Tamika greatly.

The man driving her to someplace in Tennessee really was human after all. "Can I thank you now?"

Rice said, "You're welcome, Tamika."

Tamika grinned briefly, then closed her eyes and went back to sleep...

33

AFTER WHAT COULD ONLY be described as a tumultuous wedding ceremony, to say the least, everyone sat down to a simple potluck dinner cooked by a dozen or so members from the church. It was their wedding gift to the newlyweds.

Brian introduced his mother and sister to Tom Dunleavey. "He's the former Catholic priest I told you was staying with me."

Tom Dunleavey said, "Nice meeting you, Sarah. I've heard so much about you."

"Nice meeting you, too, Father Dunleavey."

"Please, call me Tom."

"You must be someone special to have my son ask you to be one of his groomsmen."

"I consider it a great honor."

Chelsea Mulrooney kept looking down at her feet, unable to make eye contact with Brian or Jacquelyn. The newlyweds sensed Chelsea knew about Tamika. What else could it possibly be?

Sarah also noticed her daughter's sudden attitude change but ignored it for now. She would find out soon enough.

Brian said, "Why don't the three of you dine together? It's not like it's a formal setting."

"I'd love to dine with you, Tom." Glancing at Chelsea, Sarah said, "I could use the company..."

All throughout the meal, Chelsea picked at her food in total silence, looking like this was the very last place she wanted to be.

After texting back and forth with her father, and realizing she actually stood next to Tamika Moseley of all people—the very woman she'd spent many hours online chatting about with friends—she no longer wanted any part of her brother's so-called wedding. She wanted to leave this place and join her father back at the hotel.

After dinner, the newlyweds were eager to be alone. Travis Hartings drove Brian and Jacquelyn to a hotel in Sterling Heights and checked them into a room that was registered in his name.

Charles Calloway had originally reserved a honeymoon suite for the newlyweds in Ann Arbor. It was his wedding gift to them. But that plan was quickly scrubbed.

This room, not suite, in Sterling Heights was paid for compliments of the *ETSM*. Given the situation, it was just perfect.

Brian carried his bride over the threshold. Despite everything that had happened, now that they were officially husband and wife and alone inside their hotel room, they let the rest of the world fade away.

"We did it, honey," said Jacquelyn to her husband, wrapping her arms around Brian's neck.

"Yes, we did!" Gazing into his wife's gorgeous blue eyes, he cupped her head with his hands and pulled her in for a kiss. Then another. Then, "Are you sure you want to consummate the marriage, after what just happened, and knowing what's still to come?"

Jacquelyn took a moment to consider her husband's words, then gazed deep into his eyes and nodded yes.

And so it was...

Jacquelyn jumped out of bed, still energized. "Don't you dare open any of the cards and gifts until after I shower, okay?"

"Yes, dear." Brian yawned and reached for the TV remote control. It had been an emotional day and he was exhausted. The many highs and lows suffered along the way had drained him of all his energy.

After a hot shower, Jacquelyn rejoined her husband in bed to find him sound asleep. She curled up next to him in silence and wrapped her arms around him.

A half hour later, Brian woke up, "Ready?"

Jacquelyn kissed her husband on the lips and climbed out of bed. The youthful exuberance she felt for having just consummated their marriage was about to come to a screeching halt.

Jacquelyn sorted through the cards. "I think you should open this one, honey."

"Who's it from?"

Jacquelyn said nothing but handed the gift and card to her husband. On the envelope were the words, "Open gift first before reading card!" Brian pulled back the tag on the gift and recognized the handwriting: It was from Renate. He read the inscription:

To Mr. and Mrs. Mulrooney:

Congratulations!
Hatefully, Renate M.

Brian opened the small package. "A DVD?" *Hmm?* He wondered if he even wanted to view it. He hesitatingly inserted the DVD into his laptop and tapped the play button.

Renate McCallister appeared on screen looking beautiful as ever, dressed in black from head to toe. "Congratulations to Mister and Misses Mulrooney!" Renate declared arrogantly, slurring her words. She sounded intoxicated. It was apparent that she'd been weeping. Mascara was smeared across much of her face.

"I guess the way I acted at your apartment the night I first met Jacquelyn wasn't without foundation after all, was it Brian? See, I'm not so crazy after all. You kept saying you were friends only, but my woman's intuition was spot on!

"Do you know how many years I suffered hoping and praying you'd ask *me* to be your wife? Do you know how many nights I cried myself to sleep over this? Do you even care? And to think I wanted to have your children!"

Tears formed in Renate's eyes, "Yet you know *her* for less than a year and you're already married and relocating somewhere on the East Coast? That's right, I know about your secret escapades.

"I went to your apartment one night when you were away on one of your bogus business trips. I saw credit card statements from hotels in Chicago and Pennsylvania.

"Why didn't you just tell me? Don't answer that! I already know why. It's because you brought Jacquelyn along with you, didn't you?" Renate lowered her head. "I can't bear to think how many other lies I would have discovered had I only kept digging.

"Have you forgotten how happy we used to be? How perfect we were for each other? How many times we laid in each other's arms dreaming of having children together?

"It's like you've gone off the deep-end, maliciously leaving so many victims in your wake, especially me and your father!

"Well, I couldn't think of a more appropriate wedding gift for the new bride and groom. I hope you enjoy it, Brian! After all, this is all your fault!"

Jacquelyn brushed off a cold shiver. Fear twisted through her body like a snake in search of food. "This can't be good..."

Brian gathered Jacquelyn in his arms, suddenly fearful for his ex-girlfriend.

"Well, Brian, my love," Renate said, sarcastically, "it's time for the moment of truth. Time for me to explore the afterlife and see what I can discover on my own, without you or anyone else trying to direct my path!

"Hopefully Salvador Romanero will be there to receive me on the other end someday..." Renate hiccupped. "Wouldn't that be great? Then again, anything will be better than the hell you've sentenced me to on this planet!"

Brian's pulse raced in his ears. His mouth was suddenly dry. He felt a full-blown panic attack festering beneath the surface.

Renate went on, "Why should I look to you or the God you serve for spiritual guidance? I believed you all those years and look where it got me: lonely, depressed and forever bitter! There's nothing left for me here. You've stripped it all away. Thanks to you, my life's a total failure!"

Renate hiccupped again then continued, "I want you to know I have no interest in meeting the so-called God you love so much. If this is how His own people act toward others, I'd rather spend an eternity in hell with Satan than one second with your cruel and heartless God!

"Regardless of where I end up, it'll be far better than remaining here on this cruel planet with the two of you! How could it possibly get any worse? My only hope now is that I'll end up with someone like Salvador Romanero in the next life. Despite what you say, he's a good man. A real man, unlike you!"

Brian closed his eyes and shook his head. He wished he could stop the DVD and, in the process, stop what he sensed Renate was about to do. If she only knew the repercussions of her words and actions, she would never consider doing anything like this...

Renate reached for a half-empty bottle of whiskey and poured herself another shot. Throwing it down her throat, she winced, shook her head and went on, "Sorry if I ruined your honeymoon. Actually, I'm not sorry," she hissed, "you've ruined my life, Jacquelyn! You don't deserve to bear the Mulrooney name.

"You've already had your shot at marriage! I should be Misses Brian Mulrooney, not you! Who do you think you are? To me, you're nothing but a worthless tramp! I hate you!"

Renate fell to the floor and sobbed uncontrollably. The pain in her heart was intense. A few moments later she pulled herself together.

Looking straight into the camera, she said, "I don't understand what's happened to you, Brian. You used to be so stable in all ways until you found religion and lost your mind. But know in your heart that I'll always love you, even if our final destinations are different."

Renate paused a moment. Her eyes narrowed. "No, I take it back: I hate you, Brian, and I'll never forgive you for this—not in this lifetime or the next!"

Renate reached for a handgun and placed it inside her mouth. Without the slightest hesitation, she pulled the trigger and quickly fell to the floor completely motionless.

Brian's eyes grew wide in panic. At the top of his lungs he screamed, "Noooooooooooooooooooo!"

"Oh my," Jacquelyn looked away. She felt the sudden urge to vomit and raced to the bathroom, sobbing hysterically.

Brian wanted to comfort his wife but didn't know how. There was a scream on the DVD. Almost immediately, Dylan McCallister appeared on screen. He was weeping uncontrollably.

He fell to his knees. "Please, God, no!" Gathering his daughter's lifeless, bloodied body in his arms, he covered her disfigured face with a towel.

His wife, Rose, appeared a few moments later. She took one look at what was left of her daughter and collapsed to the floor. Within minutes, Rose McCallister was dead after suffering a massive heart attack.

Brian was too terrorized to move. Watching his former girlfriend blow her brains out on camera was the most traumatizing experience of his life; even worse than the disappearances. The feeling of guilt was unbearable.

It wasn't his fault, he wanted to believe, but right now it certainly felt like it was.

Brian hesitantly opened the card from the McCallisters. It was a morbid looking black card with a broken heart image on the front, with no printed words either inside the card or out.

Twelve words were handwritten on the inside: *We buried Rose and Renate shortly before attending your wedding. Congratulations, murderers!*

Brian tore the card into shreds and deposited it in the waste basket before Jacquelyn had the chance to see it.

The phone rang. Brian answered but was sobbing too much to speak.

"Is everything okay in your room, Mister Hartings?"

After a while, Brian said, "Who's this?"

"Sir, this is Ramon from the concierge desk. A guest in the room next to yours said she heard loud screaming."

"We're fine. Leave us alone!" Brian slammed down the phone and grabbed his cell phone off the bed.

"Hey, Brian! Didn't expect to hear from you so soon, especially tonight, if you know what I mean..." Pastor Simonton chuckled loudly. After a turbulent wedding ceremony, the fellowship they shared after had proven quite therapeutic.

There was no reply from Brian.

"Least one of us thought it was funny. Hey everyone, it's the man of the hour," Pastor Jim said, to the many still gathered at the church.

"Don't tell me they already need marriage counseling," Tom Dunleavey shouted, jokingly. Many laughed.

"Did you hear that?" There was silence. "Still there, Brian?"

"Yes," came the somber reply.

"Are you okay?" Pastor Jim asked, sensing that he wasn't.

"No, I'm not! Can you come here as quickly as possible?"

"Sure, but why?"

"You'll see when you get here."

The call ended.

"Hmm." The look on Pastor Simonton's face said it all: something was seriously wrong. Brian never acted like this before.

"What's wrong, Pastor Jim?" asked Rick Krauss somberly. Krauss was the one who invited Tom Dunleavey to stay at his house. He was also one of the prayer intercessors at the church.

"Something bad happened to Brian and Jacquelyn. He wouldn't tell me on the phone, but I have a very bad feeling inside. He wants me to go there immediately. This may take a while, Rick. If I'm unable to come back tonight, could you lock up and set the alarm for me?"

"Sure thing, Pastor."

"Thanks." Jim Simonton left at once for the hotel.

Meanwhile, Brian called his mother's cell phone.

"Hi Brian!"

"Mom, can you come up here right away?"

"Is everything okay?"

"No. It's horrible."

Sarah said, "Be right there, sweetie." Dick, Sarah and Chelsea were staying at the same hotel, three floors down from Brian and Jacquelyn. "Something's happened to Brian, I'm going up there."

"What is it," Dick Mulrooney all but shouted down the hallway to his wife.

"I don't know." Sarah hurried toward the elevator with a sinking feeling inside. Still in her robe, she was the first to arrive on the scene. Brian opened the door.

"Oh Brian, you look awful! What happened?"

Brian said nothing but stared blankly at his mother.

"Is Jacquelyn okay?"

Brian shook his head no, then motioned for his mother to come inside. They sat on the couch and Brian pushed play.

Sarah watched the DVD and was horrified. Her body trembled. "Oh no!" *Why did you do this, Renate?*

Brian was too numb to console his grieving mother. She sobbed uncontrollably.

A few minutes later, Pastor Simonton arrived. Seeing the door was slightly open, he went inside to find Brian and his mother sitting on the couch weeping hysterically.

Following closely behind them were Dick and Chelsea Mulrooney. "What's all the commotion about," Dick snapped, "This is supposed to be their honeymoon, not a discotheque!"

Before Brian played the DVD again, Sarah excused herself and joined her daughter-in-law in the bathroom. She couldn't bear to watch it again.

It didn't take long for Chelsea Mulrooney to see why everyone was so hysterical. She started dry-heaving and looked away from the laptop. Now that she understood what had caused Renate's father to do what he did at the wedding, she started weeping and trembling uncontrollably.

Pastor Simonton watched and was shaken to the core.

When Renate said, "It's like you've gone off the deep-end, maliciously leaving so many other victims in your wake, especially your father and me," Dick shifted his gaze from the laptop screen to his son. With eyes full of rage, it's as if he was trying to burn holes in Brian's head. His nostrils flared.

When the DVD ended, Dick inched up close to his son until their noses nearly touched. Gritting his teeth, something he never did prior to the disappearances, he said, "I hope you're happy now! You've forever disgraced the Mulrooney name. May God forgive you for the many despicable things you've done! Don't bother taking us to the airport tomorrow. We'll manage on our own!"

Dick Mulrooney stormed out of the room, much like he did at the wedding ceremony earlier. His parting words were, "Serves you right for being in a religious cult! You won't get away with it, son! God will punish you!"

Without saying a word, Chelsea followed her father out the door.

Brian dropped his head and remained silent. Jacquelyn pressed her legs up against her chest and hugged them. *We should have eloped to Las Vegas...*

The phone rang again. Brian motioned for Travis to answer it. "Hello?"

"Mister Hartings, this is Ramon again from the concierge desk." Ramon sounded a little more agitated this time. "Are you sure everything's okay? Do I need to call security or perhaps the police?"

"No need for that. We just received tragic news and we're all grieving."

"Sorry to hear that, Mister Hartings."

"Thanks for the concern, Ramon. We really appreciate it. We'll be fine soon."

The call ended.

Travis Hartings prayed, "Father, we need You now. Our hearts go out to Renate's family in this time of unspeakable grief and loss. To lose a spouse and child on the same day is a crushing blow for anyone to cope with. Our brother Charles and sister Jacquelyn both know this firsthand. Would You comfort Mister McCallister and his daughter, Megan, at this time, and draw them to You? Make Yourself known to them, Lord, as only You can.

"As we mourn, please assure the newlyweds it wasn't their fault. This was a choice Renate made on her own. Comfort and restore Brian's and Jacquelyn's broken spirits. Remove all guilt from their weary souls. Let them feel Your presence at this time and Your healing touch. I ask these things in Jesus' name, Amen."

"Amen," came the reply in unison.

Brian and Jacquelyn remained silent. Both were trance-like. It felt more like they'd attended a funeral rather than their own wedding. It was a funeral they felt happened because of them.

Brian, especially, really did feel like a murderer. He wondered if the gut-wrenching guilt and pain he felt would ever go away? He feared it wouldn't. *Help me, Lord!*

34

THE FIRST NIGHT TOGETHER as husband and wife was a sleepless one for the Mulrooneys. Aside from consummating the marriage, nothing else had gone as planned.

By the time everyone left their hotel room it was after 3 a.m. Sarah Mulrooney wanted to remain with her son and daughter-in-law all night, but Brian had insisted that she go back down to her room and do her best to calm her husband and console Chelsea at the same time.

In near total darkness, Brian clung tightly to a pillow as Jacquelyn clung tightly to him. Brian's eyes were closed, but how could he sleep with constant heart palpitations and with horrific visions assaulting his mind?

Jacquelyn felt her husband trembling. Then again perhaps it was her. Peering into the darkness the only light in the room, dim as it was, came from a digital clock on the bedside table, a small red power light on the flat-screen TV, and from a few faint wisps of moonlight penetrating through a slight crack in the curtain.

It was enough to dimly illuminate the white tissue box on the bed next to her. Other than that, it was pitch black.

Jacquelyn had done so good overcoming her emotions leading up to the wedding. The stress and tension from dealing with her parents was overwhelming enough, yet she'd somehow managed to rise above it.

But when Brian's father stormed out of the church after identifying Tamika Moseley, the last layers of the onion started peeling away. Then Dylan and Megan McCallister—two people Jacquelyn didn't even know and weren't even invited in the first place—caused a commotion as the ceremony was winding down, and Jacquelyn literally felt herself shrinking away in her wedding gown.

Now that she understood the source of their anger and grief, the onion had peeled completely away, sending everything in her life careening out of control again.

Jacquelyn felt trapped beneath a new canopy of tragedy and despair. Now on top of that, part of her felt cursed in love. First to lose Tom and their child seven months ago. Now this?

Had she already lost Brian on their wedding day? Would Renate's suicide slowly pull them apart? Two husbands in seven months?

Jacquelyn understood why Brian was grieving. She also understood why he was unresponsive to her affection. Having gone through a similar experience herself, she pretty much knew how he felt. But this was their wedding night and she desperately needed him now.

Yet, Brian was so unreachable.

Jacquelyn felt terribly alone, as if stranded on a desolate island with no one to comfort her. It was a dreadful thought to be sure.

It only intensified when Brian climbed out of bed without saying a word to her. He got dressed and left the room.

All Jacquelyn could do was cling to a pillow in the darkness and wonder in silence where her husband went, and hope and pray that he returned to her again.

Brian rode the elevator down to the lobby and left the hotel. He was unfamiliar with Sterling Heights, Michigan and, therefore, had no idea where he was going. But that didn't stop him from taking a long walk. His eyes were blurry from being so tired and from shedding so many tears over the woman he gave five years of his life to.

For the first time since he broke up with Renate, Brian wondered if he'd made the right decision. Though he no longer loved her the way he once did, they'd shared a measurable amount of time together. Had he not ended their relationship so abruptly, chances were good she'd still be alive.

It was impossible for his human side to not second guess himself.

But his spirit side told him it was the right thing to do.

Renate wasn't a Christ follower. The fact that she adored Salvador Romanero—even mentioned him in her final seconds on Planet Earth—not to mention her worldly lifestyle and view point proved that much.

Yes, ending the relationship was the right thing to do.

Still it hurt...

A few miles from the hotel, Mulrooney's phone vibrated. He thought it was Jacquelyn. It wasn't. It was a text message from Craig Rubin. After many months of silence, Craig finally decided to contact him on his wedding night of all nights.

It read: *I hope you know there's a warrant for your arrest in New York for harboring a known fugitive! I gave the police all sorts of information on you, including where you live and work.*

What a loser you turned out to be! So glad I didn't come to your wedding. And to think we used to be best friends. My father's so ashamed of you. He told me to tell you to be a man and do the right thing. Turn yourself in!

Brian didn't reply. What could he possibly say? "How nice of you, Craig, to share such good news with me on my wedding night!" Mulrooney said sarcastically to himself. "You shouldn't have, really!"

Just then a state trooper, seeing Brian talking to himself and looking rather distraught, pulled his vehicle to a near stop.

Are they looking for me here in Sterling Heights? Thanks to his own stupidity and Craig Rubin's assistance, authorities in New York knew he was in Michigan. They also knew he was getting married.

But he seriously doubted they'd be looking for him an hour drive from Ann Arbor. Unless, of course, his father ratted him out to the local police. He trembled at the thought.

Mulrooney gulped hard when the police officer rolled down his passenger side window to get a better look at him. His palms were sweaty, and his mouth was dry like cotton. "Can I help you, officer?"

"What are you doing out here at this late hour?"

"Going for a walk."

"Are you from around here?"

"I'm visiting. Why do you ask?"

"Are you okay?"

"Yes, I'm fine."

"You don't look fine to me."

"Just received some bad news. I'll be fine soon. Thanks for the concern."

After a five second stare down, the state trooper slowly drove off.

Brian took a few deep exasperated breaths and decided he'd had enough of walking. He had to get back to the hotel as quickly as possible and start packing. Even though the room wasn't registered in his name, his father knew where he was staying. If he shared his whereabouts with local authorities, it wouldn't end well for him.

Walking back to the hotel, Brian thought about Tamika and Tom Dunleavey and how their lives had drastically changed for the worst after coming to faith in Christ Jesus. *How could it possibly get worse than this?*

211

Brian pushed that thought from his mind. It would get worse, incredibly worse, in fact! He just didn't want it to begin with him sitting in a jail cell.

Halfway back to the hotel, Brian felt a sharp pain in his chest. He was so busy drowning in his own sorrows that he overlooked the needs of the woman he'd just pledged to take care of in good times and bad. *How could I leave her alone like that?*

Brian picked up the pace and started jogging. Guilt stabbed at his heart every step of the way.

When he returned, it was 5 a.m. Jacquelyn was wide awake shivering beneath the covers, staring at the wall across from her.

Brian's shoulders slumped. He was breathing heavily. "I went for a walk. Sorry for leaving you here alone, sweetie. Don't know what I was thinking."

"I need to get out of Michigan," she said, without making eye contact with her husband. "I can't stay here another day."

"I was thinking the same thing." Brian sighed. "The sooner the better."

Jacquelyn shot her husband a curious look, "Oh?"

"I just had a brief encounter with the police."

Jacquelyn tensed up, "What happened?"

"It's okay. It turned out to be nothing. A squad car pulled to a stop as I was out walking. He looked at me suspiciously and asked a few questions. What spooked me most was that it happened immediately after I read a text message from Craig Rubin."

"What did it say?"

"Basically, there's a warrant for my arrest in New York City for aiding and abetting a known fugitive, and that I'm a loser and he's glad he didn't come to the wedding, and that I need to be a man and turn myself in."

Jacquelyn gulped hard, then put her hands up to her mouth. "Oh my..."

"Yeah. Thanks to my father, I don't feel safe at this hotel. Never thought I'd see the day when I couldn't trust my own dad..."

Jacquelyn sat up in bed and tousled with her hair. "Even more reason to leave then. We can't go to church in the morning. Last thing we need is for your dad, my parents or even Renate's father to lead police there. What would we do then?

"And there's no way we can go to my parents' house. My folks already think you've brainwashed me. I can only imagine how far they'll go to pull me away from you."

Brian gulped hard. For the first time in his life he got a taste of what being on the run felt like. "I'll call Mom in the morning and tell her we're leaving Michigan sooner than expected."

"I won't text my folks until we're out of Michigan. Last thing I need is for them to make a big scene." Jacquelyn started sobbing, knowing she might never see her parents again.

Brian said, "Who will move our things out of the house?"

"Pastor Simonton already offered to help. Given the situation, I'm sure many from church won't mind helping him load the truck, so Travis and Clayton can drive it to Pennsylvania for us."

Brian sighed. He was really looking forward to his final three days in Michigan before leaving for Chadds Ford. He and Jacquelyn had planned on taking Charles and Tamika on one last tour of Ann Arbor.

And Pastor Simonton had planned a sendoff luncheon for them the day before they were scheduled to leave for Pennsylvania.

Not only that, Jacquelyn had planned on inviting Tamika to stay at her house until a decision was made about her joining the *ETSM*. Now that Charles and Tamika were en route to who knows where, those plans were scratched.

And all because they believed in Jesus....

Brian reached for his cell phone on the table beside the bed. "Let's see if I can change our hotel reservation in Pennsylvania."

Jacquelyn said nothing. She was too busy packing her suitcase.

Brian understood. Completely.

213

35

"YOU'RE WHAT?!"

"I'm a Christian," Sarah Mulrooney said softly to her husband.

"What are you talking about, Sarah. You've always been a Christian."

"What I mean is I'm no longer a Catholic."

Dick Mulrooney rolled his eyes. *Geez, not again!* "You can't be serious, Sarah."

"I'm totally serious."

Dick sat on the edge of the bed waiting for his wife to finish getting dressed, so they could have breakfast at the hotel restaurant before leaving for the airport.

Still in deep mourning over Renate McCallister's suicide, neither felt like eating. "Okay, I'll play along. So, what caused you to denounce your Catholic faith?"

"It happened even before coming to Michigan. All Pastor Simonton did was confirm it to me when he gave a clear description of the Gospel at the wedding. Never heard that kind of preaching before. His words made my soul rejoice. At least, until I watched the DVD..." Sarah lowered her head.

Dick glanced at his daughter, Chelsea. She was sitting on the couch, phone in hand, chatting with friends online looking for comfort. After viewing the DVD, she hadn't spoken a word to her parents since. Their constant arguing certainly wasn't helping.

Chelsea pushed her earbuds as far in her ears as they would go to hopefully drown out her parents' voices. Not even the Xanax pills she took after her shower could numb the pain she felt.

"Wedding, ha! What a joke," Dick hissed. Even in mourning, he was clearly agitated. "Come on Sarah, it was nothing but a sham. It was a godless event that ended up being the main contributor to Renate's suicide!"

It was still difficult for Dick to accept that she was gone. A beautiful life snuffed out just like that! Also gone was the possibility of Renate giving him a grandson someday.

What seemed so promising would never come true now. That dream died along with Renate. Brian and his false religion were to blame for it all. Surely, he was demon possessed.

Sarah still knew nothing about his dream. It was the first thing Dick had ever kept from his wife in more than 30 years.

Dick took a deep breath and tried blinking these disastrous thoughts from his conscience, but he couldn't. His heart burned within him. "How could you possibly think God was present in such an evil environment? I mean, who in their right mind has a fugitive as part of their bridal party, a fugitive our own son harbored out of New York City?

"Now there's a warrant for Brian's arrest? I dread going back home. Thanks to the internet, the Mulrooney name will be forever tainted. How will I be able to look anyone in the eye? I'm so humiliated! Yet, you seem perfectly okay with it."

Sarah searched her husband's eyes. Now that hers were open, spiritually speaking, it wasn't difficult seeing just how spiritually blinded Dick really was. "I figured you'd say something like that. You really believe I'm incapable of thinking for myself, don't you? Which means you probably think I'm incapable of understanding the Word of God on my own, without Church supervision."

Dick wasn't used to hearing Sarah's voice bolstered like this. He wondered where the sheepish figure he'd grown accustomed to over the years had escaped to? "I never said that. It's just that..." He paused, wanting to choose his next words very carefully.

Sarah was too emotional to remain patient. It was time to defend her faith. "Let's examine your comments, Dick. First, regarding your doubt about God being present at the wedding: let me remind you, dear, that God is Omnipresent, which means He's everywhere at all times.

"And come on, it's not like Tamika's a murderer or a drug dealer. Nor did she steal anything from anyone. She was simply searching for answers. Nothing more. Now that I'm a *real* believer, I understand why she did it."

"Yeah, I know, purely for spiritual reasons, right? Blah, blah, blah!"

"Precisely." Sarah did her best to ignore her husband's sarcasm. "Everything that followed was nothing more than spiritual warfare..."

Dick snapped. "Give me a break, Sarah!" His voice was so loud that Chelsea nearly jumped off the couch.

"About my experiencing God in such an evil environment; let me just say I felt His presence in that church more than any Catholic church I've ever gone to in my life. I finally got to experience true Christian fellowship, even if you didn't!"

"True Christian fellowship?"

"Yes. Funny thing is, had it happened in a Catholic Church, you'd believe me." Dick wanted to say something, but Sarah wouldn't let him. This was too important! "I mourn the loss of Renate just like you. Lord knows how much I loved her and longed for her to be my daughter-in-law.

"Who knows, had it not been for my faith in God, perhaps I would've killed myself last night too. Though I mourn, because of my new faith in God, I can feel His peace that surpasses all understanding the Bible talks about."

"What would *you* know about the Bible?" This was said with as much sarcasm as Dick could muster.

"Been reading it every day since last November."

"You what?!" The look on Dick's face resembled someone who'd just been completely blindsided. He shook his head, feeling totally betrayed.

"Sorry for not telling you earlier. But had I done so, you and I both know you would have done all you could to stop me from reading it, especially since it isn't a Catholic Bible."

You're right about that! Betrayal quickly turned back to anger. "Man, oh man, here we go again! It's like Déjà vu! First Brian, now you!"

"I'll have you know there were many former Catholics at the wedding, including one of the groomsmen. The older gentleman was a former priest named Tom Dunleavey."

"Don't you mean Father Tom Dunleavey?"

Sarah shook her head no. "He insisted that I not address him as 'father'."

"Was this so-called former Catholic priest aware that a wanted fugitive was one of the bridesmaids?"

"I believe so. Why?"

"Isn't that just lovely. He must be brainwashed just like Brian!"

Sarah felt another urge to lash out at her husband but remained calm. In a softer tone, she said, "Brainwashed? I felt so blessed to meet Tom. When was the last time you read the Bible, Dick?

"It seems you read all things Catholic, except the Book that's so transformed our son." Sarah sighed. "It took reading it for myself to finally see just how on-track Brian really was."

Dick snickered. How could he not be insulted by her comment?

216

Sarah ignored her husband and kept going, "The more I read it, the more I can relate to what Brian and Jacquelyn are going through. All throughout the Bible, God's servants were beaten, tortured, imprisoned, and even killed for their faith in Christ. Yet they firmly stood their ground, by remaining true to the faith despite the persecution and separation."

"How can you say that, Sarah?"

"I'm sorry, Dick. I respect your opinion and your beliefs. But I won't apologize for reading the Word of God or for being a born-again Christian."

Dick lowered his head. "I can't believe you would do this to me. To us!"

"I didn't do anything to you, Dick! It was a decision I had to make on my own, without your involvement!"

Sarah frowned. "I'm sorry, dear, but I've had lots of time to think this through and pray about it. There's nothing you or anyone else, including a Catholic priest, can do to change my mind."

She sounds just like Brian! "I feel so betrayed by you, Sarah."

"That's because you're spiritually blinded to the Truth. The proof is that you're more sold out to the Catholic Church than you are to Jesus."

"That's ridiculous, Sarah," Dick barked, "and you know it!"

Sarah glared at her husband, "Do I? Again, I respect your opinion. Now I'm asking you to respect mine. Whether you believe it or not, I feel so transformed spiritually despite the deep pain in my heart!"

Sarah paused to formulate her next thought. "If you wish to remain with the Catholic Church, that's your choice. But I no longer want anything to do with organized religion on any level."

Dick's face reddened.

"Now that you know will you hate me like you hate Brian?"

Dick erupted, "Hate him? How can you say that, Sarah? I don't hate him. I'm trying to save him!"

"You can't save him, Dick, only Jesus can! And He did, last November." Sarah shook her head. "Have you noticed Brian harbors no animosity toward you? None whatsoever! Sure, he's deeply concerned for you..."

"Concerned for me? Ha! What a joke!" Dick barked.

"Deeply concerned, yes, because you keep clinging to things that have nothing to do with obtaining the salvation of God. But he doesn't blame you for it. Mostly he blames the Church."

"Brian has nothing to fear from the Catholic Church, Sarah. It's the one true Church."

"Again, that's your opinion, but it's no longer mine."

Dick started pacing the floor huffing and puffing in anger.

"Calm down, Dick. You were *never* like this in the past."

"It's because of Brian!"

"Really?" In a whisper, Sarah said, "Look at Chelsea over there: her life's so off track, yet she's still your little girl. Probably because she never challenges anything you tell her.

"Brian's the most on-track member of this family, yet you treat him like an outcast! How can you properly grieve Renate's suicide when you're so full of venom? I can't take it anymore!" Sarah sat on the bed and was clearly on the verge of tears.

Dick sat next to his wife. "Are you saying you're abandoning the Catholic Church altogether?"

"Yes. I'll never try pulling you away from it. Just please don't try to pull me back in. That's all I ask."

Dick glared at Sarah. "Hello? Where's my wife? I know she's in there somewhere. Whoever you are, can you please tell her to resurface!"

You're the one with demons, not me! "Mock and ridicule me all you want, Dick, but I remain unchanged."

"I've had all I can take of this nonsense." Dick called the front desk. "Can you put me through to Brian Mulrooney's room?"

After a few moments the person on the other end said, "You're the only Mulrooney we have on file, sir. Is he related to you?"

"What about Jacquelyn Swindell?"

"Let me check. No one by that name either, sir."

What in the world? Dick looked at his receiver. "Never mind!"

Dick slammed down the phone in anger and called Brian on his cell phone. It went to voice mail: "This is your father. Why aren't you or your wife registered at this hotel? What's going on? I'm so disgusted with you both! If I never hear from you again, it'll still be too soon! Goodbye!"

"Would you please stop! I can't take it anymore!" These were the first words Chelsea had uttered since watching the DVD. She covered her ears with a pillow to further drown out her parents' voices.

Sarah should have been shocked by her husband's tirade, but she wasn't. She calmly reached for her cell phone and called Brian. It, too, went to voice mail.

"Hi, sweetie. I'm sure you're still at church," Sarah said, not knowing they'd already left Michigan, and were in Ohio headed toward Pennsylvania. "Sorry for your father's outburst. It's the last thing you and Jacquelyn need right now. He's in mourning just like the rest of us. But at least you know why it's happening. Mostly, anyway.

"Something really good happened to me this week. I wanted to tell you last night, but with everything that happened, it wasn't the right time. I'll call you once I'm back in New York. Be careful on your journey," Sarah said, careful not to mention Pennsylvania. As of yet, Dick and Chelsea had no idea Brian was leaving the state of Michigan, let alone for good. "I love you both very much. God bless you."

Sarah followed up the call with a short text message to her son: *Don't worry, I deleted all pictures of Tamika and Charles on your father's phone. As an added precaution, I threw our wedding programs in the trash down in the lobby. So, your father and Chelsea have nothing to take back to New York. Stay strong! God is with you and will see you through it all.*

Sarah sent the text and burst out in tears.

36

AFTER A FULL DAY of driving, Mr. and Mrs. Brian Mulrooney exited the Pennsylvania turnpike. It was 10:30 p.m.

Last time they drove to Chadds Ford, Brian did all the driving. With a warrant out for his arrest, Jacquelyn drove this time. Besides, he was too distraught to get behind the wheel of a car.

Jacquelyn slowed the vehicle to a stop and paid the steep toll, then drove south on route 100 until it merged with U.S. 202 south. They took it all the way to Chadds Ford.

Before leaving Michigan, she removed the EZ Pass toll transponder from her vehicle, so they couldn't be tracked by it.

The Mulrooneys were bone-tired from being on the road all day. What should have been a joyous trip for the newlyweds—their first as husband and wife—was anything but that. They held hands most of the way doing their best to console one another, mostly in silence, which was a difficult feat in itself.

Their wedding couldn't have ended any worse than it had! As much as they both tried blinking the horrific images away, the phrase, "Just when you think it couldn't get any worse, it does," kept coming true.

If the newlyweds thought leaving the state of Michigan would allow for a brief reprieve from their many problems, they were wrong; bad news followed them all the way to Pennsylvania.

It wasn't enough that Megan McCallister made a disparaging DVD blaming Brian and Jacquelyn for her sister's suicide and her mother's untimely death. After leaving the church, she teamed up with Renate's best friend, Rachel Stein, and uploaded the video onto all their social media pages, and even onto *YouTube*.

Normally, a video like this would have been removed due to its graphic nature, but since the accused were Christians, they allowed it to remain online.

To further smear Brian and Jacquelyn Mulrooney online they sent the link to everyone in Brian's circle of friends, including his former co-workers at the Marriott Hotel.

With Megan McCallister out of work and Rachel Stein three months pregnant, both women had plenty of time on their hands. They vowed to spend much of it assassinating Brian Mulrooney's character and his reputation. It was their new full-time jobs.

Halfway through the state of Ohio, just as the sun was rising, Brian Mulrooney was peppered with questions and comments on his social media accounts from friends and co-workers who'd viewed the video.

Some seemed genuinely concerned for him. But most were outraged, especially those who knew and loved Renate McCallister.

His former boss Susan Marlucci was one of the first to contact him on his *LinkedIn* business account. Brian read it aloud to Jacquelyn: *Not in trouble?! I knew you were lying all along! And to think I always thought you were a level-headed individual. You're nothing but a murderer in disguise! Had I only known you were a womanizer, I would have done all I could to protect Renate from a monster like you. Your wife must be a real psychopath to marry you and have a fugitive as part of her bridal party.*

What's wrong with the two of you? I hope you both go to jail for a very long time! Tamika Moseley too! Either way, your days in the hotel business are finished. You have my word on that! You both should burn in hell for what you did to Renate and her poor mother! Don't you ever show your faces around here again!!!

"Now I'm a womanizer? What's next, pedophile? The hits just keep on coming," Brian mumbled to himself. "Good thing the *ETSM*'s paying my expenses from here on out. Who would want to employ me with the many lies being spread about me online?"

To be labeled a murderer from so many people was a heavy burden to carry. Knowing it was spiritual warfare at the highest levels meant there was nothing he could do about it.

Brian deleted the comments, blocked all who posted them, and powered down his cell phone. He searched the Word of God hoping to be refreshed by the countless eternal promises everyone belonging to God could look forward to. He read the last chapters of Revelation three times while en route, twice aloud so his wife could hear and hopefully be comforted by it.

But it was nearly impossible to concentrate on what he was reading with visions of Renate's suicide tormenting him. To see someone he once loved with all his heart, marred and mangled to the point that her face was unrecognizable, twisted Brian's stomach in knots.

And how could he forget the level of disgust he saw in his father's eyes after watching the DVD? He really did blame Brian and Jacquelyn for her death. Brian had no trouble believing his father really didn't want to hear from him ever again.

Then there was the way Renate's father pointed his finger at him in church, scowl on his face, holding him in contempt for driving his daughter to suicide and making him a widow all in one day. How could Brian not feel guilty? Of course, at the time, he didn't know he was being openly accused of Renate's death.

Now that he knew, it was too much to bear. Especially since Renate's sister, Megan, super imposed the words, "Congratulations, Murderers!" onto each DVD wedding guests took home with them.

Now everyone knew...

Luke 12:52-53 kept flooding Mulrooney's mind: *For from now on in one house there will be five divided, three against two and two against three. They will be divided, father against son and son against father, mother against daughter and daughter against mother, mother-in-law against her daughter-in-law and daughter-in-law against mother-in-law.*

Brian sighed. *Don't I know it...*

Now here he was moving to a new state, which just happened to connect to the state in which there was a warrant for his arrest. It only added to his growing angst.

If New York City authorities ever learned of his whereabouts in Chadds Ford, Pennsylvania, would they come looking for him?

Probably. Brian shivered at the thought. He couldn't remember feeling this insecure and entirely out of place in his life.

All this mental jostling kept pushing him further away from any sense of exuberance he should have felt, having just married the woman he deeply loved.

Each time he tried thinking joyful thoughts—after all, he did have much to be thankful for—a new wave of grief, sadness, shock and fear pulled him back under, suppressing what little wind he still had left in his sails. He didn't know if he was coming or going!

"Are you okay, sweetie?" Jacquelyn said, squeezing his hands as they drove south on U.S. 202.

Brian nodded yes.

But Jacquelyn knew he wasn't okay. Even worse, she knew her husband's thoughts were centered squarely on Renate McCallister.

Jacquelyn understood, but that didn't stop her from battling constant jealousy flare ups. She quickly repented after each one, asking for God's forgiveness.

With Brian so unreachable, all this windshield time gave Jacquelyn plenty of time to lament over her own situation.

As her reputation was being assassinated online, she became terror-stricken by the potential danger she may have brought upon the *ETSM*, by telling her parents she was moving to Pennsylvania. Would they come looking for her at some point? Jacquelyn didn't know.

She didn't know anything anymore, only that Brian would never leave her. He assured her many times on the long drive that his love for her was genuine and wouldn't crumble even under the most intense pressure, because it came from above.

If Jacquelyn didn't have that assurance from her husband, she'd be fit for a straight-jacket now, no questions asked. Having gone through the same pool of emotions Brian was now suffering, when her first husband died, she knew it was normal to mourn the loss of someone who was part of your life for so long.

Brian was simply grieving for Renate. Nothing more. He was there when Jacquelyn was at her absolute worst and hadn't left her side since. Nothing had changed between them. It was her turn now to be there for him.

Forty minutes after exiting the turnpike, Jacquelyn pulled her red Blazer into the hotel parking lot. It was the same place they stayed at on their first trip to Chadds Ford. But instead of reserving separate rooms, only one room was needed this time.

The Mulrooneys walked inside the hotel, still too numb, tired and grief-stricken to bask in the elation they should have felt being husband and wife. They looked nothing like a happy newlywed couple on their honeymoon. At least they held hands.

With the final payment received from TH Corporation, the only thing left was to sign the huge mountain of legal documents. After that, the property was all theirs.

As exciting as it all sounded just 24 hours ago, the DVD changed everything. Throw into the mix that their unsaved family members and friends thought they were criminals and wanted nothing to do with them, and it was easy to understand why they were having great difficulty processing it all.

Brian opened the door to their hotel room, "Well, here we are, my love. Our second honeymoon suite..."

Jacquelyn smiled wearily. After showering, Brian sent text messages to his mother and Charles Calloway, informing of their safe arrival to Pennsylvania. He then sent one to Rhonda Kimmel, confirming that they'd be at her office at 10 a.m. sharp.

A few minutes later, Kimmel replied confirming everything was set on her end.

Brian was grateful that his real estate agent was able to adjust her schedule and meet with them tomorrow morning, rather than on Wednesday. Then again, in this new climate, her schedule was probably wide open. Still, he appreciated it.

Just as Mulrooney was about to power off his phone, he received a text message from Travis Hartings. *Charles just texted me. Glad you arrived safely. Not to further startle you, but given what's already happened, Clayton and I feel the hotel you're staying at is too close to the residence. We think it would be best if you check out in the morning and find another hotel either in New Jersey or Delaware. Make sure it's in your wife's name...*

Brian replied: *Will do!*

At that, the Mulrooneys settled into bed for the night. Instead of being intimate like they were the night before, Brian held his wife for dear life as she lay shaking uncontrollably in his arms. It was his turn to comfort her.

Much like in the car earlier, he whispered Scripture after Scripture in her ears until Jacquelyn dozed off, and her body stopped quaking from fear and from the long drive.

In the darkness, Brian wondered how many newlyweds on the planet—past and present—had ever come close to enduring what he and Jacquelyn had in the first 24 hours of being married. He seriously doubted there were many.

Nevertheless, the Mulrooneys were on a mission from God. Which meant the joy buried deep beneath a mountain of guilt and grief would resurface in time.

The key for now was to keep taking positive steps in the right direction, despite their dire predicament. Meeting with Rhonda Kimmel in the morning would be a vital first step.

Come sunrise, as Pennsylvania landowners, they would begin at once cleaning and scrubbing *ETSM* safe house number one, from top to bottom, the moment the keys were handed over to them.

With time being of the extreme essence, they'd keep themselves busy day and night to avoid going insane.

37

THE NEXT MORNING

"CONGRATULATIONS, GUYS," RHONDA KIMMEL declared, after the final signature was recorded.

"Thanks, Rhonda." Brian did his best to hide the grief on his face and in his voice. But the bags under his eyes indicated something was seriously wrong.

Rhonda Kimmel placed her pen on the desk and removed her reading glasses. "I hate to pry, Brian, but are you okay? I'm almost afraid to ask, but are you having second thoughts?"

"No. It's nothing like that. We still want the land."

"What is it then?" the Realtor said. "Not used to seeing you both so down."

"We're mourning a death."

"Sorry to hear that. And to think on your wedding week and all," Kimmel said, with an empathetic frown.

"Yeah, the timing couldn't have been worse." Brian hoped the fear in his eyes from being on the run from law enforcement wouldn't make Rhonda even more suspicious.

"Someone close to you?"

Brian looked at Jacquelyn who was staring at the floor. "You could say that."

Jacquelyn looked down at her lap.

"My deepest condolences to you both..."

"Thanks," they both said in unison.

Rhonda sensed the newlyweds didn't wish to discuss the matter any further. "If you need anything, please don't hesitate to contact me."

"You've been a great help, Rhonda. We appreciate it," said Jacquelyn, looking down at her lap again. It was difficult maintaining eye contact knowing their Realtor could become their staunch enemy if word ever got out that Brian was a wanted man.

As one of the few people who knew their exact location, if a reward was ever offered for her husband's whereabouts, would the woman sitting across from her—who was all smiles now—lead the enemy to their front door? Jacquelyn gulped hard at the notion.

Kimmel noticed Jacquelyn's reluctance to make eye contact but brushed it off. After all, they were in mourning.

Not knowing what else to say, Rhonda said, "Well, what are you waiting for? Better get going!"

The Mulrooneys rose to leave.

"Don't forget the keys to each cottage are under the doormats."

"Check."

"I wish you both many happy, fruitful years of married life together."

The Mulrooneys smiled faintly knowing, at most, they had less than seven years together as husband and wife. Unless they miraculously survived the coming mayhem. Right now, they didn't like the odds.

Just as Brian was closing the door to Rhonda Kimmel's office, she said, "Oh, one more thing: there will be fireworks in Philly and Wilmington the moment the first child's born. Might be a good way for you to get out and meet some locals. I'll be going to Wilmington. If you decide you wanna join me, shoot me a text. Drinks are on me." *Least I can do after the $37,000 commission I just made!*

"Thanks for the invite but we plan on working day and night making improvements to the property..."

"Understood," Rhonda Kimmel said with a smile. "Such an exciting time to be alive, isn't it? I can't wait to see children again."

"Us too..."

"Won't be long now," the real estate agent said. "Do you plan on having kids of your own?"

Brian and Jacquelyn glanced at each other. "Time will tell, I suppose," Brian said.

Rhonda Kimmel looked at her fingernails. The conversation was going nowhere. "Hope you enjoy your first day as Pennsylvania landowners. If I see you at the fireworks, great! If not, no worries."

"Sounds good, Rhonda. Either way, enjoy the fireworks."

At that, the Mulrooneys left for the property. It was officially their land. They were Pennsylvania's newest residents. Only they wouldn't go knocking on doors introducing themselves to neighbors within earshot.

From a geographical standpoint, this was a significant moment for the *ETSM*. They were officially on the map. With the first safe house up and soon-to-be running, many more would follow. Hundreds of others were already in the pipeline.

Initially, safe house number one in Chadds Ford was slated to be the testing grounds of sorts. While others would soon follow, Clayton Holmes and Travis Hartings wanted to take their time and perfect this location to the best of their ability, then use it as a cookie cutter of sorts, much like a fast food franchise.

But due to the recent events, not to mention the constant rumblings that Salvador Romanero would strike the U.S. next, they were scrambling to purchase as much land as they could get their hands on, most of which would end up being underground.

President Danforth was right: they needed to be hunkered down in the soonest possible fashion.

The Mulrooneys reached the residence. Brian climbed out of the vehicle and opened the gate. Now in full bloom, the sprawling property looked even more beautiful than when they first saw it last April.

Brian craned his neck back and saw Jacquelyn mouthing the words, "So beautiful", even if her face betrayed her words.

"Shall we, my dear?"

Jacquelyn nodded yes. Brian drove the car onto the property then got out to close the gate behind them.

For the first time since viewing the DVD, he felt a slight surge of excitement brewing beneath the surface.

Looking at his wife, his lips pressed into a warm smile. Even with so many imminent threats in the air—a constant threat no one was immune to anywhere on the planet—this place still felt like a Pocket of Peace.

Straight ahead and spread all about were many small cottages, which would soon to be full of Christian refugees. They went off in that direction.

The keys to each cottage were found underneath the doormats just like Rhonda Kimmel had said. Each time they opened a cottage door, their nostrils were exposed to a musty stench that hung thick in the air.

After a while, Brian started wheezing heavily. Fearing he might have an asthma attack, all they could do for now was open windows and let them air out, until air filtration units could be placed in each cottage in the coming days.

They made their way to the church pavilion and took a seat in a front row pew. Brian's phone rang.

"It's my mother. Not sure if I wanna answer it."

"Go on."

"Hello?"

"Hi, sweetie. How ya holding up?"

"Okay. You?"

"Good as can be expected, I suppose. Still hard to believe Renate's gone. My mind's still blown..."

"Mine too." Brian changed the topic. "Is Dad any better?"

"He's a little calmer now, but that doesn't mean he's okay." Sarah paused a moment to formulate her thoughts. "I finally realize just how lost your father really is, spiritually speaking."

Brian straightened up. He greatly anticipated what his mother would say next.

Sarah sighed, "The nasty message you received yesterday wasn't only due to Renate's suicide or Tamika's involvement in your wedding. I think what has your father so upset is that I've received Christ as Lord and Savior."

Brian's eyes teared up, "You did what?"

"I'm a Christian, Brian!"

"Are you kidding me, Ma?"

"No. It happened at home a few days before your wedding. All Pastor Simonton did was confirm it to me."

Brian started sniffling.

"Are you okay?" Jacquelyn rubbed her husband's shoulders, half-expecting more bad news. Brian nodded yes.

"I think what got me off the spiritual fence was another dream I had."

Another dream? "You're having dreams, Ma?"

"Yes. In my first dream I kept seeing myself in the bathtub reading the Bible you gave me, and the letter Justin included for his parents. Never could remember the content of the letter, only the anguish I felt from reading it. Each time I woke, my eyes were moist with tears."

Brian scratched his head. "Why didn't you tell me, Ma?"

"Haven't had the chance to. Anyway, frightened as I was to read the letter, I'm glad I finally found the strength. Something Justin wrote had a profound impact on me."

"What did he write?"

"The One who saves us is the very One from whom we must be saved. Justin may have intended it for his parents, but I think God intended it for me."

Brian took a moment to let it settle in his mind. "That's deep. Couldn't have said it any better myself."

"All my life I figured God was the One who had the power to save souls, while Satan was the one who destroyed them. How wrong I was! Now I understand why the Bible tells us to fear God. He alone has the power to save souls or destroy them.

"Satan is merely a by-product of unbelief, and hell is merely the final dwelling place for those whose souls are sent there by God Almighty Himself. Satan has nothing to do with it.

"Once I fully understood this, for the first time ever, I feared God. It was enough to bring me to my knees. I cried out to Jesus in my bedroom closet, so your father wouldn't hear me, and repented of my sins and begged Jesus to be my Lord and Savior.

"Like I said, your pastor merely confirmed it for me when he shared the gospel at your wedding. What a strong preacher he is! I'm sure you'll miss his teaching..."

Brian wiped fresh tears from his eyes. "Can you please tell Jacquelyn what you just told me? I'll put you on speaker phone."

"Hi, Jacquelyn. Just wanted you to know I'm a Christian now."

Tears welled up in Jacquelyn's eyes, "Praise the Lord!" *Finally, some good news!*

"As you can imagine, Dick's upset with me. We're not speaking at the moment. We need to pray for him before it's too late. Chelsea too."

"We pray for them every day without fail."

"Thank you, Jacquelyn." Then, "Are you aware of what's being said about the two of you online?"

Brian sighed. "We know..."

"It's spreading like wildfire among people we know. All of Chelsea's online friends have seen the DVD. You can imagine how humiliated she is. She hasn't been online all day. Talk about a miracle!

"Needless to say, she wants nothing to do with either of you. She thinks you really are criminals. She needs prayer in the worst way."

When Brian and Jacquelyn remained silent, Sarah said, "Take care of my son, Jacquelyn..."

"I promise to do my very best, Misses Mulrooney."

"Please call me Sarah or Mom."

"Okay, Mom," Jacquelyn said to her new mother-in-law, liking the sound of it. "I could never survive all this craziness without him."

Jacquelyn's words filled Sarah with a new sense of dread. The comfort she always took knowing Dick was always there for her at times like this was no longer available to her.

Jacquelyn picked up on it and said, "Contact me anytime, Mom. I'm always here for you."

"Likewise."

Brian said, "Thanks for sharing the awesome news with us, Ma. Couldn't have come at a better time."

"Would you like to know the other dream I had?"

"Of course."

"I think I saw the place you and Jacquelyn are living at. In my dream, Tamika and Tom Dunleavey were there too."

Brian's ears perked up, "Tell me more..."

"It looked like a campsite or something. Sort of like the one we took you to in the Poconos when you were still a boy. But I don't think it was in the mountains."

"Quite a dream you had, Ma."

"It was so real I could almost smell the grass."

"Something tells me you may be here soon. Let that comfort you for now, Ma. We'll be in touch soon. Love you."

"Love you, too, son."

At that they said their goodbyes.

Brian draped his right arm around Jacquelyn and stared out in the distance. "Do you think it's bad to feel joyous now?"

"How could we not feel joyous after the news we just got? Perhaps this is what experiencing God's peace that surpasses all understanding is all about. Think about it, the moment we arrived at the church pavilion, your mother calls informing us she's a Christian. The timing couldn't be more perfect."

"You're right. I still remember the desperation in my mother's voice when she called after the surprise attack on Israel asking me to pray for her. To think it would lead to this..."

"I think God wants us to rejoice over another soul being saved, even as we mourn. How much more since it's your own mother? Perhaps He's reminding us that He still has everything under His complete control, despite what we're going through. I think your mother's conversion is further proof of it, right?"

Brian nodded agreement.

"I mean, if it wasn't real, she probably would have abandoned her faith by now, especially knowing even darker clouds loom on the horizon. But she hasn't. And besides, the only way we can climb the huge mountain before us is by having the proper attitude, right?"

"Well said, honey!"

"Well then, if God wants us to be joyous, who are we to object? Let's do our best to rejoice and be glad in it, shall we?"

Brian pulled Jacquelyn in even closer. He felt so blessed to call her his wife.

A few moments later, they made their way to the house they planned on occupying. Much like the night before, Brian swept his wife into his arms and carried her over the threshold.

Jacquelyn bathed in her husband's affection, knowing it was merely an outward extension of his true inner-feelings for her.

It made this moment all the more priceless, deep mourning or not!

The overpowering smells of an old stone house—dust, mold, mildew and soot from a fireplace that hadn't been lit in at least a year—quickly attacked Brian's lungs, causing him to wheeze heavily. He placed his wife's feet on the floor. "Man, oh man! It's even worse in here!"

Jacquelyn said, "Definitely not sleeping here until this place has been scrubbed from top to bottom!"

"If we did, I'd be in the ER come morning."

"Here we come Delaware."

As Brian opened the windows, Jacquelyn went to the kitchen to make sure all the appliances still worked.

Though both were thrilled to experience the joys of moving into a new house as newlyweds, it wouldn't last. Soon they'd have little or no privacy. Even the house they would occupy would be full to the brim of Tribulation Saints.

But for now, they had it all to themselves, making this husband-wife moment memorable, musty stench and all.

After a full day of cleaning and scrubbing, the Mulrooneys were dirty, exhausted and hungry. After just one day, Brian and Jacquelyn knew it would take a small army of residents to revamp the property and clean the 270 cottages dotting the landscape.

If help didn't arrive soon, Jesus might return before they were all cleaned.

"Think we should close the windows," Jacquelyn said, her mouth formed in a hearty yawn.

"Why bother?"

"What if it rains?"

"Everything's gonna be replaced anyway. Besides, there's nothing here for thieves to take. And when was the last time it rained? Let's just pray for God's protection and leave it at that."

"Okay, sweetie."

38

MID-JULY

AFTER FIVE DAYS OF cleaning, exterminating and setting mouse traps all throughout the house, and with several air filtration units turned on, Brian Mulrooney could finally breathe without battling frequent asthma flare ups.

It would take a few weeks before the house was bug and rodent free. But, for now, it was clean enough that once the furniture arrived, it could be brought inside the residence.

The Mulrooneys were thankful to be out of the hotel and officially moved onto the property. The thirty-minute drive each way was robbing them of so much precious time; time they couldn't afford to lose.

On this, their first day as full-time residents, their guests were just ten minutes away. Jacquelyn thought to flick the switch on the coffeemaker before leaving the house but decided against it.

She knew they'd probably want to inspect the grounds first and pray God's full protection over it, before coming back to the main house. She would brew fresh coffee then.

This was the day the newlyweds had dreamed about since first laying eyes on this sprawling property a few months back. They just never expected so many lifelong relationships to be destroyed beforehand. It was bound to happen at some point, they knew, they just hoped it wouldn't be until after the Mark of the Beast was implemented.

The Mulrooneys reached the front gate just as the founders of the *End Times Salvation Movement* pulled onto the lot of safe house number one.

Clayton Holmes drove a dark blue fifteen-passenger van—one of many owned by the *ETSM*. Travis Hartings was right behind his partner driving a twenty-two-foot delivery truck, full of much-needed supplies provided by President Jefferson Danforth.

Brian opened the entrance gate and waved them in.

The *ETSM* leaders drove onto the premises looking completely exhausted. They left Oak Ridge, Tennessee at midnight and drove straight through the night.

"Welcome to safe house number one!" Brian said.

Barely a week had passed since they last saw each other at the wedding, but Brian was noticeably thinner by at least ten pounds. And the bags under his eyes were humongous.

Yet, there was a tinge of excitement in his voice. Holmes was certain it stemmed from what Charles Calloway had told him about his mother's recent conversion and the dreams she'd had.

"Honored to be here," Holmes said, on behalf of himself and his partner.

"Where's Charles?" Jacquelyn asked.

"Fell a little behind on U.S. 202. He'll be here shortly." Clayton Holmes yawned into a fisted hand. Just as the words came out of his mouth, they heard tires rolling on stones on the other side of the maroon wooden fence.

Charles Calloway pulled onto the lot with the U-Haul truck full of the Mulrooneys' things.

Behind him was another vehicle that Brian instantly recognized. "Is that Tom Dunleavey's car?"

Holmes nodded yes, signaling for his colleagues to enter through the maroon gate.

Brian's shock knew no bounds. "Why's he here?"

Travis Hartings smiled. "Consider him resident number four!"

Brian and Jacquelyn exchanged confused glances. Jacquelyn said, "Don't you mean number three? There's only two of us here."

Hartings chuckled to himself, "Close the gate first."

Brian did as he was instructed, then joined everyone by the vehicles. The Mulrooneys nearly jumped out of their skin when Tamika Moseley suddenly popped up from the front passenger seat of the U-Haul truck.

"Surprise!" Tamika shouted.

"What are *you* doing here?" Brian was overjoyed and became teary-eyed.

Tamika climbed out of the truck. "Mind if I call this place home, too?"

"Are you serious?" Jacquelyn shot a curious look at Charles.

Calloway nodded yes.

Brian couldn't erase the smile on his face. "Did you bring Cocoa?"

Tamika nodded yes. "He's sleeping in the truck." Her eyes surveyed her new surroundings. It looked exactly like she saw it in her dreams. To see it materialize before her very eyes was simply amazing. She knew it was God.

"Can I call it home, too?" Tom Dunleavey asked. He was having similar thoughts as Tamika.

"Of course, brother Tom." It took all Brian's strength to not start sobbing tears of joy. "This is answered prayer! Welcome to Chadds Ford! So nice having you both here. Cocoa too!"

Jacquelyn eyeballed Charles Calloway, "Where did you and Tamika end up going the day of our wedding?"

Charles shifted his gaze to Travis Hartings. Jacquelyn's eyes followed his. Hartings nodded for Charles to proceed. "We were taken to an *ETSM* cabin in Tennessee."

"Is that where you've been all this time?"

Calloway nodded yes. "After the U-Haul truck was loaded at your house, brother Tom drove it to Tennessee."

Tom Dunleavey said, "That's where Tamika and I officially became *ETSM* members. I was then invited to join Pastor Simonton wherever he ends up purchasing property. But given my situation I wanted to be as far away from the state of Michigan as possible. I pleaded with Travis and Clayton to send me wherever the two of you were." He looked at the two *ETSM* leaders, "Thanks for honoring my wishes, brothers."

Travis Hartings said, "In the end, you were right, Tom. This is a better fit for you. Tamika too. Braxton keeps insisting we should keep close friends together to limit communication from one safe house to another.

"Besides, from what I'm told, Brian and Jacquelyn need all the help they can get. After the week the four of you had, now more than ever, you need each other."

"Amen to that!" Mulrooney practically shouted.

"Just hope some of the members from my former church will be invited to come here too. Many are having dreams and have already been cleared to join the *ETSM*."

Clayton Holmes nodded, "One day at a time, brother Tom."

Travis Hartings said, "One of our staff doctors, Doctor Meera Singh, examined Tamika's leg. She was given an antibiotic injection for her leg and a dextrose IV to provide nutrition to her frail body."

Tamika smiled, "Doc said my leg's gonna be fine. She got to it just in time. Had I waited any longer, I could be in serious trouble."

"Thank you, Lord, for the medical provision," Brian said.

Travis Hartings looked out in the distance. "You were right, Brian. It sure is beautiful here."

Tom Dunleavey said, "Indeed it is..."

Everyone looked tired after the long drive; yet the joyous expressions on their faces greatly comforted the newlyweds.

After the many disparaging remarks made about them on social media, being surrounded by friendly faces was just what Brian and Jacquelyn needed.

Especially Jacquelyn. For the first time since her wedding, she was able to smile. Her eyes smiled with her. A wave of relief washed over her. "Why don't you park the vehicles at the back of the property where we're staying?"

Travis Hartings said, "Speaking of vehicles, Jacquelyn, consider them gifts from TH Corporation. But with one stipulation..."

"What's that?"

"That you trade your personal vehicles for them. They'll be sold through TH Corporation."

"No problem. Jacquelyn and I have already concluded that we need to get rid of them. Especially my car."

"That would be correct, Brian. You and Tamika both need to stay off the road at all costs."

"Can I at least drive one of the vehicles back to the house?"

Hartings laughed. "Sure. Take the truck I drove. After the long drive, I feel like walking."

Once the four vehicles were parked at the rear of the property, Clayton Holmes said to Brian, "Wait till you see what's in the truck, compliments of President Danforth."

"What's inside?"

"Everything you'll need to get started—food, water, medical supplies, mainframe computers, massive refrigeration units for food supplies, medicines, secure state-of-the-art communication centers, backup generators, and Level A hazmat suits. And this is only the first shipment. More stuff will be coming soon."

Jacquelyn scratched her head. "Level A hazmat suits?"

"Basically, they provide total encapsulation against airborne chemicals, vapors, gases, and other harmful particles in the air. In short: they offer the highest level of protection in hazmat suits.

"All come with self-contained breathing apparatuses, steel-tipped boots, chemical-resistant gloves and radios and earpiece speakers for two-way communication during an attack."

Jacquelyn shivered at the thought. "Hope we never have to use them." "You and me both!" Travis said. "Until you have a dedicated underground storage place for everything, we can store them in the basement of your house."

"We're one step ahead of you. We've already covered the cement floor with wooden crates we found in the rat-infested cafeteria."

"Good thinking, Brian."

Jacquelyn said, "Since our house is the only one clean at the moment, we can all sleep there. Would you like breakfast now?"

"I'll eat later. For now, I'd like to see what we just purchased."

"By all means, Clayton," Brian said.

"Can I put Cocoa inside the house first? He's been cooped up all night."

"Of course, Tamika. Follow me." Jacquelyn opened the front door and Tamika placed Cocoa on the carpeted floor.

Rodent infestation or not, the grounds were breathtakingly beautiful! There were a few gasps and "wows", but after the wedding disaster, everyone did their best to keep their enthusiasm in check, mostly out of respect for the newlyweds.

Seeing Brian and Jacquelyn holding hands comforted Tamika Moseley greatly. She still blamed herself for everything that happened last week. Seeing them looking so in love despite it all took some of the guilt away. Apparently, they'd found the strength to rise above their wedding day fiasco by keeping busy day and night. But by looking in their eyes, she could still see the pain and trauma there.

After touring the place, they sat on benches inside the church pavilion. Travis Hartings said, "Obviously building a new fence must come first."

Before Brian could agree, Hartings went on, "Once the robotic bricklaying machine arrives, we'll build a twenty-foot high wall around the entire perimeter, with motion detectors and cameras every ten feet or so. Once it's built, the old fence can come down."

Brian's face lit up. "We're getting a robotic bricklaying machine?"

Clayton Holmes nodded yes. "President Danforth set aside dozens of them for our exclusive use. Would take forever to build a wall without it. But you'll only have it for one month. After that, it'll be shipped to another *ETSM* location."

"The President's also authorized a tunnel boring machine to be delivered with the robotic bricklaying machine. He's also sending bulldozers, dump trucks, cranes, generators, cement trucks, backhoes—basically everything we'll need for new construction to begin. He's even sending a tanker full of fuel. Soon this place will look entirely different..."

"I'm eager to get started."

Clayton Holmes said, "That's the spirit, Brian! If all goes well, they'll be here by mid-August. Then we can begin at once reconstructing this place. President Danforth's been a real godsend. Don't know what we'd do without him."

"As much as we'd love to stay and help you guys," Travis Hartings said, "we need to get back to the cabin. We received good news while en route."

"What news?"

Hartings smiled. "The seven locations down south are now in our possession. And hundreds of other safe houses will be up and running in the U.S. in the coming weeks.

"Worldwide, we expect to have thousands under our umbrella by the end of September. Lord willing. If there's one good thing Romanero has done, he sure has lit a fire underneath us all!"

Jacquelyn looked perplexed. She had this "How-in-the-world-will-we-operate-that-kind-of-equipment-on-our-own?" look on her face. As it was, they were barely able to clean a few cottages without screaming.

Travis cracked up. "Don't worry, Jacquelyn, we plan on coming back once the big equipment arrives. And we won't be coming alone, either."

"Oh?"

"Lord willing, hundreds will live here in the coming weeks. But for now, twelve have been chosen to join us immediately, six men and six women. They've been given until the end of the month to get their affairs in order and report here the first week of August."

Brian and Jacquelyn smiled at each other. More good news...

"Among them will be Meera Singh, the doctor who treated Tamika. She'll also serve as resident dentist. You'll also have a nurse, two IT technicians, an electrical engineer, an architect, and four construction workers with lots of experience with tunnel boring and robotic bricklaying machines," Travis said, winking at Jacquelyn.

"The other two will be temporary residents." Hartings looked at Brian. "Remember Donald Johnson and Manuel Jiminez?"

"Yes, of course."

"They'll stay with you a few months until Donald returns to the Philippines, and Manuel travels to Mexico. Being here will be a good education for them. For all of you, in fact."

"We're so grateful," Brian Mulrooney said.

"Once the big equipment arrives the architects, engineers, and construction workers will begin at once building a solid wall around the perimeter with the robotic bricklaying machine."

Hartings paused. "The noise could bring unwanted attention our way. But we're left with no other choice. It needs to be done. And quickly. Soon as the wall's built, the next project will be the church pavilion. The canvas walls must go.

"Doctor Kim will accompany us next trip to help us revamp the inside with the latest secure technology. It's time for the church pavilion to be brought into the twenty-first century."

Brian and Jacquelyn both nodded agreement.

"Before we can start digging underground, blueprints will need to be analyzed by our surveyors. Once we know where we can or cannot dig, we'll build three underground locations. One will be for storage. One will become an underground operating room. The largest will be used as a fallout shelter.

"All three will be connected by corridors. After the first underground shelter's been constructed, the robotic bricklaying machine will be brought underground to lay bricks, as the tunnel boring machine begins working on the second underground location.

"While all that's going on, the rest of us will restructure cottages to sleep as many Tribulation Saints as we can. President Danforth is sending copper, so each wall and ceiling can be hermetically sealed with additional thick inner walls, to hopefully prevent the enemy from honing-in on us with their high-tech surveillance devices.

"Naturally, all cottages will be repainted to blend in more with the land. We'll also tackle the rodent problem in the cafeteria and drain the green slimy water from the pool, so we can start collecting rainwater from there.

"Finally, the daycare center and general store will be converted to makeshift clinics with small operating rooms until they're eventually moved underground. All drugs and medicines will be stored under lock and key. Only Doctor Singh will have access to that key for now."

"Understood."

Tom Dunleavey said, "I'm exhausted just thinking about it."

Tamika Moseley scratched her head, "I heard that!"

"It's not going to be easy, y'all, but what choice do we have?"

Brian stretched his hands above his head, "I think we're up to the challenge, Travis."

"Very good. After we eat breakfast, we'll unload the truck and store everything in the basement. Then we can unload the U-Haul. Best to make full use of the many helping hands while we're still here, right?"

Jacquelyn Mulrooney nodded yes.

"After we leave, your first task should be to clean a handful of cottages so new residents and helpers will have clean places to stay once they arrive. Make sure they're spread out, so we'll have eyes and ears all throughout the property."

"Yes, sir," Brian said. "Good thinking!"

Jacquelyn marveled at how Travis Hartings took control of the situation as if he'd been through it many times already. It comforted the new bride immeasurably.

For the first time since her wedding day fiasco, Jacquelyn Mulrooney felt more bolstered, more galvanized, more connected. And comforted, seeing this Christian community slowly but surely coming together.

It no longer felt like two against the world. Relief washed over her. Brian too. Both were honored to be entrusted with such an awesome responsibility of managing the very first *ETSM* safe house. It was a responsibility they took very seriously and would execute to the best of their ability.

Despite that they were still reeling, they were convinced beyond a shadow of a doubt that moving to Pennsylvania as husband and wife was where God wanted them to be. Having two good friends as their first two residents made it even better.

Jacquelyn was struck with a thought. Of the four of them, two had warrants out for their arrest and one was on the run from the Catholic church. She chuckled to herself.

Brian heard it. "What's so funny?"

"Oh, nothing." Jacquelyn kissed her husband on the cheek.

39

THE FOLLOWING WEEK

BRIAN MULROONEY AND TOM Dunleavey were on a cottage rooftop cleaning gutters and measuring the roof for the copper insulation when Brian's phone rang.

"Hello?"

Brian heard sobbing. "I need to get out of here..."

Brian wiped sweat from his brow with the back of his hand, "What happened, Ma?"

In between sniffles, Sarah said, "Your father went to see Craig Rubin today at Mitzi's."

Brian's heart sank. He steadied himself on the top rungs of the ladder, lowered himself to the ground, and started pacing back and forth. "And?"

"When your father told him I was a Christian, Craig urged him not to let me follow in your footsteps. Needless to say, he never wants to see you again."

"Yeah, I know. He sent a text message on my wedding night, informing me there was a warrant for my arrest and many other not-so-pleasant things."

"Your father also spends an awful amount of time talking to Renate's sister, Megan, and her friend, Rachel Stein. He finally got them to stop posting bad things about you online, but only after he convinced them it was having a negative impact on him as well.

"Wouldn't you love to be a fly on the wall for their conversations?" Sarah said sarcastically. "I think this is his revenge on you for destroying the Mulrooney name. Least that's what he thinks. He's even thinking of contacting your in-laws."

"Can't say I'm surprised. What ever happened to turning the other cheek?"

"He can't get over how you smuggled a known fugitive out of *his* city without ever thinking of the consequences it might bring on the family. It was a big blow to him."

"Come on, Ma, Tamika was charged with a crime she didn't commit, and you know it."

"Yes, but that's not how your father sees it. He thinks you're insane. He's not the only one."

"If I thought she was guilty of robbing grave sites, there's no way I would have helped her. It's because of false accusations against her that I'm now on the run."

"I know, son. But it's not only that; it's many things. I think what has your father most upset is he can't go outside without neighbors asking questions about you.

"We've even had reporters and investigators come knocking on our door. And we occasionally see unmarked police cars parked up the street waiting for you to show up, so they can arrest you.

"Your father's never been so humiliated in all his life. He has difficulty looking anyone in the eye, especially people at church. All because of you. The very mention of your name enrages him to no end. I think he's mad at me for not hating you, too.

"Of course, this gave Chelsea another excuse to never leave the house, let alone her bedroom. Only I don't think she's chatting much these days. Mostly out of humiliation. It's like she's totally cut herself off from the outside world to avoid defending you. I fear for her..."

"Anyway, when your father came back from breakfast, he marched upstairs without saying a word to me or Chelsea. A moment later he came back down with the Bible you gave me. He glared at me with the most hateful eyes I've ever seen, like I was a traitor or something, then proceeded to shred it apart right in front of us.

"He scattered it all over the living room carpet like confetti. He then did the same with the journal I kept with thoughts on what I was reading in it, saying he won't let me turn out like you."

Brian shook his head. "Sorry for causing you so much trouble."

Sarah started crying again, "I can't take it anymore..."

"Is Dad home now?"

"Yes. He's downstairs. I'm in my bedroom closet. It's become my prayer room. I pray day and night that God would change his heart. But he only gets worse..."

Brian closed his eyes and shook his head. "I know it's hard, Ma, Lord knows I do. The great separation has begun. This is spiritual warfare at the highest levels. Don't expect things to get better. All we can do is keep praying."

"It's like he's demon possessed or something. He must be to destroy the Word of God without a shred of remorse. And for what? Reading it without church supervision? How else could I learn what it teaches if I don't read it? In all my years as a Catholic, it's not like anyone's ever offered to read it to me. Had I not taken it in my own hands, I'd still be lost."

Sarah shook her head. "Your father took great pleasure belittling me in front of your sister. I think Chelsea enjoyed it, too. The way she looked at me; it's like she's mentally distancing herself from me like she already did with you."

"Can't say I blame her, given that she's spiritually blinded to the Truth."

"Part of me wishes I was too."

"Don't say that, Ma. You know you don't mean it. Satan's doing all he can to destroy families. It's happening to millions of other families as well. Never forget what awaits us on the other side. Revelation twenty-one, four says God will wipe away every tear from our eyes, and death shall be no more, neither shall there be mourning, nor crying, nor pain anymore, for the former things have passed away. Comfort yourself with these words, Ma. Cling to them. Take them literally."

"I know, honey, but it's just so hard." Tears welled up in Sarah's eyes, "All we do is argue day and night. Your father's temper frightens me to no end. I'm supposed to be his wife, the one he promised to protect in good times and bad. It's like we don't know each other anymore."

"How soon would you like to leave New York?"

"Today, if possible."

Brian gulped hard, then looked at Jacquelyn. "Not possible, Ma. Are you safe there?" This was a question he would have never asked his mother before the Rapture. It would have never crossed his mind! "If not, I'll find a place for you to stay until a decision's been made on your behalf."

"If you're asking if I think your father will hurt me physically, I don't believe so."

"Okay, good."

There was more sniffling. "How long must I wait?"

"At least a few weeks. The good news is you've already been cleared because of the dreams you've had. The only red flag is Dad."

"In what way?"

"Do you really need to ask? You know if you leave him, he'll search the ends of the Earth looking for you. What if you have a change of heart and end up going back to Dad, and he demands to know our location?"

Sarah took a moment to blow her nose with a tissue. "That's not what I saw in my dream. We were clearly separated. The thought of no longer being with your father is enough to stop my heart from beating in my chest. But that's what I kept seeing in my dream. There was no reconciliation..." She started weeping again.

Brian wiped tears from his own eyes. This was so hard. Now that his mother was a believer, he knew it would happen at some point. He wanted to reach through the phone and hug her. He knew this wasn't his fault, but it sure felt like it was.

"Are you sure you wanna do this?" When Sarah sighed, Brian pressed on. "I know everything inside you wants to preserve the family, but it may be impossible at this point."

"I don't want to leave your father, Brian, but I know I have to..."

Brian grimaced. "I'll make some phone calls and get back to you. For now, I need you to hang in there for me, okay Ma?"

"I'm trying my best..."

"Once you come here, you'll have a good support system. For now, you must find the inner strength to carry on."

"It's just so hard."

"It's not easy for me either, Ma. I'm going through it too. We all are. Renate's suicide has really forced me to think about the afterlife. I can't tell you how much it torments me knowing she's suffering now without hope. From a spiritual standpoint, though she was quite shallow in life, that can no longer be said of her."

"What do you mean, Brian?"

"Renate now knows more about the afterlife than even the most knowledgeable Bible scholars on the planet. She also knows she's forever doomed. You know how much I loved her, Ma. Even though I still mourn for her, whenever I rise above my emotions enough to big picture it, I always come to the same conclusion."

"Yeah? What's that?"

"That I'd rather be in Heaven without Renate than in hell with her. Now that you're a Christian, you need to understand that as much as you love Dad, you'd much rather be in Heaven without him than in hell with him, if that becomes Dad's final destination."

Sarah started crying again.

Brian sighed. "Hopefully it won't come to that. When I think of Dad or Chelsea possibly ending up in hell, I have trouble catching my breath. But in the final analysis, we're all responsible for the choices we make. I've finally come to grips with the fact that Renate's death wasn't my fault. Jacquelyn's either.

"My decision to leave her may have triggered it, but the choice to go through with it was entirely hers to make. The same is true with you and Dad. His decisions have triggered yours, not the other way around. You're not doing this to hurt him. Again, it's spiritual warfare at the highest levels."

There was a moment of silence. Sarah's sniffles grew more faint.

Brian went on, "All decisions from here on out will be difficult. You must cling to the promise that you're on the Good side of eternity. Nothing can be more glorious than waiting for our blessed hope, the appearing of the glory of our great God and Savior, Jesus Christ."

"Amen," Sarah said, halfheartedly. "Just wish I knew where the two of you were living."

"I believe you'll know soon enough, Ma..." Brian replied. "Until then, keep fighting the Good Fight. Pray for me as I pray for you. God is with us. I love you."

"Love you too, son." The call ended. "Be strong!" Sarah told herself. It didn't work. She burst out in tears again...

A few moments after Brian sent a text message to Travis Hartings explaining everything, he replied: *I've advised Braxton of the situation. Lots going on here with the properties. Might not be able to rescue her until we return to Pennsylvania in a few weeks. If anything changes, I'll let you know.*

Brian understood. *Just hope my mother does!* Brian wasn't the slightest bit concerned about his mother knowing his whereabouts. She could be trusted with such information. But if his father knew, Brian believed he would do whatever it took to destroy what they were building in Chadds Ford, claiming to be helping his son, not hurting him.

And that went double for Jacquelyn's parents.

Tom Dunleavey glanced down from the rooftop and saw Brian looking ever so distraught. He took his time climbing down the ladder to check on his brother in Christ.

Jacquelyn and Tamika were cleaning inside the cottage. They heard Brian talking on the phone earlier. Whoever was on the other end really rocked Brian's world.

The two women stopped what they were doing and joined Brian and Tom outside.

"Who was that, honey?" Jacquelyn kissed her husband's right cheek.

"My mother..."

"Is she okay?"

"Not exactly." Brian took a moment to fill them in on what had transpired earlier between his parents.

Even dirty and sweaty, the four *ETSM* members joined hands and prayed for Dick and Sarah Mulrooney...

40

FIRST WEEK OF AUGUST

JACQUELYN MULROONEY WOKE AT 4:15 a.m., and climbed out of bed, careful not to wake her husband.

But the alarm on her cell phone woke him too. "Coffee, dear?"

"Please." Jacquelyn kissed her husband on the lips. "I'll join you downstairs after I shower."

This was a big day for safe house number one. Not only would the number of residents increase by a factor of three, Donald Johnson and Manuel Jiminez would also temporarily reside in Chadds Ford, Pennsylvania, bringing the number of residents to eighteen.

While the coffee brewed, Brian walked out onto the front porch. The fresh morning air felt good on his face.

Except for the dim lights inside the house and a few faint lights in the distance, it was pitch dark. He looked forward to seeing the cottages they'd worked so hard cleaning the last three weeks being occupied by others.

As instructed, the 30 they'd cleaned were spread about the sprawling property, giving them eyes and ears in the front of the property and back.

A year ago, none of this would have seemed fathomable. Had it not been for the Rapture, Brian Mulrooney wouldn't be in the Keystone State now. None of them would, in fact.

This time last year, Mulrooney was proud to call Ann Arbor, Michigan his home. Things were really looking up for him. He had a stable job he loved and a girlfriend he planned on marrying someday.

Now Renate was dead, and he was married to another woman living in a safe house in another state, with a warrant out for his arrest. *Go figure.*

Nevertheless, despite all that, Brian was comforted knowing he was exactly where God wanted him to be. Being a child of the Most High God supernaturally placed him in the safest place in all the universe, even if it didn't always feel that way.

And this meant the Antichrist and his global forces could easily kill his body, but no one could touch his soul. Only God could.

For that, Brian Mulrooney was grateful, and totally committed to doing whatever it took to win as many souls to Christ as God would allow.

Brian received a secure text message from Travis Hartings: *Robotic bricklaying and tunnel boring machine will arrive before noon, along with various other construction vehicles. Time for the real work to begin. Expect long days and nights. Sleep will be more of a luxury than a requirement.*

Brian was replying to Travis when he was alerted on his phone that the last plane had just touched down. *Time to get a move on!* He refilled his coffee cup and walked the short distance to the garage. He placed two car magnets on the blue fifteen-passenger van advertising *Delaware Valley Budget Shuttle Service.*

Brian wanted to accompany his wife to Philadelphia International Airport, if only to help her load the luggage into the van, but it was too big of a risk. And with Tom Dunleavey soon-to-be leaving for Baltimore, to pick up the *ETSM* brass at BWI Airport, he didn't want Tamika to be left alone on the property.

Upon landing, all were instructed to collect their luggage and proceed to the arrivals section at Gate C. Once there, they were encouraged to engage in mild conversation, as strangers routinely did while waiting for ground transportation to shuttle them to area hotels and rental car agencies.

In this case, it was *Delaware Valley Budget Shuttle Service.*

With the magnets carefully placed on both sides of the vehicle, Jacquelyn climbed inside the van and started the engine.

Brian kissed his wife on the lips, "Be careful, my love..."

"I will. Gotta go. Keep praying..." Jacquelyn drove off to get the first batch of residents. The second group would arrive at Philly International between the hours of nine and ten a.m.

As the world waited expectantly with bated breath for the first child to be born, not surprisingly, most radio and TV talk shows talked exclusively about children populating Planet Earth again. It would be any day now.

With so many pregnant teenagers out there, experts spoke on a myriad of topics for the young expectant mothers to glean, from how to properly breastfeed a child, to putting mittens on a child's hands to not shaking infants or letting them get too close to pets and other animals.

On and on they went.

Prior to the Rapture, most viewers and listeners would have rolled their eyes and tuned them out. But after nine months without children, and with millions of pregnant women out there, it was like food for the starved soul. Most listened with great interest.

Jacquelyn arrived at Philadelphia International Airport and spotted the first passenger load of folks she was there to get.

It wasn't difficult since everyone was exactly where they were told to go, wearing exactly what they were instructed to wear—even down to the two construction workers wearing retro Philadelphia Eagles knit caps. Jacquelyn pulled over and helped load their luggage into the back of the van. She even received tips from passengers as instructed. It needed to look authentic.

Once everyone was buckled in and introductions were made, Jacquelyn looked in her rear-view mirror, "Welcome to Pennsylvania!"

"Happy to be here," said Tony, a construction worker from Nevada.

Eyeballing Dr. Meera Singh, Jacquelyn said, "Thanks for examining Tamika. We were so worried about her."

"And for good reason. I never told Tamika but, the red line from the infection was slowly working its way up her leg to her heart. It could have led to systemic infection all throughout her body."

Jacquelyn's eyes widened. "Thank God you were able to get it in time, Doctor."

Dr. Singh smiled and nodded professionally. "Please call me, Meera."

Jacquelyn smiled back. Then, "Hope you're all well rested. The big equipment will arrive sometime before noon. Needless to say, we'll be busy from sun up to sun down. I can assure you none of us will ever battle boredom where we're going."

"Just anxious to get started," Tony said.

"One more thing, the cottages you'll occupy will be spread all throughout the property. This way, we'll have eyes and ears everywhere in case danger ever pays us a visit."

"Sounds like a good plan," Tony said again, as if assuming the role of foreman for the group.

Jacquelyn left at once for safe house number one. Upon reaching I-95 southbound, she sent a voice text message to her husband, informing that they'd be there in roughly thirty minutes.

Brian and Tamika already were waiting at the front gate when they arrived to welcome them home.

A few moments later, Tom Dunleavey returned from Baltimore with Clayton Holmes, Travis Hartings, Charles Calloway, Dr. Lee Kim, Donald Johnson and Manuel Jiminez.

Jacquelyn ate a quick breakfast and left to collect the second passenger load of new residents. She returned to safe house number one just as the heavy equipment had arrived.

Also, an *ETSM* crew arrived from Atlanta with more supplies, including another 22-foot truck full of bottled water, compliments of President Danforth.

"They're here!" Travis Hartings said to everyone gathered in the church pavilion.

Clayton Holmes rose from his seat, "Let's go, y'all!"

Everyone rushed to the front of the property to find all trucks idling quietly in the outside parking lot. Holmes and Hartings ordered everyone to stay put as they went out to meet the drivers.

For now, only they knew the two men driving the trucks carrying the robotic bricklaying machine and tunnel boring machine were secret service agents posing as truck drivers.

"Open both gates," Holmes yelled.

Brian Mulrooney did as he was instructed. It took a while, but the trucks made it through the entryway without incident.

After introductions were made, Clayton Holmes said, "Time to get busy, y'all! After you fill your bellies, we'll need all hands on deck!"

The only one excluded from this command was Braxton Rice.

When Jacquelyn returned from the airport with the second batch of new residents, Rice removed the airport shuttle magnets from the van, replaced them with two different magnetic stickers, and left for New York City...

41

AT 2:30 P.M. BRAXTON Rice arrived at the Mulrooney residence in Manhattan. With far less vehicles on the road, he made the 120-mile trip in excellent time, an hour and a half to be exact.

The last thing Rice was concerned about was getting a speeding ticket. In a world full of turmoil, and with roadways far less crowded with vehicles, authorities had all but stopped handing out speeding citations. Their efforts were needed elsewhere.

Prior to last November, Rice hated driving anywhere near the *Big Apple*. Traffic was always gridlocked. A trip like this could easily take four hours or more. It was a breeze this time.

Rice climbed out of his vehicle and knocked on the front door. Brian assured him that his mother would be the only one to open the door. His father was at work and Chelsea was probably locked in her room chatting with friends online or sleeping.

Brian also warned Braxton to expect nosy neighbors keeping a steady eye on him. According to his mother, whenever someone came or went, neighbors were always watching. Brian also told him to be on the lookout for unmarked police cars. Last thing they needed was for someone to follow them back to Chadds Ford.

Out of the corner of his eye, Rice spotted someone peeking through a slit in the window curtain two doors down from the Mulrooneys. His eyes volleyed back when Sarah Mulrooney opened the door.

"Yes?" Sarah's eyes were joyless and filled with great pain.

"Hi, Misses Mulrooney! My name's William Fuller," Braxton Rice said, using the name he used when meeting potential *ETSM* members for the first time. He made sure to say it loud enough for the neighbors to hear. He was sure some were listening. "I'm here to drop off boxes. How many will you be needing?"

"Not sure. Five, perhaps?"

"Yes ma'am. Be right back with them."

The head of security for the *End Times Salvation Movement* opened the rear door of the blue passenger van double-parked in front of the Mulrooney residence and retrieved the boxes.

Both sides of the van donned magnetic stickers advertising:

SPREAD THE LOVE:
FEEDING AND CLOTHING
THE BIG APPLE SINCE 1973
HELP THOSE WHO NEED IT MOST!
PLEASE DONATE TODAY!

"Would you like me to carry them inside for you?"

"Okay," Sarah said softly, somberly.

They went inside. Mindful that Chelsea was also at home, Rice spoke in a whisper, "Instructions have been taped onto one of the boxes including where we'll meet after I collect your things."

"Okay," Sarah said, with absolutely no emotion. She found it impossible to maintain steady eye contact with the man. "What should I pack?"

"Things you'll need. Clothing, mostly. You already know where you're going. The climate's pretty much the same as here."

Sarah looked down at her feet. "Okay..."

"I know this is hard for you, Misses Mulrooney. You've been through a lot. But we're all suffering. It is what it is."

Sarah started weeping.

Realizing he was being insensitive, Rice placed a hand on her right shoulder and gazed at her steadily, "I wish there was something I could say to take away the pain, ma'am, but there are no words except that, as Christ followers, we win in the end."

Sarah's sobbing increased.

"You must find a way to rest in this eternal Truth, Sarah. Soon we'll be comforted in every sense of the word. The future's so bright. We just need to hang in there a little longer."

"Thanks, Braxton. I really needed to hear that."

Me too! Rice found himself getting choked up. The poor woman was so fragile. He wished there was more he could do for her. He cleared his throat and refocused, "When I come back tomorrow to collect the boxes, you'll have roughly an hour to get your affairs in order. But you must be at the pick-up location on time."

"And then?"

"You'll begin life anew."

Sarah's lips started trembling. She was on the verge of a nervous breakdown.

Braxton Rice sighed, "Are you sure you wanna do this?"

Sarah looked down at the floor, "I don't want to, I have to."

"Just checking. I should go now. Last thing you need is nosy neighbors asking your husband questions about me. If I were you, I'd get packing while he's still at work. Oh, and one more thing: don't be surprised when you see another woman in the van tomorrow. She'll be joining us for a few days before going to another safe house down south."

"Okay."

"It's showtime again. Time to play it up for your neighbors."

They went back outside.

"Thanks again for donating to the less fortunate, ma'am..." Rice smiled brightly, something that didn't come easy to him. As *ETSM* top security man, he was forced into total seriousness most of the time.

"You're welcome, Mister Fuller." Sarah looked around to see who was eavesdropping on them.

"Be back tomorrow to collect them. I should be in the neighborhood at around noon. Will that work for you?"

Sarah paused to take in her surroundings. Once she left, chances were good she may never see this street or the house she'd lived in for 35 years ever again. It was overwhelming. She nodded yes. "That'll be fine."

"Okay, then, see you tomorrow." The sadness on Sarah's face was something Braxton Rice had long since grown used to in this position. It wasn't easy leaving loved ones behind for good. This was especially true with married couples.

Sarah Mulrooney nodded. Missing was the joy most who donated to various good causes projected on their faces. Rice feared she was having second thoughts. This concerned him. But he also understood her situation.

Braxton Rice climbed back in the van and drove off. He spoke into his Satphone, "Call Brian Mulrooney!"

Brian was helping pour cement into the mixer when his phone rang. He removed his face mask. "Hey Braxton, how'd it go?"

"Your mother has the boxes. I'll pick her up at noon tomorrow. Just hope she doesn't change her mind.

"Why do you say that?"

"What I saw in her eyes..."

"She'll be fine, Braxton. This will be her first time away from my father in thirty-five years. I'm sure she'll have her moments, but she'll never compromise the organization. Her conversion's as real as the dreams she had."

Rice wanted to say, "How can you be so sure? You nearly did!" Instead he said, "Tell Charles I'm en route to Mary Johnston's place to drop off boxes."

"You got it, Braxton. Thanks again."

"See you tomorrow." Rice programmed Mary Johnston's address into his GPS and left for her apartment. This next stop would be so much easier than the first one. Unlike Sarah Mulrooney, Mary Johnston couldn't wait to leave New York City. With her lease up at the end of the month, she'd already sold or donated most of her things away to co-workers.

Like all other *ETSM* members, her life had been reduced to just a few suitcases.

After dropping off the boxes, Braxton Rice checked into a hotel and powered down his phone. The only thing on the agenda for the rest of the day was rest. Exhausted as he was, if no one disturbed him, he could probably sleep for three straight days...

BRAXTON RICE, SARAH MULROONEY and Mary Johnston arrived in Chadds Ford, Pennsylvania early the next afternoon to a flurry of activity.

As one of the two newest *ESTM* residents at safe house number one—thus increasing the number to 20—Mary Johnston, the now-former Waldorf-Astoria desk clerk was eager to take her belongings to her temporary cottage, then get busy helping her brothers and sisters in Christ any way that she could.

The adopted woman who'd searched all her life for a stable family environment, without ever finding it, suddenly had it in Pennsylvania. And it was an eternal family at that! Now about to meet her new family for the very first time, she felt so grateful to be part of something special.

The same couldn't be said about Sarah Mulrooney. She was totally glum-faced. She quietly sobbed the entire ride from New York to Pennsylvania, thinking about the twenty-page goodbye letter she left on the kitchen table for her husband before leaving the house for the last time.

She also left a five-page letter for Chelsea.

Sarah's heart was torn in so many pieces she was amazed it still worked at all. What devastated her most was knowing how devastated her husband would be when he came home from work in a couple of hours and read the letter.

Would he survive this? She dreaded the thought. She wondered if Chelsea already read hers...

Sarah Mulrooney no longer wanted to be alive. Her mind wasn't full of suicidal thoughts like it was after the disappearances, but the further the van traveled from the only home she knew as an adult, the more she prayed that God would take her out of this world.

Prior to the disappearances, a disagreement of religion in most circles was just that: a disagreement. Now it was all out war, with the casualties resulting in the separation of millions of families.

For Sarah Mulrooney, this was more difficult to deal with than even the earthquakes.

Brian silently gasped when he saw his mother. She looked even worse than the day he broke her heart in a New York City diner.

Seeing her in this extremely fragile condition, he struggled to put a brave face on. After introducing her to those who weren't busy doing something, Sarah asked to be excused so she could take a nap.

"Would you like a cottage of your own, Ma, or would you like to stay with us?"

"I don't care. I just need to be alone for a while."

Brian gazed deep in his mother's eyes. He didn't see much there. "Why don't you eat something first?"

"I don't feel much like eating. I just wanna lay down a while."

Brian grabbed his mother's belongings and she followed him inside the house and up to the bedroom closest to his and Jacquelyn's room. "Want me to wake you for dinner?"

"If I get hungry I'll let you know."

"I'll have the rest of your things brought inside so they don't get lost in the shuffle."

"Okay."

"I love you, Ma."

Sarah lowered her head, looking like the saddest person on the planet, "Love you too, Brian..."

At that, Sarah Mulrooney closed the door and Brian went back outside.

Braxton was right! Perhaps she really was having second thoughts. It pained Brian to see his mother like this. All he could do was cling to the fact that his mother had dreams. She explicitly told him going back home wasn't part of it.

Then again, even if Sarah Mulrooney wanted to go back to her husband, she wouldn't be able to. America was just days away from coming under attack.

No one at safe house number one knew it, but everyone would be stranded in Chadds Ford, Pennsylvania for quite some time...

42

FIVE DAYS LATER

ROUGHLY NINE MONTHS AFTER the Great Disappearing Act took place, there was much commotion in the coastal town of Chennai, India, a city situated on the lower southeast coast of the second most populated country on Earth.

Prior to the Rapture, Chennai was known by many as the "Detroit of India", for producing more than one-third of its country's automobiles. It was also one of India's largest cultural, economic and educational centers.

Listed by the Quality of Living survey as the safest and healthiest city in India, Chennai had become a huge foreign tourist destination long before people vanished, including all small children in the area.

Just outside the sprawling capital of the Indian State, Tamil Nadu, in a poor fishing village on Chennai Beach, lived Yogesh and Hana Patel. Hana was one of many women hoping to give birth this day.

With a huge international spotlight suddenly glaring down on the Patels, and at the insistence of Salvador Romanero, Hana was taken by limousine to Chennai's top-rated hospital days before her labor pains even started. Like all other expectant women, the *Miracle Maker* wanted her placed in the care of the very best doctors and nurses in the area.

After nine long turbulent months, the world longed for good news again, something everyone could rally around and celebrate. It was time to ignore all the craziness, if only for one day, and embrace life again, new life!

To sports fans it was the Super Bowl.

To movie fans it was the Oscars.

With thousands of women about to give birth, maternity wards were on complete lock down, worldwide, making expectant mothers some of the safest individuals on the planet.

Swarms of reporters circled the globe hoping to be the lucky journalist chosen to report the world's first human birth in just over nine months.

As an added incentive, Salvador Romanero announced that, along with all doctors and nurses responsible for bringing the first child into the world, the journalist and the cameraman reporting the story would also receive bonuses in the amount of $50,000 each.

With that motivation, reporters constantly pressured doctors and nurses to whom they were assigned, peppering them with questions: "Any progress since we last spoke?" "Has the cervix dilated any further?" "Is the patient still okay?"

And on and on they went.

Miriam Goldberg was the lead reporter for the Baby Patel story in Chennai. Goldberg was honored for having been chosen to report this feel-good story among all the turmoil in the world.

With her bank account constantly shrinking, the Middle Eastern journalist hoped against all hope that Salvadora Patel would be the first child born this day. The fifty-thousand-dollar bonus sure would come in handy.

Goldberg had reason to be hopeful. Of the hundreds of women now in labor rooms, only five were mere moments away from giving birth. Hana Patel was one of them. Along with four other women, her cervix was dilated 9.5 centimeters.

One woman was from Beijing, China—although her family had relocated to Tokyo, Japan, as bombs were falling just before the earthquakes leveled the city. Another was from Seattle, Washington. One was from São Paolo, Brazil, and another was from Nigeria, Africa.

Hospital spokespersons caring for the expectant mothers held press conferences of their own. They gushed with pride over being "blessed" to help bring forth new life.

In normal times, the birth of an Indian baby girl would go unnoticed by most. Especially in the case of Salvadora Patel.

Yogesh and Hana Patel were impoverished Indian peasants who mostly kept to themselves. They lived in a two-room shack not far from the Bay of Bengal. It was stacked side-by-side in a long row of shacks, with no space in between them. Most had no front doors, only door frames.

Like most of their neighbors, the Patels covered the entryway of the house with a curtain, allowing for a little privacy. They had no inside bathroom, limited running water and electricity that worked sporadically.

The roof was made out of sun-dried clay, then covered with brown palm branches. Many covered their roofs with large tarpaulins to protect from heavy rains.

It was a luxury the Patels could never afford.

Across the street from them, vendors sold freshly-caught fish, fruits and vegetables each morning in the most undesirable conditions. Some stacked fish on small tables that were nothing more than sawhorses topped with sheets of plywood. Many who sold fruits and vegetables used baskets and crates.

Those who couldn't afford baskets or tables laid blankets on the cement ground and placed their goods on top of it, as dogs, cats, cows and goats roamed the streets searching for scraps of food to eat.

Locals had long since grown used to the overpowering smell of fish and animal dung that always hung thick in the air. It was all they know. But visitors to this place often wore face masks to keep from gagging or even vomiting.

What looked reminiscent of days long gone to most was commonplace to the Patels. Excluding last November's global incident—when all young children in their village disappeared—little else had changed over the centuries.

Yogesh Patel worked as a fisherman six-days a week, 52 weeks a year. Hana hand-washed clothing for neighbors whenever she could find work.

Even surrounded by stark poverty living in a dilapidated shack, the Patels were just grateful to have a home. They thanked their many gods every day, knowing others had it so much worse than them.

Everything was about to change for them...

The first woman to give birth would receive $1,000,000 from the global community.

The second woman to give birth would receive $500,000.

The third would receive $250,000.

The next 97 women to give birth would receive $100,000 each.

Each gift would be awarded by an international monetary card, the first of its kind. Even after the contest ended, all women giving birth would receive free hospitalization and a lifetime supply of diapers, compliments of the Global Community.

The Patels were all but assured of winning at least $100,000. But being awarded $1,000,000 would be so much better, because it would leave them more to share with their extended family.

But Yogesh and Hana Patel were even more excited about being first-time parents than they were with winning the money.

Married the day before the disappearances, after what had happened, both were hesitant to bring a child into the world. But after a delegate from their country told the world it was a Christian thing, as lifelong Hindus, their minds were somewhat put at ease.

When Salvador Romanero confirmed he had it on the highest authority—whatever that meant—that children would repopulate the world again, even turning it into a contest of sorts, Yogesh and Hana did all they could to conceive, not knowing Hana was already a few days pregnant at that time.

Both rejoiced when it was later confirmed.

Nine months later the eyes of the world had settled upon them. It was almost too much to absorb.

This was a time to celebrate. Fireworks would once again light up the night sky after a nine-month absence. But not only in cities where children would be born. This was an earth-shattering event and, therefore, needed to be celebrated globally.

Fireworks crews in major cities all over the world had been busy preparing all week, knowing everything had to be ready to go on the day the first child was born.

After a few false alarms, it looked like today would be that day. The fireworks festivities would begin in New Zealand and slowly work itself around the globe, beginning at precisely 9 p.m. in each time zone.

To win a cash prize, the birth had to come naturally. If there was any sign of induced labor, that mother would be disqualified. In short, save for a medical emergency, the child had to enter the world when it was good and ready, not when doctors thought it was time.

To ensure overall authenticity, cameras were required in all delivery rooms to validate that each child came out naturally. Patient privacy was sacrificed at the altar of global curiosity.

The Patels weren't thrilled about having a webcam broadcasting the entire birthing process. This was a cherished moment that was supposed to be kept private between husband and wife. Now the whole world was seemingly watching, as if they were all in the delivery room with them.

The Patels could have opted out, but had they done so, they would have been disqualified from the contest.

In the end, it was all about the money...

When Salvador Romanero announced to the world a few months back that women would give birth again, online gambling sites all over the world quickly got involved. Initially, the only bets that could be wagered

261

were on the gender of the first child born, the country of that child's birth, what day, what time, and so on.

But when names started surfacing of the thousands of women nearing their third trimesters, most of the money wagered from that point forward was on who would be the first to give birth.

The odds for Hana Patel were 6:5. The same odds were given to the four other women who were now pushing and screaming then pushing again, hoping the baby would finally come out, as billions watched and were gripped with anticipation.

Many online sites had all five women on the same screen.

In the next few minutes, three boys would be born and two girls. The parents of two of the boys had already announced their sons would be named, "Salvador", to honor their great leader.

And the parents of the two girls had already announced their daughters would be named, "Salvadora", for the same reason.

But the parents of the child to be born in Africa refused to name their son, "Salvador." As lifelong Muslims, they would choose a Muslim name instead.

Thousands of other women were also relatively close to giving birth. Some were married. Most weren't.

Reporters were on standby at those hospitals, just in case.

But right now, the world was zeroed in on five women. Excitement levels were sky high, as everyone anticipated seeing a real, live baby being born again. It seemed like nine years had passed since children last inhabited the Earth, not nine months.

All speculation came to an end when Salvadora Patel was born at 7:32 a.m., India time. The world watched and rejoiced.

To hear a baby crying after a nine-month absence filled most with a great sense of pride. Even some of the world's most hardened criminals had tears in their eyes.

Miriam Goldberg silently rejoiced knowing she was $50,000 richer. She waited impatiently for Hana Patel to finish nursing baby Salvadora so the camera could be turned on and the long-awaited interview with the suddenly world-famous parents could begin.

Meanwhile, 97 seconds later, in São Paolo, Brazil, the world watched the second child being born.

The father of baby Salvador lit a cigar and, in Portuguese, said, "Boy, oh boy, ninety-seven seconds cost us five-hundred thousand dollars! Still we are thankful to Salvador Romanero for his generosity! The money will greatly help us! We proudly dedicate our son to you, your Highness!"

Up until now, Hana Patel had declined each interview request for fear of bad luck. Though nervous to the point of hyperventilation, having just received one-million dollars from Salvador Romanero, she felt obligated to agree to any and all requests for interviews.

With baby Salvadora now asleep in her mother's arms, the camera was turned on and Miriam Goldberg began, "Let me begin, Hana, by congratulating you on behalf of the entire Global News Network, on the arrival of your beautiful daughter, Salvadora."

"Thank you," came the reply, sheepishly. Her husband, Yogesh, sat on a chair next to her bed, wondering why the reporter didn't congratulate him too.

"How do you feel?" asked Miriam.

"I feel tired, but also blessed to be a first-time mother."

"I'm sure you are tired after twelve hours of labor. How did it feel to be the only woman on the planet with a newborn child for ninety-seven seconds?"

Hana Patel managed a weary smile, "Truthfully, I'm too exhausted to think about it. But I wish to congratulate all other mothers who gave birth today. Good luck to each of you."

"What do you plan to do with all that money?"

"My husband and I don't know what the future holds. We are simple people living simple lives. All we want is to raise our daughter to the best of our ability.

"The money will allow us to stay home with Salvadora, without always having to rush off to work. We also plan to share some of the proceeds with family and friends."

Goldberg had hoped for a much better reply. "Do you plan to move into a new neighborhood?"

Hana shot a glance at her husband, then nodded yes. "Before I went into labor, Yogesh and I were handed the keys to a new condominium not too far from here." Hana managed another smile. "It was given to us as a gift from a local businessman."

"Can't say I'm surprised seeing all these gifts in your room. Baby Salvadora sure has lots and lots of global aunts and uncles."

"Yogesh and I are overwhelmed by the kindness of so many people. Even corporations have given us new vehicles to drive, laptop computers, baby furniture for Salvadora and lots of clothing."

Miriam Goldberg beamed, "I'm told nearly a million cards have been mailed here to the hospital, not to mention the countless gifts. Anything you'd like to say to your adoring public for their overwhelming generosity?"

"Yes. Yogesh and I are grateful to all of you for your loving kindness. Now that we have new laptops, we plan to email each of you personally after we've had a little time to adjust to being first time parents."

Goldberg said, "Once you're on social media, expect millions of followers practically overnight."

The thought alone frightened the new mother. "It will take time for everything to settle in our minds. But for now, please know that Yogesh and I thank you all from the bottom of our hearts."

Miriam Goldberg smiled brightly again, "If anything, we should be thanking you, Hana, for being the first woman brave enough to bring a child back into the world. On behalf of everyone at GNN, congratulations again to you and your husband on the birth of your child."

At that, the camera zoomed in on Salvadora Patel, who was still sound asleep in her mother's arms. A few seconds later, the camera panned back to Miriam: "Well, that's all for now. From Chennai, India, this is Miriam Goldberg reporting. Back to you, Farouq," she said to the anchor back in London.

"What an awesome day!" Miriam Goldberg exclaimed to herself. Like the rest of humanity, the veteran reporter rejoiced over the birth of Salvadora Patel. But on top of that, she was fifty-grand richer... *Yes!*

ETSM MEMBERS AT SAFE house number one watched Salvadora Patel being born on a projector screen inside the pavilion. Like the rest of the world, they rejoiced hearing a baby crying again. They were equally frightened.

Unless these newborns somehow survived the coming mayhem and were still alive when Jesus came back to rule Planet Earth, they would never experience true security on any level.

Each day would be one horrific nightmare after the next...

After the second child was born in Brazil, Brian Mulrooney said, "Let's pray for these children."

While praying, Mulrooney felt the Holy Spirit prompting him to contact Yogesh and Hana Patel.

I will do as you say, Lord...

43

THE LAST TIME THE world came together like this was for the global vigil. It was a somber gathering meant to honor the billions of citizens who'd died or were among the disappearances, including all small children.

Much like now, Salvador Romanero was the one responsible for making that vigil happen. It was the first vital step he took to becoming the indisputable leader of the world.

Since that time the young Spaniard had towered high above the landscape of humanity with the greatest of ease. His face was suddenly the most recognized on Planet Earth.

Appearing on live television, this was the first time the *Miracle Maker* had tears in his eyes. They were tears of joy!

Sitting in a leather chair, he wore a button-down sweater trying to look grandfatherly. But at 30 years of age it was a difficult feat, especially since he looked like he was still in his mid-20's.

Ambiguous smile playing on his lips, Romanero began, "What a glorious day this is for all of humanity! My joy is such that I feel like bursting wide open seeing little ones among us again! At last count, fifty-seven births have been recorded.

"With so many women now having contractions, I'm told that by week's end, more than three-thousand newborns will be among us. With millions of women now entering their third trimesters, that number will increase exponentially in the coming weeks."

Romanero glanced back at the beautiful images on the wall behind him of every child born thus far. "I've had the privilege of speaking with a dozen or so new mothers on the phone. I'm happy to report all mothers and children are in perfect health and are receiving the very best of care.

"These little ones represent not only a very bright future for us all, but also the first stop-gap to the constantly dwindling global population. It won't be long before newborns are seen in every city, town and village on the planet. How amazing is that? The very thought fills me with the deepest sense of pride! I'm eager to hold these precious children in my arms someday.

"For those of you who aren't among the first one-hundred women to give birth, do not lose heart! Much like the little ones already among us, I will rejoice over your child as if he or she was the only one on the planet. Romanero smiled brightly, showing two rows of perfect white teeth. "I must say the nearly two-million dollars already awarded to new mothers was the best money spent since the disappearances. I'm told a handful of women in maternity rooms are expecting twins in the coming days.

"I'm not sure if they will be among the first one-hundred to be born or not, but even if not, I wish to announce the first mother giving birth to twins will receive two hundred and fifty thousand dollars on top of any other cash prizes she may qualify for.

"While I'm not aware of anyone expecting triplets at this time, when that day comes, the first woman giving birth to triplets will receive five hundred thousand dollars. The first woman to give birth to quadruplets will receive one million dollars. And so on and so forth. Just hope I don't run out of money in the process," Romanero said, with a chuckle.

"In all seriousness, when I promised that children would inhabit the planet again, I meant it! Never again will Mother's Day be a day of somber reflection like it was this year! In fact, not only will Mother's Day be celebrated to the fullest next year, I hereby announce this day will be officially recognized as 'Universal Children's Day!'

"To commemorate this most precious time, I wish to declare a week-long celebration honoring all new life. Fireworks will light up the skies for the next seven nights, honoring these precious first fruits, so to speak.

"It promises to be a celebration of a lifetime, one that won't be forgotten anytime soon! For those of you who will be attending, eat, drink and be merry to your heart's content as you enjoy the fireworks, all compliments of the global community!"

"This will be the first of three new international days of celebration. Once the first one-hundred new mothers have had time to recuperate, we will assemble at a location to be determined later for yet another celebration. What better time than this upcoming November, when we observe one full year since the disappearances?

"This second new international holiday will be called, 'The Day of New Beginnings.' Celebrating new life on what for so many will be a day of solemn remembrance, will be like a ray of bright sunshine piercing through the darkness.

"By then, we should have more than a million newborns among us. These precious little ones represent a new beginning for all global citizens! It's time to stop looking back at the past and focus solely on the future."

Salvador Romanero gazed into the camera. His eyes were glowing, "The third international day of celebration will be my new birthday! From this point forward, February second will no longer be my calendar birthday. It will now be celebrated on December twenty-fifth! In short: from now on Christmas will be known as 'Salvador Romanero Day.' But more on that another time."

"For now, let's keep the focus on the many soon-to-be venerated women for making us all aunts and uncles again! Future generations will celebrate you all as heroines for humanity.

"Because of you, fireworks will once again light up the skies beginning in New Zealand, at nine p.m., and slowly work its way around the planet. Wherever you are, enjoy the festivities. May you all be blessed in my name..."

Just like that, New Zealanders filled the streets of their country eager to see fireworks again. But mostly, they were grateful to be the first country to officially celebrate Universal Children's Day...

Much like when Salvador Romanero took all the credit for protecting Israel on the day of the sneak attack, he was now taking credit for the birth of all children.

But in truth, many women were already pregnant before the *Miracle Maker* assured humanity that children would once again be among them again. Many, thinking the world was coming to an end on the day of the disappearances, clung to their lovers for dear life. If the end was near, their wish was to leave this world in the most intimate of ways.

By the time Romanero made his big announcement, many like Hana Patel were already pregnant. But most who were still too shell-shocked— not to mention that they were under the young phenom's strong delusional power—to connect the dots.

The man who wanted everyone to think the universe was under his complete control at all times was mere moments away from experiencing a rage so intense it would make the sneak attack on Israel seem like child's play...

44

IN RIYADH, SAUDI ARABIA—one of the Middle Eastern countries not leveled by earthquakes—Mohammed Al-Mahmoud received confirmation that the last of the 1,000,000 toxic packages had been successfully distributed all throughout the Western Hemisphere, from Canada all the way down to the southern tip of Chile.

It was 2 a.m. in Saudi Arabia and 5 p.m. on the east coast of the United States of America. Like everyone else in the world, these Islamic jihadists had long-awaited this day to finally arrive, but for entirely different reasons than everyone else.

"Praise be to Allah," the Muslim cleric said, sipping his tea very slowly, looking around the room. "Now we wait."

The other men in the room nodded agreement. These were the men responsible for secretly connecting nearly a hundred thousand jihadists who'd recently relocated to countries in North, Central and South America, to various sleeper cells on that side of the world. Dormant for the longest time, now that the call was made for this all-important mission, they were ready to go.

With Israel protected from above, and with many of their cities now in ruins, it was time for the nation of Islam to retaliate by waging war on the infidels in the Western Hemisphere.

Yes, it was time to drag them into the fray and make them pay for their many crimes against Allah. Justice needed to be served for the many centuries of gross mistreatment of Muslims everywhere.

The more infidels they killed in the coming days the better...

The United States of America was clearly the bull's eye. Actually, there were two bull's eyes. The second one in their cross-hairs was none other than Salvador Romanero. He was the reason this day was chosen in the first place.

What better way to strike back at him for siding with Israel—which ultimately led to the destruction of their three holy sites in Jerusalem—than by killing many of his precious children?

With hospital maternity wards being protected better than Fort Knox, newborn children were untouchable. But they were okay with that. Their eyes were fixed on a much larger target, namely the millions of pregnant infidel women who would be out and about this night for the fireworks festivities.

If everything went as planned, the casualties would be numerous.

If they needed further confirmation from Allah that this was the appointed day to carry out the attacks, they didn't have to look too far. Of the twenty or so new mothers Salvador Romanero contacted earlier in the day, to offer his personal blessing, the Muslim woman in Africa wasn't among them.

Was Romanero trying to send a message that Muslim children weren't welcome in the new world he was creating? It sure seemed that way. It's not like the woman from Nigeria was the thirtieth to give birth, she was the fourth! Yet Salvador the Great never even bothered to call and congratulate her.

This was unacceptable, unforgiveable! Since it appeared that only infidel children were welcome, they, too, needed to be wiped off the face of the Earth with the rest of the infidels.

So determined were these jihadists to bring the Great Satan to its knees that one-fourth of the 1,000,000 toxic packages designated for the West, were distributed throughout the 50 American states—250,000 to be precise.

The 750,000 packages distributed in all other infidel cities in the West, would conclude the attacks on those countries for now.

But in the United States, this was Phase One of a four-pronged approach meant to honor the 19 exalted heroes who so willingly and selflessly gave their lives back on September 11, 2001, when they hijacked four commercial airplanes in the name of Allah and invaded a nation at peace.

Thousands of Americans were killed that day.

That mission, satisfying as it was for so many Muslims around the world, fell way short of the intended mark. Instead of killing hundreds of thousands of American infidels—their intended target—less than 4,000 perished that day. This came as a bitter disappointment to the architects of the 9/11 attacks.

This group of Islamic jihadists were fully determined not to fail this time. With their home cities in ruins and their religion under constant attack, they wouldn't fail. They couldn't! This was their last shot at world domination and they knew it.

Even with a drastically shrinking population and depleted military, with no way of excavating the weapons of mass destruction they had buried deep beneath the Earth's surface in secret places—at least not for now—they had no chance of attacking America militarily.

But all hope wasn't lost. After many years of research and development dating back long before the disappearances, Muslim scientists, chemists and inventors had perfected their skills to the extent that they now believed they had the perfect plan to potentially kill millions of infidels in a single day.

When Salvador Romanero announced his intent to sign a peace treaty with their most hated enemy—Israel—a few months back, they worked double-time making sure their contraptions would become fully airborne when the time came. The nerve gas they chose to be placed inside those contraptions was sarin.

The reason sarin was chosen over the 50 other weapons of mass destruction Muslim scientists and chemists had stockpiled over the years was that, in its purest form, it was 25 times deadlier than cyanide. Not only that, it could evaporate into a gas vapor, making it easier to spread into the environment than most other man-made nerve agents.

Even at low concentrations sarin was highly toxic, whether inhaled or through penetration of the skin. At this lethal concentration, the vast majority exposed to it would surely die.

After a series of successful tests, using non-toxic aerosols, wealthy Middle Eastern oil sheikhs were so convinced they finally got it right, they enthusiastically forked over the three billion dollars needed to fund the project.

Nearly a hundred-million-dollars was used as bribery money. Once all the right hands were greased, the process of smuggling the deadly agents to the West began in earnest. They were transported by Chinese cargo ships, by way of the Middle East.

One cargo ship dropped its load at Boston Harbor, in Massachusetts. Another ship dropped its load at a dock in Panama. The third cargo ship dropped its load somewhere in Brazil.

Members of various sleeper cells took the cargo and delivered it accordingly, then immediately got busy assembling their contraptions. Instead of using briefcases or metal canisters, which might cause panic if seen, fast food paper bags were used for this diabolical endeavor.

To the naked eye, if anyone chose to investigate, they'd discover nothing but used napkins, greasy hamburger wrappers, French fry holders, and empty soft drink cups inside the crumpled-up bags. But if lids were removed from the empty drink cups, plastic containers would be found inside that were engineered to let the sarin slowly but surely seep through them.

Once that objective was achieved, the deadly agents would be aerosol-sprayed into the atmosphere and would begin at once wreaking havoc on humanity and the environment, destroying every living being within its reach.

Since there would be no explosions to propel the deadly agents outward (like there would be with Phase Three later)—their range would be 100 feet at most—the toxic packages needed to be distributed in highly concentrated areas so many humans would be exposed to it.

Mindful of this, those chosen to carry out this mission deposited the fast food bags in trash receptacles in shopping malls, supermarkets, convenience stores, fast food restaurants, hospital lobbies, hotel lobbies and convention centers.

Many more were placed on trains and at train stations, buses and bus depots, taxicabs and airports.

Those chosen for this mission were battle-hardened veterans, fanatics in every sense of the word. Only their American friends, co-workers and neighbors didn't know it.

While most were of Middle Eastern origin, they didn't resemble your prototypical terrorists. Most had lived in the United States for many years and were highly educated, even receiving their degrees from America's top universities.

They were doctors, lawyers, government officials, business owners, religious leaders and law enforcement officials. Some were even professors at the places from which they'd received their college degrees.

These men were well-disciplined, kept low profiles and had multiple identities. They were skilled at covering their tracks, making them white collar jihadists in every sense of the word.

Because they were highly respected, any red flags that may have possibly gone up when they first moved into their communities, had long since been lowered.

In short: they were the last individuals most would ever suspect of committing such evil. Which is why they did all the running around in public, while those who'd recently relocated to America, from other countries, remained out of view of the public eye.

Now in hiding, those responsible for carrying out Phase One—also dubbed the Flight 11 Project honoring the five still highly-revered fallen heroes on Flight 11, which was the first airplane-turned-missile to strike the Twin Towers in Manhattan on that fateful day—were forbidden from contacting anyone on the outside. It was just too risky.

They would remain in total lock down for 21 days, just in case, wearing protective gear provided by the masterminds in charge of birthing this lofty plan. By then, most airborne agents would be cleared from the earth's atmosphere.

With no mobile devices, laptop computers, TVs or radios at their disposal to help pass the time, they would read the Quran day and night, fast and pray without ceasing that Allah would deliver overwhelming victory into their hands this time.

They praised Allah for choosing them for this glorious mission. They knew their god would never ignore the prayers of his bravest front-line soldiers, especially when on their knees in enemy territory. How could he?

No, Allah would never let such bravery and loyalty to go unrewarded.

With millions of American infidels hopefully hours away from being wiped off the face of the earth, this was the first step to ultimately unearthing their still-hidden weapons of mass destruction, to include nuclear weapons.

Then they would begin at once imposing their will on all infidels everywhere, starting with Salvador Romanero.

For added inspiration, four rows of framed pictures of the nineteen fallen 9/11 heroes were hung on safe-house walls.

Above them were these words, this credo: "Stand firm and inspect your weapons. Know the plan well. Vow to accept death. Purify your heart and cleanse it of all stains. Let your breasts be full of gladness. To Allah we shall return."

To further safeguard these hideouts, the walls and ceilings were sealed with a thick kerosene coating. If the enemy ever learned their whereabouts, with a simple strike of a match, any location could easily be burned to the ground in just minutes.

Phase Two, also known as the Flight 175 Project—honoring the five fallen heroes responsible for hijacking the second airplane-turned-missile to strike the Twin Towers—would actually come as a result of Phase One.

Everyone soon-to-be exposed to the deadly toxins would unknowingly help the cause by spreading it to everyone with whom they made contact.

Even the clothing they wore would release the deadly nerve gas into the air long after being exposed to it. Whether this happened at home, the supermarket, the mall, or at the many fireworks festivities planned nationwide, mattered not to them.

The main thing was that they exposed as many infidels to the colorless, odorless deadly agents as possible this day.

Even foreigners visiting the U.S. would do their part by infecting many around the globe when they traveled back to their home countries in the days ahead.

If they lived that long...

Phase Three, also known as the Flight 77 Project, would commence at precisely 9:11 P.M. EST! This part of the mission involved another group of jihadists, one thousand men and women in all, honoring the five fallen heroes on the third flight to pulverize America that day, when the plane struck the Pentagon.

In just a few short hours their actions would create unspeakable carnage. Mass hysteria would ensue, once again ensnaring the godless nation.

If everything went as planned, their actions would serve to decrease the American population even more, ultimately bringing America to her knees.

The time chosen to carry out this part of the mission—9:11 or 9/11—was purely symbolic.

Phase Four, honoring the fallen heroes of Flight 93—whose efforts fell short when American infidels stormed the cockpit and crashed the plane in a field in Pennsylvania, curtailing their efforts—would commence 21 days from now, once the atmosphere was cleared of all deadly toxins.

With customized extended-life breathing apparatuses affixed to their hazmat suits, they'd be free to move on to the next phase of their all-out attack on the United States and Salvador Romanero.

But for now, as the deadly agents slowly melted the one million plastic containers in which they were stored, Phase One was well under way, even if the outside world didn't know it yet.

Soon, very soon, as Americans and Westerners in all other countries left their homes to meet with family members and friends to celebrate the first infidel children being born, deadly chemical agents would start filling the lungs of so many.

But in the United States, the biggest bang wouldn't come until 9:11 p.m. Then the countdown would be on to see how many would ultimately become their slaves in the afterlife...

Allah willing, the first step toward that lofty goal had just been taken.

With their task completed, all they could do now was hope and wait and pray for success...

45

AT 9 P.M. EST, MILLIONS of spectators were gathered in cities and towns on the East Coast of the United States, to watch fireworks and celebrate new life. Millions more were already gathering in all other time zones in the Western Hemisphere.

Aside from the much smaller crowds—due to the fact that nearly half of the American populace was now gone—it very much resembled past Independence Days or New Year's Eve celebrations.

While there weren't any children among them just yet, seeing the numerous handheld signs, banners and T-shirts, with pictures of newborn babies on them—including the first American child, Salvador Rodriguez, from Seattle Washington—coupled by the fact that many pregnant women were out celebrating with them only added to the overall elation everyone felt.

News cameras and reporters focused more on expectant mothers than anyone else. Naturally they were given the choicest locations from which to recline.

The deadly odorless agents stored inside the 1,000,000 plastic containers had already been released into the atmosphere. Millions had already been exposed to the highly-contagious agents without even knowing it. By the time they became aware, it would be too late. Most would die gruesome, painful deaths.

Totally oblivious to it all, Salvador Romanero recorded a simulcast video message to be played in every time zone just before the fireworks went off. Finally, it was America's turn to celebrate Universal Children's Day.

The *Miracle Maker* appeared on huge screens up and down the East Coast, wherever fireworks would be lit, and said, "Greetings, global citizens! Has there ever been a better time to be alive than right now? I think not! As we celebrate the very first Universal Children's Day, let us raise a glass and toast the many brave women out there for making this moment possible!

"We are truly indebted to each of you. And now, let the celebration begin! Enjoy the fireworks! May you all be blessed in my name!"

At that, the celebration was on. Music blared through speakers as fireworks were launched into the evening sky.

Strategically placed among the crowds on the east coast were the 1,000 Islamic terrorists chosen to carry out Phase Three. Half were men and half were women posing as couples, so they would blend in even more.

The women chosen for this mission weren't of Middle Eastern descent like their counterparts were. They were radicalized Americans who looked every bit a part of the American melting pot as everyone else. But they hated America just as much as their comrades in arms did.

Each of the 100 locations having festivities on the East Coast had jihadists among them. Crowd sizes varied. Naturally, the bigger the crowd the more jihadists assigned to it.

Their orders were specific: spread out so the vast-majority of spectators would be in harm's way, and don't cause any unwanted suspicion beforehand.

But knowing what was about to happen, it was impossible to conceal the strained expressions on their faces. In just a few minutes, with powerful explosives strapped to their bodies, they would create their own fireworks spectacular of sorts and leave this planet with a big bang, hopefully killing countless infidels in the process, including pregnant women.

Allah willing, those who weren't blown to smithereens by the powerful explosives would die in the coming days from exposure to the aerosol-sprayed toxins. Either way, they would walk into eternity and have countless slaves catering to their every whim.

Every male would have 72 pure virgins assigned to them. The women involved in Phase Three wouldn't have male virgins assigned to them. But once they were reunited with their husbands in the next world, they would appear infinitely more beautiful to them.

Those who never married on Earth would be able to marry any man of their choice in paradise. Or so they were told...

Knowing death was certain, these jihadists made "last testament" videos explaining their actions as retaliation for Muslims worldwide who were victims of the daily atrocities at the hands of the infidels, especially Salvador Romanero. All expressed their willingness to die as martyrs for Allah the great.

Come daybreak, their videos would be widely distributed for all to see.

At precisely 9:11 p.m, at the height of the fireworks festivities, the 1,000 men and women with explosives strapped to their bodies shouted, "Allahu Akbar!" at the top of their lungs, just as the bombs were remotely detonated, creating ear-splitting roars at each location, sending body parts—including their own—all over the place.

Chaos ensued...

IN CHADDS FORD, PENNSYLVANIA, after another full day of reinventing the land, so to speak, some at safe house number one were too exhausted to watch the fireworks on TV. They chose to sleep instead.

Everyone else met at the church pavilion to watch the festivities in Philadelphia on the big screen. As pyrotechnics blazed above the City of Brotherly Love, numerous explosions suddenly went off simultaneously. The camera broadcasting it to viewers in the region shook violently, as if an earthquake had just occurred.

The person holding it must have been killed because the camera fell to the ground on its side but kept broadcasting at a 45-degree angle. Viewers at home didn't need to tilt their heads sideways to see the unspeakable carnage unfolding on their TV screens. Dead bodies and body parts were strewn everywhere.

The cameraman must have been relatively close to one of the explosives because the ground upon which the camera lay was severely charred and soaked with blood.

Even among the turmoil, there were no screams. After the explosions, the only sounds viewers at home heard was the music blaring through speakers and the fireworks still going off. Both were programmed and wouldn't stop until the last fireworks were shot out of the cannons for the finale.

It was quite eerie seeing so many dead and disfigured bodies on TV, as celebratory music blared through speakers.

Similar scenes were being broadcast up and down the East Coast of America.

Clayton Holmes was the first to snap out of it. "Everyone back to the main house now!" he barked. "Go straight to the basement and change into hazmat suits and gas masks. Hurry before any possible radiation clouds reach us!"

"What about the others?" Travis Hartings asked.

"I'll take care of it!" Braxton Rice raced back to the house and put on a Level A hazmat suit, steel-tipped boots, and chemical-resistant gloves, then loaded a truck with hazmat suits and drove off to the cottages where *ETSM* members were sleeping.

The first door Rice pounded on was Mary Johnston's. When she opened the door and saw him wearing protective gear, she was frightened for her life. "Put this on quickly then go to the main house," he ordered. "Don't ask any questions! Just do it!"

Rice raced back to the truck and drove off to the next cottage.

Meanwhile, back at the house, as everyone raced down to the basement, Brian went upstairs and knocked on his mother's door. He knocked earlier to invite her to the church pavilion for food and to watch the fireworks, but she never bothered opening the door.

Since arriving at safe house number one, Sarah Mulrooney never left her room. She refused to eat and didn't want to be bothered by anyone, including Brian.

Brian knocked harder. "Open the door, Ma! It's an emergency!"

Hearing the panic in her son's voice, Sarah climbed out of bed and opened her bedroom door. Her hair was unkempt, and she had deep dark bags under her eyes, from too much crying and lack of sleep. "What's wrong?"

"There were multiple explosions in Philadelphia during the fireworks celebration. Many were killed. I saw it all on TV. Looks like the work of suicide bombers. Clayton fears the air may be toxic. We need to go to the basement and put hazmat suits on, in case radiation clouds come our way!"

When Sarah hesitated, Brian yelled, "Now, Ma! We gotta hurry!"

It worked. Sarah followed her son down the stairs in total silence, sort of wishing she was among the many now dead. Being blown to pieces by a suicide bomber suddenly sounded like a good way to leave this miserable planet.

Knowing she had eternal assurance, it would be a quick and easy way to get to Jesus without committing suicide.

Upon reaching the basement, Charles Calloway handed them hazmat suits to put on.

"What do we do now?" Tamika Moseley said in a panic. Even with her protective gear on, everyone could see her chest heaving up and down. She had difficulty breathing.

279

"Pray, and constantly check for radiation in the atmosphere," Doctor Meera Singh said calmly. Her voice betrayed her trembling body.

Tom Dunleavey placed a hand on Tamika's head and started praying for her until her breathing stabilized.

After a while, everyone went up to the living room. The TV was turned on. First thing they saw were the words: EXPLOSIONS ROCK ENTIRE EAST COAST! MILLIONS FEARED DEAD!

Sarah Mulrooney dropped her head and wept silently, knowing New York City was among the death and destruction. She felt completely powerless.

Dr. Lee Kim was seated next to Travis Hartings, "What about the website timeline?

Hartings sighed, then shot a desperate glance at Clayton Holmes.

After taking a moment to think it through, Holmes said, "Shadow Revelation six, verses two through eight in a lighter shade of red like you did with Revelation four and five in the past. With so much death and destruction, it's hard knowing which of the four horsemen is responsible for what.

"For now, let's assume it's a combo of all four. Once the dust settles, if it settles, we'll ask God to sort it out for us. Until then, the light red shade will be the safest bet."

"You got it, Clayton."

"While you're at it, you might want to reach out to *ETSM* members around the world and let them know we're okay. Also, check and see if our brothers and sisters on the East Coast are safe as well."

"Already heard from Nigel Jones, Amos Nyarwarta and Xiang Tse Chiang. I told them we're safe for now. They're praying for us."

Clayton Holmes sent a text message to his aunt Evelyn, letting her know they were all fine. Holmes was relieved when she quickly replied, informing that she and Deacon Ernest Stone were both safe.

After being released from the hospital in Atlanta a few days after the peace treaty signing, Deacon Stone was taken to the cabin in Tennessee, so he could be placed in the care of *ETSM* doctors and nurses.

Charles Calloway drove him there after he confessed to having dreams for three straight nights. The original plan was that Deacon Stone would stay at the cabin until he was healthy enough to leave. Then he would join Calloway at one of the seven properties down south once they were up and running.

Then Deacon Stone met Miss Evelyn and the two seniors fell in love. They were already making plans to get married. Mary Johnston sat quietly and listened and observed. Like everyone else, she was petrified. But for the first time in her life, though they looked like a bunch of astronauts who'd been transported from Chadds Ford, Pennsylvania to Chadds Ford, Mars, Mary felt comforted being surrounded by those she could confidently call her family. Unlike everyone else in her past life, these people would never leave her.

"Should I try contacting Rhonda Kimmel to see if she's okay?" Brian Mulrooney said to his wife.

Jacquelyn nodded yes.

Mulrooney sent a text message to his real estate agent: *Are you okay? Just heard about the explosions in Wilmington. Please let me know. Stay safe out there. God be with you.*

Within a matter of minutes, Mulrooney knew she wasn't okay. Normally, Rhonda Kimmel would reply immediately, within minutes anyway. But not this time.

Meanwhile, the news on TV kept getting worse as the minutes passed. It was now feared that people all across the United States had been exposed to the deadly toxins and were becoming violently ill as a result.

It didn't take long before the impact zone was expanded to the entire Western Hemisphere. Whereas initial reports had suggested that perhaps as many as 10,000,000 casualties might occur from this catastrophe, it now looked like that number would be ten times higher than that...

"What do we do now?" said Manuel Jiminez.

"We pray..." Charles Calloway said. Everyone joined hands.

Once they finished praying, Sarah Mulrooney trudged up to her bedroom without saying a word to anyone.

She locked her bedroom door and laid on the bed sill in her hazmat suit. With tears in her eyes, she prayed for Dick and Chelsea, not knowing if they were dead or alive, wondering for the hundredth time if she made the right decision by leaving her husband and daughter.

More than anything, she wanted to be with them now, but knew it wasn't possible...

46

IN WASHINGTON D.C., PRESIDENT Danforth and First Lady Melissa Danforth were out on the White House south portico balcony watching the fireworks blazing over the National Mall.

After having a nice dinner together, the First Couple decided to shut out the world for one night and relax and enjoy each other's company for a change. They even held hands.

Then multiple explosions literally shook the White House foundation beneath them. Even though they were roughly a mile away from the National Mall, they easily felt the pulse created by the explosions.

In a matter of seconds, they were surrounded by secret service agents and taken to the fallout shelter beneath the White House. Their training had taught them they had 60 seconds to get the President and First Lady to safety before they were exposed to the deadly toxins feared in the air.

Once underground, both were checked for possible radiation exposure, which thankfully neither had, then ordered to put on gas-tight suits and gas masks, to which neither objected.

The secret service needed to remove the First Family from the hot zone as quickly as possible, to prevent toxic air from being ingested into their lungs. But until the green light was given that it was safe to fly on *Marine One*, they would remain in the White House fallout shelter wearing Level A hazmat suits.

Hundreds of secret service agents, also in protective gear, set up perimeters around the White House looking for anything out of the ordinary. Then again, with mass carnage all around them, everything looked out of the ordinary!

Even so, they needed to make sure no one was lurking in the darkness with shoulder-mounted surface-to-air missiles locked onto the Presidential chopper, just waiting for their boss to climb on board.

First responders and military reservists, also wearing hazmat suits, trudged through the mass casualties on the ground at the National Mall looking for signs of life.

The few they saw who weren't killed by the explosions lay on the ground trembling uncontrollably, gasping for air, the look of death stenciled onto their faces.

Others were choking and foaming at the mouth. Their bodies were covered with cuts and burn marks from the explosives and with hideous boils from the chemical agents their bodies had just been exposed to.

A half-hour passed before secret service agent Daniel Sullivan—who was down in the fallout shelter with the First Family—heard in his earpiece to bring the President and First Lady to *Marine One* at once.

"Time to go!"

Without saying a word, the Danforths followed Agent Sullivan out to the White House South Lawn and boarded *Marine One*. The pilots wore Level A hazmat suits, along with everyone else on board the chopper.

Agent Daniel Sullivan barked, "Take POTUS and FLOTUS to Joint Base Andrews immediately!"

"Out!" the pilot said. He flicked a switch and the propellers slowly roared to life. Once they were up to speed, *Marine One* slowly lifted off the White House lawn.

President Danforth nodded to the man seated across from him, knowing who he was, then stared out the window wondering how he would explain to his wife what he was about to do. He ignored it for now and steadied his gaze downward.

The bright flood lights trained down on the National Mall made it easy to see the numerous corpses and severed body parts scattered about. The carnage was unspeakable.

The First Lady chose not to look.

President Danforth couldn't help but recall the life-altering sensation of being flown back to the White House, from Camp David, on the day of the Rapture. It felt eerily similar to now. In his mind's eye, he still saw the thick black smoke billowing up everywhere, darkening and polluting the skies.

Whereas that incident was caused by a silent evacuation, this appeared to be a coordinated attack on his country. Also different from last time was upon landing at the White House, the eyes of the world were all on him wanting to hear the most powerful man on earth tell them everything would eventually be okay.

Who cares what I have to say now?

The President shrugged his shoulders and refocused. Now wasn't the time to feel sorry for himself. Taking a moment to think things through, he sat up in his seat and buried his still-raw emotions as deep as they would go for now.

Only his most trusted advisers knew what he was about to do...

Upon landing at Joint Base Andrews—under heavy guard—*Marine One* wheeled its way to *Air Force One*, for the trip to Denver, Colorado. But in this case, it was the President's "doomsday plane", code named E-4B.

Designed to withstand a nuclear blast detonated from the ground, it could also outpace it, allowing the Commander-in-Chief to remain in the air indefinitely, if need be, without disrupting the continuity of government.

Just when President Danforth thought the news couldn't get any worse, it did. According to his Joint Chief of Staff, William Messersmith, many in Alaska and Hawaii were also experiencing similar symptoms and were among the sick and dying...

The President didn't reply. He was too busy mentally calculating this latest mass reduction to the American populace—first the 100,000,000 from the Rapture, then the 70,000,000 who recently denounced their citizenship and relocated elsewhere.

Now this? He wondered who was responsible for this latest attack; Salvador Romanero? Islamic jihadists? Or was it an inside job? It was too soon to know...

The First Couple boarded the President's plane. Upon arriving, they'd be taken to an underground secure location where the President could still run the government. Only the man climbing the steps up to the fuselage with the First Lady wasn't President Danforth. It was one of the President's body doubles.

When the Danforths boarded *Marine One* on the White House South Lawn, the stunt double was already on board waiting for them. With everyone wearing hazmat suits, no one knew who anyone else was.

Before getting off *Marine One* to board *Air Force One*, the President informed the First Lady that he wouldn't be joining her in Colorado, that he would go to the underground bunker in northern Virginia, to continue putting the counter shadow government in place.

Hearing this, the calm demeanor Melissa Danforth had miraculously displayed while en route to Joint Base Andrews quickly evaporated. The

First Lady was *not* happy! The one time she needed her husband by her side more than any other, he was sending her away. She begrudgingly agreed to his wishes...

Once *Air Force One* (E-4B) took to the skies, bound for Colorado, President Danforth got off *Marine One* still in his hazmat gear. He unceremoniously climbed into the back of a black Suburban and was driven to the underground bunker without the usual motorcade and secret service protection.

Only Agent Daniel Sullivan was with him.

With the "real" President not on board the aircraft, *Air Force One* was inaptly named for this particular flight.

If the press only knew...

MEANWHILE, THE CHAOS UP and down the East Coast of America was unimaginable. Mass casualties were being reported everywhere. Many in hot zones who weren't blown to pieces were severely disfigured. They went in search of the closest hospitals.

But hospitals were overwhelmed with the sick and the dying. Most, fearing death was near, demanded to be seen, but were turned away with along countless others.

Hospital administrators begged for police assistance to keep the masses at bay until antidotes could be administered and decontamination units could be set up in hospital parking lots.

Maternity wards were placed on complete lock down and were protected by armed guards.

Using bullhorns, hospital staff in full protective gear up and down the east coast of the United States shouted similar messages to the massive crowds within the sound of their voices, "Please remain calm. You must receive antidote shots and be fully decontaminated before going home. Otherwise you may expose your family and friends to the toxic nerve gas. Mass decontamination units are being dispatched to all infected areas.

"Once set up, each unit can decontaminate two-hundred people per hour. Naturally, pregnant women must be the first to receive antidotes and go through decontamination. We'll eventually get to everyone!

"Until then, if any of you have open cuts or abrasions anywhere on your bodies, they must be covered immediately! Do not under any circumstances put your hands in or near your mouths for any reason, or you could risk ingesting the deadly toxins. This means no smoking. No drinking. No eating."

Once mass decontamination units were set up, everyone exposed to the deadly toxins was ordered to strip out of their contaminated clothing, including underwear.

Everyone was then scrubbed thoroughly and hosed down with warm water before being given protective gear and gas masks to put on. Everything they had with them—eyeglasses, contact lenses, jewelry, cell phones and the like—was confiscated and burned in furnaces.

Only time would tell if it worked...

But for many waiting in line, by the time it was their turn to be decontaminated and receive the proper antidotes, it would be too late. Most would die gruesome deaths.

BY THE TIME *AIR Force One* touched down in Colorado, President Danforth was in his underground bunker in Virginia. The situation was far worse than first expected.

It was now feared that millions more had been exposed to the very same nerve gas in every country in the Western Hemisphere and were also among the sick and dying.

The President's heart sank in his chest when a CDC official (Centers for Disease Control and Prevention) told him on a secure conference line, "Many who were exposed to the nerve agents would have had a fighting chance of survival, had antidotes been administered within a few hours.

"But since sarin is odorless and initial symptoms resemble a bad case of allergies or a common cold—headaches, runny nose, excessive sweating, tightness in the chest and constriction of the pupils—apparently most didn't take it seriously at first. Either that or they were so caught up in the first Universal Children's Day celebrations that they decided to tough-it-out.

"But when millions suddenly had difficulty breathing, and their vision became blurred, most fell into a state of confusion. By the time they made it to hospitals for Atropine and Pralidoxime antidotes, they were already drooling at the mouth and vomiting uncontrollably.

"Their bodies jerked violently from convulsions until they lost control of all body functions and became comatose until they eventually died. No one in the path of the explosives had a chance. Even if they survived the blast, death is all but certain for them."

"How many casualties can we expect overall?"

"Sorry to say, Mister President, but I believe the final tally in America will be in the tens of millions..."

President Danforth blinked hard. This was unfathomable! He ended the call and stared at the wall opposite him, wondering why this had happened on his watch.

No other American President had experienced anything quite like it. In fact, in the 200+ years his predecessors had occupied the White House, the many tragedies they'd endured combined, couldn't come close to comparing to what he suffered over the past nine months. *Not even close!*

Unfortunately for him, the suffering was far from over. When Jefferson Danforth left his wife back at Joint Base Andrews, he didn't know it would be the last time he would ever see her again, in this lifetime or the next.

Had he known, he would have never left her side...

47

AT 4:30 A.M., SPAIN time, Salvador Romanero was awakened from a deep sleep. He didn't know the full extent of his dream, only that something had happened somewhere in the world causing numerous casualties.

What caused him to bolt up in bed was an inner-foreboding that countless pregnant women were among the casualties. *My precious children!*

Suddenly there was a knock on his door. "You may enter, Devereaux," Romanero said, to the man in charge of managing his residence in Spain.

Romanero knew it was Devereaux because only he had the authority to knock on that door, let alone enter Romanero's sleeping quarters. But only during an emergency.

This *was* an emergency!

"Sorry for waking you, your Highness," the French man said softly, not knowing he was already awake.

Romanero squinted, then blinked a few times to adjust to the light Devereaux had turned on. "What is it?"

"The Pope needs to speak to you immediately. It's urgent. He's on the phone waiting for you." The fear in Pierre Devereaux's eyes was palpable.

Romanero climbed out of bed and started pacing the tile floor. "That'll be all, Devereaux."

"Yes, your Highness. Call me if you need anything," he said, slowly walking backwards toward the door, careful not to take his eyes off of the *Miracle Maker.*

"Hurry, Devereaux!"

"Yes, your Grace."

Romanero didn't reply. He picked up his personal line. "What can I do for you, your Eminence?"

The Pope was calm and lucid, "America has just fallen under attack."

"How?" After spending most of the night with the Prince of Darkness in his meditation room, Romanero sensed something big was about to happen. But unlike the crystal-clear vision his master had given him regarding the earthquakes, this one was rather vague.

"Well, Your Highness, there were multiple explosions up and down the east coast of the United States during the fireworks festivities."

"Were there casualties?"

"Numerous. It appears to have been a coordinated chemical attack not only on America but on the entire Western Hemisphere."

"Has anyone claimed responsibility?" Romanero asked calmly.

"Yes. The nation of Islam."

"Did they give a reason?"

"They gave three. First to strike at the Great Satan..." The Bishop of Rome paused, praying Romanero wouldn't become so incensed with the next words out of his mouth that he would send an earthquake to the Vatican.

When the Pope hesitated, Romanero said, "Go on, your Eminence."

The Pope cleared his throat, "Since children being born in this new world you're creating will never be given the chance to convert to Islam, those responsible view all children as infidels who need to be wiped off the face of the Earth with all other heretics. They vow to keep killing children at all costs."

Romanero became fidgety. "And the third reason?"

"Revenge on you, your Highness, for siding with Israel and for not allowing them to rebuild their three holy sites. Also, for never acknowledging the Muslim mother who gave birth earlier. They claim they're planning for your eventual assassination."

Really now! "Let me get further briefed on the situation. I'll get back to you later."

At that, the call ended.

Much like those from the secret society who'd helped elevate Salvador Romanero to his lofty position, both the *Miracle Maker* and the Pope weren't the slightest bit concerned about the great loss of life that just occurred in the Western Hemisphere.

Ridding the earth of billions of dissidents was all part of the plan. Whereas Planet Earth boasted a population of more than seven billion humans less than a year ago, it had dwindled down to just under five billion in just a few short months.

They were off to a rather impressive start, but the world was still overpopulated by more than four billion humans. So, in that light, the *Miracle Maker* wasn't the slightest bit concerned about the countless millions now feared dead across the Atlantic Ocean.

But pregnant women were altogether different. Deep down inside, Romanero feared perhaps as many as a million expectant mothers were killed. Many were just days away from giving birth.

He could already hear the unborn children crying out to him from the grave for justice. The very thought caused his temper to go from zero to mach speed in the blink of an eye.

They ruined my week-long celebration!

This was the second time his enemies had tried ruining his plans. First it was the failed sneak attack on Israel. Now this, on Universal Children's Day? Whereas what happened in Israel was a coalition of many nations, this was a coordinated attack carried out by Muslims only, and no other demographic.

On the failed attack on Israel, their goal was to kill many Jews. Had they succeeded on that front, Romanero would have silently rejoiced. But the attack on the West placed many who did matter to him in the path of their destruction: pregnant women.

He looked up at the ceiling, "Why didn't you warn me in advance?" he shouted to his master, feeling completely betrayed. "The world expects me to be omniscient, especially after the earthquakes miracle! Some may now question my deity again for not seeing this coming? How could you let this happen to me?"

The fact that Satan was his master, but certainly not his Maker, meant Romanero should have been looking downward instead of up when communicating with Satan.

The final straw was when Romanero watched one of the "last testament" videos made by a now-dead terrorist. He said, "Every hardship we face is but a test of our faith and an example of our ceaseless dedication to Allah. It's the duty of every Muslim to defend the brotherhood of Islam.

"While we expect mass retaliation for our actions, we will not fear. Our lack of fear is what unites us and divides you. In the end, our fate doesn't rest with Salvador Romanero or the infidel world he is creating, but in the hands of Allah. To Allah alone be the glory!"

The comforting glow that was on Romanero's face all day was replaced with a fury that was mostly dormant up to this point.

The *Miracle Maker* wanted blood! An hour later, Romanero appeared on live television. Gone was the total elation everyone saw on his face a few short hours ago, after the first child was born.

Without greeting anyone he said, "The attack carried out on the West a few hours ago was done in the name of the Islamic religion. The so-called infidels they massacred were our precious citizens! I'm told as many as one-million unborn children were among those killed at their hands!

"Now Muslims everywhere will pay for their actions. For every person they killed, three Muslims must die! And for every pregnant woman they killed, a thousand Muslims must die! If I must kill every-last Muslim on the planet to finally bring those who did this to justice, I will do it!"

"Since the next generation will be our torchbearers, nothing can be more important than protecting life in the womb! It's with that in mind that I wish to announce an international law abolishing abortion. From this point forward, anyone caught in the act will be punished by death. This includes doctors, nurses, and all who are deemed enablers and supporters."

"Further, anyone causing harm to a child already born must die. No exceptions! This universal law supersedes the laws of all countries, including dissident countries. May all who are with me be blessed in my name..."

Within minutes of Romanero's universal declaration, Islamic mosques, universities, and religious training centers were being set ablaze by fire. Anyone found inside those buildings were ordered outside then killed by firing squad.

This was only the beginning...

48

TEN DAYS AFTER THE ATTACK ON AMERICA

AS IT TURNED OUT, the only silver lining found behind the dark cloud that had invaded America was that no radiation clouds were registered anywhere in the U.S.

After ten straight days of constant testing and not finding a single trace of radiation in the Capitol City, the President and First Lady were cleared to return to Washington.

President Danforth considered it a minor miracle that they were able to outsmart so many in the U.S. Government, and the media, by making them think he was in Colorado all this time when, in reality, he was only 50 miles away from the White House.

The President was notified by Vice President Everett Ashford that the First Lady had boarded *Air Force One* and would be en route back to Washington in a matter of minutes.

The ten days spent apart from each other was the longest Jefferson and Melissa Danforth had gone since their college days.

They yearned to see each other again.

Because the world thought the Danforths were together out West, and with two shadow governments in place, communication between them the past ten days was kept to a bare minimum. Even the most secure lines couldn't be trusted at this time.

As it turned out, President Danforth wasn't alone underground. The adjoining sub-terrain shelter was already full of *ETSM* and *AFK* members when he arrived. Shock filled their faces when he made a surprise visit and explained to them what had just transpired on their side of the planet.

Upon learning that more than 30,000,000 American citizens were killed, and another 70,000,000 were killed all throughout the Western Hemisphere—totaling 100,000,000 human beings—there were many gasps, followed by tears and deep grieving.

Their mood only worsened when they were told they might be stranded underground an additional three weeks.

Everyone was relieved when President Danforth—who made sure to spend a few minutes with them each day to update them—explained ten days later that the air outside was finally safe and they could leave the underground bunker.

After personally witnessing the last busload of passengers escorted from the mountain and taken to their vehicles, the President returned to his sub-terrain location, to meet with National Security Adviser Nelson Casanieves and Joint Chief of Staff, William Messersmith.

Afterward, all three would drive back to Joint Base Andrews together. When *Air Force One* landed, the real President would already be on board *Marine One* waiting for Melissa and the President's body double.

Upon landing on the White House South Lawn, the real First Family would enter the White House together, as the President's body double remained on board the chopper.

This final underground meeting was centered on the handful of military options they were considering. While everyone was in agreement they had to retaliate, the question was where could they possibly strike? Thanks to Salvador Romanero, many of the countries in which the perpetrators had lived already lay in ruins.

There was a knock on the door. "Who's there?"

"Sir, it's Agent Sullivan. I need to speak to you. It's urgent..."

"Come in, Sullivan..."

Agent Sullivan entered the room with an expression on his face that brought President Danforth straight back to Camp David. He was the same agent who informed him that people were missing on the day of the disappearances, and that his mother had died of a heart attack. What he saw on the secret serviceman's face nearly stopped his heart from beating.

"What is it Agent Sullivan?"

"Sir, there was an explosion on board *Air Force One* over Kansas."

President Danforth gasped, then blinked hard. "Primary or decoy?"

"Primary, Sir," said Agent Sullivan, closing his eyes and slowly shaking his head.

For security purposes, whenever the President of the United States of America took to the skies on *Air Force One*, an exact replica accompanied the President's plane, to throw any potential danger off his scent, so to speak. Hence, the decoy...

"Oh, no!" cried the President. "What kind of explosion?"

"Don't know, Sir, but it appears to have been an inside job. The fact that there was no evidence of vapor trails coming from the ground or in the air means the bomb was most likely detonated from inside the plane. This points to an obvious security breach in Denver."

President Danforth closed his eyes. Panic rose in his voice, "Were they able to safely land the plane?"

Agent Sullivan dropped his head. "It crashed to the ground soon after the explosion. It's believed everyone on board was killed. I'm sorry, Sir."

This can't be! The President buried his face in his hands and sobbed uncontrollably. "Not my Melissa." The room grew eerily silent until Jefferson Danforh said, "Take me back to the White House immediately!"

"You can't go there, Sir," Vice President Everett Ashford implored. "At least not until we think things through. Everyone thinks you were in Colorado with the First Lady." He paused. "Mister President, if this was an inside job as it appears, it means there's a coordinated effort to, well...you know..."

"The Vice President's right, Sir," Agent Sullivan said. "For now, the V.P. needs to get back to Washington immediately. Until your fate has been confirmed one way or the other, the appropriate measures must be taken for the continuity of government." Seeing his boss lower his head and shrug his shoulders, Agent Sullivan felt like weeping. "I'm sorry, Sir, but that's how it must be for now."

The room grew silent again. The anguish on President Danforth's face had little to do with the fact that his days as President of the United States may have just ended.

That wasn't it at all. It all came down to the seven words he kept hearing in two separate dreams before coming to faith in Christ: *This is your last shot at redemption...*

Only this time it was eight words and they were now past tense: *You missed your last shot at redemption, Melissa...*

The President wept uncontrollably again...

49

ELEVEN DAYS LATER

AFTER BEING LOCKED DOWN in total isolation for 21 straight days, the thousands of jihadists responsible for the widespread carnage in America were ready to carry out their next round of attacks on the Great Satan.

Forbidden from making contact with anyone while in hiding, they were totally unaware of the widespread carnage their actions had created on Universal Children's Day.

Upon hearing that more than 20,000,000 Americans had died as a result of the quarter-million toxic packages they had placed all across America, they rejoiced.

When they heard another 10,000,000 American infidels were killed by the explosions, they saluted their fallen comrades who blew themselves to pieces for the cause.

When they heard another 70,000,000 had died in all other Western Hemisphere countries, they praised Allah with everything that was in them for delivering overwhelming victory into their hands.

A hundred-million infidels dead at their hands...

What more could they ask for?

Would they even need that many slaves in the afterlife?

Their mood quickly soured after seeing footage of millions of their Muslim brothers and sisters being dragged out of homes, mosques, universities, and even out of prisons—starting the day of the explosions—and killed by firing squad.

The news hit them hard. They expected serious blow back for their actions, but this was beyond the scope of anything imagined.

The more they watched the more enraged they became.

When they saw the file footage of Salvador Romanero ordering the killing of three Muslims for every infidel killed, and a thousand Muslims for every pregnant woman killed that day, they were incensed like never before.

When Romanero declared if every last Muslim on the planet had to be killed to finally bring those who did this to justice, they shook their fists toward heaven, crying, "Salvador Romanero is the devil incarnate!"

They were even more determined to carry out Phase Four. They prayed without ceasing that Allah would bless this next wave of attacks on the Great Satan.

They left their hiding places and piled into passenger vans with tinted windows. Now that Romanero had declared war on Muslims everywhere, they wore protective gear to conceal their identities.

If seen out in public, they would be shot and killed on the spot.

The last man out of each hideout struck a match and lit a fuse which slowly made its way to the kerosene-coated walls.

From there, they firebombed many other houses in America's largest cities. It didn't take long before thousands of buildings were engulfed in flames all across the United States of America.

This coordinated "Scorched Earth" campaign—scorched America to be more precise—would honor the fallen heroes of flight 93 whose efforts fell short when brave Americans stormed the cockpit and crashed the plane in a field in Pennsylvania, thus curtailing the terrorists' efforts.

With firefighters stretched to the limits battling numerous blazes nationwide, these terrorists roamed the American countryside looking to cause as much death and destruction as they possibly could, before being caught in the act and forever silenced for their efforts.

With chemical-laden bombs hidden beneath the protective gear they wore, they would go out with one last bang, hopefully taking even more infidels with them in the process.

With their home cities in ruins and so many slaves awaiting them in paradise, these brave soldiers were more eager to leave this world than ever before and be ushered into paradise.

And what better slaves to have in the afterlife than Americans?

Or so they thought...

What they would learn upon slipping into eternity was the wretched place to which they would be sent wouldn't be paradise. Nor would they be welcomed warmly as heroes. There would be no slaves to serve them in the afterlife.

No friends.

No allies.

Only suffering.

They would also learn the man they hated more than any other back on Planet Earth—Salvador Romanero—actually served the same master as them.

Eternally speaking, they were on the same side all along.

Even worse, they would learn the god they worshiped was merely Satan in disguise, and the prophet Mohammad they faithfully served was nothing more than one of the Master Deceiver's many false prophets used to deceive humanity.

If their souls had skin upon learning this, it would crawl or shrivel up, seeing the false prophet Mohammad cowering, begging all who followed his teachings to repent of their sins and trust in Jesus before it was too late; not out of compassion for them, but because those who died following his false teachings would heap even more judgment upon his soul.

For all Muslims sent to that dreadful place, the false prophet they loved and venerated back on Earth would be someone they would detest for all eternity, even more than the so-called infidels they were bent on killing back on Earth. This hatred would only intensify as the ages passed without end.

To hear the desperation in their fraudulent leader's voice echoing throughout the deepest chambers of hell, would cause them to hate him even more...

Only those now executing Phase Four back on Earth couldn't hear his desperate cries. All they had were the written words the false prophet had left for them to follow; words that would ultimately lead to their eternal destruction. The moment they breathed their last in human form, the torment would begin.

Without mercy, they would share the very same fearful expectation of judgment and eternal fire as every other condemned soul sent there. The wrath of God would burn against them forevermore. Only they would never die.

Totally blinded to what awaited them on the other side they marched on, hellbent on killing millions of more Americans, not knowing they were being duped by Satan all along, disguising himself as the god they called Allah...

MEANWHILE, IN JERUSALEM, THE number of Jews sitting under the direct tutelage of the Two Witnesses had grown exponentially. Despite the many Jews cramming the Western Wall to protest against the two men, this group of young virgin Jewish men listened very carefully to everything they had to say.

These were the first of the 144,000 prophesied in the Book of Revelation, who would soon be responsible for leading a multitude that no one could number from every nation, tribe, people and tongue to faith in Christ Jesus.

Only they didn't yet know it...

50

FOR NINE MONTHS CHELSEA Mulrooney did her best to cope in this strange new world. Nothing worked.

Even the online community she was part of—virtual friends she spent copious amounts of time with—couldn't pull her out of the rut she felt trapped in. How could they possibly help her when they were just as lost themselves? As it was, suicide frequently came up during their chats.

With her family in shambles and the planet crumbling all around her, as a last-ditch effort, Chelsea thought that perhaps seeing children again would rescue her out of this rut and give her a reason to feel hopeful again.

When Salvadora Patel was born, Chelsea's spirit soared with the rest of the world. For a brief-moment, she even saw a bright future in the eyes of an innocent child. It was enough to convince the divorced woman that she should have a child of her own.

All she had to do was find the right man. Even though most women cared so little about who impregnated them, Chelsea wasn't the type to sleep with just anyone. She wasn't wired that way.

But the thought of living vicariously through someone she could actually bring into the world outweighed the fact that she was a divorced woman who hadn't been on a date in years.

When a chat mate from Sweden offered to impregnate her, Chelsea seriously considered traveling there for that very reason.

The very thought filled her with hope again. She felt energized and wanted to start living her life again.

She even planned on going to the fireworks festivities in New York City, to celebrate new life with everyone else, but she fell asleep and woke up just as it was starting.

Watching America falling under attack on her TV screen took all the wind out of her sails again. Not only that, it convinced her that her brother, Brian, was right on at least one front: life wouldn't get better on Planet Earth, only worse!

The long and winding road the youngest Mulrooney family member had traveled on all those months now felt more like a grave with both ends kicked out.

Chelsea Mulrooney was tired of going back and forth in this rut. Back and forth. Back and forth. Had she only gone to the fireworks festivities, perhaps she, too, would have been blown to pieces from the explosives and wouldn't have to do it herself.

It was said that brainwashing was nothing more than repeating the same thing over and over until even the most stupid person finally understood it. Chelsea Mulrooney now understood that statement perfectly clear. Convinced there was only one way out of her misery, the only thing left was choosing which option to take.

With the decision made, her means to this particular end would never make it onto the video.

The last thing she wanted was to expose her family and online friends to another devastating suicide video. Renate McCallister's video was enough to scar a person for several lifetimes.

Chelsea's message was short, to the point, and completely void of drama. Clinical would be the best way to describe her voice.

She looked in the camera with eyes that already looked dead and, in a soft-spoken voice, said, "I hope you can forgive me, Mom and Dad, for doing this to you. You already have enough to worry about than coping with yet another family tragedy. But I see no other way out.

"With so much bloodshed in the world, I've finally concluded that life won't get any better. No matter where I look, I see no evidence of a brighter future. Society's walls keep crumbling all around us. The many ongoing wars. The earthquakes. Now this deadly attack on America?

"Don't get me wrong: I'm sure Salvador Romanero will do many good things for humanity, but one thing he won't do is create a new utopia that's free of evil. And I'm okay with that. Truth be told, I never thought he could do it anyway.

"But what I'm not okay with is having to choose between family members. Not that you left me much of a choice, Mom. Yes, I'm mad at you for leaving Dad and for abandoning me. I can't understand for the life in me why you did it. I thought I'd never see the day when my own parents would separate.

"As a divorced woman myself, I know I have no right to speak on this topic. But after thirty-five years of marriage, you leave Dad a goodbye letter? Seriously? Do you realize how devastated Dad is? He's been in a fog ever since you left him. He looks like a zombie!

"I know we haven't communicated much since the disappearances, but that never changed the fact that the two of you were always my peace in this crazy world. My life was supposed to be screwed up, not yours!

"I always took comfort knowing you and Dad would always be together. Even when you disagreed on things, there was always this mutual respect the two of you had for each other's feelings and opinions. What happened Mom and Dad?"

Chelsea started weeping. "I'm sorry, but if I have to choose between either of you, I choose death instead! I see no other way out. This recent catastrophe was the icing on the cake. It robbed me of the will to want to continue on. I can't possibly fathom living on this planet another day.

"As for you, Brian, I still love you. But how can I forgive you for destroying the family the way you did? What you did to Renate was downright criminal. I will forever mourn her death. And moving to Pennsylvania without telling me or Dad was a low blow. Then to brainwash Mom to moving there with you. It's unforgivable?! It's like you've sucked all the life out of Dad. I'm so ashamed of you!

"Try as I might, I can't seem to wrap my head around the many bizarre things you've done of late! I know you're sold out to your religious cult and you'll never change. But I can't accept how you used it to destroy the family. We were a good family, a happy family. I was always so proud to call you my brother. All my life I looked up to you! Then your brain went haywire and you tore us all apart. This is something else I can't forgive.

"Who knows, perhaps in the next life God will hit the reset button and we can be a happy family again. Then I'll forgive you. Since I'll be the first one on the other side, I'll keep myself busy preparing things to the best of my ability until the three of you join me, whenever that time may be. That's the only hope I have left.

"That's all I have to say. Until we meet again, dearest family, just know in your hearts that I love you and already miss you all so much. Goodbye for now..."

At that, the video ended. Chelsea Mulrooney slit both of her wrists in the bathtub, then emailed the video to her father. The last thing she saw before closing her eyes and breathing her last breath in human form, were the words, "Message successfully sent!"

Then the world started spinning away and Chelsea was no longer part of it...

DICK MULROONEY WAS DOWN in the living room watching the breaking news on TV, of the 127 house fires burning all across New York City's five boroughs, when he was notified that he had a message from his daughter.

At first, he ignored it. On the night of the explosions, Dick wanted to take Chelsea to a fallout shelter, but didn't want to chance leaving the house without the proper protective gear.

The next option was to seal all doors and windows with the strongest adhesive tape he could find down in the cellar, and hope and pray it would work.

So far, so good.

Now this? Thousands of house fires blazing all across America, including Alaska and Hawaii?

Dick Mulrooney buried his face in his hands. He was already on maximum overload, at his wit's end, really.

He turned off the TV and checked his email.

It was a video message from Chelsea. Seeing the hopelessness in his daughter's eyes, suddenly the thousands of out-of-control house fires in his country seemed more comforting to him.

He braced himself.

Before the message even ended, Dick raced up the stairs and found his daughter lying in a bloody bathtub with her head resting on the tile wall. He lost all strength. "No, Chelsea! Please God, no!"

It was too late. She was gone...

After three hours of inexpressible agony, Dick Mulrooney finally found the strength to call 9/11, then pulled himself together just enough to make a brief video of his own.

When Brian was notified that he had a message from his father, his legs turned to jelly. When he saw his father looking completely out of sorts, as if he'd just lost his best friend, he braced himself for what he knew would be even more tragic news.

Without any sort of greeting Dick gritted his teeth and came straight to the point, "I want you to know your sister just committed suicide. I found her dead in the bathtub with two slit wrists. I thought about calling you but wanted you to see first-hand the pain and anguish you've caused me.

"Thanks to you, I'm all alone in the world. You've cost me a wife and only daughter. And a grandson!"

Grandson? Brian thought, not knowing to whom his father was referring...

"If your plan was to destroy a beautiful family, you've succeeded. Congratulations, Brian! Are you happy now? Whatever happened to honoring your mother and father?! Isn't that one of the Ten Commandments?! I'm quite sure it is," Dick said sarcastically, in between sniffles.

"I never knew I had the capacity to hate someone as much as I hate you right now! You're nothing but a monster! Because of you and your false religion, I no longer have a family."

Dick Mulrooney shook his head. "You've destroyed so many lives and caused the deaths of at least three people that I know of. Who knows how many more deaths I might find at your hands if I started digging. Perhaps I will. At any rate, it's because of you that two young women, including your own sister, took their lives."

After taking a few moments to collect himself, Dick Mulrooney wiped his moist eyes with his shirt sleeve and looked straight in the camera, "Remember when I said I never wanted to see you again? Well, I take it back. I do want to see you again.

"Let this message serve as fair warning that you won't get away with this, son. Son, ha, what a joke! You're not my son; you're the devil in disguise!

"I want you to know I've become quite close with your in-laws, and with Renate's sister, Megan. The one thing we have in common is a shared hatred for you. You already know Megan wants justice for what happened to her mother and sister. The only thing the Leglers want is their daughter back. Nothing more.

"But that's them. As for me, finding you is my new mission in life. It's time for you to pay for your many sins! Thanks to the Leglers, the search has been narrowed down to Pennsylvania. You have my word that if universal authorities don't find you, I will! And when I do, I'll kill you! May God have mercy on your soul!"

The message ended...

"They will be divided,

father against son

and son against father,

mother against daughter

and daughter against mother,

mother-in-law against daughter-in-law

and daughter-in-law against mother-in-law"

(Luke 12:53).

Epilogue

Now that Phase Four had just been unleashed, what will be the full extent of the attack on the United States of America?

Will President Jefferson Danforth remain the leader of America or will he be forced to live out the rest of his life in hiding?

Now that Chelsea Mulrooney took her life, will Sarah Mulrooney follow in her daughter's footsteps?

When will the 144,000 be sealed by God and sent on their global missions?

What role will the Two Witnesses play in it all?

Find answers to these questions and so much more as you continue in this prophetic series...

Thanks for taking the time to read the fifth installment of the CHAOS series. I would be most grateful if you shared your thoughts on Amazon. Even a short review would be appreciated.

May God continue to bless and keep you.

To contact author for book signings, speaking engagements, or for bulk discounts, email @ patrick12272003@gmail.com.

About the author

Patrick Higgins is the author of *The Pelican Trees, Coffee in Manila,* the award-winning *The Unannounced Christmas Visitor,* and the award-winning prophetic end-times series, *Chaos in the Blink of an Eye.* While the stories he writes all have different themes and take place in different settings, the one thread that links them all together is his heart for Jesus and his yearning for the lost.

With that in mind, it is his wish that the message his stories convey will greatly impact each reader, by challenging you not only to contemplate life on this side of the grave, but on the other side as well. After all, each of us will spend eternity at one of two places, based solely upon a single decision which must be made this side of the grave. That decision will be made crystal clear to each reader of his books.

Higgins is currently writing many other books, both fiction and non-fiction, including a sequel to *Coffee in Manila,* which will shine a bright, sobering light on the diabolical human trafficking industry.

To contact author: patrick12272003@gmail.com
Like on Facebook: https://www.facebook.com/patrick12272003
https://www.facebook.com/TheUnannouncedChristmasVisitor
Follow on Twitter: https://twitter.com/patrick12272003
Follow on Instagram: @patrick12272003

Made in the USA
Columbia, SC
23 March 2019